RICHARD WALKER

Richard Walker spent much of his childhood in Ghana, read English at Oxford and has since worked in Canada, Kuwait, Spain and Thailand. He was until recently Deputy Director of the British Council's Literature Department in London and is currently working for the British Council in Lagos, Nigeria. He has published one non-fiction book and several of his stories and plays have been broadcast on Radio 3. This is his first novel.

sceptre

Richard Walker

A CURIOUS CHILD

First published in Great Britain in 1989 by The Bodley Head Ltd.

Sceptre edition 1990

Sceptre is an imprint of Hodder and Stoughton Paperbacks, a division of Hodder and Stoughton Ltd.

British Library C.I.P.

Walker, Richard
A curious child.
I. Title
823.914 [F]

ISBN 0-340-53722-1

The characters and situations in this book are entirely imaginary and bear no relation to any real person or actual happenings.

Printed and bound in Great Britain for Hodder and Stoughton Paperbacks, a division of Hodder and Stoughton Ltd., Mill Road, Dunton Green, Sevenoaks, Kent TN13 2YA. (Editorial Office: 47 Bedford Square, London WC1B 3DP) by Clays Ltd., St Ives.

For Lauren

CONTENTS

I have seen
A curious child, who dwelt upon a tract
Of inland ground, applying to his ear
The convolutions of a smooth-lipped shell;
To which, in silence hushed, his very soul
Listened intensely; and his countenance soon
Brightened with joy; for from within were heard
Murmurings, whereby the monitor expressed
Mysterious union with its native sea.

William Wordsworth
The Excursion Book VI

OVERTURE

The Crucifixion
How Far Back

THE CRUCIFIXION [illegible] tomorrow [illegible] the street. And when [illegible] the consolation of being [illegible] two or three friends. When [illegible] wildly [illegible]

[illegible]

You [illegible] Christ [illegible]

[illegible]

What [illegible] knows the pain [illegible] the saving [illegible] and today is the last day I have been able to [illegible] When [illegible] whether it was [illegible]

THE CRUCIFIXION may have been more agonising. Just. But it didn't last as long as this pain. And when mine is over I will hardly have the consolation of being called the Redeemer except perhaps by one or two of my friends. When this physical anguish has finished I will have to admit that I suffered the torment not to save others but only to try to rescue myself from a body to which I did not belong.

You say the reference to Christ is blasphemous and that there is no comparison to be made. Let me tell you before we go any further that I am what would be called a spiritual rather than a religious person. In my position there is no choice to be made. I am obliged to believe in the existence of some presence other than my mere body. If I fail to affirm this then what has just been done to me is a travesty of nature, a perverse interference on the part of the surgeon and myself. Indeed, it is only my faith in the invisible, the untouchable that can't be examined by probing Vaselined gloves, or X-rayed, or reveal itself as a lime-green blip on an oscilloscope, only my knowledge that something lies beyond these medical surfaces that has brought me this far. So if anyone accuses me of contravening the Church and its teachings I tell them that their doctrine is irrelevant to my case. I have gone through purgatory, harrowed by where my body stops and where my soul begins. This has not been some theoretical discussion conducted over a glass of wine (though I have done that too), it has been necessary for me to get it absolutely clear where the division lies if it exists at all. Work out your own salvation is what I say to the critics and what I will say to the judges. And there will be judges, both legal and other, I have no illusions about that.

What concerns me now is the pain. It has been five days since the last and, thank God, final operation, and today is the first day I have been able to think through the pain. When I am asked whether it was worth it I will say, 'Yes, yes, of course it was,' and in this way I will be like a mother who has erased from her memory the anguish of childbirth. And the comparison is apt for the wounding of my body has brought a new person into this world.

Not only am I beginning to string a few thoughts together at last but the outside world can occasionally be glimpsed when the pain recedes and draws open its curtains a fraction. I can sometimes hear the *muezzin* calling the worshippers to prayer and once or twice his voice has even reached me in my drugged half-consciousness which is neither sleeping nor waking. We are in a quiet place here away from the city and so the *muezzin* does not use a loudspeaker and reaches me using nothing but the power of his own vocal cords. If he can do that then I must be getting better.

I try to picture him standing at the top of the minaret with his hands cupped and his chin raised, his Adam's apple bobbing up and down under the chestnut-brown skin of his throat. What is Adam's apple in the language of the Koran? They recognise Christ as one of the prophets announcing the coming of Mohammed. Does Adam figure in their sacred book? I would not be surprised. After all, Moslems are so acutely aware of the force of a woman's attraction that they wrap them in layer after layer of material like some exotic present.

Away to one side and below where the *muezzin* stands I conjure up the dome of the mosque. I say conjure because arriving at night I noticed very little. I only remember the stars that could be seen everywhere above the flat roofs, burning white and glinting like chips of ice. I had never seen so many stars blazing together. Oases of cool in the blanketing warmth of a North African night.

Was the dome of the mosque an inverted bowl of hothouse colour like the mosque in the main square at Isfahan which I had visited on an assignment? I remember standing in that square craning my neck and shielding my eyes from the sun to try to get a better view of the many-coloured dome when a voice came out of the shadow. 'Sss, sss,' and a hand beckoned me frantically to come and join it in the dark. I moved close enough to make out a figure in a tattered, shapeless garment which fell from his shoulders to his bare feet in one swoop. 'You go up, you go up,' he gibbered, pointing to the minaret thrusting up above the dome. 'You see good. Here no see good.'

Before I could answer he took me by the hand and led me down a dark passageway to a door no bigger than a half stable door. From somewhere inside the folds of the grey material he produced an enormous iron key and hurriedly pushed it into the lock, all the time looking up and down the passageway to see if anybody was about. He swung open the thick studded door and hitching up his robes and tucking them in a pair of khaki shorts he was wearing underneath he jumped up into a gloomy alcove.

'Quick. You up,' he hissed and held out a hand. He pulled me up into the alcove, grazing my knee badly, and then shut the door behind me before I had time to catch my breath. So for a moment I was crouched at his sandalled feet panting and able to see nothing in that dark. I started to say, 'Look, I don't like confined spaces especially ones that I can't see in. A doctor once told me that I might even have a mild form of claustrophobia. Let me out.'

Although he didn't understand the words he knew what I was saying but continued undeflected from his purpose. He felt for my hand and when he found it directed it on to a cool stone, letting me explore it for a while. It turned out to be the first in a flight of steps which I could tell were both steep and curved round a central column in a tight spiral. 'You number one,' he said, pushing me up the first of the steps. I had to walk sideways with my knees bent and shoulders hunched. There was no light to decipher the climb and the gradient and tightness of the ascent made me stop every few steps to get my breath and let the dizziness spin itself out of my head. Once I stumbled and panicked.

'Down, please let me down. I can't breathe. I'm suffocating. Please, let's go back.' But he ignored me and gently pushed me up. 'No worry, no worry, you see good from top.' I didn't know then just how well I would see, all I could feel was an endless sense of being smothered not only by the dark and the climb but also by the enforced nearness of this Persian who had appeared as my unsummoned guide. Climbing with a stranger in the dark, nothing but the brushing of our feet and bodies on the stonework and the musty air rasping into our lungs, lent our enterprise an intimacy, a sense of conspiracy which his earlier behaviour had confirmed and to which I did not know how to react. So my response was to push on upwards to the top of the minaret but slowly, painfully, afraid.

Would I do that today knowing what I know about myself? The answer is yes but easily and relaxed. Without fear. Lying in this cool white room it is clear to me now (apart from the pain) that my life was a long climb in an obscure, constricting shaft. From this distance in time and place how repressed and inhibited my actions seem. The very clarity of the light mocks the twilight in which I once lived. How grey it all appeared and how simple and illuminated things are now in the purity of the Egyptian sunlight. The plain bamboo table with its vase of unknown flowers splashing their yellows and reds in the quiet; the deep shadowed windowsills allowing the lemon rays to pierce the wall and draw a primrose square on the flags; the braying of a mule refusing to budge in the dust outside. How much longer before I am allowed to take up my bed and walk in a world that has been reborn?

As we neared the top of the minaret I grew fainter and fainter, almost asphyxiated by the restriction of air and space outside my body and the lack of room to manoeuvre in my own psyche. Hunched, stumbling and airless in the dark, my outward circumstances were a perfect reflection of the state I had reached in myself. The spiral became so tight that I was forced to curl my head and shoulders round the column and let my legs and feet slither behind me as best they could. It was as though I were a snake inching its sinuous way up a branch to strike at the open air when it arrived. A harmless gesture relieving nothing but its own venom.

Suddenly above my head there were the sides of a square pencilled in the darkness, just as if someone had etched the four lines into a blackboard. 'Now we here. You push,' said my guide, at the same time putting his hand on my buttocks and propelling me upwards to indicate what he meant. It took all my strength to prise open the trapdoor and I was trembling from the exertion before it finally yielded and disclosed its secrets.

The impact of the glare was so intense that I shied away back into the eclipse of the minaret. It was several moments before I dared to lift my head and confront that dazzle again. When I did so it was with barely open eyes and only at the insistence of my guide. Where is he now, that scruffy waif? If he only knew what I have become he would know in what other manner he was my guide and would doubtless be confused about what he had led me into. How I would greet him if I saw him now; I would hold him and squeeze him tight until every undernourished bone in his body was about to snap. Thank you, thank you, thank your god or whoever you put your faith in, thank you.

The light bathed my eyes, washing out the dark of the long climb up the minaret. And with my sight cleansed the first thing I saw was the dome of the mosque pulsating below me. How hard I had tried to discern its true pattern and colour from the square below and how little resemblance the picture I had seen bore to what I now saw. It was like looking at a poor reproduction of a painting and then being taken into a room to find youself in front of the real canvas. You are not sure whether you are even looking at images bearing any relation to one another.

Were I a Platonist I suppose I would subscribe to the notion that what we can perceive of the world is nothing but shadows on the wall of the cave we inhabit. And, therefore, anything we produce as a response to this world can be no more than a shadow of a shadow. But I am not a Platonist, for among other things I trust my heart too deeply and have no time for those who wish to try to reach the truth by discussion, by argument and logical counter-argument. And the dictionary defines it as an art! Had I followed that path where would I be today? I would still be twisting myself on your spit of what seems right and wrong in theory rather than following what is natural to me. I would still be climbing the minaret.

'Look. See good now. OK.' But my guide had no reason to cajole me any longer for I had already forgotten the horrors of the climb and was entranced by the vibrancy of the dome. The turquoise and gold swirling in arabesques, in flowers, swooping round the smooth cheek of the dome and soaring up, aspiring to the golden needle at its peak. The petalled intricacy of the design and its complexity, restrained by the purity of colour and the simplicity of its outlines. Beyond in the middle distance the sun-dried mud blocks of the city seemed to be on their knees in supplication and in the background the mountains, dwarfed by the majesty of the dome, were as flat and one-dimensional as a child's drawing. The dome was the very hub from which the life of the city radiated and all roads appeared to lead to the square below, where – it is said – they first played polo. The square where you could sit in a cane chair and drink mint tea looking out through the stone arches into the aching light. And behind the square wound the labyrinth of the *souk* with its nougat makers spinning their pink-white strands across the alleys like wool unwinding on to outstretched arms. But I was above all that noise and half-light and instead I could barely hear the city's humming as I stood in the brightness, fixed by the aura of the dome.

Yes, I look good now, I see good now, I see how something must give and assume the intricate simplicity of the dome, not the twisted, constricting darkness, the stumbling up the minaret. The dome so easy in its outline, the grace of its silhouette, a complexity contained without torment in its curve. I had to hold on to that memory when I was enclosed and lost, blinded by working out the details of the change that would have to be made.

And back in my bed I look across to the window. They have placed me so that I can see without turning my head or having to move in any way. Have they done this before? If so, how many times? If not, I must be the first, but they would have told me surely? The surgeon is a charming but practical man. He is not an idealist. He has sensible brown eyes. He is compassionate but he has a living to make and he would not have used me as a guinea pig. Would he? Would he?

The windowsill is deep and holds a shadow of itself. Like looking through a telescope. Yes, the world is magnified now, brought closer to me as though before I were looking through glasses with fingermarks on the lenses. (The drugs, they keep pumping them into me and then all sorts of things happen, only the pain remains constant. The agony in the area of my lower abdomen and groin which the drugs are supposed to deaden, it is that agony which holds me here.) All I can see is a piece of blue sky. Someone has crayoned a piece of cardboard and stuck it over the window to fool me. I am not in a room in Egypt at all but in the school sickbay with its chipped enamel bedsteads and worn steel-blue blankets.

I was confined to a room of my own. What a rare privilege for someone accustomed to sleeping in a dormitory with nineteen others. I loved it. I loved being ill, for if whatever it was that you had caught was contagious, it meant the privacy of isolation. How I longed every term for some particularly infectious and long-lasting illness so that I could be tucked away from all the others. How they disturbed me and left me on edge. I never felt at ease in their proximity, especially when it was a question of close bodily contact.

Aah, here you come with your dense psychological textbooks on the nature of adolescence. 'It is perfectly normal for boys and girls to pass through a phase in which they are attracted to members of their own sex, even excited by them to the point of wishing to express their feelings through physical manifestations of friendship.' Do not worry, there is no need for alarm. This is only a temporary aberration.

These words and others of their kind have made it their business to call on me at all manner of times, knocking on my door and disturbing the peace. My life would have been as restful and quiet as any other without such echoes following in my footsteps. At first, the problem was that I believed them – those cruel generalisations written to hold the social fabric together and stop it from tearing apart – they held me in check, too, so that I was as tightly wrapped and bound by the material of their words as the feet of any Chinese girl. But how they chafed, making me more nervous and agitated than I would have been without their impositions. It is easy to understand how my later mistrust of anything that smacked of scholarly or academic endeavour came about. The great minds, the labour of decades, the weight of public institutions with their gargantuan reserves of manpower and finance had since the turn of the century (if not long before) gone into the business of investigating the nature of human psychology, especially as it related to sexual being; and then, when they pronounced their verdict, they had in my case got it wrong. At times I wanted to believe they were right: temporary or passing perversion, deviation or aberration – at moments crammed together and living through my adolescence cheek to cheek with so many ostensibly the same sex I wished that my feelings for them, about them, were no more than the fleeting distortions I was assured they were.

Assurance was never direct, only implicit, for I was unable to voice what I felt about myself. There was an unspoken understanding permeating every level of the school's hierarchy that maybe, perhaps, well, it was just possible that one or two individuals might, unluckily, succumb to this . . . illness. But they would soon get over it, soon recover and get back on their feet and it would all be forgotten. This, I know, did happen to one or two of them but not to me because, as I later understood, there was absolutely nothing for me to recover from. I was quite healthy and the sole cause of my suffering was the tacit assumption – more insidious and debilitating because it was never openly questioned – that I would get better from an illness that I didn't have.

The nurse has just been in to see if I am all right and ask if I want anything. I said, 'Yes, the sheets feel clammy, wet, even though I don't feel hot.'

'Perhaps the drugs are making you perspire,' she said, smiling, with her hair illumined by the saffron light sliding in a shaft through the open window. But she was lying. 'Lie still. Close your eyes and relax. I'm going to change the sheets.'

She must have thought that the drugs and pain between them had such a grip on me that I would take her at her word. Wanting to believe that what she said was true. Perspiration no. Blood yes. At first they had to change the bed linen every hour or so along with the dressings. When I came to (the first of so many times) they had just finished changing the sheets and out of the corner of my eye I glimpsed a heap of carmine cloths – my sheets which as they were carried out of the room left a trail of vermilion spots, tiny blood-red suns on the sage-green floor tiles.

This time I was fully conscious of what the nurse was doing and yet somehow she contrived to remove the sheets with the gentlest of pressure on my hip and shoulder. Such grace. This nurse is a true artist. She is not crisp and starched as would be demanded of her in so many other places. She is curved and soft without a hat and the spirit of vocation shines through all her movements. She makes sure that I have fresh flowers every day and the gentleness of her arrangement speaks to the blooms, willing them to colour and lighten my recovery. In the beginning, when I surfaced again and again from the pools of my anguish, she was unfailingly present at my bedside. The *muezzin* calling, the mule braying, the children yelping to one another outside the window all entered briefly and left, but she stayed.

'What is your name?'

'Leila.'

'Is that an Egyptian name?'

'My mother was Lebanese, my father French.'

'But you speak English perfectly.'

'Not perfectly. Well enough.' She took my hand and held it in her palm. 'I went to the American school in Beirut.'

'But your accent isn't American.'

'No? My English teacher was English. From Oxford, I think.'

'Have you been there?'

'To England? Never.' She laughed and exerted the slightest squeeze on my hand. 'But I would like to. If I save enough money perhaps.'

I saw us walking arm in arm through the meadows beyond Christ Church on our way to sit by the Cherwell and be admired by the occupants of the punts gliding past. On May Day Eve we would stay up all night and celebrate the dawn at Magdalen tower and then have breakfast at George's café in the market. Or was it the other way round? Is it the passage of time or the drugs? Does the order of events matter so much any more? Whichever came first, the scenes are etched in my memory with cupboards unnumbered and to be opened at random. So who cares about temporal order when the spatial has long since disappeared?

'When I'm better I'll take you there. A thank you for looking after me so well.'

'Ssh, you must get some rest now.'

'But really. I would enjoy it myself. It would be a convalescence for me too.'

'We shall see, we shall see. Now lie back and sleep.' She returned my hand to me, placing it on top of the other already becoming a vacant shadow on the turned-down linen.

The body distances itself so firmly and insistently from oneself that how could one fail to believe there is some entity other than flesh? This divorce between the matter of skin and bone and whatever it is that it houses seems to become most heightened at moments of physical crisis or extremity. We have all read or heard accounts from individuals who state that they have left their bodies whilst maintaining some sense of personal self, of identifiable consciousness. Most of these reports concern moments when the individual has, technically speaking, died and subsequently returned to what has been for a while his or her corpse. Accompanying these descriptions there is often a commentary describing the effect this experience has had on the individual concerned. And what is central to almost all of them is the renewed sense of self with which the whatever it is comes rushing back into the body, as though it has been separated from the one element that can sustain it. This separation infuses the absentee owner with a revived zest for the old home: the body. What relief, what joy there is in the rediscovery of what had perhaps been too long neglected and unappreciated! But things have changed.

What is startling is that some or even many of these changes are made after such a short period away from the body. People return after a matter of minutes or just seconds and want to make radical alterations to the way they live. And how do they live through their body? They become Zen Buddhists or decide to run a small-holding or even if they remain the same to all outward appearances something fundamental that is invisible has been transfigured. All this comes through a relatively brief time spent away from the body.

What would happen if from the moment of your conception you had never once managed to enter your body and been given one to which you did not belong? This is not idle speculation but true in my case. I have never felt at home in the body conceived alongside me so I have, until now, spent my time with it in two ways.

Ar first I tried to ignore the conflict between us and pretend that we were in harmony and had no quarrel. This led me into some painful contortions both mental and physical. The other way has been to tinker with the body assigned to me so that it more nearly approximates to my self. Most tinkering has something of the element of window-dressing about it and does not really get to the heart of the matter, being in essence a temporary stop-gap which may appease for a while but is, ultimately, only a frustration, an insubstantial mockery of what ought to be but isn't.

Let me stop for a moment and ask you to tell me what sex you are. Good, you know, no dilemma or messing around, you are unequivocally sure about it? And how do you know? Is it because you trust in what others tell you? I hardly think that if you have come this far with me you are quite so willing to accept another's verdict on the matter – you, I imagine, do not consider yourself male or female because others so define you. True, there are elements, traits, which are traditionally or socially thought of as feminine or masculine. But these, as we are all aware, change from society to society both in time and place. Think of the women in the dust outside my window: swathed and mysterious. Now compare them with the women on the northern shores of the Mediterranean. The further north you travel the fewer garments they wear or rather the more revealing their clothes become. So that even when it is bitter and cold, when these women have the opportunity – central heating or two weeks in the sun – they choose to wear that which exposes and lays bare rather than attire that conceals.

Let's get back to specifics. You, or most of you, tell me you know what sex you are. Have you yet asked yourself what sex I am? And if you have, do you know the answer? And if you do know the answer how did you come to it? And can you be certain that you are right? You cannot, for example, have made your choice on the basis of appearance. You have none to go on and I have not told you myself. And neither do you solely define yourself in such a way. If you have made a decision already then I allow you a much clearer perception than I had for many years – too many years. I didn't know. The person they all saw was from birth, on the standard basis for classification: genitalia, assigned to one sexual group. I accepted this quite readily and to do otherwise at an early age would have meant suffering even more mocking accusations than I had to undergo later (and they were withering enough when I was convinced of the nature of my dilemma, let alone when beginning to explore it). It was when the body neither developed nor responded according to its blueprint that the doubt formed and sidled in through the door left ajar by some natural – yes, natural, exceedingly rare maybe, but still natural – caprice of our mercurial mother nature. Even before outward bodily signals failed to broadcast or do so on the wrong wavelength I had inklings which these later transmissions only confirmed.

And now we are approaching that time when . . . I know it

will be so easy for you when you hear the facts, those little nuggets that you like to cling on to, holding them between your thumb and forefinger, turning them round in the watery sunlight; they are yours and you think at last, 'I can judge, come to my own estimation as long as you give me the evidence, present the facts of the case clearly. One can't be fairer than that, can one?'

But I don't want to give you them because by the very handing over to you, through their presentation, they are transformed, losing their uniqueness (as part of my experience and only mine) and acquiring a seemingly public objectivity which is nothing more than your distorting, ever-widening eye.

And yet I am bound to give you 'the facts'. Without them you will assume a guilt and with them . . . probably the same but at least you will have had the opportunity to reach your own conclusion. You don't see that your conclusion made in the light of 'out there' must inevitably fail to match mine reached from in here, here somewhere in me where the one just solution rests.

Congratulate yourself on your impartiality right now and then forget it. It is a sham, cloaking prejudice. 'Those are the true baffling prejudices for man, which he never suspects for prejudice' (*De Quincey*). And whatever you say, however you protest, there will be something in most of you whispering, 'Oh no, not that. It is just the wrong side of the pale. I mean I'm as open-minded as the next person but . . . ' Yes, this will call forth a host of qualifying 'buts', 'howevers' and 'on the other hands', conjunctions of liberal doubt and hesitation.

How meticulously have I placed my feet dancing round what doctors call one's case-history. At the beginning I drew the curtains open just a fraction giving you a glimpse of my case and a morsel of history, a radiating web which casts almost invisible lines everywhere: events throwing pencil-fine shadows across my path. But then I grew reticent, fearful, and retreated into the ditches of generalisation, non-event, thinking that you wouldn't like what you saw, or worse, would misinterpret.

Show courage, get back, tell staring them straight in the face just as you had to acknowledge yourself to someone who didn't look like yourself in the mirror.

* * *

HOW FAR BACK does one have to go to get at the roots of a truth? Were I to trace my history back to those paradisiac days of Adam and Eve that would, I suspect, not take us far enough. Too many imponderables would remain. Let me come a little closer to home within generations I can almost grasp, or else the prospect of a feasible reconstruction grows remote. A litany of names resounds chanting through the pain, as unfamiliar to you as the mass to a Quaker, but they sing a ritual incantation which underscores and counterpoints the early discords and later harmonies of my life.

Two women were the poles I swung between, confused and spinning out of control like giddy sycamore wings at the mercy of a high wind. Had you some slight acquaintance with my family you might well jump to the conclusion that I am referring to my sisters, Dorothy and Anne. The first a madam of convention, the second a mistress of rebellion. The older and the younger, the established and the usurper. But no. Their role is obvious and immediate yet it lacks the depth, the force of the other women in me.

It is hard for me to gauge which of the two women has exerted the stronger influence. At times I felt like the seas of the earth, sloshing this way and that, sucked from one part of the globe to another by the magnetism of the moon. Now, I hope, after the tumultuous waves of pain, that things will settle down and become a little calmer.

The arms of my mother, Virginia, enfolded me and while we were both standing I buried my face in the front of her dress and began to sob. From somewhere, her coat perhaps, came the tang of camphor mingling with the salt of my tears. 'I don't want to leave.' She knew that I didn't want to leave but we stood, powerless it seemed, in the hallway waiting for the car to be driven round to the front of the house. We were both caught up in the motion of an event spinning from a source beyond ourselves. I had said goodbye to the others who tactfully remained in the drawing room; through the folds of mother's blue dress the murmur of their chatter, punctuated by the occasional volley of laughter, reached me from behind the closed door. No doubt my departure was already a matter in their pasts while it persisted as my present. I pulled my wet face back from the soft creases of her dress, a shaft of light slid in through the window and poured like a spotlight on to the dark green of the hall carpet. It indicated depths like those in a pond illuminated for the first time.

'Are you sure you don't want me to come?'

I nodded my head. Did I mean yes or no? I meant, 'Yes, I do want you to come,' but I said 'No. I'd rather go on my own.' I thought it sounded braver that way. She took out a handkerchief and wiped my face.

'Are you sure?'

I nodded once more.

'You promised you'd write. Regularly, once a week.'

The sound of tyres crunching over the gravel outside stalled my answer.

'Better go now,' said the woman, who was already becoming Virginia not 'mother' any longer. She clicked up the latch on the heavy door. The light flooded in. I was leaving home. As I walked to the car I caught sight of a face at the drawing-room window. It was the face which had sent me from home. A face which, like a Janus sun and moon, has beamed down wherever I have walked and before that too. It was the face of my grandmother, Emily. It did not smile or give a sign that it had seen me, it only watched me climb into the car, then the driver closed the door behind me. As the engine started up I turned round. Through the rear window there were two faces. My mother's, anguished and impotent as she stood at the front door waving. From inside the house, behind glass, the visage of Emily, a passive observer whose face seemed to loom larger, in inverse proportion to the distance of her generation.

Of course there were other women too – my aunts Margaret and Jean, my grandmother's then my mother's friend Julia – but these are the two women whose stories are mine as much as their own. I am the final destination of their narratives which is why I invite them to speak. Let Emily, the oldest, address you first while I try to conquer this pain.

EMILY

EMILY was looking down the [illegible] to the [illegible]

[illegible]

EMILY sits looking down the wintry garden to the sundial which casts no shadow, for there is no sun today but a uniform mist swirling grey as though her son Cyril has lit a bonfire that is running out of control. She reaches out her arm, her fingers drum, chatter without rhythm on the glass to check that it is there for sometimes she is unsure about whether she is inside or out. She tries to wrap the blanket more tightly around her legs but her hands scratch feebly and to no avail. One feathery sheet of an airmail letter drifts from her grasp while its ragged envelope lies in her lap. Opposite her is a second chair which, like hers, faces down the garden, only it is empty. Yet time and time again she addresses a figure she constructs for herself in this chair. She is alone so often now. She must have someone to talk to. Her eyes narrow.

God forgive Ronald for he has no idea what he's done. Why did he have to go and change? Why not stay as he was born, keep what God had given him? Yes, it might have been difficult for him but then it's hardly been easy for any of us, me included. There was so much he might have had. For a start the business. I built it up for the family, for him, something to work for, to pass on. But how can I leave it to him now? How?

She does not consider herself exempt from her own judgement. She is willing to admit that there have been times when she too did not know what she was doing. Business, even a successful one like hers, can, she knows, only take one so far. Indeed its success has come, she feels, because she has recognised its limitations and not demanded more than it could possibly give. She has on the whole enjoyed the comfortable if unspectacular life it has given her.

I always left the fireworks to others. Ronald's father helped with the bonfire once. That was the beginning of the end, how he met Virginia.

If you asked Emily she would tell you that she did not regret working out of the limelight. That she liked to get on and do whatever was necessary without making a fuss. Planning, building slowly year after year, never in a rush because she knew that it would come in time. She has worked hard, too hard some might say, though she would deny that, claiming that all her efforts had been directed to one goal.

The family. Always the family. I wanted to hold it together at all costs.

The corners of her mouth twitch, pushing back the arguments, the bitternesses and recriminations, the lack of comprehension. She wants to feel the river of family blood flow through her but this letter in her lap seems to have put a stop to that. She does not know whether it was a gradual leaking away with the century itself or a more sudden drought. Whichever, the very notion of selves and family relations has drained away with the bold writing on the tissue-thin airmail paper. What brought her to devote her energies to maintaining the family web with herself at its hub?

Albert and Robert were Emily's brothers. They were both killed in the Great War which she remembers, after a fashion, while swathed in a tartan blanket she waits for . . . what is she waiting for?

How proud I was of Robert, so correct in his naval uniform. One ear – the left – sticking out more than the other, just like father's. The brass against the deep ocean blue made me think of telescopes and portholes, the surf-white of his hat. I was going to ask him why he had joined the navy but I knew the attraction.

Emily's neck inches forwards with the caution of a tortoise. She addresses someone we cannot see in the chair opposite. It is her dead husband Charles to whom she talks of her brothers, her daughters and son.

After all, didn't I marry you, a naval man, Charles? At least Robert survived longer in his uniformed glory than Albert. Robert had two or three years. I can't remember, was it 1916 or 17? I know it was June because cook had baked a cake for Margaret's birthday which is, as you know, midsummer's day. There were two or three candles, I think. Jean was younger and Cyril and Virginia weren't born, of course. You were at sea but you were always at sea, Charles. I heard the clattering of hooves – father, he would never ride in a motor car if he could help it. 'You know why I've come,' he said. I made him sit before I would listen. Whenever he stood and talked I always felt I was being lectured. His boots shone in the full afternoon sun. The gardener, I remember, was spreading horse manure just outside this window.

Emily turns her head to look out as though she might still see him there forking manure.

There was muck on her father's boots too.

'Yes,' I said, 'I know why you've come. You're here to tell me that Robert has died, drowned under the command of Admirals Beatty and Jellicoe.' You made me learn the names of all our admirals then, though the second time round I didn't know them so well. Had the novelty worn off for those of us who'd been through the first? Or did you, Charles, lose your enthusiasm for teaching me the names of the admirals and their fleets? Father scratched his ear like he always did when he was nervous or apprehensive.

'You already know?' He was surprised and slightly offended.

'Yes, I already know.'

'But how?' He was puzzled. Dear father, so literal, so material. How could I know about anything that went on in the world unless someone told me or I read about it in the newspaper? Where was the sense of outrage I wanted him to show? If he had any it was hidden from view.

Emily learned this behaviour from her father, bridling her emotion with the reins of public decorum. Her brother's death, her father's second son to be killed, provoked neither outrage nor a heartfelt display of grief in her father but the rigid posture of an unflinching duty. The Owens and the Rosenbergs through whom some like to interpret the Great War were a sideshow. The reaction of Emily's father was the one they lived by; held in, steeled by duty and a faith in the order of things. Emily's father had been born in the middle of the nineteenth century, 1849, when Victoria had been on the throne for a decade – in what other manner could he have reacted? His life had coincided with the great peace. Decade after decade oozed with the plenty, the security, the fruits of this peace. His half of the century had been a long summer's afternoon waiting for the apple to drop. It was only at the end, when the apple lay unpicked and bruised on the grass with a wasp buzzing round, that there was a whiff of something rotten in the air.

I wonder, thinks Emily, if Cyril's apples have kept better this year than last. He seems just recently to have lost the knack of storing the fruit to keep it crisp through the winter.

At first, the faint odour of decay was something one couldn't quite catch, it was merely hinted at in the Boer War – first nervous gesture of a nation unsure of itself and losing its grip. Then came the full-blown stink of Albert's death in a trench followed by Robert's at sea. (She thought of the lungs filling up to the last bronchiole and alveolus with brine.) Yet still Emily and her father both refused to acknowledge their senses and pinched the fingers of duty and obedience to their noses, clenched shut their eyes and hugged their shoulders to their ears.

I remember standing up from a chair near this very window and seeing the gardener walk past with mud and manure on his boots. I thought of my brother Albert in a trench with horses somewhere nearby.

'You're very quiet,' said father.

'I was thinking of Albert,' I told him. He looked at me very hard, staring as though he hadn't heard me correctly.

'Emily, my dear,' he said, 'Albert is dead. He died last year. We're talking about your other brother Robert now. I've come to tell you . . . but you know.'

I stared back at him. 'Does it make any difference that Albert died last year?'

He was embarrassed and turned away.

Outside the window I can smell the gardener's boots – a stench like the clouds at Ypres even now when I had hoped winter might sanitise my senses.

Emily continues to address her husband, a habit which she finds herself pursuing more and more. Although he is dead she brings him back to face her – something he had managed to avoid when he was alive.

He asked me, Charles, how the new gardener was. One moment we were talking about Robert and Albert – dead – the next I had to tell him the gardener was willing but too old. All the young men had gone, hadn't they? Do you recall what trouble we had finding even that old man who couldn't hold a pair of shears without shaking? So I had to ask father, 'How did Robert die?'

'I thought you knew.'

'Details, I mean.'

'You're too morbid, Emily,' he said. Then he swallowed, his Adam's apple swelling like a frog's bloated throat. 'I don't know but I imagine that he drowned.'

Emily's father, in fact, imagined too little. He thought the death of his sons was an interlude and not the beginning of a new act. He knew, of course, that there had been skirmishes before this one – 'skirmish' was the word he was still using when the gas was blowing around Ypres – and he recognised that there had been before then hiccoughs in the years' breathing, but with the death of his second son he was still unable to grasp that the old century had died and the new one was already exhausted and broken. It would have been unfair to ask him to predict that things would never return to what they had once been before the 'skirmish' began. How could he have anticipated that more than half a century later his daughter would have in her lap a letter whose contents horrified her more than the deaths of her brothers, Albert and Robert?

'I think he was below deck at the time. It must've happened quickly. He wouldn't have known very much about it.'

I never asked you, Charles, were you afraid to go below deck then? You never told me what it was like on your ship in the war. Oh yes, you told me about the spirit and the way you all worked together but you never said to me how you felt. I wanted to hear you say you were afraid to die, that would've meant something, but you never said it.

A large black bird which is probably a crow alights in the garden though Emily, twisting her head that way, is not sure – she has never learned to tell the difference between a crow and a jackdaw. It flutters like a charred sheet of newsprint from one of Cyril's bonfires which it could not possibly be for, although Emily does not know it, Cyril has other things in mind today.

* * *

A STREAM runs through part of the garden surrounding the house where Emily sits. As the youngest child, Robert was forbidden to go there when Emily and Albert were old enough to be allowed to wander where they liked. There was something in their mother's fear that he might drown, as he did years later and fathoms under at Jutland.

Emily had a doll called Alice named after the adventures in Wonderland. One day Albert, older and taller than his sister, stole the doll from her and, teasing, waved it above her head out of reach. Emily danced round Albert beating him on the chest.

'Please, please, Albert, give Alice back to me,' she cried.

'And what will you do if I don't give her back?' came Albert's laughing reply.

'I shall . . . I shall, I shan't pray for you any more!'

'What a wicked young lady you are.' Albert laughed more loudly and whirled the doll just out of Emily's reach. On his upper lip there was the thin line of his first moustache which prickled Emily when he kissed her goodnight. It sometimes smelled of tobacco which, as their father detested it, was a secret between them. Albert continued to tease her.

'What good do you think it does even when you pray for me? Why don't you stop and see if it makes any difference!'

'All right, I will and you see what happens.'

Emily had never told anyone what she had said to Albert because she was afraid that she might be accused of heartlessness and cruelty and that it might be true. It might really have made a difference. She remembered the words and she did stop praying for him at night and on Sundays. Later, of course, she included him once more in her list and when she remembered mentioned his name twice to try to make up for the times he had been omitted. When she heard of his death she did not recall the incident but after the war was over she remembered it again and contemplated its effect. She could not escape a sense of betrayal, however short-lived it might seem to anyone else. This may have been one of the first sources of her guilt but it was not the last.

Albert skipped away from Emily still holding Alice aloft in the soft blue air and her hair streamed as he ran. Emily cried after him, 'Albert, come back. Stop! Wait for me.' Albert had reached the bank of the stream when he stumbled and tripped headlong in the grass. A bird flew up and Alice was flying too. For an instant Emily could not tell the difference until one of them dropped and plummeted into the stream where the doll was carried away through the small eddies swirling round rocks and stones. The tears which streamed down Emily's face shattered the grass, the trees and the sky into confusing prisms.

Emily was thinking of this while her father stood reporting Robert's death.

I told him I was thinking about Albert and Alice. I knew he thought I was temporarily cracked. He wanted to tell me about Robert but it didn't make any difference to me which brother I talked about.

It could be seen in the way Emily's father shook his head that he was thinking: poor girl, it's all been too much for her. Charles away at sea, a skirmish on, first her brother Albert is killed, she has two youngsters to care for, no shoulder to cry on and now this business with her second brother killed has knocked her for six.

He tried to respond and asked Emily whether he had met or knew Alice.

I told him Alice was about a foot high with a porcelain complexion and raven-black hair. That Albert had drowned her, by accident of course. How the doll face down in the stream was recalled by Robert's drowning. He didn't know what to say or do. It had been an age since Emily's father had fully embraced his daughter, now married and a mother of two herself. She must have been twelve or thirteen years old when he had last folded her in his arms. Now they moved upwards and out, stiffly at first, like a rusted machine suddenly oiled by Emily's tears. He too trembled and shook as he held his daughter who, glancing up into his face, caught a look of dumb and petrified horror, an animal incomprehension that disappeared when it felt itself observed – the old century enfolding the newly born one in its arms, but arms which were already frail and feeble, arms that could no longer grip, apprehensive and half-senile arms.

* * *

THE RUG wrapped round Emily's legs is a tartan. She is gratified that it is one she herself bought from one of her own shops. She remembers taking three crisp pound notes out of her purse and waiting for five shillings – two half-crowns – change. That was more than ten years ago and she is pleased that it still looks fresh and bright. It was a line she had helped the buyer choose. She prided herself on her ability to select and sell products that she knew would last. People never understood why she insisted on paying for things she could have had by walking into a shop and picking straight from the shelf. Charles was always saying that she was a fool – though he knew she wasn't – for not taking advantage of her position and walking out of any one of her shops with whatever she wanted. But she would never do it, not even in an emergency. It would have been too much like stealing from herself when she wasn't looking.

But there is this letter from one of her daughters, Margaret. Which makes Emily's eyes blaze.

I thought I had done it, finished. I brought my family – all of them, Margaret and Jean, Virginia and Cyril – through it all. The war and the depression, the war and austerity and they are still here. I thought I had done enough but not so. Now Ronald has gone and cut the link in the chain I worked so hard to forge. Ronald has cut the family off from its future.

Although she does not admit the question there is also the matter of what now happens to the family business. Her labours there have run into a cul-de-sac. She had assumed without stating it that Ronald would continue the line of inheritance by taking over the business and passing it on. Naturally, this is no longer possible.

Emily's passion subsides and she focuses once more on her husband,

Charles, dearest Charles. Who would have thought seeing the dribble run down your chin that you once helped to supply us in the scarce years of the war. That you kept the provisions coming in one of your ships to feed and clothe us. You bringing things across the sea and my selling them. It gave me a sense of continuity, of our working together – you probably don't know what I'm talking about – as though we were both providing in our different ways what the community needed. You know what our granddaughter Anne used to say? Capitalists! Mind you, she was happy enough to use the money to buy time to shout us down. Do you know what this letter says, Charles? Can you hear me? It's about Ronald. He's had it cut off. Do you hear? Cut off, I said. I know you can't answer but what am I going to do? I was depending on him, Charles. I thought he'd come right in the end but he didn't.

Emily picks a sheet of airmail paper from her lap and holds it up to the window. Through it she can make out the garden overlaid by the words of Margaret's letter. As though the place where she has lived for more than sixty years is a palimpsest and this letter the latest contribution.

You see, Charles, this letter Margaret has sent me from Spain – what is she doing there, I ask you? I have to hear it from a daughter in another country not Ronald's own mother. Where is Virginia? I hope she hasn't let the milk run over.

Emily reads from the letter with contempt, mimicking Margaret's sonorous twang: 'I've just had a letter from Ronald's sister Dorothy . . . ' Does she think I'm going gaga that I can't remember who Dorothy my first grandchild is? 'Dorothy who says that your grandson is no longer your grandson. He's gone and done what some of us suspected him capable of all along. He's changed his sex. In any case, I am sure that Virginia has told you all this by now.' You know, Charles, that Virginia hasn't said a word about this. Surely she knows.

Emily leans forward because she has noticed that Charles is cold and shivering.

Would you like my rug, Charles? No? Perhaps we'll ask Virginia to bring you one when she comes. Would you like that, captain? Do you think, Charles, we ought to have the chestnut cut back, or perhaps it should be felled completely? It doesn't look as though it could survive another winter. I know it would be a shame. Ronald and the girls often used to sit under it. And you've always loved the flowers, you once said they reminded you of fireworks or was it candles floating in a river ceremony somewhere or other? Where was it? Shanghai? Bangkok? You went to so many places I get them mixed up. But safety first, don't you think? Cyril's probably right that it should come down altogether. And you know how he hates to uproot anything. Remember the fuss he made when I told him to get rid of the blackcurrant bushes. You'd think I was asking him to commit murder. But there were just too many of them and we don't eat them any more like we used to. So when it's convenient we'll get someone out here to cut it down, it's best to be on the safe side, I think.

The paper in Emily's hand whispers in a draught blowing under the oak door on the far side of the room.

I was telling you what Margaret said about Ronald. You know why she wrote to tell me this? It wasn't from sympathy or concern, it was out of pure spite. She was always jealous of my affection for Ronald and never understood why I didn't care for our other grandsons, her boys. Now she's gloating.

Somewhere in the house there is the crash of china shattering.

* * *

MARGARET AND SONS were expected 'home' – this, at least, was what Emily had said although her grandsons had never been 'home'. Margaret had left pregnant with her first and with her GI at her side sometime between VE and VJ day. That was seven years before and she had not returned to England since then; this was to be her first visit. Charles was not there when they arrived. No one could remember whether it was because his ship hadn't then docked or whether he had disappeared into the garden to help Cyril.

Emily stood at the front door waiting for the car she had sent to the railway station to return. They were travelling from Southampton to London and from there to Guildford where George would meet them. George was the odd-job man who sometimes drove the car. It was not that Emily was unable to afford a full-time driver, she could by then, but as there was very little driving required she considered it wasteful to employ a man who would spend most of his time polishing radiator grilles and hub caps. It could not be said of Emily that she ever spent her money on the upkeep of a frivolous appearance.

When she heard the car, still hidden by the trees and hedgerow, crunching up the drive, she straightened her frock and patted her bun to check that it was in place. Unusually, a strand of her hair had come loose and there was no longer time to retie her hair so she would have to tuck it back in as best she could. Which she was doing as the car made its circular approach to the house. The car door swung open not at all sedately but as if there had been an explosion inside which threatened to blow the door off its hinges. Emily's grandsons tumbled out, pulling and poking at each other as they continued their brawl quite oblivious of their grandmother at the top of the steps. They were followed by a shining, radiant Margaret who somehow seemed to vibrate an even larger presence than her mother recalled. Emily thought for a moment how she might seem a trifle dusty and ragged round the edges. Nevertheless, she stepped forward confidently to greet the daughter she had missed, the grandsons she had never met.

Who could censure Emily for her momentary misgiving at the top of the steps? After all, life was still a pinched and hollow affair for many in England in the aftermath of war. There was the sense of people clinging on, the notion of rationing and hoarding just in case hung in the air. Indeed, meat was still rationed. Things were accumulated and sparsely used in case it happened again. The customers in Emily's shops looked around as if they mistrusted what they could see in front of them on the shelves, as if it were a mirage that could fade at any moment. They weren't accustomed to spending, to being able to spend. They stood goggle-eyed, in awe, like a group of convicts suddenly given their freedom and unsure what to do with it. Emily hardly stocked and no one bought 'luxury' goods – that came later. They wanted sensible things: soap, bread, sugar, butter, eggs, cheese, milk, tea. As yet there were few frivolities.

But Margaret looked as though she could and did have every possible indulgence. The make-up, the clothes, the nylons, the very flesh on her bones was humming with an unfamiliar zest. Emily, stepping forward to meet her freshly coiffured and perfumed daughter, tripped and stumbled down her own steps.

'Larry, Andy! Your grandma!' Margaret's voice rang out. The two boys stopped their scuffle and turned to help their grandmother, but Emily had already picked herself up and was dusting down her frock.

One boy with bristles on his scalp – Emily thought of the nail brushes they sold – held out his hand, smiling. 'Hey, you OK, grandma?' Emily stared at the unknown creature. 'Anyway, hi, I'm Larry.' In Emily's ears it was another language. She took the creature's hand in her own which was trembling. No doubt, thought Emily, he will put this down to my age, my infirmity, which is not the reason at all.

Have you noticed, Charles, that on a good day I can still put a teaspoonful of sugar in my cup without spilling a single grain?

So the New World arrived in Coronation year to find the Old

World teetering on its doorstep and shaking not in decrepitude but in rage. Emily was ashamed that she felt it but she was insulted. Who was this presumptuous child behaving as though it were an adult? She knew that she should not blame Larry because his scalp was shaved like a monk's but she felt an abhorrence for it that she was never able to expunge and this was compounded in her eyes by the child's grotesque aping of an adult's familiar manners as if the child had known her all its life! She knew then that she was being unfair, and even later, but however hard she tried she could never overcome her initial revulsion at this affront to her dignity.

Then Margaret was calling to her.

'Hi, Mom! It's great to see you!'

Whatever had happened to Margaret's tone and diction? To one side of her the other grandson piped, 'Gee, Mom, doesn't she look old!' Margaret did not contradict him. Emily knew she should laugh and dismiss this but the little boy's words seemed to echo and taunt her. Margaret and Emily embraced. Emily could smell the perfume heavy as roses on a summer's afternoon – she never used the stuff herself now.

'Mom, you're looking great. Don't worry about Larry, he's just funny.'

Emily detached herself. 'Let's go in, you must be exhausted.'

'Oh no. I'm just so excited to be back, everything looks so . . . so cute.'

Emily wondered if Charles who had travelled all over the world might understand Margaret better than she was doing.

'You know the kids are really looking forward to seeing her.'

'Seeing who?'

'Queen Elizabeth, of course.' The boys bounded up the steps two at a time. 'It's great to be back.' Margaret followed her sons up to the house.

Emily stood on the drive looking up. Was it possible that one's own flesh and blood could alter so radically and in such a short period of time? Come to think of it, had Margaret really changed that much? She was still big and bold. Emily began to climb the steps, her heart sinking.

In the weeks that followed Emily noticed when Larry and Andy talked about her they never used the name she ached for.

They forever whispered about 'her' or 'she'. She thought that perhaps she should say something but decided it was Margaret's task and not hers. In later years neither of her American grandsons knew what to call her and it became a matter of unease, an awkwardness whenever they wrote to her.

I wanted them, Charles, to call me 'grannie' or 'grandma' or 'nana' but they wrote 'Dear Emily . . . ' and I felt dissatisfied, incomplete. I wanted to be a part of a family that I'd never had. When you get old people think you've used up all your emotions; that because your skin's dried out then your feelings must have too. If anything your need is greater.

Emily's grandsons saw the English queen and left with their mother. Emily never met them again. The funny boy, Larry, was, with longer hair and no smile on his face, killed in Vietnam. Or was it Cambodia? Nobody was quite certain where the border lay. Andy crossed several state boundaries and found himself swallowing a drug that was fashionable for a time. Then he was a carpenter north of the Golden Gate Bridge in a county that later became fashionable too. Where he snorted cocaine rather than swallowed LSD. What were families to him? But there was Margaret, their mother Margaret.

Margaret, you know, Charles, could have eaten Cyril for breakfast. Where is Cyril? Somewhere in the garden, I suppose. That's why she had to leave England which wasn't big enough for her, and settle somewhere with a bit more space. And now she's in Spain, what is she doing there? Drinking her alimony, I imagine, trying, and pretending she isn't, to forget. That she has lost both families.

Emily fingers the rug and looks through the thin glass between her and the world outside. If she could she would stay like this forever with all the movement of her memories as she sits. She would only ask for the memories and welcome their imperfections, no more. Charles, it seems, has a dribble of spittle running through his unshaven chin. She leans forward to wipe it away.

* * *

RONALD, in contrast to his American cousins, used to call Emily 'grandma'. It made her feel there was a belonging, however tenuous the connection. Even when he had last visited and told her he was to be away for some little time and the conversation had run:

'Anywhere interesting, darling?'

'Egypt.'

'Cairo, I suppose. But you should try Luxor too. A little boat trip down the Nile, that's fascinating, or so I understand, because as you must know it's not a journey I've ever done myself.'

'I don't think I'll have time.'

'Working?' Emily had always been curious, wanted to know what he was up to.

'Sort of. Not a holiday in any case.'

'Films?'

'Not exactly.'

'Otherwise I might've asked if you wanted to show me the pyramids, the desert. I don't get out much these days, your mother never takes me anywhere.'

'Another time perhaps.'

How could Emily have failed to notice his agitation, his evasiveness. Ronald had been reluctant to tell her anything about his forthcoming trip when normally he was so garrulous, enthusiastic. Now she understands why. His fingernails had been extraordinarily long and beautifully manicured though she'd said nothing at the time. It was the last occasion she had seen Ronald, the real Ronald who was now gone from her and the rest of the family forever. It was one thing to discover that your parents were no longer the people you had imagined they were, but to find that your grandchild was no longer the boy you had thought he was . . . Ronald knew Emily was bluffing. In spite of the fact or perhaps because Charles had spent so many years at sea, Emily's voyages consisted of a single Channel crossing – 'once was enough to give me the idea,' she had said, 'and I don't understand the attraction.' She preferred to travel in England and Scotland only and to know about anywhere further afield through talk or books and latterly television.

But then with Ronald in Egypt, or anywhere else for that matter, as long as he continued to call her 'grandma' the thread remained uncut for her until Margaret's letter arrived. Of all her daughters it had to be Margaret who broke the news. Amazing that she herself had produced such a creature as Margaret, loud and elbowing in while the others – Virginia and Jean – stood back and were so quiet compared with the first, large-boned sister.

* * *

JEAN. How much longer can Jean stay in that godforsaken place, Charles? Did you see her last letter? It was written by someone whose hand was shaking. Her writing looked even more trembly than mine sometimes does. I'm sure she had some sort of fever when she wrote it and it was later than her normal monthly letter. I do hope she hasn't caught anything serious.

Emily clears her throat and looks at the chair hoping she will hear concern expressed for her own health but there is none forthcoming. She wonders whether Virginia has deserted her forever. But no, she's never had the will to leave since that first abortive attempt. Emily strains to try to catch the sounds of her third daughter moving about the house. Perhaps she is picking up the broken pieces of porcelain and placing them one by one in the dustpan so they do not tinkle.

Perhaps Jean's got leprosy? It can do horrible things, attacks the nervous system and parts of you just wither away through lack of use. Why doesn't she come home? She must have done all she can by now. Surely there's a limit to what one person working in those sort of conditions can do. You can't forever knock your head against a brick wall. I remember you telling me, Charles, that you thought charity had its limits otherwise it was a matter of pouring yourself into a bottomless pit.

Emily had not objected when Jean had made what she, Emily, now thought of as 'Jean's sacrifice'. She thought it would in time wear off and Jean would come scuttling back home with her conscience salved, but it had not happened like that. Jean had remained in Africa and Emily started referring to 'the waste of a woman's life'. When Emily realised that Jean was not coming back, at least for a very long time, she cried. There had been nothing specific, it had dawned on her for no reason at all.

She remembers how Cyril found her sitting in a deck chair one September evening. She knows it must have been September for she had been to put flowers on the grave – she always remembered her father's anniversary. It was almost too dark to see anything and she was sitting in the garden staring back towards the house where she was now encased. She thought it should be getting cold though she didn't feel it. The first lights came on in the downstairs rooms and she could see Virginia pulling the curtains to. She felt excluded. Then came Cyril's voice from somewhere behind her.

'Mother, what are you doing out here at this time? And dressed like that.'

I was wearing a frock, the one I bought for your retirement party, Charles, the one with a high neckline that you liked. The first time I wore it you said how aristocratic it made me look. I remember it wasn't too often that you noticed or commented on what I wore. There was some pretty lace round the cuffs . . .

Cyril had seen his mother's face wet with tears and stooping low over her had whispered, 'What's the matter, mother? What is it?' He picked her hands out of her lap and held them between his own. 'Mother, you're frozen!'

'Am I?'

He rubbed her hands and blew on them. 'You should go indoors now.'

Emily looks down at the backs of her hands which are not, as she feels, translucent, fragile; she expects to see her thin blood running in the veins, aqueducts over the tendons that criss-cross the area, but surprisingly there is no evidence of such a flow. Her hands are a little coarse and gnarled like a carpenter's. They amaze her with their lack of delicacy, their matter-of-factness: hands, no more or less. She feels cheated by them.

Cyril put his arms round his mother's shoulders and helped her out of the deck chair.

'I know,' he said. 'I know you still love him.'

Which was not the reason for Emily's tears though she did not contradict Cyril. She left him, as she did so often, comfortable in the illusion that he knew how she felt and understood her. It tied him to her, for who else might he claim as his own?

By this time Jean must have been in Africa for seven or eight years. And Emily's tears were for Jean's tossing and turning. Emily had imagined her daughter exhausted but unable to sleep; pot bellies, sagging and sucked-dry breasts, pigeon toes, huge staring eyes, heads perched on necks almost too frail to support them, all parading through her nights as they did her days. Jean had once written that a mangy three-legged dog had been chased by a mob through the village. It had been stoned to death because it was suspected of having rabies and had already bitten someone who was waiting to see whether he would find himself hysterical at the sight of water in a part of the country where fresh water was God's own nectar. Jean wrote how the dust settled in their throats and lungs like dust in an unused room and filmed the furniture which had to be dusted at least once a day; how the mosquito net hung round the bed shrouding one's vision; how the geckos when caught by the cat would scurry away leaving their tails in its paws; how the houseboy never used a handkerchief but openly hawked his phlegm on the veranda; how the flying ants would batter at the shutters after the rains and in the morning the boy would gladly sweep them up to cook for his breakfast; how . . . these were, in fact, incidental asides in Jean's cheerful and optimistic letters home but they were the ones on which Emily fastened as though she wanted to confirm the horror of the life Jean had chosen for herself. She was aware that she had perhaps schooled Jean too well in a Christian teaching. That the daughter who had followed the straightest and narrowest path had gone furthest from home – culturally if not geographically – was an irony not lost on Emily who inscribed at the top of her list that charity began at home.

Were you here when she came on her first home leave, Charles? Probably not. What a shock it was. True, she's never been as well-built as Margaret but she was painfully, pitifully thin. She looked to me half-starved, like the people she was supposed to be helping. Did she think it an insult to look well-fed in a place where there was a shortage of proper food? No make-up of course. Not that she'd ever used much before she went. Takes after me like that.

Emily's fingers feel for her cheeks. She uses a moisturising cream though she never admits this to anyone except Virginia who has to buy the jar for her. She is pleased with the suppleness and the wrinkles seem to be less in evidence now than they were a few years ago. Visitors who are twenty, even thirty, years younger than her have skins that look, she thinks, like creased maps.

I swear Jean was wearing the same pair of shoes and carrying the same handbag as on the day she left five years before. Not that a man would notice that kind of thing. You once said, Charles, that men never notice until a woman stops taking care of herself. Then you might've noticed a change in Jean, though you never said anything, at least not at the time. Which was . . . how long ago was it? A quarter of a century.

1949, when there was still rationing in her mother's shops and the customers complained. Before Jean left for Africa she heard her mother's reports : surely, their customers said, you could let me have just a little more sugar; or, one would've thought that four years after the end of the war one might be able to pick and choose a little more; or, I expect they get more eggs in Germany than we can here. So when Jean left she did not feel she was missing out. People were grumbling, people seemed grey to her. She anticipated the vibrancy of a tropical light.

In the autumn of 1954, when she had a home leave and returned sapped by that very light, how different things were. People were buying from the shops and wouldn't stop. Jean herself had almost forgotten how to go shopping, it was all sent up from the coast to her. It was an orgy in which she did not know how to take part, where to begin.

Emily, determined that Charles will not sit and vegetate, rifles for a topic she thinks might interest him. Not that the matching blue of Jean's handbag and shoes some quarter of a century before will hold him. Business might. She pulls herself up in the chair, the rug slips down to the floor but she ignores this, speaking in what she considers her forceful voice, a tone that in fact rasps; the hairline cracks can be heard throughout her delivery.

* * *

PROFIT. We made a greater profit in the year Jean came back on leave than we did in the three years before. We kept running out of stock and not because there wasn't any. People were suddenly buying, Charles. Am I telling you something you already know? Is it boring you? You were never a great one for profit and loss, accounts you said were my speciality, something finite, reducible. You, I suppose, thought you were the philosopher, the mystic at sea. But the balance sheets, Charles, were the thin ice I had to walk, forever, without your asking, knowing what lay underneath.

She sees the shelves empty in a dizzying whirl of packets, bottles, jars, tins, boxes, cans, chests, pots, cartons. The back of the shop knee-deep in waves of paper, cardboard and wrappings.

They took on a casual labourer at the Haslemere shop to help with the unloading and stacking. Emily used to love visiting that shop, especially in autumn, driving round the Devil's Punchbowl in a horseshoe of reds, russets and golds. The man they had temporarily taken on said to her, 'Whoever would've thought, ma'am. That it'd be like this,' and he nodded at the piles of boxes stacked outside the shop. 'Last time I unloaded this many boxes it weren't no groceries. Live ammunition. They taught me to be careful of 'ow I 'andled it. No good throwing that sort of thing around, if you'll excuse the expression ma'am.' He heaved another box out of the back of the van and started a new pile. 'Don't want any accidents, do we?' The boxes carried the Tate & Lyle insignia – a knight bearing a shield and brandishing a sword.

'Sugar?' asked the man.

'Syrup,' said Emily. 'You're out of work then?'

'Not right now, ma'am.' He grinned.

'There's plenty of work about for a willing fellow like you.'

'True, ma'am. But when they 'ear what 'appened . . .' He trailed off but Emily prised his story out of him.

The war was all but over and in a few weeks there would be unconditional surrender in Europe. He had been loading up a lorry at the depot in Aldershot where he had worked for most of the war – he hadn't been able to go and fight because they said he was too short-sighted. He had left his mates still loading the lorry while he went to find the sergeant to sign his chit. He was, he said, about sixty or seventy yards from the spot when there was an explosion whose force knocked him to the ground. This was followed by a second much bigger explosion – 'the whole ruddy hut going up, if you'll excuse me ma'am.' He explained that it was like someone squeezing your head between their hands or swimming too deep underwater. Then he passed out and woke up in a hospital bed and there were soothing voices telling him not to worry, that he was all right and that there were only one or two pieces still left in his legs but that the worst were out. There was a pain like nothing he'd ever experienced before in his head and a shadow was hanging above his eye as when a cloud passes overhead on a sunny day. He had tried to move his hand up to his head where it hurt but the nurse had been too quick for him and told him not to touch. When he asked her why she said that he'd had a piece of metal in there and though it was out now it would be tender for a while. He asked if he could see it but she misunderstood and said there was nothing to see but the bandage. He told Emily that 'these nurses have a knack of playing things down,' because when, some days later, he first saw the thing himself he was shocked.

Emily grew conscious that he was telling her this with the left side of his face turned away from her and, in fact, during the time she had been speaking to him she could not recall seeing that part of his head. But he swung round to face her, removing his cap at the same time. There she saw a crater where his hairline should have met his temple. She imagined a bomb ripping up a meadow, the ragged edges of turf and weeds hanging limp at the crater's rim.

'So you see, ma'am, I was the lucky one. The rest of the poor blighters, three of 'em, was killed outright. And I'd seen fellows coming back from all the worst places without a scratch on 'em.'

They had, in the end, kept him in hospital for months and naturally enough he came to know the nurses well and married one. He explained how people got frightened when they saw his sunken skull, assuming he was a half-wit or something.

Emily asked him if he would like a more permanent job.

'If you don't think it's a cheek, ma'am, I think you could answer that question yourself.' And he turned away to continue with his stacking of the Tate & Lyle boxes. Mr Johnson became a loyal employee and after a dozen years of doggedness and persistence manager of the shop in Haslemere. He inched his way there and died a year later of a brain haemorrhage. At the funeral there were youths lounging by the lych gate with hair below their collars and bell-bottomed trousers flapping in the breeze. One of them had stencilled on the back of his denim jacket, 'All You Need Is Love'.

When it was over, Charles, I went up to the youth and said, 'I'm sorry about your father. He was a good man. He was loyal and worked hard for us. If you're ever out of a job like your father once was . . . ' but he cut me short. Do you know what he said? 'Can't you stop, even when he's dead, talking about business, profit?'

Emily thinks she hears someone at the door of the room where she is sitting and turns her head in time to catch, she swears, the door closing and its handle released. It could only have been Virginia and she knows that her daughter has a habit of checking to see whether she is all right. If she appears to be then she, Virginia, disappears again. She thinks she has better things to do than listen to her mother talk, is how Emily puts it to herself; and yet if she listened there is plenty, Emily is sure, that Virginia could learn. She shrugs her shoulders inwardly and lets out an inaudible sigh. This daughter has never been willing to listen to her, though in the end, Emily smiles drily to herself, she has usually come round to her mother's way of thinking. Would she, for instance, be living in this very house had she not accepted her mother's wisdom? And though she may sometimes avoid conversation with Emily she would never desert her, not now. In any case, there is always Charles who is a willing listener and Emily is suddenly gladdened that he spent so many years away from her at sea since there is still so much at which he was not present, which he does not know, or if he does, only dimly. The thought brightens her. She clears her throat to speak to him.

* * *

FATHER'S FUNERAL was quite different from Mr Johnson's. You were definitely away then, Charles, or I would remember you being there. It was such a solemn affair. Because we couldn't find enough able-bodied male relatives the bearers were some of father's longest-serving employees and they were shaky enough as it was. I thought they were going to drop the coffin. Thank God it's all cremations these days. Who will carry me? Certainly not you.

It was an evening in November 1918 that the Armistice was celebrated by a crowd at the Angel Hotel in Guildford. Emily and her father were among the guests of Bertrand. Bertrand who? Many of the guests could not have answered the question. Just as they could not have told you what it was that he did. There was, of course, money in the family which was in some way connected with the import and export business and this was how, apparently, Bertrand knew Charles and hence Emily and her father. Not that Bertrand wasted much time consolidating the family's fortunes in trade. Which was probably why everyone knew him as Bertrand.

That night Bertrand proposed a toast to you, Charles. 'Here's to those absent friends who aren't with us tonight because they still have a job to do. And especially to my friend Charles wherever he may be now.' That's what he said, smiling at me at the same time. You know what I thought? I wondered why your friend Bertrand was still here and not doing his bit for King and country. There were balloons on which someone had painted 'Victory' in white. Mine burst on one of the candles in the centrepiece of the table. Though everyone laughed the sudden explosion made me tearful. Bertrand asked me if I was glad that it was all over. 'Of course,' I said. And do you know what he replied? I remember every word because it sounded so wicked. He said, 'I wouldn't have been unhappy had it continued just a little longer.' He shocked the other ladies at our table but I understood him.

Bertrand handed Emily into the carriage standing outside in the yard. He joked with her father, 'Why don't you get something more up-to-date?' 'One of those infernal contraptions!' came the answer. 'They're the coming thing,' said Bertrand. 'But I'm not!' was George's retort, and Bertrand stood admiring the carriage and the clatter of wheels and hooves as it turned down the High Street over the cobbles which felt exceedingly bumpy whenever he travelled over them in his motor car. The following morning Emily's father did not get up from his bed which was where she found him, dead.

It was as though he had seen what was then thought of as 'the worst of it' through. Having ensured that the old order had been preserved intact – which it hadn't, though if one didn't look too closely one could imagine – he could give up his own struggle with the world. Perhaps there was something in him saying that it would never be the same again however much he pretended. Shortly before he died he cited the case of women. How some of them had already got the vote, how they were still working in factories though the war was nearly over, how they were in jobs as 'clippies', as clerks. It was a wave which threatened to drown the world he knew and understood. He carried about with him, literally speaking, a picture of his wife, Emily's mother, who had died before the old century had finished. Whenever he took out his watch to tell the time he would flick open its case and find himself gazing at the image of true womanhood, his dead wife. It was often said about him that he concerned himself too much with hours and minutes but those who said it did not realise he was contemplating an eternity. Somehow he knew by instinct that things on earth were changing. How carefully he chose the right time to stop living.

The telegram I sent you, Charles, didn't reach you in time or you couldn't get away. Which wasn't clear and doesn't matter now if it did then. But in my defence I did send it hoping that you would arrive. Now you're wondering what this is about 'my defence' and you're thinking Emily has gone a little bit gaga. I haven't. Perhaps I shall tell you about it after lunch. Where is Virginia? Not still clearing up the mess, surely.

Emily hopes that Virginia is not burning the lunch but then reflects that she will not mind since today it is her own turn to do the dishes. Which she likes and if the pans are burnt it is more of a challenge. It is nice, she thinks, to feel that one is contributing even in a small way. She does not like the way in which Virginia tries to dismiss her efforts by suggesting that she or Mrs King will do the washing up without her. Really, sometimes Virginia considers her a complete nincompoop. A recent conversation comes to mind in which Virginia upbraided her for saying how nice Guildford used to be. She told her mother how she was talking about the past more and more, contemplating the present less and less. Margaret's letter concerning Ronald has stirred Emily into imagining action.

We don't go outside the house much these days. The garden is as much as we can manage. I think we ought to make more of an effort. Don't you? I think I might have made a mistake bequeathing the business to Ronald. It has made us all too complacent.

She looks out of the window. There is a sign that the mist may be breaking up as if a light can be glimpsed shining faintly through a half-translucent curtain. You know this is the first year that I have not changed them completely by myself. I had Mrs King help me though I made her swear not to tell Virginia that she had. Don't look at me as though I'm raving. The curtains of course! What else would Mrs King help me change twice a year? The cushion covers, perhaps, but then you wouldn't think of those anyway. I don't imagine you even know that I ran them up myself. That I didn't have them made to measure at some exorbitant price. Or did you think I bought them ready made? As if one could find ready-made curtains for windows that size. You most likely never considered the matter.

Emily twists the top half of her body to look at the curtains drawn back behind her. To put the lining in was a devil. She reaches out to finger the rich warmth of the velvet but she cannot stretch far enough and drops her arm in exhaustion. She will get up now! Just to do it. And clears her throat to cry:

Virginia! Virginia!

* * *

TAKE FOUR SHOPS situated in the parts of Surrey where London had not yet crawled. Scribe an arc some thirty-five to forty miles distant from Marble Arch and you will find that in a south-westerly or south-south-westerly direction it runs through towns called Dorking and Guildford and further west through villages like Chobham. These are areas noted for their prosperous gentility with something of a rural air attaching itself; there is, however, nothing which could be considered wild, remote or threatening about the region. It is the kind of place where two high spots on the Surrey downs, the Hog's Back which leads west to Farnham and Newlands Corner on the ridge between Guildford and Dorking, are visited by families with their picnic baskets and more recently by ice-cream vans though such disturbances were, of course, unknown in Emily's childhood and youth. The sheep on the downs look – as they still do – as if their fleeces have been freshly bathed and the potential wool as though it will need no preparation before it is turned into cardigans or socks. The grass on the slopes of the downs appears to have been evenly trimmed with a modern machine like a hover mower when, of course, it has been neatly chewed by those ruminants. The compact hedgerows seem to be as precisely boxed as any of those yew hedges on the estates which are scattered across this lush part of the country; a difference between the rural and domesticated hedgerow might be that the former are thick and abundant with flora and fauna which apparently prosper as richly as the inhabitants of the grounds where not a flower or leaf is out of place. The russet brickwork of many of the buildings reflects that mellow ripeness of the landscape itself which is plentifully blessed by natural bounty and comfortable growth.

This is the place where Emily's father, George, opened his shops in the final decade of Victoria's century. Emily's mother died giving birth to her younger brother, Robert, in 1894.

George was heartbroken and lost. It was not his wife's physical presence around the house that he would miss. After all there was a nanny to look after Albert, Emily and Robert as well as a housekeeper, a cook and a gardener. It was her company that was lacking, her ability to occupy him and sketch out his codes of thought, behaviour and emotion. It seemed as if the areas of experience she had created for him ceased to exist except in his memory. There was a void and he knew only one way to fill it: business, enterprise, profit. Not that there was any shortage of money. The family was sitting quite content and satisfied on wealth accumulated through the shipping trade which had begun with the West Indies route a century and a half before and latterly had drifted to India.

The shops were set in the High Streets of the three towns – Guildford, Dorking and Farnham – and a village – Chobham. They sat on well-chosen sites without ostentation but with dignity. There might be a gunsmith's on one side and a saddlery on the other. They were double-fronted in oak with the words running the breadth of the shop: G. Harrison. Retailer of General Groceries and Provisions.

If one stopped to look in through the front window one might catch a glimpse of a selection of items on offer: Cheddar, Double Gloucester, Caerphilly, Red Leicester and Stilton cheeses; orange, lime, redcurrant, strawberry, damson and blackcurrant jams, jellies and marmalades; raisins, dried apricots, currants and prunes; shortbread, gingerbread, crumpet and muffin; oatmeal, plain flour and baker's yeast; Chinese and Indian teas; breakfast and after-dinner coffee roasts; Worcestershire sauce, horseradish and powdered mustard; cinnamon, cloves, mace and nutmeg. If you stepped up and pushed open the front door there would be a gentle tinkling to herald your entrance and most probably a voice would be heard asking you if there was any way it could be of assistance. You might look down the length of the shop and find two counters running into the back, underneath them cupboards and behind them more cupboards and shelves. The brass of weights, scales and cheese wires might be glowing against the marble counter. If you went upstairs you would find two rooms: an office and a storeroom, though unless you were a tradesperson you would naturally never have ventured further than the customers' side of the counter. The shop's staff would most probably consist of a male manager, a lady assistant of 'mature years' and a young boy, who would be eager to please you for they worked still in a world where the notion of service did not imply indignity.

Emily thinks that Charles needs a shave. How long is it since Virginia came with a brush and soap in her hands? She oughtn't to allow her own father to look forgotten as though he were a resident in some second-class nursing home. She asks her husband:

I wonder who helped my father stock the shops? He chose so well, it seems out of character. Perhaps it was mother's voice whispering to him from beyond the grave. He didn't or dared not understand others' feelings yet he judged their material needs so wisely. Was it simply a question of gauging his chosen market accurately? What do you think, Charles? How did you know which goods to freight in your ship, which ones would bring you a profit?

A third of the men recruited for service in the Boer War were rejected as unfit and unhealthy mainly on account of their miserable diet. One had to be well fed and watered to die *pro patria*.

I've never cared much for asparagus. Though we've always had a good reputation for it. You know it was only first grown commercially at the end of the century. Father's shops captured the market for it early on. It may be that without knowing it I felt guilty. You've never said to me, Charles, that you ever felt guilty about anything. Girls in foreign parts, boys below deck. Have you nothing you'd like to confess now? There's something I will tell you later.

At the end of the Great War Emily was left with a decision to make about the direction which a high-class retailer of food and perishable goods might take. The most obvious route was the one her father had originally taken – to continue selling the cream of the cream – which is probably what he would have done had he lived. The choice was not as simple as it may seem now. It was not then apparent that their customers would have less money to spend. Although the government had to increase its spending it did this by borrowing rather than increasing taxation, so for the time being the gentry's feathers were unruffled. The demands the war placed on industrial production meant that before the end of 1916 a Trade Card Agreement was reached which handed over the control of factories to shop stewards' committees.

Most people said Emily was foolish to try and attract a wider clientèle. They claimed it would lower the quality and come to no good in the end.

Did you ever hear, Charles, of a war waged by a government which had to cajole not demand the co-operation of its workers?

Here lay the heart of the changes to come, occurring not on the battlefields but in the factories and industries at home. Which Emily felt though she could not articulate, only intuit, at the time.

The word 'workers' rolls round Emily's tongue. She has always considered herself one even at the pinnacle of her power when, some ten years before, she exercised absolute control over more than two hundred retail outlets. She would tell you if you asked her that it is her willingness to work at, work on the trivial details with her own hands – the curtains, the washing up, the weeding, – that has made her a success in the less tangible fields of finance, management and marketing.

She suddenly feels very cold and thinks Charles must be too. In spite of the pale citrus sun she can make out through the window she will have to get Virginia to bring in some kindling and a scuttleful of coal. Later she will enjoy kneeling by the empty grate twisting paper, laying the wood criss-cross, plunging the tongs into the scuttle while she calculates dividends and considers how much Charles should know.

Her father's establishment of the shops had begun as a means of distracting him from the loss of Emily's mother but while the new century grew out of its infancy they did not. The shops assumed the role of monument to his memory of her and as his tactile sense of her faded their original purpose ossified. When Emily inherited ten outlets, more than double the number of the prototypes, she found herself in control of an organisation that was already archaic. Only those who refused to recognise the scars, wider than trenches, claimed Edwardian Britain still lived. Emily was not one of those.

'Virginia, coal please!' she calls.

* * *

MISTRESS. The word is synonymous with a glamour that rarely pertains, though here love lies down too. Emily's father took a mistress because he loved her mother so completely. To marry another woman, giving her the status of his dead wife, would have meant if only by implication the desecration of his wife's shrine. It must have been easier for him to take a mistress than to accept a second wife with the fundamental shift of ground that would have entailed. It was simpler to resort to the petty subterfuges demanded by the maintenance of a mistress than to opt for the open difficulties of remarriage. Such inflexibility was a characteristic of the time. Brought up to the notion that love like other abstracts was fixed as a tongue in aspic how could he have done otherwise than remain a widower?

You know, Charles, that father had the emotional manoeuvrability of a rhinoceros. That's what appealed to me in you. Lumbering, yes, but steadfast too.

Suddenly she catches sight of a small blue rectangle on the carpet at her feet. An image of the swimming pool they had started to build but never finished floats up. She imagines the pressure and stiffness oozing from her joints as she bobs on the surface of the warm turquoise water. One spring some men had come and dug a hole but they had gone away and never re-appeared. Charles was away at sea and she didn't know where they might be contacted. Through a dry summer the sides of the hole cracked and crumbled. By autumn the bottom was rustling inches deep in leaves; in the months following the hole filled with rainwater and froze. Anne nearly drowned trying to walk across the ice. The next spring she had the hole filled in and never again spoke about her swimming pool. She knew, in any case, that Charles would not mind. After all, didn't he spend most of his life surrounded by water? She reaches down towards the blue paper as if she is about to dip her hand in the limpid pool she never realised.

I was always grateful to get your letters, Charles. You wrote so regularly. There was never anything exciting or unpredictable about them. I knew what they would say before I opened them but I was glad they came all the same.

Two years after the end of the Great War and before Ronald's mother, Virginia, was a year old Emily received a letter in an unknown hand. It was from a stranger who said she had known Emily's father and had always wanted to meet Emily but the months somehow had flown by with her doing nothing about it. She hoped that Emily would not be offended that she was, after all this time, getting in touch with her. It was a courteous if somewhat formal letter and Emily replied in similar fashion inviting the lady to tea.

When the lady was shown into the drawing room Emily had difficulty in hiding her surprise. She had been expecting someone of her father's generation but the lady was, if anything, barely older than herself.

Did I tell you, Charles, what Julia was wearing when we first met? Probably not. It wouldn't have interested you, I suppose. A matching jacket and skirt with a fox fur slung over her shoulder. A pillbox hat cocked to one side with a dark veil shading the upper part of her face. One of the fox legs was pinned across her lapels – it made one think the leg was holding the whole thing together. Her hat was the same colour as her suit, a deep pine green. Her shoes and clutch handbag had a hint of burgundy to pick up the fox.

Emily's own long hair was tied in a bun and had she been wearing a hat it would have been one of the flat, broad-brimmed variety which was all her wardrobe held. Her dress was long and a dark blue indistinguishable from black, with a white lace collar. She wore flat-heeled shoes and only the form of her ankles could be guessed through thick stockings, unlike Julia's calves which were fully visible. Emily's concession to ornament was a brooch made of gold and representing a galleon.

I was wearing the gold ship you gave me. It was one you hardly ever saw. I always wore it when you were at sea but the moment you docked I put it away. Like an armband of mourning, I suppose. Reminder of an absence.

The stranger was dressed for post-war England while from Emily's appearance one could not have known the new century was twenty years old. Emily's father had encouraged her to assume the same attitude in relation to Charles as her mother had borne to him. It was a role Charles had done nothing to discourage. At thirty years old she was dressed in the apparel of a deceased mother whom she had hardly known. Her conversation too was formulaic.

'My dear, do come in and sit down. I'm sure you've had an exhausting journey.' She would have said the same if her guest had walked from the other end of the village. It did not betray a lack of concern; rather it underscored a sense of ritual to which Emily then subscribed. The stranger's reply twisted the convention.

'Not at all. It was great fun coming down on the train. I met a charming man who insisted on bringing me all the way from the station in his motor car. I would have driven myself but I felt like a change. Trains can be such fun, can't they? One meets such interesting people. The man who brought me here was a surgeon. He had some ghoulish stories but I can't blame him. I did ask.'

This was all said without pause for breath. Emily thought about the last time she had travelled by train with Charles. They had sat next to a vicar from the adjacent parish and conversation had centred on the vicar's difficulties in finding a new housekeeper, could they recommend anyone? But she did not allow the stranger to perceive her observation. The stranger seemed quite at home.

'What shall I call you? It can be so difficult with people one has just met. Mrs. . .'

'Oh no, I'm not married. Not yet. I haven't met the right man. Or if I have, well, you know . . . ' Emily did not take up the thread. She felt she ought not to know what the stranger was talking about though, in fact, she knew very well.

'Please feel free to call me Emily,' she said. The stranger held out her hand which was without a glove.

'Julia.' The stranger paused for a moment. 'Look, I'm sorry. I didn't mean that about marriage. I'm sure you're very happily married. Most people are, it seems. I know you're happily married. Your father used to tell me how well matched you and Charles were.'

'Are,' said Emily too quickly.

Did you know, Charles, that Julia knew your name before I met her? Didn't that strike you as odd? It did me. Funny when you hardly ever met, even later. Have you thought about lunch? Would you like soup? Or cheese? Your right eye looks bloodshot. I shall ask Virginia to bring you some drops.

She thinks that Charles's skin looks greyer today and the cowls hooding his eyes make him owlish. She had once thought of asking him to have them lifted through cosmetic surgery though in the end she had never dared mention it. She knew that his response to such a suggestion would have been scornful and short. She wondered why she wanted to make the proposal. She thought that it might have been as a displacement of her own apparent lack of vanity about her appearance. She had always turned herself out scrupulously but never flatteringly, preferring a clean to an artificial look however disguised. Charles had been handsome but now he stooped and his face was a hillside of beaten paths and sunken hollows or mounds. It was, she knew, the sort of face one too easily took for granted because its changes were slow and almost imperceptible. Each time he had returned home after months at sea the focus of his face had altered slightly but she had ignored it until recently. Now that she could observe him daily and without interruption the landscape seemed to shift by the hour, or was it that she was for the first time seeing the accumulations of nearly half a century compressed in minutes. And was this how Charles saw it too? Or was she a constant, her features and skin unweathered as a piece of sculpture kept indoors? She could not believe that herself though she suspected that Charles would say, if asked, that she remained unblemished as the day they had first met. The thought revolted her because of its lack of perception or truth. Did Charles really regard that as honest and, still more insultingly, did he imagine that her vanity would be sated with such sweetnesses? Yes, she had her vanities, but they did not concern her appearance and she doubted whether Charles would ever discover what they were or for that matter ever attempt to find out; she had long ago given up the expectation that he was still interested in turning over stones about herself. If there were any revelations to be made they would have to be of her own volition.

Julia moved to the window and it seemed to Emily that she had temporarily stopped breathing, then she turned with a beatific smile.

'I love gardens. Can we go outside?' Six of them went into the garden. There was Julia with Virginia who was only just learning to walk. Margaret and Dorothy ran off somewhere. Cyril kept close to his mother, Emily.

Julia flashed emerald green through the ochre of an autumn afternoon like some caged parakeet that had escaped and found itself flying through the exotic closeness of an English country garden. They walked round one side of the house where a recently chopped pile of logs had been stacked. Julia bent and picked up a chip of wood which she placed between her teeth as though she were about to chew and swallow it. They passed the dovecote where the pastel birds whirred upwards like pages torn and scattered in the breeze. Virginia cooed with delight and Julia held her up so that she could look more deeply into the dark caves of the cote. She waved frantically and her laughter sent more doves fluttering into the sky. Cyril was wary and shrank back into the enfolding darkness of Emily's skirt.

'Cyril,' cried Julia, 'there's no need to be frightened. It's only the doves. Look at Virginia, she's not afraid.' Virginia was still squirming in Julia's arms waving her tiny fists at the birds. Cyril turned away and hid behind his mother.

Cyril never liked Julia. Not from the very first day. I think she frightened him with the birds. I don't know where he got his shyness from. It wasn't you or me. With Virginia it was quite the opposite. She and Julia took to each other from the start. Virginia grabbed the veil on Julia's hat and pulled the whole thing off her head.

It whirled in a spiral like a milliner's sycamore seed twirling its wings before coming to rest.

But she wasn't in the least cross. She laughed, which only encouraged Virginia more. I was so embarrassed. I scolded Virginia and then Julia picked up the hat and sent it wheeling away over a rose bed. If you lean forward, Charles, you'll see the one I mean. Down there near the holly tree.

Emily's forefinger uncurls itself and crooks somewhere in the garden's presence. She is once more holding the stem of a rose-bush with a pair of secateurs poised and glinting.

'Who,' asked Julia, 'prunes your roses?'

'I do it myself.'

'You've no gardener?'

'If I let him do it he always leaves it too late. Roses aren't his strong point.'

'You haven't spared them. I'm afraid I shouldn't have the heart to be so brutal.'

'Most people are far too gentle with roses and then next year's blooms are not what they should be.'

They walked on to the far side of the rose bed and Julia picked up her hat but didn't put it on. Emily tried to ask the question she had had in mind since receiving Julia's letter.

'How did you know my. . . ?'

'Don't worry about that. There's plenty of time for that.' Julia was casually dismissive. They walked in silence until Julia turned and looked back towards the house. 'It's magnificent. How happy you must be here.'

How could I tell her? Yes, I am content. I have a husband who loves me dearly in the ways that he knows. There are four children, a beautiful home . . . But . . . What was the 'but', Charles? I tried to see the house as Julia was seeing it, for the first time. A home with a sense of history rooted in a landscape to which it belonged. I didn't tell her how you had said it was I who must choose where we should live because you would only be spending a few weeks a year there, wherever it was. How easily and glibly you handed over your responsibility, or what should have been yours. And I didn't and I don't resent that I had to make us a home alone. The work was satisfying and pleasurable. But I did want to tell Julia that it hadn't always been like that. I'd had to work at it. I would have liked some credit for that, especially from you, Charles, but you never seemed to notice.

Instead Emily said to Julia, 'Yes, living here all the time one forgets what a wonderful house it is. It's the garden that we have to get right now.'

'But the garden's wonderful. I can see so many little paths leading off. I'm sure they all go to secret places, hidden areas where you can't be seen.' Emily frowned, Julia continued with zest, 'I would've loved a garden like this as a child.'

'Really?' Emily's bewilderment was not in the least ironic. She pointed towards a small copse that lay at the far end of the formal garden. 'In there, for instance, it's an absolute jungle and it ought to be sorted out.'

'I should love to go there.'

Emily drew back her long blue sleeve to look at her wristwatch.

'It's really the children's teatime,' she said and noticed that she was trembling slightly. She said to herself that she must be cold.

'And what about those fields over there?'

'Yes, they're ours too. As far as the third hedgerow.'

'Which?'

'Do you see the large oak?'

'I'm afraid I'm not very good at trees.'

'On the left there's a holly tree. See?'

'Sorry.'

Emily took Julia's hand and raised her arm in the right direction.

'There. Can you see now?'

'Mmm . . . yes.'

They were standing close together by now with Emily's arm resting on top of Julia's and their cheeks brushed as Julia bent to focus on the third hedgerow. They stood thus for some seconds before separating slowly as if bound together by an invisible, unknown adhesive.

Sometimes the threads connecting us still vibrate like rails humming with the imminent approach of a train, thinks Emily.

Julia chased Virginia who, chortling, had disappeared behind the stables. Cyril, still half enfolded in his mother's dress, said, 'Mummy, who's that lady?' Emily watched Julia trying to run in her tight, fashionable skirt. 'I don't know who she is but I will,' said Emily. 'I will.'

The tea table had been immaculately set to provide a complete replica of an adult's dinner party except that instead of wine there was water in the glasses. Sandwiches, toast, biscuits, jam, crumpets and cake took the place of grown-up soups, meat or fish, poultry or game and vegetables, cheeses or soufflées. The tablecloth was linen and fresh, the cutlery gleamed and good china was in evidence. All this meant that teatime had become a test of the children's ability to mimic what they could of adult table manners; an event to be treated with solemnity out of all proportion to the occasion. Emily would look on as nanny attended to ensure that Margaret, Jean and Cyril sat correctly, held their implements in the correct manner, ate rather than spoke and that if they did speak they said such things as, 'Would you mind passing me the toast please, Margaret.' 'Not at all, Jean.' Or, 'Cyril, I think I'd care for another biscuit.' By the time of Julia's first visit Cyril had only recently been allowed to sit at the table proper with his two older sisters and Virginia was not yet regarded old enough to perform satisfactorily.

I occasionally wonder, Charles, whether Virginia's eating habits are so slapdash because we dropped our teatime routine before she was old enough to learn it. I'm sure your men on board benefited from regular meals served at regular hours and being expected to eat properly. Sometimes I think it was a mistake to let all that go. Even after all this time she's an age with our lunch.

When Julia saw the doll's-house precision and play-acting of the tea table she burst out laughing. Emily could only ask, 'What's the matter? Is there something wrong?'

'Emily, dear, you are too serious. Next time I come, I will arrange tea for the children.' She picked up Virginia who had been trying to climb her legs. 'And next time this one will have tea with her sisters and brother.' Virginia gurgled with delight.

Bathtime followed teatime after an interval of fifteen minutes to allow the children's teas to be sufficiently digested. The routine demanded that the children lined up in the long, narrow bathroom and stripped down to their underwear. Then nanny would instruct one of them to step forward and the prickly woollen vest and pants would be removed by her cold and bony fingers. The child was told to sit in two inches of tepid water while nanny soaped its neck and upper torso, afterwards the child had to stand and wash its bottom, pubic area, legs, especially concentrating on the knees and feet, under nanny's steady supervision. A final dip in the water was intended to remove any remaining lather and the child was given a towel to dry itself in the corner of the bathroom while nanny started on the same process for the next child. Being third in line was a misery; not only was the water grimy and it was difficult to raise any lather from the soap but it was also cold. Margaret had asked why there couldn't be more water and why it couldn't start hotter. Nanny had told her that hot water did not grow on trees and that too much of it would not only entail unnecessary expense in itself, it would over a prolonged period cause the bathroom paintwork to peel necessitating yet more expense. And besides, she said, it was not good for you to have a hot bath, though she gave no further explanation.

Having seen the teatime ceremony, Julia must have guessed the nature of the bathtime ritual and said to Emily, 'Why don't we bathe the children ourselves?'

'But nanny . . .'

'It'd be such fun.'

'Won't you miss your train?'

'Blow the train!'

'I think you should allow the best part of an hour to get to the station.'

'Let's get started then.'

They shepherded Margaret, Jean and Cyril upstairs with all of them dragging their feet and saying nothing, anticipating a cold wait and wondering who would be last tonight. Virginia clung to Julia as though she had never known anyone else. Emily went to fetch towels and Julia took the children into the bathroom which she immediately felt was uninviting and institutional. It smelt of the business of cleaning bodies, she said later. She turned the brass hot-water tap full on and soon the mirror misted over and the porcelain tiles were beginning to sweat. Behind her stood Margaret, Jean and Cyril stripped to their undergarments and waiting for instructions. As she undressed Virginia, with clouds of steam wreathing about their heads, she asked, 'What are you waiting for? An order or something?'

The children look at each other in embarrassment and bewilderment. Then Margaret spoke: 'Normally we do it one at a time.'

Julia smiled to herself but did not let them see her amusement.

'Jump to it then.'

'All of us?'

'Yes.'

Margaret and Jean removed their vests and knickers and dropped them on the linoleum; only Cyril stood unmoved. They waited for further orders.

'Come on then.'

'Together?'

'We haven't got all night.'

Margaret and Jean could hardly believe their good fortune. So no one was going to have to wait and climb into cold, dirty water. They raced to the side of the bath and Margaret put a foot into the water.

'Ouch, it's hot!' But it was a delicious sensation she had never had before and she was more than willing to feel and watch the pink then red warmth ring her ankles as they drew out the water's heat. Hot water! She splashed some at Jean who was now climbing in too. They sat facing each other in a tangle of legs which was further complicated as Julia dropped Virginia in and out of the water like a human yo-yo. They thrashed and dived, twisting round each other's limbs, as they pretended to grab for the soap which they had no real intention of trying to find. Who dreaded bathtimes now? Who thought about getting clean? Who cared if there were puddles on the lino? Not Margaret, Jean or Virginia.

When Emily finally opened the bathroom door she would, in the normal course of events, have been astounded by the shouting and laughter, the tangle of limbs glimpsed through the banks of steam, but she was already preoccupied with another matter. She was flushed and agitated.

'I'm sorry I was so long. There's been a telephone call. His ship, Charles's ship. It's docked early. He expects to be here later tonight.'

'I ought to be going anyway,' said Julia, taking a towel from Emily and starting to dry Virginia.

It was only then that the two women became aware of Cyril who, still dressed in his vest and pants, was standing by the toilet on one leg, like a forlorn heron which has not caught a single fish all day.

When you came home that night I suppose it all seemed perfectly normal to you, Charles. As it always was. Or did you sense how the order of things had been disturbed? I expect not. At first you didn't know what was happening. Of course, you knew later that Julia came to stay but you didn't know how much she mattered. Whenever you appeared she melted away. As far as you were concerned it was 'out of sight out of mind'. You never guessed how important she was to me until it was too late for you to do anything about it. And then when you realised what it meant you wanted to keep the peace. You thought that if you drew attention to Julia and me that might devalue the currency we dealt in: the family. You were tolerant, some would have said weak. Was it a sense of family politics that kept you quiet or were you blindly oblivious to the affair? Did you fail to see us because you didn't want to or because you couldn't?

A squirrel scurries across the lawn and stops near the base of the sundial. It is the first one Emily has seen in several months and she would like to see it as an omen of a springtime renewal, when the stores of memory are abandoned and a green future is promised, but all she can contemplate is a bushy-tailed creature that bobs and ducks in a grey fur coat like a secret agent at a cold border. Her unwillingness to draw a parallel is, she is sure, one sign of her age, an acceptance which is readily labelled apathy by those too young to understand otherwise. She is content to watch the slatey animal twist and bound away and draw no conclusions from its appearance. Only she recalls another squirrel some half a century ago when she lay down under a dripping beech and frightened the animal collecting nuts. It had been the middle of winter and she had wondered then why it had been out and about and not curled up hibernating somewhere. It had momentarily stopped on the bare branch of the beech tree. She could still see its nose quivering and claws twitching in fear and excitement before it scampered round the far side of the tree and disappeared. She wonders whether the squirrel she has just seen is a direct descendant of the one she knows from years before. How long do squirrels live for? Do they live in family groups? She must ask Virginia whether she knows.

The night after Julia's first visit and Charles's early return Emily was woken by screams. She found Cyril sitting up in bed, sobbing, but only half awake so she calmed him down and knelt at the bedside until he had gone to sleep. The next morning she asked him whether he could remember his nightmare and he told her that there had been a lady dressed in vivid colours standing at the end of a long corridor pointing at him and laughing. Which she, however much he pleaded with her, would not stop.

Every mistress is someone's friend or wicked aunt.

Emily tries as she has done so many times before to trace the route of Charles's feelings towards her friendship with Julia. He chose a life, the sea, which took him away from his wife and family for the greater part of each year. Why should he have objected to the friendship with a friend of her father, no less? Indeed, there had been reason for Charles to rejoice that she had someone to turn to when he was absent. She imagined how it must have been on board when everything had been dealt with and he had slipped into a routine with weeks between the port he had just left and the one to which he was sailing. As the keel rippled the glassy calm of the Pacific had he found himself on deck with a rage and resentment welling up in contrast to the tranquil scene before him?

Was he frustrated by his absence in the face of their friendship or gladdened that it meant there was a vacuum which he no longer had the responsibility of attempting to fill? Or, more likely, did he not consider the matter at all? He would never tell her now. His silence would last beyond the endless rollers of the oceans he had sailed. And as she sees the grey ball of spittle gather in the corner of his lips her own tongue darts out in sympathy, as well as to ensure the same occurrence is not happening to her.

* * *

JULIA'S FURTHER VISITS took their shape and tenor from the first one. Appearances out of nowhere and equally mysterious vanishings into . . . It was not until she had made half-a-dozen visits that she allowed Emily any glimpse of her origins or her connection with Emily's father. And even when she did allow the veil to part it was at first only for the briefest instant, tantalising Emily with the brevity of what she had seen or thought she had seen.

I was always asking her when or where or how she had met father. I was persistent and if I didn't ask then the questions were always on my lips. When I did ask, Julia would wave an arm or shrug her shoulders in a gesture indicating vagueness. Of course, it wasn't that at all. She knew exactly what I wanted but she wouldn't give it to me at first. It was an endless current of 'Oh I can't quite recall . . . it might've been . . . I'm not sure . . . '

Here Emily's voice breaks off, not on account of her losing the train of her thought, but because her memory is focusing too clearly on it.

'Father loved the chestnut tree. When we came here he thought it was the best thing about the house,' said Emily to Julia.

'Yes, I know. He told me that, and that he hadn't wanted you to take on the house. That he thought it was too much for you to do on your own but you proved him wrong.'

The summer after their first meeting Emily and Julia were both in the garden with Cyril and Virginia who was digging in a rose bed and throwing out dirt on to the grass. Cyril was telling her that she should, if she wanted to be a good girl, put it back. Julia had abandoned her former metropolitan elegance in favour of a rural bohemianism which meant looser blouses and skirts. Or, as now, trousers! She was sitting on the grass making a daisy chain and laughing at Virginia's soiled face. Emily, who could never bear to be out in the garden unless she was busy, was weeding nearby. Cyril ran over to tell her what his naughty sister Virginia was doing.

'And did father tell you why he didn't want us to move here?'

'Oh yes, he was perfectly honest. He didn't think you were capable. Or at the very least that you couldn't manage without Charles.'

'Then why did he leave me the business?'

'Perhaps he thought you could cope by then. In any case, what else could he have done?'

'Sold it and left me the profits. Instead the terms of the will stated that I had to keep the business intact.'

'Perhaps he judged you better than you give him credit for.'

Suddenly Julia stood up as though something had bitten her. In fact, the conversation was coming dangerously near to the centre of her emotions and she was anxious not to come to the point too soon, before she felt that Emily trusted her. She was agitated to be skirting round the edge of all that was still dearest to her and toiled with an infinite caution towards the time when she could set her burden at Emily's feet in the hope that it would be taken up.

Much later, of course, she said she'd had no choice in the matter. She'd had to keep it a secret or we would never have become friends. Is that true, Charles? Do our friends know everything? There are things about you that I don't know, that I don't wish to know. We're still friends, aren't we? Aren't we, Charles? I think I would still have loved Ronald if I hadn't known about this. I'd rather not have known Ronald's secret. Wouldn't you?

Her voice has the edge of a rasp, the bones in her face tighten.

Emily fingers the light-blue airmail paper and then screws it up into a ball which she does not throw away but clasps in her fist.

As Julia's influence grew more marked Charles began to notice, however infrequently, the changes in domestic detail.

'I see, dear, that you've changed the children's teatime arrangements.'

Emily blushed.

'I didn't think you'd mind, Charles.'

'I don't. After all, you are the one, the main one, the arbiter of family business. Of how things are or should be run.'

Emily grew agitated, unsure whether Charles was being facetious or direct. The latter it seemed as he went on.

'What is the point in my saying such and such should be done in such and such way?'

But I wanted him to care. To say, no, this isn't right, do it this way. Instead he withdrew as easily as he weighed anchor.

'I'm hardly ever here. It would be wrong for me to lay down the rules. No. You go ahead and do as you think fit. I'm sure that's best in the long run.'

You were liberal to the point of indifference and disinterest.

'After all, I have a large enough crew of my own to worry about when I'm away. It's rather restful not to have to worry about anything while I'm here.' He pulled on his jacket. 'Just out for some fresh air. See you later.' He touched his lips to her cheek and was gone.

Emily watched him from their bedroom window. Wrapped against the cold he strode across the lawn, leaning forward into the wind with a glow on his weathered cheeks. She could see his lips pursed in the shape of an 'o' and guessed that he was whistling as he went, conducting himself in a hearty, affable fashion as he did everything else, including their lovemaking, which he attacked as though it were some compulsory exercise to be performed on deck. Emily knew then that this marked his abdication of the responsibility he should have claimed: their family. His shore leaves became less of moment to her, dying into routine, while Julia's visits brought with them an excited emotion and trailed anticipation in their wake.

There was laughter and chatter and bread and cake on the table and floor. They had the old stained cutlery and cheap china that was cracked and chipped, which nanny and the gardener had always used. Margaret's spaniel was yapping and begging under the table. It was so different from before but you said nothing. They might have been naked, eating off the kitchen floor with their bare hands and you would have said . . . nothing. And now Ronald. You sit there and say nothing.

Emily would like to reach out and shake Charles. Take him by the shoulders and rattle something, anything out of him. Then to her disgust she finds rising in her throat like a nausea the cripple of love she despises, pity.

It was Christmas, 1922. Charles was away and Julia was staying with Emily and the four children. Christmas night and only the tree remained in the corner of the room with the paper cross Jean had made tied to its tip. All the children were in bed and they sat watching the coals pulse in the grate as though someone were quietly breathing on them. They had been quiet for some time when Julia spoke.

'What do you think of the election result?' Emily shook her head.

'I don't know.'

'You're a business woman. You own several shops.'

'I have a manager who looks after them. I hardly have enough time to run things here as it is.'

'You don't make time. You could get involved if you wanted to. You're as capable as anyone else of doing it.'

'With four children, a husband who's away most of the time? I don't care to.'

'What would your father have thought?' The appeal was too much for Emily.

'I'm sorry. It's not that I don't care. I . . . '

'What did you vote?'

Emily was embarrassed. 'I voted as father would have done. For Curzon and Baldwin.'

'Are you always going to do what your father would have done?' Julia was not mocking. Emily shrugged and stood up.

'I should go and check whether the children are asleep.' And she left the room with a high colour on her cheeks. Julia sat staring into the fire until her eyelids began to droop. She came to with a start, unsure whether she had drifted out of consciousness for a moment or some minutes. There was no sign of Emily so she went out to look for her. As she opened the drawing-room door she heard a faint sobbing coming from upstairs. She found Emily on the landing with a tousled Virginia in her arms. But it was Emily who was weeping while Virginia, settling on her mother's shoulder, was smiling from her sleep. Julia took Virginia from Emily who did not resist her and returned the sleeping child to her bed. When she returned to the landing Emily had gone but she could hear water running from a bathroom tap. She went downstairs to the evergreen with its paper cross.

Julia waited in the drawing room for me, Charles. I wasn't going to tell her. But she was so kind. She held my hand and we sat over there.

Emily nods in the direction of the fireplace where ashes, not a fire, lie in the grate.

I think Virginia ought to light us a fire, don't you? I know it's earlier than normal but suddenly I feel there's a chill in the air. Lean closer if you can. I don't want to strain my voice. I told Julia how when father died, your ship was delayed. It was a strong wind and the currents were wrong, you said. The elements were outside our control. How the night before he died I saw your friend Bertrand at the Armistice celebration. He asked to see me alone but I refused. He was insistent but I said no. I wanted to be faithful to you, Charles.

It was Bertrand who spoke. 'But you promised that you would see me at least once whenever Charles was away.'

'I don't have the time. Besides, it's Charles you come to see.'

'Is it?'

'I'm too busy. You've no idea what it's like to be on your own and run a house and look after a family and . . . '

'That's why I'm offering to pay you a visit. To relieve the burden just a little.' He smiled. And continued to look her in the eye as he emptied his glass of wine.

Emily thinks how Charles has never questioned, at least to her face, her faithfulness to him. She wishes she were too barren to feel guilt but it rises in her like pitch seeping to the surface of the desert. She continues in a whisper as though she herself cannot bear to hear what she is telling Charles.

The day we buried him I was so lonely, so lonely. As though I were in a glass bubble and nothing could touch me. A needle in the artery of affection for the world. I saw Margaret and Jean playing as if they were someone else's daughters, not mine. I had lost what I never knew I had. Within hours father was a stranger to me. A man I didn't know, but he had encircled me and kept me safe. I thought that Robert's and Albert's deaths had inoculated me against the discasc of suffering. They hadn't.

Emily shivers. How can she inflict this on her unmoving, dumb husband?

Rattling home in the coach on Armistice night she said to herself – oh Christ you're a liar. Why don't you admit how he excites you? Go on, touch him just once before he has gone and your chance with him. She imagined stroking his golden skin in emerald shadows. How he had arrived out of an impossibly lush and fecund spot pacing with a natural, oiled grace. And how the sunlight poured between the trunks as if through the bars of a prison.

And now especially she remembers how it had been Julia alone who had shared this with her. The ashes in the grate flutter on her tongue as she attempts to share it with Charles. She assumes a lighter, brisker tone.

* * *

MEN FRIENDS. That's what Charles and Bertrand were. Who needs talk of emotion? Share and feel it. Is this how it was, how it is always for men, wonders Emily.

She said to Julia that Christmas night under the paper cross, 'It was difficult for me to refuse him entry into our house. He was a friend of Charles's. He had been even before I met Charles. I didn't encourage him. I swear I did the opposite.'

'Who is he?' Julia asked.

'Does it matter?' Emily looked up at a portrait of the mother she barely knew, thinking, I am being torn apart by the insubstantial wings of angels. She continued, 'When Charles is here he still comes to see him. They go out for walks together, sometimes they take a gun.'

'So?'

'I hear shots coming from the wood.'

Julia realised that Emily could say no more. She imagined her standing at the window waiting to see if it was one or both of them who appeared in the garden. Whether there had been some kind of accident. Of course, they would both reappear, strolling out from under the fringe of the silky beech with the clang of the iron kissing gate telling their arrival.

They would often have a couple of rabbits slung head down and dripping blood on the grass as they approached the house. In the kitchen with the rabbits' eyes unglazed and still with the appearance of sight Charles held them up by their hind legs.

'Look at these. Aren't they beauties? We'll have them for supper. Where's Mary? She knows how to cook a decent rabbit pie.' He addressed Bertrand. 'You'll stay for supper, of course.'

Bertrand shrugged. 'If Emily . . . '

'Nonsense,' said Charles, taking Bertrand's arm and guiding him towards the study. 'Let's get out of here. It'll be the children's teatime in a minute. And you wouldn't want to suffer that!'

After the children had had their tea and been bathed they were lined up in front of the drawing-room fire which had usually just been lit. They were ranked in order according to their ages but this did not correspond to their heights. Margaret was already spreading outwards rather than up whereas Jean was too much bone, and a fraction taller than her older sister. Virginia was going to be tall, too, though better built than Jean. She was two while Cyril was a four-year-old and yet she seemed taller.

There was always something about Virginia which made her loom very large. And the same thing, whatever it is, made Cyril shrunken and dwarfed. I know I shouldn't talk about our only son that way; compare him with his sister. Tell me though, which parent who cares doesn't do that? Only the indifferent, thinks Emily staring at Charles, take no measure.

In fact, had one taken a pair of scales and a tape measure the statistics would have been found quite in order. Cyril at the age of four was both taller and heavier than Virginia two years his junior. So they were lined up to receive their goodnight kisses, including one from 'Uncle' Bertrand. It was Charles, against Emily's protestations, who had insisted on the endearment. Bertrand kissed each child in turn beginning with Margaret who wobbled and shook; then Jean who received his offering as though she were a priest taking the necessary evil of a collection plate. Even before Bertrand had bent down Cyril blushed and winced, casting his eyes down as Bertrand kissed him on the cheek. All this while Virginia had been hopping from one foot to the other in excitement, agitated as she waited her turn so that when it came she threw her arms round 'Uncle' Bertrand's neck and refused to let loose her grasp until she heard the sharpness in her mother's voice telling her to stop.

Didn't you ever wonder why Virginia always clung to Bertrand so? Did you ever remark on it to yourself as anything more than a breach of the decorum you thought was necessary for our children's upbringing? Or was it sufficient to notice that the rules had been broken, that the offender should be dealt with accordingly and the motive ignored? Emily has long since forgotten the pact she made with herself not to think along these lines. Now she admits that it is broken daily.

After Bertrand Charles started his round in a ritual unaltered by Julia's aura, at least, for the times he was present. He descended from an infinite altitude, grazing their cheeks like a grater falling from a kitchen shelf. The only sensation they knew which was comparable to the touch of his beard was when nanny used the pumice stone on their skins at bathtime. Cyril was the only one to avoid this torture of the bristling embrace. In its place he had been coached to hold out his hand and shake his father's as if they were meeting for the first time. This formal, minimal gesture forever characterised their posture to one another and it became an attitude impossible for either of them to erase however much they might try to do so through the years. In the end they both abandoned the attempt and admitted to no more than the handshake. Lastly, Virginia's cheek was scratched no more or less than her sisters'. Then they filed from the drawing room and upstairs; Margaret and Jean to the bedroom they shared not because they had to but because they wanted to, Cyril and Virginia to their solitary rooms. Though when the chance was there Cyril would get up from his bed and pad to Emily's room where he would slip between her covers and drift to sleep in her curves, her warmth. Whenever Julia was in the house then Virginia would leave her bed, too, only if she crept into Julia's bed there would be a hushed chatter and giggling before they fell asleep, not the humid silence of Cyril's comfort. And if their father were absent and Julia was staying this also meant a difference in their goodnights, done in the bedrooms and not in the drawing room. There would be a flurry of sheets and blankets, the bedspreads it seemed thrown up by the timbre of Julia's voice like a soft breeze. Even Cyril could not resist the sense of exultation sweeping along in front of her, a swell on which they all bobbed up and down, which gently rocked them to sleep. Later Emily would go upstairs and if one of the children half woke they would catch the scent of her soap so different to the pungent tang of their father's and 'Uncle's' whiskied breaths.

Emily looks out of the window into a sky that is clear, clearer than she has seen for weeks. In the blue beyond the copse she can see the vapour trail left by jet engines. It is beginning to break up and fade but the rings of smoke are just visible. She recalls the droning and black plume of a wartime aeroplane, a Spitfire, she supposes, though she never knew the difference, curling down in the same spot on the horizon beyond the copse. She must have been at this window then too, only standing and without Charles. When she focuses again the distant puffs of white smoke have disappeared. She was going to tell Charles but first she must say:

My sight is still good, excellent I'd say. Half the time Virginia doesn't believe me. It's simply that I can't always be bothered to focus on what she's talking about. Then she says I should wear my glasses more. She doesn't understand that I only need them for reading and the television. If only you'd tell me what you can see, Charles. You know whenever Bertrand was here you never seemed to notice me at all. You used to talk to him as if I were invisible but he looked, he saw. Did you think he was listening to you?

Emily finds the words have tumbled out in a way she hadn't intended at all. But she is not anxious, she is ever so slightly relieved. After all it is hardly momentous to admit in passing that Bertrand looked at her while he pretended to be listening to Charles some fifty years ago. And Bertrand had only to listen to Charles's talk to be free. And talk Charles did. On the following . . .

In 1920 Charles's discourse to Bertrand included such topics as the Railways Bill, reducing the number of companies from a hundred and twenty-four to a mere four; the Agriculture Act guaranteeing prices for four years; dockers refusing to load coal on a ship sailing to Poland at war with Russia (Bevin the scoundrel!); the Government of Ireland Act creating the province of Ulster and (much too generous!) allowing Dublin its own Parliament.

In the following year Charles held forth on the return of the mines to private ownership; the emergence of an independent Communist Party of Great Britain and the unemployment figure which stood at over two million. In 1922 he expounded on the general election following Lloyd George's fall; the establishment of a new Tory committee; civil war in the nascent Irish republic; the birth of the British Broadcasting Company and the discovery of the tomb of King Tutankhamun.

Even when you were speaking on something which interested me, thinks Emily, you never tried to draw me in, to include me.

She finds herself fingering the double string of pearls at her throat, twisting them round and round as a Catholic might do with a rosary. In spite of her later loyalty to the Church it is these family gifts, not a religion, to which she clings. Charles had had the necklace made up by a London jeweller from pearls he had acquired on a voyage to the Far East. She sees the pearl fishers, boys, skins the tone and texture of tanned leather with their legs pumping like frogs on their dives to the sea bed. She would like to have seen such water threaded with sunlight and now that she won't its clarity speckled with grains of sand grows more acute.

Charles was relentless in his pursuit of world affairs. In the next year his themes were: attempted legislation on arms control and limitation; the dispatch of marines to Canton to protect trade interests; protest against Russian involvement in Persia and Afghanistan and Baldwin's first cabinet with seven Old Harrovians.

In the new year, 1924, he could grasp the nettles of the first Labour government taking office with the son of a Scots farm labourer at the helm, shortly followed by its collapse. (MacDonald ought to be ashamed of himself. Allowing his political leanings to enter into a matter of King and country.) And in the wake of the fall the first election to be contested over the wireless.

Bertrand glanced across the room to Emily as Charles droned on, but she refused to acknowledge his stare and continued to read with a rush of blood coursing up her neck, reddening her throat and pulsing into her cheeks. Hot, too hot, it must be the fire, put something on it, damp it down, it doesn't need so much coal – and when Emily said this to herself she knew as the words formed themselves that she was lying unsuccessfully.

How the grand events in the world beyond slipped by like some demented race of frogs in a hurry to spawn and then outjump each other. One voice released Emily from this cycle but Charles did not hear it. 1925 and he pressed on, insistent in his determination to pursue the decade and squeeze its happenings dry. Which, of course, he was eager to share, with Bertrand; after all, what interest could Emily be expected to take in Chamberlain as Minister of Health setting up the infrastructure of state responsibility for care of the sick? Or Churchill at the Treasury scrabbling to revert to gold and pushing up the value of the pound to its pre-World War One level? Charles's commentary ran along the lines, 'British exports are already too expensive compared with our competitors. Our fleet is only working at about half capacity when the holds should be full. For once, I agree with Bevin that keeping unemployment high is bound to lead to trouble. It's the City's talk Churchill is listening to and not industry's.' Bertrand, with half an eye on Emily's flushed neck, could not resist the temptation to reply. 'But I thought you were all for a return to pre-war standards.' Charles was oblivious and ploughed on. 'In values, yes. In money, no.' With the British Empire Exhibition Charles warmed to this theme, agreeing with *The Times* about the sense of adventure and space lent by the overseas pavilions but that it was no use for young men to be sent to the open skies of the bush or prairie unless they first found markets for their produce. Bertrand said, 'I thought climbing the Nigerian tower rather fun. What about you, Emily?' Emily looked up, her expression a mixture of pride and humility, but she was not quick enough. 'She didn't go,' said Charles. 'Too busy with the shops and children, weren't you, Em?' The question was rhetorical as so many of Charles's questions seemed to be. Moreoever, she hated Charles calling her 'Em' and especially in front of Bertrand, it made her sound like a hesitation or an apology. But Charles glided on. 'Baldwin's subsidy is giving us time to equip ourselves. Enquiry into the mining industry my foot. It's the Organisation for the Maintenance of Supplies that interests him, not the coal industry. You don't set up an enquiry with four men who know nothing about coal if you want a sensible answer. And sticking a dozen Communists behind bars has given them a warning too. They won't strike now,' came Charles's pronouncement in the last month of 1925.

And at each moment Emily felt Bertrand's eyes boring into her like some insistent and voracious insect. How could Charles not see or feel it? She wondered whether shooting and Charles's perorations on politics were the total of their friendship. Or were there things between them hidden from her as there were things which she and Bertrand concealed from Charles? She did not conceive of a consistent deception by Charles but surely there must have been moments in the months when they were apart which shook the resolve he always displayed at home? There were things, she felt sure, that occurred between his ship's embarkation and its docking on return about which he told her nothing. Then she had a desire to know but not the temerity to question him.

Now, she thinks, I could look him directly in the eye and ask, have you ever wanted to kill me? Or, was there much buggery on board your ship? And he would be compelled to answer her, unable to escape the steadiness of her gaze. She no longer has any wish to question him. It seems doubly removed from her concern by the dimensions of space and time. What happened long ago and happened across seas where she has not sailed or places she has not visited has lost its urgency; to enquire now would be like reading a fiction with the sole intent of voyeurism. How can she reduce their pasts to that?

Something flashes at the rim of her vision and her head swivels to try to catch whatever it is. A young deer stands by the vegetable-garden wall, half disguised by the tones of the rust-rose brick, cream dabs of mortar on its coat. Emily wonders what Cyril is doing behind the wall for without doubt that's where he is, occupied in bending, sowing, digging, raking or some such action, considering perhaps which seedlings might go out under glass without suffering the risk of frost. Has he spent so many years cultivating plants to avoid the attempts one is obliged to make at nurturing people? Emily thinks so and is too conscious of her own role in Cyril's behaviour. She has too much that she wants to say, that needs to be said, to pursue this avenue with herself or anyone else. That is how she justifies it to herself, quickly formulating a list of priorities which does not include Cyril at its head. There is a blur and she is aware of the outline, the space where the deer had been standing and from which it has gone. This gives her an excuse to say to Charles:

It's clear now why Ronald and Cyril are so fond of each other. Like you were with Bertrand once, perhaps, different generations I know but . . .

For once her voice trails away for she is embarrassed by the transparency of her effort to wrest the topic round to Bertrand and Charles once more. She wants to elaborate the deceptions practised on Charles; does not imagine Charles's and Bertrand's on her.

At Bertrand's club a shadowy figure poured amber liquid into their tumblers and Bertrand asked for the decanter to be left on the small table in front of their armchairs. He allowed Charles to talk on at some length about the state of the world and later, when he paused for breath, said, 'I'm taking you somewhere special tonight. Drink up,' and he replenished Charles's tumbler with the malt. Charles knew exactly what Bertrand intended. He had spent most of his weeks in ports around the world refusing similar invitations.

Once as a young officer he had been taken into a building that must formerly have been the property of some colonial settler. But when Charles arrived rampant orange bougainvillaea had been allowed to grow where it wanted, hiding the windows and almost preventing entry into the house. One of the pillars by the doorway seemed to have crumpled, looking as though it might collapse at any minute, and inside the plaster was damp and crumbling from the walls. Before he had gone any further Charles had wanted to leave. He was amazed at how readily his two senior officers accepted the squalor of the building. They perched on cane chairs, a bottle and three glasses – two of them chipped – were placed on a low table which rocked on the tilting slats of the floor. The madam, thin to the point of emaciation – an opium addict most likely, Charles thought – clapped her hands saying, 'You choose now, have drink then enjoy.' The girls filed past, some yawned, some made a half-hearted attempt to pout in their direction, they all shuffled along the dusty boards on bare feet though they looked freshly washed and manicured with their long dark hair swinging in the paraffin light which flickered and fumed. One of them hesitated a moment and smiled at Charles who nodded to the madam that this would be his choice. He wanted it finished quickly. His companions were more discriminating and spent some minutes discussing the girls with the madam and each other. When they had finished the bottle on the table she led them upstairs and showed each in turn a bedroom. The doors were teak and heavy. Charles pushed his open and there was a whiff of damp. The room was bare except for a mattress in the far corner and as he closed the door behind him he heard something scurry across the floorboards, claws pattering in the musty silence. The girl was already there, sitting on the mattress with her knees up to her chin. As Charles approached she stood up, allowing her sarong to slip away. In the rank light he could see, under the small breasts, the belly crossed and re-crossed by the tracks of the surgeon's scalpel. He put his hand in his pocket and held out some notes which she took without a word, only bowing her head slightly. Shutting the ponderous door behind him he could hear laughter along the landing. Waiting downstairs for his companions he noticed that one hand was black from the banister-rail dust. He felt nauseated but not on any moral grounds. It was the filth, the squalor that made him squeamish and his lack of substantial moral objections made him in turn more uncomfortable; he realised that had his entrée, the ambience, been more conducive, less naked, he might well be laughing in one of the bedrooms off the landing upstairs. When his companions eventually appeared, tucking in their shirt-tails and flexing their shoulders, he did not tell them how long he had been downstairs waiting for their return; they assumed everything and suspected nothing deviant in his actions. Who, indeed, could be so perverse as to visit a brothel and fail to engage? Charles left his aesthetic objections under cover, ashamed of what, he guessed, would be regarded as a weakness amongst men friends. He did not want to seem perverse, he had an urge to belong so he kept quiet.

Therefore, when Bertrand made his suggestion, although Charles had refused similar invitations on countless voyages, he said nothing. Charles had reached the point when he considered that a denial would have exhibited a betrayal of what he deemed a close, a deep friendship. Besides, he thought that on this occasion in central London the decor and furnishings might be more to his taste. Emily was not a factor in this brief calculation. And why should she be? In London clubland he was as removed from her and the family as if Tenerife were astern *en route* to South America.

With the letter from Spain scattered, pages in her lap, others on the carpet, Emily walks down the narrow, cobbled lanes between the whitewashed walls which, against their nature it seems, throw blue shadows in her path. At one point she finds herself stretching above her head to pluck a small cluster of green globes. Then she stops; she is looking into a photograph which Margaret sent in her last letter. After all, she has never been to Spain and will say:

I thought that we might take a holiday in those islands where there are bananas and palm trees. Only you never wanted to travel. Even years later when we might've flown.

The taxi hummed through the drizzle comforting Charles with its soft whooshing. Bertrand led the pliant Charles up between the fresh white pillars to a door which without their ringing the bell glided open to reveal an Aladdin's cave of gilt and polished walnut. He knew at once that unlike the occasion of his first such visit he would not only succumb to the pleasures of the house but he would positively enjoy them. His conscience rapidly added the rider that he was present through the strength of his friendship with Bertrand and that had any other man made a similar invitation he would not have entertained it. In fact, he was already convinced by the silver tray and the crystal glittering under the chandelier.

Emily knew nothing and were she told now it would be too late.

A jay swoops down on to the grass and immediately takes off again in a flurry of sapphire which mocks, needles the grey. Emily finds her voice unaccustomed to the bitterness of the tone it adopts.

If only you had shown a weakness, just the slightest chink, it would have made it so much easier for me. Instead I have had to live with the impossible gloss of your perfect picture of me.

Did you know?

She trembles, remembering the inflections of Charles's voice and her attempts to catch whether they carried an undertow. Or gestures; times when he had loved her to help him into his jacket or hand him his gun changed to moments when he would shout through a door that he was going out. And when she came to help him on with his coat the room would be empty and she would hear his boots scattering the gravel like a platoon heard tramping in the distance.

In the beginning there had never been silences or if there had been they were full and rich not empty or hollow. Later it sometimes seemed as if he were swimming through the room, muffled behind glass with that grotesque and exaggerated dumbness which belongs to people under water. She wondered whether he had forgotten how to speak to her. The result of years at sea trading with men who could not speak his own language; on board with a crew distanced by the tailor-made vocabulary of merchant shipping and restrained by its hierarchy. Or, she asked herself, did he forget his early words not because he had spent too many years at sea but too many years at marriage? Would the same have happened if he had stayed at home and bought the adjacent fields and farmed them? Or was it the third option which she simultaneously exulted in and dreaded; could his neglect of her stem from his knowledge of her, that he knew, that he knew about Bertrand?

* * *

BERTRAND'S SILVER EYES, mercurial, able to pin her to the spot with their tempered, calculated incision – he should have been a surgeon with those eyes. She felt staked by their weight, thought how she had seen a thermometer break on a parquet floor and the silver globules had danced in all directions at once, unassimilable and quixotic. She had stood transfixed, mesmerised, like a frightened rabbit not by light but as if a knife were sliding between her ribs. The sensation was not unwelcome, did not include pain, only presence as she marvelled at the blade's urbanity and how when it withdrew, as it had to when he had to turn to someone other than her, she was amazed that it left no trace visible to others.

There were further comparisons to be made: silver eyes, the far rumble of an avalanche and then she was buried in wave after wave of snow; she was drawn out of a solution attracted to the wires of his eyes and she had no conception of where such force was generated; a bird's feather she had found and stuck in a jar not knowing for years what it was; the papery bark of a birch tree.

Under the Christmas tree already dropping its needles in the corner of the room where she now sits she remembers how Julia held her hand.

'I, we, it was after the funeral. The reception. Everyone had gone away, gone home, left me alone; I thought I was alone and then I don't know how, I swear it, I wanted no one.' How she had been sitting on the edge of a chair rocking herself backwards and forwards into a numb forgetting. Suddenly wondering where the children – Margaret, Jean, Cyril – were and who with. How the light had thickened and feeling a presence she had turned to find the silver ladders streaming down from his eyes pulling her up out of the dark,

'You're alone,' said Bertrand, 'I didn't think you'd want to be; do you know how long you've been sitting there?' Emily shook her head. 'Hours. The children are in bed, asleep.'

She stood and his arms closed round drawing her to him with her head resting on his shoulder. A tear ran down the back of his jacket and fell on to the carpet with its pink roses swirling, a threaded whirlpool, stitches weaving down to the flowers' throats, sharp wool thorns piercing out of the woven stems.

'He picked me up and carried me into the hall,' she told Julia. 'I felt I was a child again. He held me tenderly, as protective as if he were my father – father whom we buried that day carried me upstairs to bed.' The stairs rose and fell like waves swelling and she flew, skimming and dipping over them in the dusk, until they reached the landing where the dark through her half-closed eyes enveloped her in soft plum tones. He carried her past the grandfather clock, warm time ticking in its walnut case, and past the light swimming out from under Cyril's bedroom door – she allowed him this indulgence when Charles was absent – Emily remembered then being carried past her mother's bedroom door late at night when a light shone and she heard the stifled groaning that she later knew as the cries of labour. Bertrand's shoulder angled down and nuzzled the door gently like a pony rooting for sugar. The curtains were undrawn and there were moonlight rhomboids and trapezia marking out the room. He lowered his arms and rolled her on to the bed so that the buttons on the back of her dress winked like coffee beans.

'He couldn't undo the hook at the back of my dress. I had to help him.'

Emily's arm twists round reaching for the place where her neck meets her shoulders but she can no longer stretch that far and her arm comes to a halt, trembling as if held back by some invisible weight on a nylon cord. She brings it back to rest in her lap and looks at it with a faint disgust as though it did not belong to her at all but to someone else.

The first button popped out of its hole and the others followed quickly so her dress split open in Bertrand's eyes like a knife running down the scales of a fish which part to reveal the delicate flesh ranged within, the geometry of spine and smaller bones, an exquisite formation of calcium embedded in tissue. Emily heard him gasp softly. The black skin of her mourning slid away and rustled on to the floor in a pool of magnesium light.

'I asked him where my father was and he told me not to worry, that he was somewhere close by. I was afraid of the dark, of being alone. I didn't ask him to go.' As she fell asleep the thud thud of his heart echoed the pattering of earth on her father's coffin.

In the dawn she found his silver eyes still watching, the dark had been kept at bay and yet there was something more waiting in her self which she could not refuse.

'I opened myself to him,' she told Julia. It happened as naturally as a bee seeking nectar, the petals parting pushed gently aside, the creature's proboscis readied in the absolute concentration of search, discovery and achievement. They lay in the bed given by her father as a wedding present under the sun carved in the oak headrest and with fingers of light etching out the details of the room. The wardrobe with roses carved in its front panels, her dressing table with its central mirror flanked on either side by two more mirrors reflecting each other's view forever.

'I can still see the angle of the hairbrush, the patterning of the lace coaster, the inlay of my jewellery box, pins; double images of them all in the polished wood.'

Then splinters of ice pierced their ears, an intrusion of notes from the piano downstairs randomly played by one of the children. She thought of the youngest, Cyril; who had put him to bed and where was he now? She was half out of bed when the door snuffled open and in staggered Cyril, drunk with the intoxication of learning to walk. He came to a halt swaying in the middle of the room, hesitant, and wondering whether he was in the right place, whether he had entered the guestroom by mistake. He tried to hold himself erect, upright against the mystery of his father's friend, Uncle Bertrand, in the same bed as his mother who held out her arms and whispered, 'Come here, darling, everything's all right,' and saw with Bertrand's silver eyes the dark, damp patch spreading out through the carpet under Cyril's feet.

Emily said to Julia, 'That was the first and only time.' Which was true when she said it. 'I've felt so guilty. I've lived with the day my father was buried, its night, its next morning. Lived with it for four years. Should I have told Charles?'

'What? About Bertrand?'

'I've had to see him when he's been to visit Charles.'

'You've never talked.'

'I've been too afraid to tell him. I wanted to make up for it. For Charles, the children.'

'But you wanted to be near him.'

Emily could hardly believe that Julia understood her feelings; she began to smile but it split, cracked into tears and they held each other.

'Stay with me tonight.'

And they trod the stairs holding hands.

* * *

JULIA'S SECRET TOO.

There is sun angling through the glass making Emily squint and screw up her face. She thinks about moving from her chair but instead she turns her head away from the window. The brightness and magnified warmth cheers and gives her courage.

Charles, you can't imagine how happy I was the morning after I had told Julia. So happy. I felt my life, our life was beginning again until Julia told me her secret.

She stops. How is she going to put it to Charles?

They decided on a walk before Julia was to return to London and swathed the children and themselves in layers of vests and woollens, jackets and coats, socks and stockings, gloves, mittens, hats, scarves and boots.

I pulled Jean's hat down over her eyes so she couldn't see. I tied Margaret's scarf around a peg. I put Cyril's mittens on the wrong hands. I stuffed a piece of paper in the toe of Julia's boot. How could I have been any happier?

The family gambolled across the starched white sheet of the lawn grown from seed. The gardener had had to put up lines of fine black cotton to stop the birds. Like a spider's web.

Only Julia clumped, out of character, with shoulders hunched and hands dug in her pockets. They stopped at the edge of the pond with the exhalations of their breath boiling in clouds as though for a moment they might manage to thaw the ice. Not only was the air brittle and glassy but every twig of every tree was iced, the blades of grass stiff and sharpened ready to cut; the surface of the pond looked as if cook had been there before them with her sugar shaker, webbed tracks crossed the ice to disappear on the far side of the pond in clumps of petrified bulrushes. Virginia stepped on to the ice, pointing at the tracks.

'Look, mummy, look. Auntie Julia, look!'

Before she took more than a couple of steps Julia was on the ice, grabbing her and pulling her back as the frozen sheet creaked and coughed. Emily's fear provoked her anger.

'Never, never go on to the ice. Any of you. Ever.'

'I wanted to see where . . . '

'What would happen if it cracked and you fell in?'

'She can't even swim,' said Margaret. 'I can. So I can walk on it.'

'You can't, it's too cold,' said Jean. 'Daddy told me. A man fell in and they threw him a lifebelt and even though it was very near he couldn't reach it and he drowned.'

'I want to see the footprints. Where do they go?'

'Not on the ice. You have to walk round the pond. Not across,' said Emily.

Julia picked up a clod of sparkling earth and tossed it up into the pearly air. It landed on the ice and burst straight through. A faint lap and a creak were heard as the ice readjusted itself and for an instant Julia's action had silenced the children.

'See.' Cyril peered round Emily's legs. 'You should do what mummy says. It's dangerous.'

Virginia was already skipping off to find her way round the edge of the pond, determined to discover where the bird's tracks led. Margaret and Jean scuttled after her from a mixture of curiosity and protectiveness leaving Cyril fidgeting, hovering somewhere in the background, reluctant to leave his mother's side but drawn by Margaret's shout.

'Come on, Cyril. We're not going to wait all day for you.'

'All right then,' and he ran to catch up with the others calling, 'Wait for me. I bet you can't find anything without me. I said wait.'

Julia stubbed her toes into the ground as she tried to stop herself from setting, hardening like the ground itself.

'Emily, you're always asking me how I knew George.'

When Julia said George I didn't know who she was talking about. How light-headed I must have been.

Emily's attention was fixed on the girls now disappearing behind the clumps of bulrushes. For once even the mention of her father's name failed to stir her as it usually did but then she began to come back.

'My father, yes. What about him?' she murmured. Julia gestured to a fallen tree trunk, brushing the fine white crystals from the ridges of the bark. Cyril was playing at the far end of the trunk trying to dig a stick into the sealed earth.

We sat on an elm that must have been blown down. It was only much later I noticed how cold I felt.

'We met just before the war broke out. At Ascot. My fiancé had taken me there. We were in a box with a lot of people I didn't know. Your father was there wearing tails and a top hat like everyone else.'

She said she had wanted to reach out and stroke his hat.

Julia took Emily's hands between her own and through their gloves they could feel the other wrapped against the cold.

'My fiancé was a prig. He got upset when champagne splashed his jacket. Everyone was concentrating on the race.'

I pictured ladies with their arms gloved to the elbow, their pearls tick-tocking, chins up, the criss-cross of veils hatching their cheeks, white hats with a dark ribbon cocked on the side of their heads fragile as bone china, thinks Emily.

'I dropped my programme and your father picked it up. I could smell the carnation in his button hole as he handed it back to me. There was no wedding ring on his finger.'

He removed his wedding ring the day my mother died and left instructions that when he was buried next to her they put it back. But it wouldn't go on, so they put it in his palm and closed his fingers over it.

'When the race was over he turned and asked me whether I had won. I hadn't. "Let's see if we can pick the next winner together," he said. He told me there was nothing worth placing a bet on and suggested we took some refreshment.'

They stepped out of the box and left the buzz of the crowd discussing the race and potential winners behind them.

While Julia was speaking to Emily, Cyril knelt on the pitiless ground against the tree trunk where they were seated as if he were in silent prayer at the communion rail. Instead of a priest he listened to Julia, who had never been so wired and taut with squirms of red daubed on her cheeks like some hastily made-up circus clown. Cyril saw her staring straight through his mother at someone he couldn't see. In the posture of devotion behind his mother's back his knees began to hurt on the stone-hard ground and he chattered in the cold.

'So you see we met in the year before the war started.'

That was the year in which Charles and I were married.

It was the same year in which another Emily, Davidson, threw herself under the hooves of the Derby horses in a protest for the vote to be extended to women. Julia was at her funeral and was knocked to the ground in a scuffle as police arrested Sylvia Pankhurst jeered at by spectators. Julia did not then include this in her confession to Emily who had only the vaguest notion of Julia's liberal tendencies.

'And I fell in love with him among the glassy chins and shoes of Ascot.'

One of Julia's friends said about her: Julia's paradox – passion and politics, political about her passion and passionate about her politics. Whoever gets involved with her will have to watch his servants.

It was Emily's father George, successful entrepreneur, long-suffering family man, embodiment of decade after decade of infinite material and commercial expansion, for whom Julia had a sexual passion, and loving the old order gave birth to a new one.

'We had a child. A boy, at least, that's what they told me. I was in a coma for weeks. When I knew what was happening again they had taken him away. Your father told them to. He refused to tell me where. I begged him again and again but he never relented.'

The last time Cyril had seen his mother in this frozen posture, her limbs set as though she were caught forever in this attitude drained of all life, had been as she stood in the middle of the bedroom, the bedclothes suspended in mid air.

'George never allowed the faintest hint of intimacy between us in public. Once I laid, no, brushed a gloved hand on his arm and he shrugged it off as though it were some nasty insect. I know it's because he still worshipped your mother. He couldn't shake her off however hard he tried.'

There were whisperings after George died. They ran something like this: Julia, poor thing, has taken George's death rather badly and insists that they were lovers! The absurdity of it! She's young enough to be his daughter. Besides, George was in love with Emily's mother until the day he died.

Emily was rigid and Cyril, who was still genuflecting behind his mother's back, his sisters absent, twisted and turned against the log like some beetle seeking food and a home. Julia was saying something to his mother which he didn't understand but he did recognise the arrangement of his mother's features like the rabbit he had seen frozen in the gardener's torch. As the torch was dipped and the creature bolted the expression on his mother's face cracked and her laughter burst into the white, threatening to shatter the ice on the pond and snap the branches over their heads. The laughter shook the ground and pierced the brittle air, scattering a moorhen from out of the bulrushes. Then the girls came back into view on the opposite bank of the pond with Jean's thin voice piping, 'Mummy, mummy, what's happening?' and Margaret chiming, 'Mummy, stop that horrible noise,' and Virginia saying nothing, only running back towards Julia and her mother.

Emily's laughter rang on through that incandescent January morning of 1923 while Cyril prayed that the grotesque sobbing and churning pouring from his mother would stop. And that the agony of her hysteria would not penetrate the Surrey hedgerows scribbled round the banks of the pond.

Julia tried, thinks Emily as she shifts her legs going to sleep under the rug, tried to prepare the ground for me in unobtrusive, trivial ways but I was too naive to notice her passing references to his favourite whisky or where he had his suits made. She says to Charles:

Julia blew the dust from father's portrait. I saw for myself the cracks in the varnish I'd used.

What Emily didn't, still doesn't, know is that her father had offered to leave the business to Julia who had refused to accept it. She argued without having met her that it should go to Emily, and besides, she said, she had more than enough money of her own. But this made her more determined to ensure that Emily should be encouraged to do something about the shops she had inherited.

* * *

CHANGE THE BUSINESS. Julia realised that even the influence of their love had not been great enough to effect a permanent cure of the hardening in George's conservative arteries; and that any radical change would have to wait for the next generation, his daughter Emily.

Do you know what she said to me? After I knew about father and her? What are you going to do about the shops? They're a disgrace in anyone's terms. They don't even make you any money. They provide a living for the dozen or so people who work in them, make enough to cover your overheads and that's it. Does that sound funny, Charles? That Julia with all her ideas of equality helped to make us very rich. She didn't intend to, of course. She was interested in me, what I could get out of it, not how much profit we would make. In two or three years she showed more interest in me than you've shown in a lifetime. I never gave her enough credit and you didn't know.

Emily seems to have lost all feeling in her left leg. It has happened before and she is not frightened though she wishes Virginia would come and help her out of her chair. With her leg dead she is incapable of standing, a prisoner at the window through which a patch of red bobs and jigs then stills on the rim of the sundial. The bird waits with its head cocked on one side, listening, waiting for me to speak, thinks Emily, then it lifts off and dips over the crimson wall to where it will perch and watch Cyril in the vegetable garden. Virginia can't still be clearing up the mess in the kitchen. Is she upstairs in one of the bedrooms though surely she made the beds earlier in the day?

Julia suggested that the business was catering to the wrong sort of people who were dwindling, dying on their feet, and that she needed to extend the range of customers the shops brought in. Emily had told her that profits had been down every year since the end of the war and Julia replied that she should increase the size of the premises, keeping a corner of select items for her old customers but appealing to a wider clientele.

I told her, Charles, that I was a wife, a mother and not a business woman. Remember how you said I should sell the shops but I kept them out of sentiment and respect. I had no intention of making money. I left it all to the manager.

Mr Drewitt was a slight man with a falsetto voice which the telephone did nothing to improve. Although he had to ring Emily to consult her on matters of staff or stock, he hated using the instrument, knowing that it made him sound younger than his shop boys. In consequence he spoke too quickly as though he were afraid that all his words wouldn't fit on to the cable if he didn't cram them all together in one go. If he called without warning on a shop and found one of the boys idle he would make him stack boxes, jars, tins or packets in an elaborate pyramid which threatened to topple every time someone passed nearby – Mr Drewitt's words were like that, too, perched and trembling they wavered as if they might tumble at any time. He telephoned Emily, voice tremulous as a chorister.

'It is a question of the utmost urgency and you see delicacy, too, well I am not at all sure that this is the right but on the other hand something should, really ought to be done about it at once before she, it is a matter of some, how can I put it, and now that I come to it I am not at all sure that I, we, should be discussing it over the telephone.'

'Yes, Mr Drewitt. What is it?' A dry resignation in Emily's voice.

'Ma'am, do you remember or perhaps you don't, she is the sort of girl you wouldn't necessarily recall.'

'Who, Mr Drewitt. Who?'

'Her name is Betty, Betty Greenwood, she came to work for us in the Haslemere shop about a year ago.'

'Yes, a big strong girl,' with forearms like best lean bacon thought Emily, 'A no-nonsense workhorse I should think. And sensible too.'

'You are quite right, ma'am. How very right you are, very correct . . .'

'Yes, what is it, Mr Drewitt?'

'She, the girl, woman really, is embarrassed, ma'am.'

'Embarrassed? What about?'

'She is, begging your pardon, ma'am, in the sort of way in which she might be if she were a married woman, ma'am.'

'Are you saying that she's pregnant?'

'Aah! Yes I am, ma'am. How clever of you to guess. You are absolutely right.'

'Well, Mr Drewitt, what does she expect me to do about it?'

'I, we, thought that it might, wondered if it would be at all possible if she could leave on a temporary basis, our, your employment that is. And to come back when it was all over, aah, out of the way.'

'Why not if that is what she wants.'

'Yes, ma'am, that is exactly what I was thinking myself, only I wanted to confirm it with you. There is one other thing, ma'am.'

'Yes, Mr Drewitt.'

'It is that Betty, Miss Greenwood that is, is not married, not that is in the normal sense of the word.'

'I don't care whether she is married in the abnormal sense of the word, Mr Drewitt. If in your opinion she is a good employee of the business then it is worth the trouble of finding a replacement for her until she can return to work. If on the other hand she is not worth the trouble . . . '

'Oh no, ma'am, she's an excellent worker.'

'In that case the decision is yours.'

'Thank you very much, ma'am. I'm sure Miss Greenwood will appreciate it and take the trouble to thank you herself. I'll make sure she does.'

'Don't trouble yourself. I'm sure you have far more important things to attend to.'

'Yes ma'am. I wanted to tell you that our sugar in the Dorking shop has gone damp and that we ought . . . '

'You deal with it, Mr Drewitt.'

'Yes ma'am. Thank you again, ma'am.'

'Goodbye, Mr Drewitt.'

'Goodbye, ma'am, and thank you.' He replaced the receiver while Emily imagined Betty Greenwood's thick forearms bunched from the wrist like sausages and her hunkers like immense hams swinging from hooks. She saw Mr Drewitt with Betty in the shadow of stockroom tea chests tasting her salty flesh; she knew how whenever Mr Drewitt came near Betty his voice would pitch an octave higher and he would start to gibber and then she realised that Julia was right: she could do better than the Mr Drewitts of this world.

From the time of that iron day in the January of 1923 when Julia shattered the portrait of Emily's father which she had always carried with her the business began to expand. She opened three more shops in the next three years, a steady if unspectacular progress, and they edged almost imperceptibly in the direction Julia had suggested. They started to attract a few people who actually did their own shopping – who didn't send their housekeepers but came carrying their baskets themselves. They were often more discriminating and demanding than the servants alongside whom they shopped and as a result the quality of the service and stock started to rise.

I wasn't completely convinced, Charles. I still thought that ladies, real ladies, did not engage in trade. But Julia was so enthusiastic and you were never here. She egged me on but I held back. I suppose you think that it was devotion to the family, our wonderful family which has gone and cut itself off. No, it wasn't that and neither was it you, Charles. Don't flatter yourself. Do you want to know what really held me back from the business? I'll tell you.

* * *

YOU, CHARLES, WERE ASLEEP by the fire in this room after a long and heavy lunch. All the children were occupied in the nursery or elsewhere. Bertrand's eyes were on me, sparkling. I'd ignored them, refused to take his gaze since father's funeral. I was forever turning away but then I yielded. If you'd been awake . . .

She herself wonders what might have been had Charles not been slumped and oblivious. She has wondered ever since. She looks at the spot next to the fireplace where she sees him still, his head lolling on one side, unconsciously shifting in the chair as if something disturbed his dream. She thinks that it was the innocence, not of a child, but belonging to some species of animal, a being unaware.

I agreed to go outside with him. To stop ourselves falling asleep, he said, looking at you. He offered me his arm. We walked through the mist and stopped under the beech tree. Neither of us had spoken since leaving the house.

How much do I need to tell him, Emily asks herself now, before he jumps up and cries out. Instead he is bent awkwardly in his chair, his limbs twisted and splayed like a doll that is never truly mobile and cannot speak. That will only move as she moulds it. Should she hand over the remembered images as they develop? How Bertrand drew her to him under the beech and their tongues slipped into each other's mouths, how her coat buttons popped and the coat split apart, his knees were between her legs and her back against the beech which rose and lost its crown in the wreathing, damp mist like a stick of spinning white candy-floss; then her head lay by its roots and the trunk shot vertically up from beside her while she could feel the damp rising even through Bertrand's thick overcoat but she pulled up her dress for him thinking, quickly yes quickly, I've held you away from me for seven years, I will come to you Bertrand I will come, soon in the summer when the leaves are out on this naked tree we will be together; push hard now and make it come, now.

Then, Charles, I stroked his forehead and we lay together gazing up at the bare twigs scribbled and dripping in the grey sky. The wind was bitter, scything.

She trembles, teetering on the brink of worse still. Dare she tell Charles that in the new year of 1926 she agreed to leave him for Bertrand? Which is worse? The thought, its execution, or the telling, the last attempting a mimesis and failing miserably, creating the event anew as though it were happening for the first time. How our words betray us, as for those of someone else . . . the words of Margaret's letter jar her far more than those of Ronald himself would have done, and his words would have disturbed her more than the act itself. Should one then act but not tell, move through life in a dumb show? After all, isn't that what Charles had done, at least, it is the profile he has always turned to her. She wants to shake him, find some way of provoking something, a dry rattle in the throat, anything. In the beginning was the word but before that there was a cry, surely? She sees him in front of her, his lips twitching, working over toothless gums. Why did Virginia persistently forget his dentures? Her tongue runs round her mouth, the ribcage roof shading into fleshy palate, and she still has her own teeth. She would like to feel contempt for Charles's dentures but despicably, she thinks, she is beyond such emotion.

Through the glass she watches one of Virginia's two cats stalking unseen prey. It wriggles across the grass on its belly like a soldier moving into position to snipe. Unlike her daughter Emily has no time for cats which she regards with suspicion. She prefers the solid predictability, the slavishness, of dogs. Ronald, with too much of his mother in him, had always liked cats. She supposes it was their aloof waywardness that appealed to him, remembering how whenever he came home from school he would insist on having a cat to sleep with him. In the morning suffering a mild allergy to their fur he sneezed and sneezed but that never deterred or lessened his affection for the creatures and sometimes he could be seen clutching a piece of string at the end of which a cat was made to prance along behind him. He did this not out of cruelty but from a desire to court a graceful feline poise. She had to go and tell him to untie the knot for surely the poor thing might be strangled. She remembers the expression of horror on his child's face as he realised that what his grandmother was saying could well be true. He had never intended to kill the silken animal and loosened the string with a hot face and tears in his eyes. Now the ginger snakes across the lawn and slides under the yew hedge where Emily hopes it will spend the remainder of the morning out of her sight and off her lap – she will on occasion tolerate its presence there but she knows that if it tried to scramble up this morning she would brush it back down to the carpet in which it would flex its claws then settle on an empty armchair, not in the least resentful but superbly indifferent.

She turns to Charles but his eyelids are flickering, he is already beyond the range of her voice so that now she will not tell him how Julia encouraged her to think that women could, should do as they wished and make decisions for themselves. She applied these words, not to the business as Julia had intended them, but to the chance of her own happiness as she saw it. Although she thinks he will not hear, she tells Charles what she had once told Julia.

* * *

I AM LEAVING, Emily said. 'We're going away together. Somewhere I don't know.' How thrilled she was to be telling Julia.

'Are you sure that it's . . . ' But Julia could not finish her sentence; instead she wrapped her arms round Emily who buried her face in Julia's neck and shook; Julia gently prised Emily's arms away from her and stepped back. Emily started to laugh until she was gibbering like a frightened gibbon chained to a post; she circled and skipped, rattling the chain with her lips drawn back in a snarl, and she bared her teeth ready to attack anything that might encroach on her territory. This was in April 1926 when there were events massing whose sounds were then a faint rumble in Emily's ears, but their reverberations would echo through the Surrey hedgerows and make themselves felt in the very room where Emily is sitting.

The strike fund ran out at the end of April and still Baldwin hadn't taken sides, refusing to stand accused of partiality. He told the miners and the employers to negotiate but no agreement was reached and the miners would not return to work without the guarantee of a minimum wage which the employers refused. The miners were locked out and the TUC brought out some of the front-line unions – transport, printing, gas and electricity. They made the mistake of holding some in reserve when they should have for maximum effect have called out the second line on strike too.

Where were you, Charles, then? Had you reached the Canary Islands by that time? My telegram never found you in Las Palmas.

When the food picketing worsened they called in the troops and on the third day of the strike Churchill's *British Gazette* could print on its front page: *Nation Calm and Confident. Food Supply Normal. Volunteers in Large Numbers*. Among this last group were the specials, that is, emergency police quickly recruited and drafted in to assist the regular force in dealing with the strike. They travelled through the capital in open-topped buses commandeered from the regular bus companies. Glancing up at them standing over advertisements for Sandy Mac whisky or Heinz 57 they could easily be mistaken for regular passengers in their assortment of rain- and overcoats; it was only their tin hats and armbands that gave them away. From within the ranks of these specials individuals were pulled out who were competent on horseback. Although this supplementary force of mounted constabulary did not wear uniforms either, its members appeared far more threatening in their pith helmets and riding boots than their counterparts on the buses. In addition, they carried two-foot six-inch truncheons over their shoulders and this lent them the air of a properly organised and well-drilled unit in spite of the fact that they wore their own jodhpurs and jackets.

Afterwards it took months before I would go near a horse.

The strike was on the verge of collapse and, therefore, one group of mounted specials was slightly surprised to find itself called out to deal with a crowd at the East London dock which, as Reith's BBC would have phrased it, was threatening to turn into a mob. Nevertheless they left their barracks at a smart trot, realising that this disturbance probably represented the final twitches of a dying corpse. When they arrived at the dockland gates they were faced with a large group of strikers blocking the entrance. From horseback they could see over the gates into the yard where lorries were, according to *Daily Graphic* headlines, *Safeguarding The Meat Supplies*, protected by more specials on foot as well as regular policemen. The strikers were not attempting anything more than to block the entrance and so prevent the lorries from leaving once they had been loaded. The men stood and talked quietly, smoking, there was even the occasional burst of laughter as someone told an anecdote or joke. However, with the ringing of horseshoes on the road the conversation dropped to a murmur and by the time the specials were within thirty yards the strikers were completely silent. They had all turned their backs on the locked gates to face the men on horseback who reined in and halted about twenty yards away.

A large group of horses in the paddock can still make me nervous. You didn't know, did you? You've always considered me the complete horsewoman but I've had to fight to appear like that, struggle against memory's instinct.

The specials' leader then walked his horse forward so that he was only five paces from the strikers. He spoke firmly but without raising his voice, telling them to stand aside and clear a way allowing the lorries to leave the yard. He said that he would return to his men and give the strikers one minute to step back and let the lorries through then he wheeled away and rejoined his men. For the first time since the specials' appearance the strikers bent their heads and spoke quickly. They decided that a group of twenty-five on foot could not offer serious resistance to more than a dozen on horseback wielding truncheons, not to mention those specials behind the gates. Shuffling reluctantly they parted and left a channel just wide enough for a lorry to pass through. The leader of the mounted specials then stood up in his stirrups and called to those inside that the route was clear. The gates were unbolted and swung back as the lorries, six in all, edged out. The strikers were tight-lipped, bitter about the eyes yet silent until the last lorry pulled out when someone shouted, 'Scabs, Traitors, Bastards!' The cries were not taken up and the specials congratulated themselves on having released the meat from the docks with so little trouble. The crowd of strikers had after all turned out to be a more reasonable group of individuals than anyone could have hoped; they doubtless knew when they were beaten.

Julia told me how at the end of the strike the official strike news bulletin, *The British Worker* I think, said, *Miners Will Now Get a Fair Deal*. It was nonsense she said. The miners' Council did bugger all for them, were her words. And now we've got no coal because they're on strike again. I wish Virginia would come and light a fire.

With the meat lorries safely on their way the specials saw no reason to remain at the docks and as the last of the lorries disappeared round the corner they tightened their reins and prepared to leave. They were not in a hurry and took the time of those who can savour an efficient victory. Later Julia told Emily how the specials as collaborators were more despised by the strikers than the regular police force and that it had been an error to call them to the docks instead of the regular force. As their reins tautened and they settled into their saddles, flexing the stirrup leathers, one of the watching strikers put a hand in his pocket. He drew out a stone which he threw in their direction; he was aiming at no one and had no other motive in mind than the release of his own anger and frustration. He was incensed that their vigil had been ended by a posse of amateurs on horseback who had the funds, the leisure and inclination to trot about the city as though on the estates where they doubtless rode. The horses were untrained and ill-prepared for such an incident, one of them shied and reared, throwing its surprised rider to the ground. In spite of its strap the pith helmet flew up in the air and the rider's temple smacked into the cobbles killing him outright. It was the sole death of the General Strike.

They told you about the strike at your club months later. What did they say? Did they tell you that the poor devils would now be wishing they hadn't made such a fuss in the first place?

Long before Charles had docked club conversation had moved on to Hobbs and Sutcliffe opening for England against Australia at Headingley. Hobbs, the shorter, wore his cap with the peak set to shield his eyes which were downcast and paid no attention to the crowd. Walking from the pavilion he was already absorbed, dropping the end of his bat on the outfield with each step while Sutcliffe carried his lower down the handle and swung it from the neck. His chin was up and his shoulders thrown back, conscious of the crowd he was to play to; there was a hint of tension, adrenalin about the nose and mouth. Later in the autumn of that year Charles stepped from his ship to admire the Cox's Orange Pippins in his orchard. Their russet the colours of England, such should be the ruddiness of a true Englishman's cheeks.

Julia told me about the ghosts working underground; anaemic, hollow, skeletal and wasted.

Charles had followed the events at a distance, reading the telegrammed reports flung out to him as he ploughed up the Atlantic – Lisbon, the Canaries, Jamaica. Once he had regained the kingdom, heard in detail how events had been deflected and turned back on those who should never have acted in the first place, then he was able to nod; paternal with a few months' history he could say, What did I tell you?

I still see him lying there. I didn't know for days, not until the black-edged card arrived, addressed to you. They thought Bertrand was your friend not mine. Perhaps they were right. I kept him at a distance too long for us to be friends. I wouldn't compromise. We were leaving . . . together.

Emily's voice trails away in a whisper. She is watching a trickle of blood drain away in a cobbled runnel and wind round quoits of khaki dung, taking two lives with it.

* * *

BUSINESS AND CHURCH are given in alphabetical sequence not in order of priority. The business of church, though not identical to the church of business, runs parallel at certain points. Emily found that her increasing involvement in both activities fed a spiral in which they seemed at times to be indistinguishable from each other.

What was there left to me? The children you say but that year the youngest, Virginia, was already seven years old and Margaret more than twelve. I had to find something to fill the years ahead. I shut out the decision I had made to leave you and the children. Even to myself I said it was nothing more than a girlish infatuation, to admit anything else would have been too painful. I pushed that Emily away. She became a third person I barely knew, glimpsed walking in an unfamiliar landscape, a figure about whom there were all sorts of disturbing rumours . . . Emily's thoughts run on unspoken. Is it time she said something?

I never walked under the beech tree again. When Ronald was a child he tried to make me collect nuts with him. My refusal made him cry but even that couldn't draw me there.

Emily who had previously been a passive member found herself playing an increasingly active role in the parish. She occasionally caught herself wondering about the nature of her faith but then action was demanded of her: could they afford to re-roof the almshouses or would that have to wait another year? Christmas presents for the children of families who were means-tested had to be found. Was there any chance that Reverend Bates would attend their group meeting on the role of Christ in the modern world? The vestry door was almost off its hinges and needed re-hanging.

The Bible needed replacing. It was so tattered that when the vicar or anyone else read from it I was terrified that the whole thing would come away from its spine and crash to the floor with its pages fanning like the doves in the cote. I donated a new one and read the first lesson from it. Let him cast the mote. The new vicar read it in church again the other day. Perhaps that's what's prompted me to say what I have this morning.

Emily ruffles the feathery azure sheet on her lap. How, she wonders, the most gossamer networks can bind faster than any cord.

But there was no time to question her faith. She became more than ever a doer without allowing herself the leisure to brood on what might have been, or be. If she argued with herself at all it was to say in a brisk manner that doubting the quality of one's present, 'given' as she put it, existence was in the end to court self-destruction. After all, hadn't she nearly ruined a perfectly acceptable marriage and family circle with such contemplations? Where would that have led her? The stones of the church offered a rampart where her emotion might be protected from further assault and the wounds in the agonised body of Christ a route by which she could leave this world for a better. And when she had gathered her strength once more she could talk to Julia of her faith, her hope in the business.

And, of course, there was always the family; until now that is.

Emily's expansion of the business had, before 1926, sounded in a minor key. Although there were now thirteen shops the three she had just opened in as many years had not fundamentally altered the nature of the business she had inherited. In spite of Julia's advice the conception remained her father's, still serving the customers from a restricted register.

After a brief pause in 1926 as if to gain a second wind the

number rose in the next thirteen years to sixty-seven. Part of this growth can be explained by a real increase in wages, a fall in the cost of living, low rates, low taxes, non-union labour, cheaper land and property and improved transportation. The new industries, including food, were expanding to cater for those with more money and leisure and Emily retailed for them. There was something schizophrenic about the rate of growth for it was achieved at a time when Emily was, if she had stopped to ask, furthest from her self.

In this division she was not unlike the nation. 1936, for instance, which was the year of the most dramatic increase in her profits began with the death of King George V and closed with the abdication of Edward VIII, in between whiles sandwiching the Jarrow march. How could any business expand so spectacularly when more than three-quarters of a town were unemployed and marched on the capital in protest? They converged capped with coats under an arm or over a shoulder. Some of them wore waistcoats. 'Proper little gentlemen,' said Charles. Those who had ties rather spoiled the effect by wearing them round their necks without collars. They brewed their tea and cooked their sausages outside on open fires, drank from and ate off enamel mugs and plates.

'What's all the fuss about?' asked Charles. 'It's nothing we haven't all done at some time or another. I expect it tasted much better in the open air anyway.' The Minister at the Board of Trade, Viscount Runciman, had it right according to Charles. He told the marchers not to bother the capital, to go away and work out their own salvation. A couple of years later it was the same figure in a bow tie who boarded a train for Prague to negotiate a peace between Hitler's Sudetenland Germans and the Czechs.

But Emily's business in London and the Home Counties, with less than half the unemployment rate of the North of England, Scotland or Wales, was in the right location for taking advantage of what surplus cash existed. And yet the pre-war surge in her business was not only attributable to the geography of national economics. It was something personal.

I mastered fat ledgers thick as a bible. I spent years poring over them. Month after month I read and re-read legal documents until my eyes ached and my head spun. I interviewed every single person who worked for me. If we changed a supplier I personally checked the deliveries of new stock. Butter, wine, sugar, pickles, cheese, marmalade, coffees and teas, I tasted them all. Not a month went by when I didn't visit each shop. I knew all my staff by name. Could you have said that of the men on your ships, Charles? Your teeth have fallen out and you suffer agonising digestive problems and yet you didn't taste a hundredth of what I've consumed. Where is the world's cause and effect?

It was a trinity, muses Emily, of business, church and the family. Each one plastered over gaps left by the other. The only element left out in this construction was her self.

From outside there is a distant chug-chugging of an engine. Emily realises that it cannot be a vehicle approaching the house on the drive at the front for the sound is definitely coming from somewhere at the back of the house. It would seem to be blowing from somewhere in the direction of the vegetable garden. It sounds like a petrol engine. Cyril is surely not going to try to cut the grass at this time of year and while it is so wet? Emily strains, listening to the engine's throb; it is not after all the motor mower but the higher-pitched whine of a chain saw she can hear. She remembers the silky grey beech leaning and the buzz-buzzing of the tree surgeon's saw all morning. How she watched from the bedroom window upstairs and saw Charles out there trying to help but getting in their way. He offered them mugs of tea and they conspired to fell more than a century of growth. Did Charles think she refused to go and watch because it was a man's work? Or that she had an easy nostalgia for what was old and natural? Emily knew that the tree had to come down because it was dangerous but as there came a dulled thunder and the glass in the bedroom window rattled she shook and shivered herself. Looking out of the window she saw the tree stranded on its side like some prehistoric creature washed up by the tide into another age.

If that's Cyril with the chain saw I do hope that he's careful. Do you remember that silly child we had billeted with us? I know you weren't here but I'm sure that I wrote to you about him.

Cyril was using a spade and the boy was without his shoes and socks – don't ask me why – down came the spade and the boy lost one of his toes. Fortunately, it was only a little piggy. He was soon back with us though I have to confess he did have a slight list. Years later, after the war, he came back to see me. I gave him a job in the Croydon warehouse.

Emily considers how in the end it all came round to the business. There was, from the moment of her committal, no escape. Even Julia came to be defined by her relation to it. Poor idealistic Julia! How she must have winced! She had prepared the ground for Emily to break out of one pattern only to see her poured into another mould. Exchanging the sacred books of matrimonial law for those of commerce and the church was not what Julia had had in mind. It was a double-edged sword which she had helped Emily draw. And she felt the distance between them heap up, accumulate slowly but inevitably like an icicle lengthening itself through its own drip drip drip. Emily did not allow herself the opportunity to take note of this icy separation. She was bound to Julia by what they knew about each other but with a newly established sense of propriety she hated any reference to those aspects of her past which she considered she had abandoned, sloughing it off, a dried-out, brittle skin for which she no longer had any use. On account of her sense of indebtedness to Julia, Emily kept at arm's length the one person with whom she had once shared her self and found towards the end that she was nurturing an insidious contempt for what she now regarded as the weakness she had formerly presented to Julia; and her feeling spread in a cancerous manner so that the shame she felt for her own weakness grew to be associated with Julia whom she began, unconsciously at first, to despise.

Nevertheless Julia was for a decade after 1926 still a regular if slightly less frequent visitor. What then continued to draw her there? Two things. One of them was their share in Emily's father, Julia's lover.

* * *

OF GEORGE. Emily kept her memories of George locked away and brought them out less and less frequently as she grew more and more absorbed in the business. When they did surface it was unwillingly, they had to be dragged up like a fish at the end of a line. Julia found it increasingly difficult to talk to Emily about George so she clutched her own memories of him all the more tightly until they threatened to snap in her grip. She would talk about how he mounted a horse with a bark to the groom who would go down on one knee and cup his hands to take George's boot. Then the groom would rise slightly, shaking as he raised George into the saddle.

'He wasn't, of course, a light man when you knew him,' said Emily.

'But he wasn't fat or really overweight, considering his age.'

'I don't know. I really can't remember. You would naturally have more reason to recall what father's figure was like.'

'He was a handsome man.'

'He was my father.'

And so the difference in perceptions continued unbroken.

For Emily George was frozen in postures of correctness: starched canapé of a wing collar; tan boot soles clattering on cobbles or crunching up gravel; his head bowed over the table for grace, the hairs bristling in his scalp like a hedgehog's coat and the forwhatweareabouttoreceive murmured from underneath; seated behind a newspaper with a photograph of two coffins on its front pages and his legs and spine set square straight; the scarlet flag of his hunting jacket teasing a monochrome day; him dropping sovereigns in the collection plate then standing in the porch complimenting the vicar on an excellent sermon; being summoned to his study to be told it was the anniversary of her mother's death and standing by the shadow of the yew watching him place the wreath on her grave.

Charles, as Emily sees him, seems to be slumping and sliding down his chair more than usual. She remonstrates.

Do sit up, Charles, we shall have to order you a new chair if you can't see out of the window from that one. It would be a shame for you to miss the spring. Cyril said there'd be some of your favourite crocus this year. He's planted a ring of orange, mauve and white round the stump of the beech tree. You know when they cut it down I felt that something was being amputated I'd forgotten had existed.

George for Julia was the soft black dashes on the backs of his hands that ran over the furrows of his pores; taking off the collar of his shirt and its stud whirring quietly on the dressing-table top; the caress of his walnut tones purring over the sound of the occasional motor vehicle beyond the curtains; the vibration of his cuff-links on the polished oak; the scar – result of a riding accident – on his shoulder; the slight curve in his spine as he sat on the edge of the bed, his posture loosening and relaxed; his toe next to the big toe longer than all the others; how he leaned over and pulled the cord to turn out the light whose softness seemed to hang in the air with an image of his crooked arm in the afterglow forever bowing and circling round her.

Given this difference why did Julia continue to take the train from London south to Guildford?

* * *

VIRGINIA is the second answer. Virginia who, from the start, was attracted to the air of something foreign and mysterious which attended Julia's presence. And though it may initially have been the peacock's feather which caught Virginia's eye something deeper and more permanent took root; and Julia came to love Virginia.

Where do you think Virginia is now, Charles? She can't have gone far. Have you noticed how little she goes out these days? I suppose she's no longer a young woman herself. She must be fifty-four. Or five is it? Should I mention it to her? Margaret's letter about Ronald I mean. Surely she knows. Ronald couldn't have kept it hidden from his own mother. Or could he?

Emily wonders whether she should reconsider. Why, after all, should she feel an obligation to hand on the business to a man? What difference would that make? Didn't she build it up single-handed without any help from Charles? If she could do it why not Virginia? And yet she feels disappointment. She has been waiting an age for Ronald to come back home to take over from her. She has been relying on the lure of the empire she created to draw him back and now that he has so obviously rcsisted its attractions what is there left to her? Certainly not Cyril whose loyalty is not open to question but who is otherwise completely unsuitable. Virginia would have been a capable candidate, once, had Emily shown her sympathy and cultivated her but now it is too late for her to learn. What remains except to sit and watch her husband slide down in silent opposition to her?

When Virginia comes perhaps she will adjust your cushion for you. I copied that design from one my mother left. Father said she had sewn it herself before they were married. Roses in a heart. How simple! And it's still one of our best-selling lines. Imagine how many sitting rooms and bedrooms, chairs and settees it occupies across the country. And we have the original. Just think there are only a handful of homes, if any, where our stock has never entered! Yet now we're in a cul-de-sac and can't turn back.

The oak-panelled door swings back and Virginia enters carrying a tray with the following reproduction of an English country cottage: bristling, neatly sheared thatch overhangs the whitewashed walls and like the brim of a good fitting hat it affords welcome protection from the sun, wind, or rain. The upstairs windows are distant bullet holes set deep in darkness, the heavy but stunted front door is studded and squats ajar to reveal two or three uneven flags as though they had been dropped at random and left to settle as best they could over the centuries. The garden is a tightly patterned profusion of hollyhocks, the stippled yellow of golden rod on green fingers; down below nestle marjoram and thyme, basil and rosemary; rocks are half hidden under cascades of green – sage, jade, pea and bottle; as if someone has flicked a damp paintbrush, creams and pinks are splattered throughout; lavender marches its upright mauve into ranks of scent. There is a pond with inverted dustbin lids of lily leaves and beside it constructed from silver birch offcuts a bench is stretched out. Behind this a clematis mounts the cottage walls and trumpets a triumphant purple.

All this can be purchased in hard-wearing melamine with a wicker lip from any one of the hundreds of retail outlets belonging to Virginia's mother. In the century which is seventy-four years old it costs one pound and twenty-nine pence in the new currency. Emily knows that people want a modern and durable technology, hence the melamine, with a touch of the natural, the craft of it all, thus the wicker frill. Its decorative aspect a mythical English existence, echo of a past that never existed.

Emily remembers how she went into one of her own shops and bought that very tray herself without being recognised. It is a long time since she knew the faces let alone the names of all her staff.

So here is Virginia bearing present, functional and half-streamlined form, claiming a content with its roots in tradition, a simulation of the past, a façade to which Virginia, unlike her mother, has refused to submit for several decades. For her there is no cottage and garden though on this image she is bringing her mother a cup of coffee and two biscuits – her mother's favourite, their own brand of wholemeal and one of their leading lines. The plate covers the pond and part of the garden, the cup and saucer are perched on the thatch.

Margaret's letter to Emily lies scattered on her lap, about the floor at her feet. Virginia sees the lips weaving but she can hear nothing that Emily says. She places the tray on the small table beside the armchair where her mother's hands claw the armrests. Virginia sits in the chair opposite, Emily's hands unclench and she focuses on her daughter in whom she discerns Bertrand's silver eyes, the mercury still running half a century later. She observes how Virginia's cheekbones shadow a rebellion, a revolution which she, Emily, could not manage to sustain and which Virginia has inherited, half-caught from Bertrand.

Emily says, 'You've been such a long time. What've you been doing?'

'Only making coffee for you.' She looks at the pages. 'What does Margaret's letter say?'

Emily scrabbles and hands Virginia the envelope and sheaves in her lap.

'Spain?'

'Yes, she's left America at last. Why she ever went there . . . I'm sure she'll be home soon.'

Franco's bald head with that moustache – dictatorial emblem of the century – stares out at Virginia from the eggshell blue of the airmail envelope. Emily watches Virginia remove the fly-weight paper that whispers between her fingers in the faintly dusty room. Virginia reads, immobile, only her eyes moving like a lizard's; she shows no reaction. When she has finished she slides the paper back into the envelope and returns it to her mother's lap.

'Margaret doesn't change,' she says, 'Even her handwriting's overblown.'

'Why?'

'You aren't drinking your coffee.'

'Did you know?'

Virginia nods, her attention momentarily caught by the distant buzz and whine of a chain saw.

'Why didn't you tell me?'

Virginia shrugs. 'I thought you'd rather not know.'

'For God's sake,' says Emily, thinking, I am still the head of one of the largest retail stores in Britain and yet my daughter treats me as if I were a half-wit.

'I thought you might not find out.'

'That his letters would come just the same? That I wouldn't notice the change? Is that it?'

'Yes,' Virginia lies. She thought Emily would have died before she had to learn about Ronald. 'I never knew if you knew about Ronald. Or Cyril for that matter.'

'Cyril is a very devoted son.'

'Devoted to his garden. Anything to take him outside. Away from the house.'

'Cyril has remained loyal. Not like Margaret in America or Jean in Africa.'

Her own name is missing from her mother's list; Virginia knows that her mother knows the reason she is here is that inertia and apathy set in. It grew too late and now there is nowhere else for her to go.

'What,' asks Emily, waving the letter in a surge of energy, 'are we going to do about this? This, this dismembering. It is a profanity.'

Virginia shakes her head. 'Nothing.'

'I knew, I knew it would happen,' cries Emily. 'I could have told you before he was even born.'

Oh, thinks Virginia, why didn't you warn me and save us the trouble?

'Because you are your father's daughter and your father is not who you think.'

Not the man who stayed for brief spells then disappeared for months, thinks Emily. Not the man who after his retirement spent his time with Cyril in the garden. Not the man who bought you a donkey, not the man you visited in hospital with the tubes up his nose and needles in his arm. 'Your father is an impostor and that's why Ronald has acted like this. You are not one of us; how could he be? There is nothing left of me in you.'

Virginia's gaze is directed through the window into the garden and lights on the mossy sundial at which Julia taught her to tell the time, then she turns her head and looks down at the wrinkles like crow's feet on the undrunk coffee. A glimmer of light catches Virginia's forehead and in it Emily watches a trickle of blood snake from Bertrand's temple and in one hand he is clutching a stone that would fit snugly into a pocket.

Emily and Virginia both imagine that they hear a strangled cry from outside the house.

Virginia thinks at last she might begin to understand and starts to weep.

VIRGINIA

THE KITCHEN is cavernous, not well-lit, and in those corners distant from the Aga a chill invades if one lingers too long. Which is why Virginia leans on the Aga's rail and nestles into the cast-iron boiler as far as its heat allows her without scorching clothes or skin. Her right foot is crossed over the other's ankle and her arms are folded across her chest in a posture which suggests that her stance is habitual and signals waiting. It does not appear as if she is in any hurry to move or expects to have to do so; the heavy looseness of her limbs indicates an intention to remain in this position for some while. Her body faces the kitchen window but presently her chin points down to the square red tiles on the floor where her eyes are directed but not looking.

I ought, I suppose, to have known all the details – exactly when, how, where – but they are, after all, an afterthought, almost. It was a matter of time and Ronald's own will to put into practice the fact as he envisaged it. Though I've never said anything, who could be a mother and fail to know? What benefit would there have been in speaking out except to relieve my own tensions? Certainly not to change anything, quite possibly to accelerate it. Only to have been there, be there, to comfort.

From the chipped enamelled saucepan on top of the Aga puffs of steam putter as bubbles of oxygen gather and break the water's corrugated surface. She thinks about the letter which she gave unopened to her mother this morning. The large, looping letters told her it was Margaret's hand and although she hasn't read the contents she knows what it says and imagines the rage which she herself does not feel boiling in her mother's thin blood. It will make her even more tetchy and difficult to handle over the next few days.

Sixteen years before there had been another letter addressed to her from Ronald's headmaster which had materialised as the first public acknowledgement that Ronald was not all that he might seem but more. Then too she had intimated to herself the essence of what she was about to be told not through any psychic skill but because she had known about it all along.

'So Mrs Wilkins,' the headmaster's conversation ran, 'it is simply a matter of asking whether or not your son, Ronald, is how shall we say somewhat . . . Let us put it this way, do you think that you yourself would describe him as, in fact, how would you describe your son?'

'He is a boy, headmaster, a boy or perhaps you hadn't noticed.'

'Very good, Mrs Wilkins, very good.'

How the poor man was obliged to play the fool, lumbering through intricacies of which he perceived and understood so little and when he would rather have been out watching his first fifteen splashing through mud.

'We are, you see, Mrs Wilkins, a little, not a lot, I stress a little, concerned about Ronald. He is not, would I be correct in saying' – here his gaze fixed on the housemaster at his side – 'not what one would call an outgoing, an extrovert boy. There is a slight tendency to, how should I say, withdraw?' Was he being so evasive because of an embarrassment in having to discuss such a matter with a boy's mother? Or was it that a public school needs its revenues, especially one that was about to begin work on a new gymnasium and swimming pool?

'Are you saying he isn't happy here?'

'Not at all, not at all. Far from it. It's just that we feel his attitude, his behaviour, shows a bias to the, to the oversensitive.' The headmaster's hairless skull shone, translucent; one could almost make out the brain throbbing beneath like the skin of some reptilian membrane that betrays pumping organs. 'I think Ronald's housemaster ought to explain. After all, it's his pigeon, if you see what I mean.'

The housemaster pulled at his grey flannels, tugged at his greenish tweed jacket and leaned towards Mrs Wilkins in a too-confidential manner.

'We're having trouble getting him to undress, aah, take off his clothes.'

'Yes, housemaster, I know what undress means.'

'In public, I mean, when there's anyone else about. We thought it was just a passing phase. I have tried to speak to your son about it but . . .' he sighed and shrugged his shoulders, 'he won't say a word.' Then the housemaster prayed that Mrs Wilkins wouldn't ask him how they had found this out.

It was the screaming which had first caught his attention. One was used to the ceaseless, growling undertow of boys herded together mingling with grunts, bellows, snorts, the occasional snarl, but one didn't normally hear screaming like that. It was streaming from the washrooms and he stopped to listen for a moment expecting it to die away but it continued to penetrate the dormitory. He didn't like to override the house prefects but the jagged squealing did not diminish, rather it increased.

Naked bulbs hung inside the washrooms to illuminate the foxed mirrors, sinks huge enough to serve the week's laundry jutted from the damp walls down to the quarry tiles which would freeze unslippered feet. Along the walls pegs beckoned, each with a name tag to accommodate a boy's mean towel, his wash and linen laundry bags. Beyond lay the showers which ran at scalding or icy temperatures, never warm, and the toilets with doors barely high enough to shield a squatting boy. In the centre of the drying room were four wire cages back-to-back designed to house rugby, cricket and wellington boots, indeed, any footwear that was prohibited in the dormitory.

The housemaster peered through the sweating windows and saw a cluster of boys grouped round these cages from where the screaming seemed to be coming. When he first entered the room no one appeared to notice though the jeering gradually faded into a hush still pierced by the screaming. The housemaster was shocked by its incisive waves flooding the pitiless, echoing room. Through the criss-cross wires, the mounds of twisted laces and boots caked in mud, he could make out a boy, a junior probably by his size, curled in the centre of this tangle of wire and footwear in a foetal position and foetal too in his nakedness. The screams poured from the boy's mouth, a tide of vomit that would ebb to leave a line of scum.

He recognised the boy on the floor as Wilkins; he had remarked before on the boy's absolutely hairless nudity and this lack had in his mind featured as a possible reason for the boy's reticence. It is true that many thirteen-year-olds are not shaving but there are normally hints, predictions of where the dark tangles might sprout. Yet there were no such shadows on this fair boy and the housemaster had noticed that even when spattered by mud from a cross-country run the boy's skin still glowed cream and peach. Or was it the defenceless curve of his spine in its embryonic form on the cold tiles that lacked the customary surge of aggression harboured in boys of this age?

'What is the matter?' He hesitated so the ring of boys was unsure whether it was they or Wilkins the master was addressing. 'What on earth . . . where are Wilkins's clothes?'

But there was little need for him to ask, he could see a blue and yellow tie wound round a dirty rugby boot, a grey shirt that peered from the top of a wellington, a pair of cream underpants stuffed in a black shoe and dark grey shorts weighted down by tennis shoes. Behind all this Wilkins scrabbled up from the floor. Oblivious to everyone he tore at the wire cages ripping his fingernails and making them bleed in an effort to reach his clothes. He was still screaming.

'How on earth did he get there?'

'Please sir, if you climb on the top you . . .'

'Get him out!' The housemaster was almost screaming himself. 'Now!'

Two boys scaled the wire cages though in the end it took four of them to drag the hysterical, flailing Wilkins out and dump him at the housemaster's feet still thrashing.

'Please sir, perhaps he's having a fit, sir.'

'Don't state the obvious, Brotherton, go and fetch matron.'

The boys began to fade.

'And the rest of you don't disappear. I want a full explanation from all of you.' Though he knew none would be forthcoming, not because the boys would prove deliberately evasive; they would say things like: Just a bit of a game, sir, that's all. He never lets us see him without his clothes on, sir. Or: we thought he might be hiding something, sir, and then there would be titters all round. There would be nothing more comprehensive to be said and the housemaster sympathised. He couldn't run a house on the premise that little boys didn't like other little boys seeing their willy but it would prove his duty to try to extract the semblance of coherent reasons for Wilkins's behaviour and present them now to Mrs Wilkins.

'So you see,' he said to her, 'it isn't simply a question of shyness, we're accustomed to that. But he has been here for two years now and we expect by then that if there have been any problems for them to be ironed out.'

'Isn't that your job?' she asked, knowing that she was being awkward, a bitch probably in the schoolmasters' eyes. She could see her upright, unyielding reflection in the headmaster's bifocals. What did they expect her to do when her son had been left in their charge? She had never had any problem with him; if there was one surely it was of their own making?

'And, by the way, you still haven't told me exactly how this so-called problem came to light.'

The housemaster winced.

'Is there any history of epilepsy in your family, Mrs Wilkins?'

'None.'

'Your husband's side?'

'None.'

She won't give an inch, thought the housemaster; in that case she can have it unadorned.

'I was crossing the yard by the washrooms . . . ' He told her the story.

'Matron is very good with a syringe, he slept all night like a baby.'

Behind Virginia the water is now boiling steadily in its saucepan but she is unaware of the cloud of steam at her back. She remembers how she had asked herself on every day that Ronald was away at school whether or not she should be bringing him home. She knew, all things being equal, the obvious answer but all things were not equal. How she twisted and turned attempting to wriggle out of her dilemma.

* * *

A BARGAIN STRUCK with her mother as atonement for blunders she was taunted by; a whispering wherever she went, I told you so, now do as I say or you'll be in trouble again. How mother said it would be so much better for Ronald to be sent away to school because she thought he would receive a much better education with fewer distractions and besides, she argued, there were no other boys at home; she took Virginia's counter-argument that Dorothy and Anne both adored him and turned it against her saying that was exactly the point, Ronald was too much one of them and should be in the company of men not women. Charles's absence added credence to this view and when Virgina reminded her mother that she had not sent Cyril away but kept him close to her at home she said, quite truthfully, that Cyril was altogether different and that Ronald showed promise of a rare quality which should be tempered away from home. Virginia's father, as he invariably did, left the decision entirely in Emily's hands. Virginia was helpless in the face of mother's imperatives. The disguise of suggestion wore thinner and thinner. Mother's will be done. She had the home, she had the money, she had a grip on Virginia who was unable to resist even when she had been a child. This was the reason that Ronald was sent away to a school where the wind drove rain down from bleak heights, and snow lay in the shadows until March.

Virginia moves away from the Aga towards the kitchen window and looking out sees the only person she has ever been able to speak to, Julia.

It was such a long way away. I only went once a year on speech day and all mother could say was that it was better to leave them alone. Visits only disturbed their concentration and upset them. What she was unable to visit on me, exile, she brought to bear on Ronald instead as retribution for my attempts at defiance.

At this time in the mid-1950s her mother's power was absolute, not solely in the domestic sphere but beyond it too. Tens on tens of Harrison's – Emily kept the established name of the business, her maiden name – were opening in every major Home Counties' town: Canterbury, Dover, Folkestone, Tonbridge, Tunbridge Wells, Gravesend, Sevenoaks, Ashford, Margate, Sheppey, Gillingham, and Maidstone in Kent; Hastings, Lewes,

Eastbourne, Haywards Heath and Brighton in the east, Worthing, Littlehampton, Arundel, Bognor Regis, Chichester, Midhurst, Horsham and Crawley in west Sussex; extensions in Surrey to blanket the county; a loop through Hampshire taking in Petersfield, Winchester (not then as far as Southampton), Alton and Basingstoke, working up to Newbury, at that time eastern end of the empire, and across to Reading, Wokingham, Ascot, Windsor, Maidenhead and Slough for Berkshire, with Henley the sole Oxfordshire representative; pushing north into Buckinghamshire as far as Aylesbury including Marlow, High Wycombe, Beaconsfield and Chesham, only Luton in south Bedfordshire; Hertfordshire well-covered with shops in Watford, Hemel Hempstead, St Albans, Hatfield, Welwyn, Hitchin standing as the most northerly point of the boundary, Hertford itself and Cheshunt; then crossing over the meridian into Essex, Epping and skirting the metropolis to Brentwood and Basildon, the coast once more at Southend, north to Chelmsford and finally closing in on the great knot of the capital itself; the outer satellites of Greenwich, Bexley, Bromley, Croydon, Sutton, Kingston, Merton, Richmond, Hounslow, Uxbridge, Hillingdon, Harrow, Ealing, Brent, Barnet, Haringey, Enfield, Waltham Forest, Redbridge and Havering, reaching at last the chambers of the heart – Kensington and Chelsea, Islington and Camden Town, Belgravia, Brompton and Knightsbridge . . .

Virginia's vision is disturbed by Cyril walking past the window and she recalls how in 1956, when Ronald went away to school, Cyril's body in its fortieth year had already begun to sag and a pot belly protruded from his thin frame as if stuck there as an afterthought. Nearly twenty years later he looks leaner and fitter for not a day has gone by without his spending hours outside the house in his shed or greenhouse when driven there by the weather. Though it doesn't seem to have stopped his hair falling out so that he is forever smoothing it across his baldness like a woman whose skirts have lifted in a gust fearful that people will catch a glimpse of something they shouldn't, as if they might penetrate his thinking through a hairless skull.

Virginia remains unaware that behind her on the Aga the saucepan has boiled dry; she has been caught up in her contemplation of Cyril as he disappears through the door in the garden wall and she cannot stop herself asking, Why does he wear that silly little cap making him look even more like a gardener than he really is? Why do I find myself saying to him when he comes in from outside, Cyril, you shouldn't be wearing your cap indoors? And then he will take it off because he's afraid of me, his younger sister, one hand nervously raking his hair then meeting the other to twist the cap round and round like potato water swirling away down the sink. Virginia pictures how his eyes start to bulge, his jaw sets and his cheeks puff out like a toad about to have a fit but he doesn't. It is held back, stored up for future days and some undisclosed expression. When this happens he turns away and goes back outside, replacing the cap as he shuts the kitchen door with just enough of a bang to register his resentment. How she wants then to cry out to his defeated figure, Cyril, come back, I didn't mean it, you can wear your cap in the house for all I care. What do I care about caps? I who have committed far greater misdemeanours than wearing a cap indoors. But she remains mute and fails to call out to her brother and she knows why. It is because she has been living in this house for too long, obeyed its laws and followed its restrictions as part of the agreement for being allowed to come back. She had tried to break them, did break them, once, but it didn't work and she found herself back not only respecting the rules but adding to them with ones of her own making like Cyril's cap. How happy she would be if Cyril turned round and told her to get stuffed and wore his cap to dinner or church. Instead he slinks perpetually through the garden and ducks for cover when he sees her approaching. She recalls how when father retired he was treated by Cyril as an intruder in his own garden, so possessive had he become about his territory.

Was it then her mother's jealousy which prompted Emily to insist that Ronald be sent away, an attempt to erase her failure with Cyril by removing a potential figure of comparison? Or was it a punishment for the mistakes of her own history? The marriage she made in the face of Emily's opposition has been the shadow in which she has lived for three decades.

Edward: a name in the news in 1936. Ascending in January,

descending in December, he didn't go to church and wanted to marry a forty-year-old who had suffered one divorce and was pursuing a second. Ever after it could be said, and was by Virginia's mother, that there were some nice similarities between those two Edwards. Most prominent was that both wished to marry outside their circle and both did. Only, she had said, you could hardly blame the other Edward, poor man, bewitched by that woman, an American, he never stood a chance! But that could not be said about Virginia's Edward, insinuating, as her mother suggested, himself into the family and marrying a Harrison-Russell which was, of course, the pinnacle of his scheming. But their marriage would like so many events in Virginia's life never have occurred without Julia.

* * *

A RESIDENT SPIRIT. Virginia turns to see that the saucepan has not only boiled dry but is beginning to glow. She moves to try and pick the thing up from the Aga but its handle burns her hand which she has to run under the tap before grabbing a tea towel to wrap round it. She tosses the scorching lump of metal into the sink ignoring the plastic washing-up bowl there; seconds later an acrid burning fills her nose and throat, the saucepan and bowl have fused. She is unsurprised and does nothing except to step back from the stench a couple of paces. She has always been accident prone and long since accepted the results of her thoughtlessness. Lack of concern for her immediate surroundings is, she considers, neither something to be proud or ashamed of, it is simply her. How when Ronald was in nappies she put a safety pin through the foreskin of his willy or when she was a girl the head of her croquet mallet flew off and knocked Jean unconscious or when, terrifying her, the first spots of blood appeared on her frock at a tea party. Then, it was not her mother who held her hand showing her what to do and explaining what was happening. Virginia returns to the window and shares the memory with Julia.

You told me not to be frightened and showed me your own blood. Mother refused to discuss it and I found it oh so difficult to talk to God in a pewed, vaulted room with cold stone flags. And when I did he gave no more answers than mother.

Do you remember midsummer 1932? It was my thirteenth birthday. Quiet trickled in from the garden to my bedroom upstairs. I could hear all of you preparing my birthday tea on the lawn – which mother now stares at for hours on end – I'd thrown my boater in the corner and stepped out of my leaden black shoes, my wrinkled black stockings lay in coils, sleeping but venomous snakes. Even in summer I still had to wear a blouse with a high collar buttoned right up to the throat. It reflected the demure order of the church school, high Anglican, for girls. I was exhausted from the excitement of the day and running all the way back from school knowing there was to be a special outdoor tea for my birthday and you here too . . . on the bed drowsing I almost tumbled into sleep. Voices floated up from the garden; mother's precise and controlled, yours abundant and luxurious, Margaret's already booming and confident, Jean's thin and barely audible. It was part of a denser texture of sound: a thrush fluting, the tinkling of china as you laid the table, the faraway whinnying of horses, a hammer knocking somewhere – Cyril had already learned how to extricate himself from such events – doves fluttering about the cote . . . I found my hand between my legs, it was examining with more of a scientific than prurient interest. It was the first time I had prodded and delved so deeply, so intently. I sat up with my knees pressed back into the candlewick bedspread, my back arched forward, my head dropped, twisted down and in to see what I could see, I pulled the lips apart trying to let a splinter of light enter this dark mouth and ringed throat. Where was the mechanism controlling that now regular flow of blood? I couldn't find it but I saw at the pinnacle of the arch a bud of flesh, forever on the point of opening, bursting out, but however often I examined it in the following months it remained wrapped tight around itself, unchanging except to grow in proportion with the rest of me, like a tiny onion. I would perhaps still be puzzled now but you explained that too.

Virginia supposes that she ought to do something about the fused saucepan and bowl in the sink so she picks them up and pulls them apart. The pan has a solid wedge of plastic stuck to its bottom and it looks as if it will require an age to remove it. Has mother smelt the burning? There is no doubt she will have to purchase a new washing-up bowl. If she gets one the same colour the substitute might escape Emily's attention. If not, how many questions will have to be answered? In any case she will have to find an excuse to prevent mother doing the washing up today. Perhaps she can bribe or tire her out with the promise of an afternoon drive. She must put some more water on for mother's coffee. But that birthday will not relinquish its hold.

The sounds outside the window rearranged themselves and Margaret's voice rumbled through, Virginiaaa, where are youuu, we're ready. She hurried down the creaking backstairs, into the dining room and through the french windows, crackled over the gravel path and skipping the three steps flew past the sundial to where they were waiting for her. They stood in a cluster beside the tea table with its pink and white cloth; there were plates of sandwiches, small cakes, biscuits, jellies and in the centre a cake with pink and white icing which had the words, Happy Birthday Virginia, piped also in pink around its edge. Thirteen yellow-orange flames streamed vertically into the hanging June air, only wavering where the tip of each flame disappeared, lost in that other invisible light which illuminates everything except itself. Oh, isn't it pretty, said Virginia, can I blow them out? Before she could do so Julia stepped forward and produced a parcel from behind her back.

'Can I, shall I open it now?'

'Of course. I didn't have time to find any decent paper.'

The present was wrapped in stiff brown paper but beneath this lay something soft and yielding.

'Oh Julia, it's, it's beautiful, it must have . . . Where did you. . . ? Look at the colours.' Lemon flame was the predominant shade with a floral pattern. 'It feels so . . . ' Artificial silk crêpe de Chine. 'And this . . . ' A Robespierre collar of white organdie muslin. 'And lace round it, too, the cuffs match don't they? And the skirt is all fluttery . . . ' With a scalloped outline edged in stitching to match the design.

'Look, it's the same colour here and there's a belt too! Julia, these darling little buttons like baby teeth!' (Completed by a line of imitation pearl buttons.)

'Julia, it's wonderful! I'm going to go and try it on, wear it for our tea.'

'Don't you think, dear, that your tea might spoil if we wait any longer?'

'Oh mummy, pleeease.'

Julia came to the rescue. 'It's all right. I'll go with her and help her put it on.'

'If you insist,' said mother. 'The other presents will have to wait then.'

Off they went, gliding hand-in-hand across the grass. In Virginia's room the suffocating church school clothes were discarded into a corner, a heap of stifling material at last abandoned.

'Oh Julia, it's so beautiful . . . '

'Ssh. Let's put it on.'

Virginia's fingers shaking and damp could not undo the pearl teeth buttons which Julia unfastened then held out the frock for her to step into.

I felt like a chrysalis bursting out into the bright gauze wings which you offered.

The belt twisted.

'Do something, Julia.'

She untangled the belt then her fingers ran down the length of Virginia's spine to turn those teeth, twist them back into their sockets.

'Here, let me straighten the collar.' Which she did and then bent and kissed Virginia on the forehead.

'There, you look ravishing. Look in the mirror.'

Outlined by the dark oak frame, oblong of sombre solidity where there had always been a reflection of her uniform (cold whites and coal-blue-blacks) there shimmered a flame which illuminated the whole room.

You stood behind me looking over my shoulder into the mirror, your face radiant. You seemed so warm, so protective.

Julia was lost in contemplating the world beyond the room, the garden, Shalford, Surrey. How riots against the means test or Nazi youth marching would impinge, extinguish that flame.

You were right that something in me would burn out but not in the way you imagined. Not on account of police batons or bombs but a weakness in myself. And when you spoke to me about these things I understood as little then as I do now about Mr Heath and the miners, except that we're short of coal, of fuel. What I did understand was the way in which you whispered furiously, the urgency and alarm in your eyes. The way you placed your arm round my shoulders or gripped my wrist. These were the signs that showed me I could trust you, not the significance of the words themselves. I knew that you cared, that you understood. Hadn't you after all bought me the frock that mother refused me, that she would always deny me, even now?

The frock that wrapped Virginia in flame made everyone's eyes turn in her direction as she approached her loaded birthday table on the lawn. She could see it written in their faces; on mother's – how dare Julia buy a frock designed for a London hussy, one that she herself might wear but quite unsuited to a child, my youngest child what's more; in Margaret's – well that isn't a very sensible first frock for Virginia, the sort of thing that'll get torn to pieces in no time. I would have chosen her something more practical. And besides it would look far better on me; on Jean's already burdened countenance could be read the lines – it is very pretty I must admit though it makes her seem so much older, older than me, almost a young lady in fact – Jean had never expressed the faintest desire to wear any other frocks than those chosen by their mother.

Virginia's return to the party was a *succès de scandale*, at least in her mother's eyes. Later, she wondered, as she does now, whether Julia had stage-managed the event in the full knowledge of her mother's response. Whether she was being intentionally provocative or whether it was Julia's natural exuberance merely spilling over into her choice of a present for Virginia's birthday. Virginia invariably answered her own musings in the negative. Julia was not, she felt, ever malicious enough to plot in such a manner and had without doubt been carried along on the tide of her own enthusiasm, forgetting momentarily the impact such a garment might have on Emily. Nevertheless it acted as a signal to Emily of what she had once glimpsed and later chosen to ignore, disguising it behind the twin covers of business and the church.

I can hear Julia thinking as she must have done:

Does it hurt, Emily? Is the pain at what you've lost making you angry with me, with Virginia? Now it's coming back to you with your daughter you won't be able to stop it. There is no way in which you can stem that tide which is beginning to flood in earnest like the blood from her womb which you refuse to recognise. Are you ashamed of what you think was your weakness here in this very garden? Has that shame soured to self-pity and jealousy?

I didn't know then, I only knew I was a pillar of lemon flame bending to blow out thirteen candles.

Virginia turns away from Julia's image and roots in a cupboard in search of another saucepan which she finds – an unused one which she bought some time ago. She tries to conjure up Ronald's thirteenth birthday and what it meant to her: baking a cake which boys with birthdays were allowed to receive on condition that they shared it with others. The silver foil in which she wrapped the sponge before packing it in a box still glitters, winking mockery of a celebration spent apart. Holding the saucepan under the tap Virginia is disgusted with herself. Has her rebellion come to this?

* * *

A SAUCEPAN bought from a shop which is not her mother's. She cracks it down hard in the stainless steel sink and lets the tap run. From the kitchen window she can see one corner of the crumbling stables that were once in constant use but are now used by Cyril for storing vegetables and garden implements. She recalls one dusk being sent to find Cyril for tea and standing on tiptoe to peer through the cobwebby window into the stables. In the gloom she saw him slumped over one of the saddles with his trousers and underpants round his ankles, his thin buttocks arched in the horsy air. His head hung down so she couldn't see his face but to one side of him with his legs apart and sleeves rolled to the elbow stood his school friend, Butcher, testing the give of a crop. He picked several from the rack, flexing them until he found one that satisfied him. Through the dusty glass Virginia saw his lips shape, Are you ready? Cyril's head bobbed up and down like a cork in water. The crop sliced the thick air and knifed Cyril's buttocks not once, not twice, not three times but again and again until she had lost count and finally Butcher's arm dropped, not because he had punished Cyril enough but through exhaustion – it was, after all, hard work imitating one's masters. Throughout the scene Virginia had not caught the faintest sign of emotion from Cyril beyond the clenched whiteness of his knuckles and the jerking of his head with each stroke of the crop. It reminded her of the seaside booth in which she had once seen Punch batter a victim with a stick. Cyril's unprotested agony and affliction now prompt reflections of her own. The stable dissolves and Julia's face appears at the window.

At first I carried on where you, Julia, left off but then things started to go wrong. It was force of circumstance. You have no idea what circumstance is like when there are children involved. That's what kept your ideas pure, your commitments undiluted. There is in the end never a choice if you're a mother. Things are both more simple and more difficult when you have children. I don't want to exonerate myself for how things have run in the last few years. I hear you say, What! Still at home though your children have long since left! Shame on you! Should I have left mother then, alone, finally, after so many years? Perhaps these are excuses but they are the best one will ever have. If I didn't believe they were, how could I look you in the face? Not excuses then but reasons are what I'm offering you. How then both more and less complicated? It's when you have children. Yes, I know you were a mother to me in a sense and showed me so many of the important things but someone has to provide the clothes, food, money, somewhere to live. Having your own children clarifies that – it becomes for them and not for yourself any more. They make the choices for you. One goes on making this decision and that, saying we will do this and that, or even I will do this and that but one's only acting as their ventriloquist's dummy. Forget 'I', it is all down to the family and that means you hedge, never coming to a quick decision because there is now a committee in session. So things get fudged, blurred at the edges and out of focus. Those ideas born in your own head are subject to amendments and voting beyond your control. At first I carried your banner, holding it high and letting the wind blow through it, never mind that I didn't understand what was written there. I was in love and acting as I knew you would have wanted me to.

Virginia has not noticed that the saucepan is brimming with water and the sink filling up as the tap still runs. She continues to address Julia.

Mother wore me down, in the end even sending Ronald away from me. I was fool enough to let us be separated on the strength of a compromise. A compromise made in the first instance for 'the sake of the children'. It wasn't that I lacked the courage, will or determination to break from the purse-strings of mother. I wanted security, a future for my children. And look what the future has brought for Ronald. There are great swathes of time we didn't spend together like dark holes in the night sky.

Splashing breaks in on Virginia and she looks down to find the sink about to overflow. Removing the saucepan she turns off the tap and crosses to the Aga. She wishes mother would have it replaced with one of the chrome and glass cookers which are sold by the thousands in her shops but she has persistently refused to part with it. It was installed some twenty years ago at the dawn of a new era: her father's retirement, and now it squats in the kitchen like some heathen god from an uncivilised age. Virginia supposes that because her mother no longer has to operate the beast she has grown sentimental about its presence in the kitchen. It surely will not be long before her legs refuse to carry her this far; already on her bad days she does no more than sit staring out of the window and takes her meals on a tray. Which reminds Virginia that she hasn't yet thought about mother's lunch. Dare she slip down to the shops and get her something without her noticing? The virgin saucepan hisses on the ring as if in protest at the unaccustomed heat.

* * *

ESCAPE did come for a while. During Edward's home leave they looked at a 'superior semi-detached property' in Epsom. It cost one thousand, four hundred and seventy-five pounds to be secured by a seventy-five-pounds deposit and paid for at thirty shillings a week.

'Do you like it?' he asked her. They were standing on the concrete drive beside one pebble-dashed wall of the house. She had already put Dorothy in the second bedroom next to where she and Edward would be. Anne would go in the small room across the landing. If the next child were a boy then Anne would eventually have to move in with Dorothy. She knew that Edward would think her foolish if she told him that she was pregnant again as she hadn't even missed one period by that time so she said nothing, wondering if it were a boy or a girl. In response to his question she nodded silently and he said, 'We'll take it then,' and they borrowed the money from her mother.

In September 1945, with Ronald not eight weeks old, Virginia left her mother's house with Dorothy and Anne each clutching a doll, a blanket and a small paper bag. The taxi driver shut the door behind the woman clutching the baby and deposited three suitcases – one bound with twine – in the alcove for luggage beside his seat. They went and set up home for a hero to return to now that the war was over.

Virginia went for walks near the race course at Epsom and this gave rise to nightmares. In her dreams the thunder of hoofbeats drummed and pounded the carpet. Ronald squirmed on the turf of the race track. The horses' lathering sprayed up, foam like washing-up liquid spewing through the air. They had yellow tombstone teeth and slobber dangled from their lips and blew through the trumpets of their nostrils. Still Ronald lay on the vomit green of the track while divots rained as if land mines were exploding and the ground trembled. Triangular, square and star purples, oranges and greens hugged the chestnut cages. Shins and hooves screamed down the hallway flanked by curving luminous rails and the surge of the crowd rumbled, the thunder of surf on a distant beach.

Virginia rarely slept well in her new home. She thought perhaps that it was the new baby causing her troubled sleep for though in the end he had slipped out, as she recalled someone saying, like a cake of soap, it had been an exceptionally protracted and exhausting labour – all the more surprising as it was her third. And since that day, August the sixth, she had been quite drained and sucked dry. She would lie in the late afternoon too exhausted to fetch in Dorothy and Anne who were playing in the street outside with the neighbours' children. They used the streetlamp to secure one end of their skipping rope so that only one of them need stand looping the cord for the seemingly endless line of girls who bunched up jostling one another and gently whispering, which in turn would break into giggling and shrieking.

I had no neighbours' children to play with unless by special request. I remember one of their skipping rhymes: The wind, the wind, the wind blows high, The rain comes falling from the sky. She is handsome, she is pretty, She is the girl of London city. She goes a-courting one, two, three, Please will you tell me who is he? . . . says he loves her. All the boys are fighting for her.

Virginia finds that she is humming the tune aloud.

But she wanted Edward to stop fighting, to come back home to the nice quiet cul-de-sac and their house with a drive big enough to park one car in. There seemed to be no escape from horses for Virginia even in her waking hours. Unable to get back to sleep one night after feeding Ronald she thought of how Julia had told her that she had met Virginia's grandfather, George, at a race meeting:

'But how,' Julia asked the fifteen-year-old Virginia, 'how can I go to races now that Hitler is re-arming and we're following suit? When I met your grandfather on the brink of the first war to end all wars I thought there was some justice, that it could get better, but I was mistaken. I loved your grandfather, do you see? Loved him so that it hurt and while I was loving him do you know what was happening? Do you? Come on, answer me. Don't they teach you history at school?'

Virginia could only think that in 1066 there had been a Battle at Hastings or that Shakespeare –they were doing him then – had been born on 23 April 1564 in Stratford and married Anne Hathaway after which he went to London where he worked in the theatre and wrote some poems and a lot of plays.

'Shakespeare wrote *Romeo and Juliet* and *A Midsummer Night's Dream*'.

'That's what it was, an idyllic, intoxicating dream. But do you know what was happening while I was asleep?'

Virginia shook her head, dumb and serious, awed not by what Julia was saying but arrested by the peculiar intensity of her delivery and Julia's grip on her wrist.

'Of course you don't because I didn't either. Two young men, boys, who would've been your uncles, died, one in mud and the other in water. You see while you're in love someone else is not just dying, they're being murdered; then if you look further you find out that it's not only someone else who's being murdered, it's thousands and millions of someone elses and it's not being done in back alleys by thugs with knives or broken bottles or madmen with bricks, it's being done on fields in broad daylight by someone's uncle or father or brother. What's more, it's not only tolerated by mothers, wives, sisters and aunts, it's supported by them, applauded by whole nations. And that's what happened while I was tied and blind in love.'

Julia paused for a moment not because she had finished what she wanted to tell Virginia but to try to gauge her reaction. She was not hoping for a rational appraisal to come from a fifteen-year-old girl, she wanted nothing more than Virginia's empathy, her intuition that what she was saying made sense.

'Now they're massing and they hope that the distraction of love will make us tolerant a second time. It's too late for anyone to lose themselves now. Guard, we must be on our guard. In love your guard is too easily dropped and the world outside too quickly forgotten.'

Virginia, faintly embarrassed, did not of course understand Julia's references to the fascist boot and heel that was about to tramp throughout Europe. Nor did she apprehend that unlike the boots of her father's generation these were not worn by amateurs for the sport of hunting but by professionals in full pursuit of their livelihood.

Julia sensed Virginia's awkwardness and changed the mood completely. 'Come on. I'll race you to the stile.' She was already five yards into her stride before Virginia knew what was happening. With her arms and legs flailing in all planes it was almost impossible to overtake her in the narrow hawthorn lane but Virginia swept past her a moment before she reached the winning post.

'Once,' she was saying, 'once I would have . . . ' But with her breath coming in huge sobs she could not continue. When her gasping had subsided she said, 'Ask your mother about horses too. For me they were a beginning, for her an end . . . ' Then she collapsed on the stile unable to speak for several minutes.

Virginia asked her mother what Julia had meant about horses as a beginning and end.

Emily replied: 'Julia, you know, can conjure stories, make something out of that,' and here she held her thumb and forefinger together to form a circle and raising it to her lips blew through it as though she were breathing a bubble into the air.

'She said you'd know what she meant.'

'She was probably talking about your grandfather, giving you snippets which are half-digested and meaningless to you.'

Virginia shook her head slowly. 'I'd like to know.'

'She met him at a race meeting apparently.'

'That's the beginning. What about the end?'

'She was probably talking about how your grandfather rode a horse until the very end of his life and refused to go in a "horseless contraption", ever.'

Virginia has had to wait the best part of forty years to discover, as she soon will, that she had still not heard the final spark of horseshoes ringing on cobbles.

At last the water in the saucepan has come to the boil and she slides it from the centre to the edge of the plate. Now she should try and find the jug, the filters, the ground coffee, but cannot for the life of her remember where she last saw them. That, she thinks, is the trouble with having someone in who helps by clearing everything away so that she has no idea where to find it. Were she given the run of things by herself then they might be a trifle more organised, but she knows as she says it that she is fooling herself. Nothing in this house will ever be more organised, at least not by her. Her heart is not in it, that's all. She squats to open a cupboard door thinking, as mother told her so often, how charity begins at home. How mother has assumed that the charity of provisions will see the family, all of them, through. She knows that she could not have managed without it but as with some strong drug the initial pleasure soured to a bleak and necessary dependence. No expense was spared, only love was missing

The cupboard door opens

presumed dead

and a blue and white china jug crashes into dozens of pieces on the kitchen floor tiles. Instead of bending to clear the fragments Virginia stands and gazes through the window.

* * *

HOME. I couldn't bear waiting alone any longer, that's why I came back here. It looked so fine as we swung into the drive by the gate house where our house-help and handyman lived – now it's let to students from the law college to stop the place from turning rotten – smoke was puttering out of the chimney, it must have been late afternoon, bath and wash time. When I left it had yellow paintwork that hadn't been touched since before the war. When I came back it had been repainted navy blue, as though one could expunge the last six years and continue as before. The garden was neat and fenced in white – it had never looked so well cared for or was that because I was seeing it for the first time in months? The yew hedge still lined both verges of the drive – later, mother made Cyril pull it up, she said it was too gloomy and made the approach seem like a graveyard. Once I found Ronald hiding in the purple hedge enclosed in its sea-green light, thinking himself untouched and undiscovered by the world outside – we'd all been playing hide and seek but the game was over long before . . . but I hadn't, I wasn't hiding in the hedge. I'd given myself up and was coming back, raw and exposed to face mother whose eyes said in accusation, the game's up and I've won.

Virginia clutched Ronald to her as the taxi crunched up the drive, newly resurfaced she noted. The house ahead of them could not be seen on account of the bottle-green tunnel through which they had to pass before swinging to the right after more than a hundred yards. As the taxi nibbled round this final bend Virginia produced a compact and mirror from her handbag. No one should be allowed to think that she cannot cope. Balancing Ronald in her lap she dabbed and licked.

I told myself I was only coming back because of the children.

Dorothy and Anne sat unspeaking and staring straight ahead.

'Isn't it fun to be going back home, back to grandma's? There's much more space and room to run about outside, isn't there? I said, isn't there?'

Dorothy could hardly say it, squeezing it out like some profanity she has promised never to utter.

'Yes mummy. There is more space than in our other house in Epsom.' Enunciating each word too deliberately in case she stumbled over the script which was Virginia's and not her own.

Dorothy was always quick to grasp what others wanted and give it to them.

Anne sat with her lips and knees pressed tightly together refusing to say it just because somebody, although somebody was mother, wanted her to. Nothing would induce her. Ronald was starting to grizzle because he was hungry. Virginia asked herself if he would ever be satisfied, stop wanting to suck her and suck her dry. His gums were so much harder than the others'.

A splosh of vanilla sunlight dolloped into the taxi making Virginia look up from her mirror to the house on the far edge of the circular front lawn. It was the first time she had been away from the house for more than a few days, the home in which she was born, to which she came with her husband after marriage.

I said I would wait here until Edward returned. I knew I was fooling myself. If I'd believed he was coming back I would've stayed in Epsom. What would you, Julia, have done with a ten-month-old baby and two young children and no help, no friends, no real friends? I know – you wouldn't have been Julia and found yourself married to a husband missing presumed dead with three children to look after and a mortgage to be paid off. Mother had the money but she wouldn't lend it to me.

'Come back and live with us,' Emily had said. 'It'll be so much better for the children than being cooped up in that postage stamp of a house. Playing in the street! They can run and run for miles here without seeing a soul. And so much better for you, too, Virginia. After all, who can you expect to look after Dorothy and Anne now that you've got another one? I don't know how you got yourself into this mess but there, I'll not harp.'

So Virginia mimicked the sentiment of her mother's words and the children could detect the falsity of her tone.

The house had never seemed more attractive than on that day. Someone, Cyril I suppose, had mown the lawns. I could smell the tang of cut grass hanging in the air, doves fluttered from the cote which mushroomed from the centre of the lawn, a geyser of wood spraying feathers.

The half-timbered house looked as though it would withstand the elements for another four hundred years. The two sets of chimneys at each end of the house rose, soft red brick, gently climbing to heaven. The porch at one end of the house was moored like an ark with its wooden struts supporting a miniature tiled roof purpled with moss. The virginia creeper planted to mark the birth of Emily's last child clung and waited for flaming autumn and winter. The stable and tack-room doors were ajar and from inside the taxi Virginia glimpsed the chestnut saddles, the ebony tackle and the honeyed gleam and caught the smell of used and polished leather, the tang of sweat, felt the brush of cacti blankets, and the hats nuzzling the walls like moles, the flexible, whippy crops.

I remembered Cyril's acquiescence in the stable. And later I saw how his tears were not of rage or pain but of submission, of a head bowed praying that it would be all right in the end, a faceless not an individual humility. I felt the same thing creeping up on me like some grey mildew descending from the damp air. I promised that my stay would be short-lived, that the warmth of Edward's love would dispel any such insidious growth.

The taxi ground slowly to rest. How would Virginia have reacted had she known that this was her first and last homecoming? And that she was to live in the house for another thirty years – more, in fact, in years than the life she had already lived, waiting for someone to come and release her. She considered the antiquity of the house and sensed its past weighing her down, its history rising and blurring the clearer picture she had momentarily held. Her mother, smiling, had opened the door and was leaning forward to kiss her.

'So nice to have you back.'

Virginia could see nothing.

'Here, let me take him,' and before Virginia could say anything or move, Ronald was being carried in his grandmother's arms and Virginia was stepping out of the taxi empty-handed.

'Now that,' said Emily, 'is a sensible frock that you're wearing. Did you make it yourself? I expect you found out a thing or two on your own about managing pennies. Not quite so easy then, is it? Two children to look after and a new baby. No money to splash around on fancy frocks then, is there?'

Emily had never forgiven Julia for giving Virginia that party frock nor her daughter for liking it and ignoring all her other presents. Virginia had been captivated by the butterfly wings she had grown.

And though there was money splashing around a decade or so later Emily continued in many respects to run the house on a wartime economy. Even when they had, as they were told, never had it so good – 'What, raped by a Tory MP was she?' Virginia heard the butcher's boy say – she turned her back on the inundations of money and insisted on making her own clothes, expecting Virginia to do the same.

'It's not simply a matter of economy but a question of pride. Pleasure taken in work done by one's own hands. Then to see the children wearing what you've made . . . it's not the same as buying something ready made. I know people haven't got the time . . . ' Emily trailed off sighing and shrugging. She did not consider how others were working to earn to spend in her shops. Which gave her the time to make clothes by hand.

The blue and white fragments of china are winking on the tiles. Virginia thinks how Humpty Dumpty and all the King's men who couldn't put him back together again was Ronald's favourite nursery rhyme. Now there was no putting Ronald back together again, he was broken forever. She crosses to a cupboard to find a dustpan and brush which are both plastic and come from the business. They used to have metal dustpans, tin she supposes, and wooden brushes. She has no preference for these and does not indulge in a nostalgic remembrance of domestic implements. Wood or plastic, what's the difference, she has had to use them both at another's beck and call. As she stoops to sweep up the pieces she is dazzled by a morning and more with Julia. Somewhere in Virginia's memory a jug of lemonade reassembles itself.

* * *

IN A JULY already shimmering and threatening to sew them all up in its sack of heat, Julia threw back Virginia's bedclothes.

'Come on, lazy, we're going for a picnic.'

'Who is?'

'Just you and me. The others aren't interested.'

'Where?'

'Over the hills and far away. I thought we'd take the bikes. I'll use your mother's. Wear something loose and cool, it's going to be hot.' Virginia pulled on another of Julia's dresses – one which Julia had helped her order from the catalogue where it had hummed in the pages, an imitation linen for sunny days, tucked shoulders for military squareness; had the designers caught a whiff of something before the politicians?

We chose Harvest Gold, anything light and sunny you said suited me. Look at me now trying to keep warm circling the Aga in a thick blue sweater.

They wheeled their bicycles out from the barn, big, heavy machines like outsize bats surprised and blinking in the sunlight.

The picnic wrapped in tea towels nestled in the wicker baskets which stretched and yawned throughout the day, unaccustomed to the exercise. The drive slipped away under their whirring spokes.

'Where are we going?'

'Down towards Sussex.'

'Good, not too many hills,' cried Virginia, streaming ahead of Julia. 'Come on slow coach.' Their laughter coloured the warm air.

They stopped at a post office and drank the mistress's own lemonade. She came outside holding a white and blue porcelain jug and with a wooden spoon stirred the pale straw contents in which the lemons knocked and lumbered like rocks adjusting themselves on the sea bed. They had to strain out the pips and flesh with their teeth.

I remembered then the sunlight in rock pools and plants waving, rocking endlessly back and forth, shaking their fronds in gestures of fury as their sinuous dances were disturbed in a frenzy of froth and foam. How Julia and I spent all day crouched over rocks and their pools, the wind whipping our hair into knots, seeking what we didn't know – periwinkle, the brown, black and red ones you said could be eaten; slipping on the kelp, look at the bladder wrack you said. I didn't know what it was, you pointed at green seaweed stuff with bubbles which I popped between my toes. And you showed me the white-grey barnacles which once they've found a rock never move again unlike the limpets which, in spite of their name, set off in search of food once the tide's up and covering them; only you'd never know, you said, because they always return to exactly the same spot when the tide goes out. You explained how whelks were cannibals that lived off other shells. Think how the barnacle resists the pounding of the sea year after year then along comes a dog whelk and bores straight through its shell. Yum yum. Off the rocks the lugworm excavated like beach moles burrowing the sand in search of food, their casts strewn like mouse droppings. And in the lee of a dune how you wouldn't tell me the name of a pretty flower, a cross between pink and purple, saying that if you didn't tell me the name I'd remember the flower itself more vividly. It was Seaside Centaury.

They pedalled south and eastwards out of Surrey into Sussex where once across the county boundary many of the houses had weatherboards, their upper storeys clad in strips of narrow planking and their lower parts hung with scalloped tiles, a contrast of candyfloss white and pink with ochres in red and brown. Virginia was now behind Julia who often had to take her feet off the pedals and freewheel while Virginia caught up with her. They cycled past cottages, a grocer's shop, another post office, then there was a rumbling that closed down on them, a shadow descended and roared past, almost knocking Virginia off her bicycle. Julia cried out but her protest was lost while they tried to control their wobbling machines and bring them back to an equilibrium as their palms slid and slipped across the handlebars. They passed a cricket pitch where the green was already suggesting yellow and brown; the cuboid score board squatted like a dice from *Alice in Wonderland*, Home 159 for 9 declared, Visitors 157 for 6, left them wondering whether the match was drawn or the Visitors had won, and the scorers didn't have the heart or time to signal their victory. An Aylesbury duck was parked in the centre of the road like a dollop of ice cream and Julia lined up her thumb in readiness; the bell jangled out of its rust, sending the fowl waddling and half fluttering out of the way, a feather floated in the warm air and was still buoyed up as Virginia rode past. They glided into shadows of trees on both verges, jade and emerald, sage and lime light weaving in and out, stitched in the spaces between trunks and branches.

'Julia, please wait for me, you're going too fast,' and though she was too far ahead to hear Virginia she did slow down and stop to look at something in the lush verge. Virginia caught up.

'What is it?'

'I don't know.' She dismounted, swinging off the saddle and lowering the bicycle to the ground in one movement. Virginia was so tired that she slipped off her own saddle and stood astride the frame and pedals; unable to muster enough energy to leave the bicycle altogether, she used it to flop against. Julia poked in the knee-high grass with a stick, prodding at something Virginia couldn't see; she bent to look more closely.

'What is it?'

'Nothing, let's go.' But her answer was too quick for Virginia who caught the edge in Julia's voice. She too lowered her bicycle to the verge.

Julia half steered Virginia back towards her bicycle.

'We'll never get there before lunchtime if we don't press on.'

'I thought we were stopping when we felt like it.'

Julia released Virginia's arm and she made for the spot where her companion had been jabbing with the stick. She could see nothing but the still grass so she stopped and parted the stalks.

Stench, acid in my nose and throat and my head jerked back. The matted coat, little yellow things crawling all over, clots of flies swarming over the rust with a darker crust emblazoned, the steel incisors and chain winking at me. I was on my knees retching and retching but nothing came. You massaged my shoulders and neck. I kept heaving and I couldn't speak.

The wheel of Virginia's bicycle was still circling slowly in its almost horizontal plane.

'Do you want to turn back?'

Virginia shook her head; her breathing, though too shallow and rapid, had steadied and the grass, the spokes, had come back into focus.

'Are you sure?' Virginia nodded tentatively as if afraid that her head might fall off if she did it too fast.

'All right, we'll stop for a rest at the next place we come to,' said Julia and picked up Virginia's bicycle for her. They both remounted and set off with Julia holding back to keep an eye on an unsure Virginia.

'Right at the fork,' she guessed, which led them in a few minutes to a public house set back off the narrow road.

'Ideal,' she cried, 'let's stop here,' for the one thing they had not brought with them in their picnic was something to drink. They leaned their bicycles against the fence and walked down the path to the battered front door where on either side there were benches facing the flower beds that bordered the path. Julia made for the door while Virginia held back and eased herself on to a bench.

'I'll wait here.'

'But you're right in the sun there. Let's go and sit inside, it'll do you good to be in the shade for a while.'

Virginia shrugged but remained where she was seated.

'What's the matter?'

'I've never been inside one before,' Virginia mumbled. Julia stared, incredulous for an instant, before breaking into laughter.

'One shouldn't go inside one, especially if one is a young lady, should one?' she spluttered. Virginia stared at the ground and flushed. Julia took her hand.

'Nothing'll happen to you,' she murmured.

The dark-oak door swung back creaking.

I remembered dungeons and ogres, sleeping beauties and dragons, magic potions.

And as if someone had stolen up behind them and slipped sacks over their heads the dark enveloped them, a velvet blackness after the pure clover honey of the light outside. They stood in temporary blindness waiting for shapes to develop and print themselves out of the darkness.

Sombre forests of sticks ran in all planes but predominantly vertical and horizontal with an occasional curve. Lumpy animals with four legs squatted balancing columns of transparent distortion, these transparencies themselves holding other and further transparencies of amber. Once or twice the columns were grasped and rose in the shade to tilt and drain away the amber which ran into bristling caves. Over the heads of these dark holes ran concentric circles crossed with spokes emanating from a tight rosebud and unfurling petals in an ordered sequence of beiges, reds and greens edged in a black rim. Jutting into gloomy space at Virginia's chest height was a wooden barrier from which rose snouty shapes like skittles the shade of tar and from beyond these came a voice, 'Can I help you ladies?' The cyclists' footsteps echoed on the tiles.

'Yes, we'd like something to drink.'

'You're in the right place then.' Two heads nodded from one side of the room accompanied by grunts and hands touching caps.

'We'd like anything as long as it's cool,' said Julia.

'The coolest thing I got,' crackled the salt and pepper beard, then hesitated as though suddenly realising it was speaking to strangers, 'is this.' He tapped the truncheon which rose from the wooden counter.

'What is it?' Julia asked.

'It's our best bitter. Only comes from a mile or two up the road. You come further than this bitter I expect. You don't want to move beer like this around too much. Especially in this weather.'

'Why not?'

'It gets all shook up and begging your pardon, ma'am, goes all cloudy. A barrel of beer's like a river I always say. Treat it right and proper and it'll run as clear as a stream. But you know what happens if you start poking around at the bottom of a river bed.' His neck uncoiled from his shoulders and his head inched forward to stare at Virginia.

'I . . . the mud.'

'Exactly, young lady. Mud. Only in beer it's not mud, it's yeast. Now what'll you have? Two halves?' Julia said yes and Virginia nodded.

'What's the matter, young lady, lost your tongue?'

'I, no, I . . . '

How I hated myself for performing so badly, for letting you down in that brown world.

There came a gurgling and splashing, a glass column holding a walnut liquid appeared on the bar. The neck and beard screwed round again.

'You're old enough of course.'

'She's my sister,' said Julia.

'If you like to sit I'll bring your drinks over to you.'

'How very kind.' Julia made for a corner of the room away from the two heads silently bobbing.

'Why did you say that?'

'What?'

'That you're my sister.'

'Why not?' She squeezed Virginia's hand and did not release it until the beard wagged over their heads.

'You come far?' it said, creased hands placing the two glasses on the table.

'From Shalford.'

'Up near Guildford way is it? Do you hear that, Harold? These two ladies have come down from Guildford way.' The heads swivelled in a slow arc of disbelief.

'Ain't never been as far as that. Went to Cranleigh once. Don't see what all the fuss is about.' The throat was cleared, the column raised and tipped, the chestnut liquid drained.

'That's as much as I've heard Harold say this summer; must be this heat, expect he'll be needing some refreshment after that little speech, won't you, Harold?' Harold nodded and the landlord lumbered into the shadows behind the bar.

'I thought he'd never leave us alone.' Julia drained more than half her beer in one swallow. Virginia raised the glass to her lips and tasted its bitterness. Was this the mud stirred from the river bed? But she drank because like Julia she was thirsty.

'My goodness, you're thirsty,' and they both smiled, remembering the last occasion when Julia said that.

Mummy and me climbed the High Street cobbles under the gilt town clock which looked like something Louis Quatorze though I wasn't sure when that was. In Jeffreys & Sons, gunsmiths originally, they squeezed my fourteen-year-old feet into heavy, lumpy footwear which they kept calling Best Quality Hiking Boots. I thought they were suitable for walking on the sea bed, not for climbing in. My arms even ached when I carried them round the town. I complained, mummy said that she wasn't having me let you down, unable to keep up with you because I wasn't wearing the correct footwear. At the bottom of the hill she decided I needed another pair of thick socks which could only be bought at Jeffreys. She made us trail all the way up again but I didn't dare protest again in case she refused to let me go with you. My first holiday away from her and Margaret and Jean and Cyril. I only ever wore the boots on our last day there. Do you remember, Julia, how you said I'd better wear them once or she'd know? It was on the day we trudged up to Rydal Mount and pushed our way through the rhododendron bushes to stare at the house, not at all grand like the landscape you showed me that he'd loved. It took a woman, his sister you told me, to reveal the intimate details of petal and moss that he'd missed in reaching for the stars from his lonely outcrop of Cumbrian rock. It was later on that day when finally we stopped at a café sometime in the afternoon and I drank not one, two or three glasses of water but four. You said, 'My goodness, you're thirsty,' and then you said things I didn't understand about the Oxford Union voting for peace and how it was already too late for intellectuals like Huxley and Brittain to be joining a Peace Council; what was wanted was action to stop things going further than they had. I drank and the café proprietor assured us the water was from the stream which fed Rydal Mere which had been muffled in drizzling mist as we sat by the spears of sedge grass and you murmured to the gunmetal water.

The noise of wood and water, and the mist
Which on the line of each of those two roads
Advanced in such indisputable shapes,
All these were spectacles and sounds to which
I often would repair and thence would drink,
As at a fountain . . . I drank the water and quenched my thirst.

As Virginia quenched her thirst and drained the first glass of beer she had ever drunk Julia asked, 'Would you like some more?' and glanced in the direction of the landlord who was immediately at her elbow.

'Same again ma'am?'

'Please, thank you,' and away he lumbered clutching a glass in each hand as if to keep him steady.

'Julia, what was it?'

'What was what?'

'The thing we saw just now that made me feel sick.'

'A fox that had been caught in a trap. It must have dragged itself there to die.'

'Poor thing. It's so cruel to kill them like that. But how did you know it was there? I mean you didn't see it crawl there. I would have cycled straight past.'

There was a faint thud followed by a tumbling and rattling, then 'Well done, Harold boy.'

In the light now turning from a dull brown to a shade of orange as the sun forced its way through the dusty glass Virginia saw a pole with a cord still swinging from it like a gallows and noose. Nearby and on top of a wooden dais two wooden figures were shaking but managing to keep upright while below them their fellows were scattered, some still quivering or spinning on their axes with their barrelled bellies pointing skywards. Harold plucked the small globe dangling at the end of the cord and crouched down to pull it taut while holding it out at an angle to the vertical pole. His head was skewed and he squinted as though along the barrel of an invisible rifle; he shuffled on the soles of his feet and shimmied himself into position for his shot, making a practice movement with his shoulder angled down and pointing forwards. His fist clenched the globe which he swung out taut on its cord and it curved away from him in an anti-clockwise direction. It made a direct hit in the neck of one figure which crashed into its companion so that they both careened over the edge of the dais to join the others already knocked down and 'dead' in the bottom of the box.

'Good shot, Harold,' boomed the beard.

'What is it?' whispered Virginia.

'Bar skittles,' said Julia.

Virginia hears a crack outside the kitchen window; she looks but can see nothing which might have caused the sound. Cyril, perhaps, breaking up old branches. She pictures Ronald running winded into the house because a branch on which he'd been swinging had snapped and he'd fallen to the ground. He was pale and clutched his side. 'I almost died, I couldn't breathe,' he whimpered.

'How did you know the fox was there?' Virginia was persistent.

'I smelt it,' said Julia.

'You couldn't have smelt it, not riding along in the middle of the road at the speed we were cycling.'

'I smelt it.'

'But Julia, there must have been something else, some other reason.'

'I've told you, I smelt it.'

'Please Julia, tell me the truth. How?'

'I smelt it. I smelt it like I can smell it everywhere. Every time I turn around it's there stinking to high heaven with a dull coat and crawling with maggots, a trap and a chain that it's dragged for miles locked on its leg.' She lowered her voice and hissed, 'Why should anyone's who's never been as far as Guildford worry?'

The landlord loomed out of the gloom with two more glasses of his best bitter.

'Hot work then, cycling from Shalford?'

'Yes.' Julia's hand reached for the second draught which seemed to Virginia more golden than the first. 'We're looking for somewhere to have our picnic. Is there anywhere you could suggest?' Her words sounded ochre in Virginia's ears.

'If I were you I'd carry on through the village, then about half a mile on you'll see a lane on your left. There's a sign, Lakeside Farm. Go down there and leave your bikes by the stile. No one'll take 'em here. Follow the path for about half a mile and you'll be there.'

'Thank you very much.' He nodded and went to watch Harold swing his rope.

A shaft of sunlight illuminated the wooden figures on the dais and the air no longer seemed to be suffused in that deep mahogany it had possessed when they entered the room. Instead a light maple danced over the table tops, through the backs of chairs, up and down legs and pillars and scurried along beams, along the counter and leaped into the murk to find a barrel, massively rotund and powerful, like a beached whale.

'Are you ready?' asked Julia and Virginia said that she was hungry. They stood and Julia skated over the dark red tiles but Virginia was rooted to the spot.

'What's in the barrel?' Was that her asking? Her chin appeared to be jutting out at a ridiculous angle, her hands podgy and insensitive as if she were wearing boxer's gloves. She asked herself whether her centre of balance was in her stomach or her head but couldn't answer her own question. It didn't feel like it was in either place so perhaps like God it was nowhere and everywhere at the same time. The brambly beard shook.

'What! Now that you're going the young lady finds an interest in something and opens her mouth!'

Virginia runs her tongue round the inside of her mouth remembering how the large and rubbery organ seemed too big to be contained there and threatened to slip out and away from its prison. She notices a desiccated fly in the corner of the windowsill and Cyril appears to her kneeling on the wooden slats of the greenhouse floor.

Cyril was so absorbed that he didn't hear me approach. I paused and watched him through the greenhouse door. It must have been sometime in early summer because the tomato plants were tall and thick-stemmed with their broad deep-green leaves shading the young light-green tomatoes which were just at that point when you think, tomorrow I will see the first one turned faintly pink. Cyril had offered to water the tomatoes for the gardener but the bucket he had filled from the stable tap was glistening untouched beside him. A piece of cardboard lay on the slats and on top of it an inverted glass inside which something was struggling to escape. There was barely enough room for the poor dragonfly to extend its wings idly entrapped and yet their gauze colours still shimmered. I didn't know how long Cyril had had the creature imprisoned but it must have been for some while because as I watched its double-decker wings beat more and more slowly until they fluttered sporadically and then stopped altogether. With extreme caution Cyril tilted the glass on its rim and grasped the abdomen of the dragonfly between his thumb and forefinger. It jerked twice then grew motionless. Cyril carefully peeled off in turn each of the insect's four wings. I had cried out softly when the first wing was detached but was too shocked to move or say anything afterwards. I was even more astounded when instead of taking up the wings and examining them with a misguided but natural curiosity he ignored them, looked up at me and frowned. He stood up and came towards me, able to look down on me from the vantage point of the raised greenhouse floor. He whispered, 'You won't, will you? You won't tell anyone. You didn't see anything. I didn't do anything wrong. I didn't. Say I didn't. Say.' From that moment I either despised or pitied my brother. Not only for the meanness of his actions but for the cowardice of his words.

'That is what we call our double-header.' The landlord genuflected towards the barrel. 'And it's not a drink I'd offer to strangers, especially lady strangers.'

'And if we weren't ladies or strangers?' Virginia found herself asking.

'Remember, Harold, the last time we had strangers here who had a drop too much double-header? They had to be fished out of the lake, so you be careful when you go down there.' He grinned and wiped his palms down the growth of his beard as if stroking a dog or cat.

The door swung back and a brick of sunlight whistled over their heads making them duck and squint. The garden path to the fence where their bicycles rested seemed to heave with the swell of the grass. Somehow the throbbing concrete would not allow Virginia to walk on it quite straight. The leather bicycle seats smelled scorched and the rubber grips on the handlebars were pungent. Julia mounted first and pedalled off, crying out at the heat. Virginia waited until she had gone some distance before daring to try to mount her own cycle.

'Come on, Virginia. What are you doing?' Julia had stopped and seen Virginia standing beside her machine.

'I was adjusting my chain. It was a bit loose.' She made an excuse. She mounted and pushed off jerkily, wobbling for the first few yards but knowing that if she could set up a steady rhythm soon enough she would be able to maintain her equilibrium. They passed through the village set back on either side of the road, the shell-pink and white weatherboards of the dwellings divided by the sizzling tarmac. As they approached the edge of the green the houses funnelled closer to the road into which stepped a lady who had safely seen Julia cycle past but failed to take account of Virginia.

I saw her quite clearly, too clearly, as in a slow-motion sequence on film. It wasn't only that someone was stepping through the sun's yellow rings straight in front of me.

It was in this month that Parliament passed the Government of India Act which was a first step to losing three-quarters of the Empire and one which would have a profound effect on Britain's and thus Charles's trade. But on this particular day when his wife's friend Julia and his daughter were riding in the Sussex countryside he was preoccupied with loading his cargo of mixed textiles and assorted goods destined for India. It was a shipment containing the sort of goods that British policemen and civil servants could only buy if imported, like typewriters, firearms and parasols.

On the quayside stood an unsmiling figure wearing a white hat which rested on hair gathered into a bun. She wore a navy-blue dress and held a strapless handbag under her arm. She did not wave but stood and watched Charles's ship until carried with the tide it melted in the dazzling sun on the horizon. She frowned. It was bad enough that he should be going and for such a long time, though neither of them knew that it would be more than a year before Charles, skippering a different vessel, would breast up the Thames and moor alongside where Emily now stood. She felt the tears of which she did not approve starting to prick and hurried away through the stanchions and cables hating herself for her weakness. Why hadn't she stayed at home with Julia and the children? Why had she stayed staring at the ship for so long until she could see it no longer? She ought not to have come. Her heels tapped out these messages for her on the cobbled yard, faster and faster she went until she was half-running as though fleeing a ghost. The cobbles came up to meet her, her handbag and hat went flying into the air and she met the stones with her palms outstretched; her cheek was turned to one side and her head lolled on its neck like a chicken whose neck has just been wrung. Her ankles crossed and threw off her shoes to reveal the soles of feet unstockinged on account of the heat. She lay face down with her arms outstretched and her ankles crossed watching a trickle of blood running through the crevices of the cobbles. It didn't look like her own.

'Are you all right, ma'am?' It was the voice of a docker and in the corner of one eye she could see the toecap of a boot.

'No I'm not all right.'

' 'Ere, let me 'elp you.' The boots grated and shifted into position to raise her.

'Keep your filthy hands off me. Do you hear? Keep them off. Don't you dare touch me. Leave me alone. Go away!' She screamed and dragged herself on to all fours.

'Poor girl. Tumble like that. Sent 'er batty it 'as.' He bent once more. 'C'mon girwl, up you get.'

She screamed again as she saw the stone clutched in his fist and fell back as the man's boots clunked away across the yard, clattering, clattering like hooves sparking the cobbles.

The woman walking across the road in front of me was wearing a white hat and a navy-blue dress and held a strapless handbag under her arm. She turned her unspectacular brown eyes on me as, failing to ring the bell, I crashed into mother.

Julia heard a crash behind her and looked over her shoulder to see Virginia lying in the road and the wheels of her bicycle on its side spinning in frustration. She jumped off her own machine and ran back to Virginia.

'Does it hurt anywhere?' Virginia had begun to shake and cry. 'Here or here?' She shook her head. The front wheel of her bicycle spun like a roulette still agonising where it would come to rest. Julia turned her over and gently raised her into a sitting position. The sun dazed down on them and no one else was about in the English village at noon on a day in midsummer.

'Where is she?' Virginia enquired.

'Who?'

'The woman who made me fall off, who I crashed into . . .' She gestured towards the fallen bicycle and scattered picnic.

'Never mind. As long as you're not hurt. That's all that matters.'

'But there was someone.'

'All right now. Can you stand up?' Virginia stood but shakily. Julia led her to the grass of the verge and made her sit while she inspected the bicycle, test cycling it down the road then looping back.

'It's fine. There's nothing the matter with it.' Then she gathered up the scattered picnic packages and put them back into the basket on the front of Virginia's bicycle.

I could hear mother saying, 'I told you, I told you, I told you so, I told you to be careful. Look what happens when you don't do as I say.'

'How are you feeling? Do you want to continue?' Virginia nodded that she did. She rode with exaggerated correctness, sitting very upright with both hands wrapped tightly round the handlebars, and as they approached the sign to Lakeside Farm she looked behind her before indicating her turn with a left arm that was held out and away from her in an almost perfect right-angle.

'Are you feeling all right?' Julia could see that Virginia's face was still pale and tense; absorbed in the mechanics of cycling she did not reply.

They turned into a narrow lane which dropped sharply between banks that rose above the level of their heads. It was completely overhung by trees forming the arch of a dappled and rustling tunnel through which there was no need to pedal. In fact, they had to apply their brakes every few yards to stop themselves from gathering momentum too quickly and running out of control. The canopy formed by the trees gave them the shade that Virginia needed to soothe her throbbing head. Whizzing down the lane with its deep sienna banks on either side of them and the sunlight flashing through the mosaic of leaves and boughs erased the shock of the last few minutes and brushed away Virginia's fears.

Father when he was home used to tell me a fairy tale in which children lay down to sleep under the trees and animals covered them with leaves so they didn't get cold. When they woke up, he said, they were in a cave with a good fairy who let them choose any present they wanted; then when they woke up again they found themselves at home in bed where they were safe and nothing could touch them. In the morning they said to their mummy and daddy, do you know what happened to us last night? And the children told them what exciting dreams they had had. It was the only fairy tale father knew but I loved to hear him tell it for it felt like we were a proper family once more.

Virginia thinks about Emily who is waiting for her to bring coffee and biscuits. This is her family now: an old woman gazing out of the window and no doubt muttering to herself.

They propped their bicycles against the stile and climbed over it to walk through the wood. Pools of dark shimmered in the light filtering from above. Fungi turned up their throats, showing delicate edible gills that would crumble, Julia said, if you tried to pick them. The boles of trees made grotesque faces at them and the billowing emerald bracken threatened to flood the path, glistening in wave after wave.

Virginia tips the fragments of china into the yellow-gold pedal bin which, she must tell Emily, needs replacing. The pedal mechanism has stopped working and she has to raise the lid with her hand. She wonders if her mother will agree to their having one delivered for she retains a notion that such service is sinfully extravagant. As though, thinks Virginia, they have not all paid enough to excuse an indulgence. Lifting the lid makes her think of the autumn bracken and how Dorothy and Anne would play in it with Ronald. Once he appeared in tears; I can't find them, he said, so she went with him and held his hand as they stalked through the dying ferns. They found a fresh track where the plants were flattened and twisted and followed it. They both heard the distant giggles of the girls and she whispered to Ronald that they should stay down and keep out of sight. It was slow, hard work crawling on their hands and knees through the tough, wiry stalks. They came to a clearing but by now the girls were quiet or they had crept in the wrong direction. She put her finger to Ronald's lips and they waited in the russet silence hoping for some indication of movement. A bird started to flute then abruptly ceased, something scurried in the undergrowth. She saw that there were tears in his eyes and he showed her his forefinger which had somehow been cut quite deeply. She held the finger to her mouth and sucked it clean, keeping it between her lips until the flow of blood had eased. Shall we stop, she asked him, and he nodded in agreement. She had her arm round his shoulders and they made their way slowly back to the house. It had been, she recalls, the last time she tasted his blood.

Beyond the bracken and under the fringe of trees they saw the lake flickering and jabbing in the early afternoon light. The edge of the wood lay some twenty yards from where the lake lapped at a sandy soil. Julia dropped her picnic basket, slipped off her shoes and ran into the water raising her frock above her knees. Virginia, slightly embarrassed by such girlish enthusiasm, hesitated, unsure how to react.

'Come on, it's wonderful,' she called. So Virginia unbuckled her sandals and walked across the hot earth which made her break into a trot to reach the water. Although murky it was cool and she lifted her frock as high as she dared, to within an inch of her knickers, then stepped into the water. Julia gently scooped handfuls of water in her direction which pattered down like a small fountain. She suggested they have a proper swim and moved towards the spot where they had left their picnic baskets. She was already unbuttoning her frock as Virginia approached with both arms twisted round behind her back to unfasten the buttons in a manner that suggested she was accustomed to performing the action unaided.

I felt I should look away but the fingers running up and down the back of your buttons fascinated me. You know that still I have never seen mother undress herself. Whenever she's been ill she's had the nurse do it for her. Only lately she's had to call me in to help her with one of the dresses that she can't manage on her own. But she makes sure that I retreat before she entirely disrobes. Is it dignity, modesty, a sense of shame? Or similar to what I thought was Ronald's simple embarrassment in refusing to let me see him undressed after the age of seven? A body I haven't seen for more than twenty years. Which remains in a sole photograph of a boy holding an innocent bucket and spade on the curve of beach at Studland Bay. We talk about black and white photographs but this, like the rest, is inevitably grey.

Virginia had seen Margaret naked when her sister was thirteen but then her breasts gave only the faintest suggestion of bud and later, on their mother's instructions Virginia was sure, Margaret studiously avoided allowing herself to be glimpsed with anything less than a petticoat. And though Jean was four years older than her, Virginia's breasts were already fuller than those of her thin sister. In short, Virginia had never seen a naked adult body.

'What are you waiting for? Don't be silly, no one will see us here.' Then Julia was standing with her frock and underclothes at her feet. How could Virginia tell her that she was embarrassed, that she had no point of reference except her own body?

Virginia sees herself in the kitchen window as Julia must have done: feet apart with the toes turned slightly inwards, knees pressed forcefully together, long, antelope legs – at five feet eight inches she now feels shorter than she did then at five feet six – at their apex the soft charcoal triangle, hips wide for her age though she doesn't know it; and though she is leaning forward slightly with her arms swinging across her tummy her full breasts are firm and do not hang. Above them her face with a nose longer than she would like is framed by dark, coppery rings still damp from their riding and walking. The auburn is lit by blue eyes.

And when those eyes came to light on Julia they illuminated one difference before all others: etched in the region of Julia's navel she saw the white squiggles of some mysterious hieroglyphics as in some ancient and unfathomable decoration. Then they were gone.

'Race you!'

Virginia reached the water ahead of Julia and stepping high until she could no longer raise her knees, she tumbled into the cool murk head first. When she surfaced yards ahead Julia was pursuing a sedate breaststroke just behind.

'What's it like down there?'

'Couldn't see a thing. Try it.'

'No thanks. I don't like putting my head under water.' It was the only occasion when Virginia heard Julia express a fear of something physical. They swam quietly for a while in the dark green water until Julia said that she was cold and would turn back. Somehow her entire manner had become graver, tenser, as if chilled by the water.

'I'll swim back with you.'

'No, you carry on if you want to.'

When Virginia finally regained the shore she found Julia face down on the ground and not yet dressed.

'Sorry, I suddenly felt awfully cold, I . . . '

'Look, I've got goose pimples,' said Virginia showing Julia a forearm.

'But I still feel cold even in this sun.' She gestured upwards and took Virginia's hand to pull the young woman down beside her.

'What's the matter?'

'I don't know.' Her arms opened and Virginia slid inside their hoop. They clung together and Virginia could feel those white corrugations rubbing against her own smooth belly. She wondered about the taut squiggles like embryonic tadpoles. Had there been an accident of some kind? Burnt when she was a child? She had heard how a saucepan of hot oil could leave terrible marks. Or tripping through a glass door or window, splinters of glass could leave marks like that.

Though naturally Virginia discovered later that it was none of these that had caused such drum-tight marks on Julia's skin. Almost from the instant of her conception Dorothy had twisted and kicked, pulled and turned, stretched and flexed her limbs to prove that her mother Virginia's flesh was tough but elastic as the canvas of a trampoline.

You held me tightly, so tightly I could hardly breathe. The salt and our dampness mingling. I wondered if those pale doodles were hereditary like multiple birthmarks. Then you released me. We both felt warm again. And mother, bruised, entered this kitchen to find the house deserted.

* * *

IT WAS NOT A QUESTION OF, Mr Edward Wilkins, how do you do? Pleased to meet you I'm sure. In any case, had there been formal introductions to be made it would have entailed Edward Wilkins standing on ceremony, cap in hand, waiting to be introduced to his employer's daughter. There were, however, no such manoeuvres entertained.

Virginia remembers the water boiling on the Aga only now she has to locate a second jug into which she can filter the coffee. Or could she get away with making Nescafé? Would mother notice the difference and if she did what would she say or do? Virginia remembers a time when Ronald had laboured, for hours it seemed, to produce a cup of tea. Which Emily tasted then poured into a nearby plant stand. 'Ugh, sugar!' she had exclaimed. 'Make me another cup please, Cyril.' Afterwards Ronald had always drunk coffee in preference to tea. How many, she wonders, of our seemingly arbitrary tastes and habits are determined by such incidents? Now where was the jar of instant coffee?

I would like to say that there had been a single moment when it came to me that Edward was the man I would marry. Do you, Julia, forgive my lack of consciousness in the matter? You who insisted, at least that's how it seems now, on responsibility for the effects of our own actions. Perhaps there was a moment when it dawned on me what I was doing but Edward was in a sense accidental and peripheral to it. Like in a well-tended garden when your attention is for some reason distracted from the obvious, the intended display of flowers and shrubs, and turns to the surprising and unplanned corner where a dog rose blooms in spite of the gardener. Mother, of course, didn't see the attraction at all. Mr Edward Wilkins, she snorted, is most certainly not the sort of man whom I would have thought a young lady in your position and with your undoubted prospects could have been expected to marry. Perhaps in the end she was right but for the wrong reasons.

The first time that Virginia saw him was in the March of 1936. It was a windy, wet and cold mid-morning when the trees in the garden were swaying and there seemed to be more gaps than growth in the hedges. She was sitting in the window seat of an upstairs bedroom and supposed to be working with her needle – a task which she loathed. Virginia never grew to like sewing because her mother was so good at it. Emily insisted on its use and virtue. Two words which were synonyms in her vocabulary.

Emily had given her one of Cyril's shirts which had lost a button and because an identical one could not be found to replace it she had insisted that every button on the shirt be unpicked and a completely new set of buttons sewn on. Snipping the buttons' threads, trying to be careful not to cut the shirt itself, Virginia was attempting to do as neat a job as possible. The material of the shirt was thick, heavy cotton – Cyril was not permitted to wear a lighter cotton until the first of May each year whatever the weather.

Virginia muses how nearly four decades later the same cycles repeat themselves, for this year in the middle of the miners' strike, a three-day week and power cuts, Cyril's flannel shirt keeps out the cold. And, she knows, he will continue to wear it until Emily says, Cyril, I think you could wear a lighter shirt now, the weather seems a little milder these days. Virginia is aware that the weather has nothing to do with it. The calendar is all. Look at it, look at the clock, look at your diary, look at your watch, look at your almanac, note the days of the festivals and holidays, the times of the feasts, the weeks of abstention, listen to the radio and hear that yesterday or tomorrow or today is the first day of spring, the last day of winter, the height of summer, consult your charts and learn that it will be a full moon, a low tide, a partial eclipse, watch the television and learn that a comet not seen in the northern hemisphere since the last century will be visible if you stand out in your garden with a telescope and your houselights switched off, read in the newspaper that it is the King's, the Queen's, the Prince or Princess's birthday – celebrate! Do all these things, Emily, as you have always done them, because the time is fixed, is laid down, has been established so that this day or that day or that moment and none other is when you will do what has already been decided, whatever the circumstances are, then act at the moment appointed. Virginia realises that this has its admirable aspects which so many of her mother's acquaintances admire – she never forgets a birthday, she is always well ahead of everyone in thinking what flowers will be needed for the church on this saint's day, that festival. She knows when things should be done. Had Virginia herself followed the calendar as punctiliously as her mother she would have kept herself safe from the day-to-day, the moment-to-moment hazards of decision.

So Virginia sat with Cyril's shirt, a marker of the season, watching the rain gust as though someone were sowing handfuls of the stuff from an invisible basket; it galloped down the window pane and through its refractions a figure assembled itself in the background where the drive appears at the far edge of the lawn that Virginia can see through the perspiring kitchen window. The figure stopped and looked about it, tentative in unfamiliar territory, then pulled up its overcoat collar and made its way round the drive. It was hatless and its hair blew up above a pallid face but it walked on firmly without bowing, its chin out and shoulders thrown back in spite of the rain.

Later I thought that perhaps he walked in that defiant manner because of the rain.

Who would choose to come out on a day like this, Virginia wondered, unless they were desperate or mad or both. She tried to see it as the figure must have done. The drive – a long one if you had to walk in a rain that stung; the yew hedge that lined it could seem over-protective as if it had secrets to hide; stepping out from its cover it must have felt as though someone had blown rice from a pea-shooter into the figure's face but it had continued with an instinct like a salmon leaping upriver to arrive at the porch of the house soaked and smarting. It turned down its collar and smoothed its hair before it rang at the first door it had come to. When she first saw the figure Virginia had wanted to open her window and shout, No! Go back, you've come to the wrong house. This isn't where you want at all. Can't you see that you're not in the right place? But she didn't. She returned to her thread and buttons while listening for the ring which would come from the porch with a roof that looked like it belonged to the ark.

Opening cupboard doors she is confronted by nearly empty marmalade jars and half-used bottles of disinfectant gathering cobwebs. She will have to ask Mrs King to help her clear them out. Mrs King is her domestic conscience, making Virginia fuss about in the house whenever it is one of Mrs King's days to come and 'do'. In the end she makes things worse than if she had left them untouched. Opening another door the words her mother spoke in this same room, the kitchen, still vibrate through her.

'I knew it. I knew we would have trouble when I had to go to the front door, not the back or the tradesmen's entrance. But I suppressed that feeling, against my better judgement I might say. I was too tolerant, too kind. It might never have happened if on that day instead of being so generous, a generosity which has been taken advantage of, if instead of being well-meaning I had followed my instincts and sent him round the back or better still sent him packing!'

The figure stood there dripping wet and dripping all over the hallway floor. He had insisted on being seen at the front entrance although the housekeeper had tried to usher him round to the kitchen. When Emily passed down the passageway to meet him she saw a young man without hat or cap and with his hair plastered down across his forehead. He lowered his head and inclined his body slightly forward but not overmuch, most certainly not obsequiously. Emily sensed that here was a polite but impoverished stranger who though courteous would respond to her as an equal. She would normally have treated any such visitor with a reined-in contempt and she would have done with this one but for one thing. She thought that in his stance, his aspect, she saw something of her father. The figure had full possession of its own identity and yet in a curious manner this made him resemble George in Emily's eyes. It was the posture of that wet and bedraggled figure which refused to surrender or be intimidated that reminded her of her father. In an instant she allowed herself to be drawn in and it was only later that she regretted succumbing to the stranger's independent charm. Virginia had to suffer her mother's lamentations in the years that followed. They ran along familiar lines: I was nice, nice as pie, too nice for my own good.

Virginia stood on the landing upstairs and listened to the following exchange.

'Good morning, ma'am,' he greeted Emily.

'Good morning to you, if we can call it that.'

'I'm sorry to disturb you on a day like today.'

'I fear it is you and not I who have been put out. Your clothes are soaking wet and you must be frozen.'

'No matter, ma'am.'

'But it is. Why don't you find our visitor a towel and perhaps some dry clothes? Something of Cyril's might fit him,' Emily suggested to the housekeeper, who was as surprised as Virginia to hear her mistress welcome what she took to be a total stranger into the house.

'Really, ma'am, I am quite all right.'

'No, I insist. I couldn't have your catching pneumonia on my account. Mrs Rylance will show you where you can change your things.' And without a further word he disappeared with the housekeeper as though he were an old family friend whose visits in the pouring rain were nothing out of the ordinary.

Virginia wonders whether her mother still regards Edward in the fashion she came to adopt. Which consisted of self-recriminations and regrets – I should have been more wary but if you're a practising Christian there's no other option but to be hospitable and welcome a stranger into one's home, is what she once said to her youngest daughter. Do these ancient bitternesses still linger in Emily's blood, poisoning her contemplation of the garden? Or have they run their course? Can one person hold such a virulence for so many years and retain their sanity? Does this account for the relentless harshness which has only latterly begun to abate in Emily?

When Virginia came downstairs having quickly and untidily sewn Cyril's buttons on to his shirt she found that the figure was once more in the hallway but that now he was wearing a dressing gown – one which she had seen hanging in her mother's cupboard but never seen anyone wear before now. Emily had told her that she must never touch it because it had belonged to her mother's father George and was, therefore, invested with an aura of ancient worship. This only made Virginia more curious when she discovered that the stranger had been given the garment to wear. She could smell its faint mustiness mingling with the odour of moth balls. It had the texture of felt and was bottle-green with a white piping round the collar, the cuffs and its hem.

She thinks how once Ronald must have slipped it from the hanger and drawn it round his shoulders, losing his hands in the enormous pockets as though they were tumbling down endless shafts of darkness. She had found him parading along the corridor in it and hurriedly whispered, Take it off, take it off! If she sees you wearing it we're both for it! And she had bundled the dressing gown up before Emily could discover her grandson's trespass.

As Virginia descended the stairs she asked herself what had possessed her mother to offer the sacred raiment to a stranger who moments before had been struggling in the wind and rain outside. She did not receive an immediate answer but she felt an immediate response. She could be nice to strangers too. Then when he turned and looked at her she blushed.

'I'm sorry, I didn't mean to . . . '

'No, don't apologise. I'm the intruder,' he offered. 'But there's blood on your hand.' She looked down and saw that she must have pricked her finger in her haste to finish the sewing.

'Sewing,' she said. 'I'm not very good at it.'

'Never mind. There are other things . . . ' His voice trailed off and she wondered whether he wanted to say 'that are more important' but had then considered that too forward. Then she sucked her finger to take away the blood.

'That used to belong to my grandfather.'

'It's very warm and it fits. Your mother said she would be in the drawing room.'

Virginia crossed from the last stair and opened the door for him. The dressing gown brushed her as he walked past into the room. A fire which had recently been lit was stuttering in the grate. It flared up and died down like a kite pulled and loosed in the gusts of wind that scythed about the mouth of the chimney. This was curiouser and curiouser, thought Virginia. The fire was never lit in the drawing room in the middle of the morning except on Sundays to greet them when they returned from church. A fire lit for a stranger. Things were running away from her too quickly.

'Aah, there you are. Come in and get warm,' said Emily, indicating Charles's favourite chair beside the fire.

'Thank you, Virginia, that will be . . . ' Virginia did not hear the end of the utterance for she had already closed the door behind the stranger who was being treated with such intimate respect.

Virginia thinks of Emily sitting now in the same room where ashes fur the grate. Ought she to go and light a fire? That is, if she can find enough coal. She wonders whether, if her mother had acted in her customary manner instead of displaying a courteous concern which excited Virginia's curiosity, she would ever have seen the stranger again, except perhaps for his departing back lashed by the rain. Later, as she was increasingly magnetised by the stranger, her mother's warmth grew cool. And worse, save for rare occasions when Emily revealed her contempt to her daughter, the matter was dealt with through oblique innuendo.

Their world at large, that is the village of Shalford mixed in with a sprinkling of the Surrey gentry, had a perfectly good explanation for Emily's growing bitterness which satisfied all those who had thought about the matter and some of those who had never considered it at all. It went on the lines of:

The utter brazenness of it, wanting to marry into her family. Who in their right mind would want their daughter to marry a shop manager? I ask you? A different breed of person altogether.

And to add insult to injury the scoundrel works for them. He's a manager in one of their own shops. I mean, really, how embarrassing. But what can poor Emily do? I always said there was something odd about that daughter of hers. I mean look at the way she was intimate with that friend of her mother's, awful woman, and interested in politics too! She must have been at least twice the girl's age. Three times I would have said. If one allows one's children to mix with types like that then one is asking for trouble. And now, of course, that she's got it there's very little that can be done. If I were her I'd tell the fellow that if he faded quietly into the background, it could be made worth his while. Quite. If she puts her foot down and gives an outright 'no' that's only more likely to push the girl into the fellow's clutches. She's got to tread carefully, what else can she do?

Nothing was going to stop me marrying Edward, it was the one act I would execute with perfection.

Emily's treatment of Edward was a condensation of the way in which her attitude to Julia changed over the years. With Julia it took more than a dozen, with Edward three years, before the cycle from intimate stranger to distant familiar was complete. A dominant factor in Emily's disaffection was, simply put, jealousy. Virginia attempted to sympathise as far as her own feelings for Edward allowed her yet it was the very innocence of this sympathy which further enraged her mother. How dare a teenage girl patronise her mother in such a fashion? Virginia was astute enough to realise that her mother's protestations – I never have a minute to myself with the business and the church – were asserted too keenly; that they were, in fact, offered to cover any admission of loneliness and formed a refusal to confess that the texture of her emotional life had worn threadbare.

I understood that her interest in Edward was more than professional. That she needed a man friend who would charm, flatter, even flirt with her a little. But that she should take her affection for Edward seriously . . . He wasn't even half her age! And when the balance of Edward's attention tilted in my favour I treated her resentment lightly at first. Only later when it hardened to a naked outrage of jealousy did I find it obscene.

After Edward's first meeting with Emily, Virginia constantly pondered what had been said by the fireside in the unprecedented midday glow. The result was clear enough: soon afterwards Edward became the manager of the Guildford shop. But the precise nature of what had been said to achieve that eluded her. When they knew each other Virginia would ask him how it was that he had been able to persuade her mother to take him on and he would laugh in a way that reminded her of Julia's laughter which was often inexplicable but mercifully blotted out the awkwardness of silence.

'But Edward, people have been waiting for years to become a manager in one of mother's shops. They have to prove themselves before they're considered. How could you, a perfect stranger, walk straight into the position?'

'It must have been my references.'

'She never took them up.'

'Perhaps she liked the colour of my eyes.'

'That's more like it.'

Edward laughed and ran his fingers across Virginia's forehead. It was shortly before they were to be married.

'Never mind. What's important is that if she hadn't given me the job we'd never have met.' He bent down and kissed her lightly on the temple. His lack of concern in the matter, his nonchalant avoidance of the issue, frustrated all Virginia's efforts to probe any deeper into the case.

In the kitchen with an Aga that needs stoking – she notices the temperature gauge has dropped below sixty-five degrees Fahrenheit – and looking for a jar of Nescafé to make coffee for an old woman, Virginia can after so long admit that it would not have happened if Julia had still been there.

* * *

JULIA'S ABSENCE left a vacuum that something, someone had to fill. Virginia told her about the stranger who had been so warmly welcomed and given the managership of the shop in Guildford. Since then Virginia had seen him twice, fleetingly, not to talk to, but she had become intrigued with the speed at which he had established himself on the scene and most obviously in Emily's affections. Julia too was delighted to hear of this young man's effect on her once intimate companion. She held a hope that whoever he was he might re-kindle something of the humanity and warmth which seemed to have drained away from Emily like the sap in a withering plant. Virginia consulted Julia in the matter to see what her opinion might be and whether she could offer any explanation.

Anything for which I cared and I turned to you.

Julia said that she would stop in at the shop in Guildford on her way down from London before coming to stay with them at Shalford. She had not, she said, seen inside the business for an age – she confided this as though she were confessing that she had omitted to go to church and that the experience of such a visit following on a long period of absence might prove salutary. 'And I might not have another chance for a while,' she added.

It was the start of August when the train left that ornate greenhouse of iron and glass, Waterloo station.

Virginia tries to picture Julia standing on the platform. Tries because it meant nothing to her at the time. Funny, she thinks, how events at which one was never present can assume a clarity and significance far greater than the scenes in which one participated. She wonders whether Julia realised that this would be the final occasion she would travel along this track. But how could she? How can any of us know that?

The platform was crowded with holidaymakers at the beginning of their journeys to Portsmouth from where they would embark for the Isle of Wight to spend, if they were lucky, fourteen days of unaccustomed, slightly awkward leisure.

Do you remember, Julia, how we sat on the stones in the shelter and shadow of wooden battlements growing green fringes, light above the dark below the water level? How boys would squeal and slip there or were scolded for throwing stones too near the bathers? How all the children pleaded for and most received money to buy ice creams from a wooden hut on the beach? On the top it said Soda Fountain and in large capital letters below CREAM ICES. They ate them beside their mothers and fathers who for the most part sat in deck chairs fully dressed, though some might have ventured to take off their shoes and stockings or socks.

They shuffled, a shade restless, on the platform; some sat on their suitcases, others waited in clusters with their arms crossed or hands in the pockets of light summer trousers complemented by dark blazers, carrying raincoats over their arms; nearly all of them wore hats as they manoeuvred under one of the four-sided station clocks that still hang in front of the platforms, their Roman numerals reflecting the solid grandeur of the station's columns and arches, the entrance fronted by monumental sculptures to the dead of the 1914–1918 war. Already before nine o'clock in the morning there was a fug in the air through which the train loomed, rattling. The holidaymakers boarded, lugging their cardboard cases up and over the gap between the platform and the step up into the train. Without a suitcase and evidently not going on holiday Julia felt herself to be a conspicuous outsider. She sat with her back to the engine – she felt safer that way – and beside her a woman sat down who was wearing a white beret and a light raincoat which she didn't take off. Opposite them sat the woman's husband in a dark-blue blazer and with the huge collars of his cream shirt flapping down the blazer's lapels like dangling white tongues. He was nearly bald and had a bad cough. Next to him sat their son who was dressed in the same fashion as his father except that he wore short trousers. The train jerked, sighed and then jolted forwards. The glittering tower of Big Ben slipped past on Julia's left.

'I always like to see that, don't you?' said the woman beside Julia to no one in particular but hoping that she would take up the remark. 'Check your watch, Albert,' she said to her husband. 'Seven minutes past nine. We should've left nine minutes ago. Now Thomas, stop knocking your heels like that. We don't want to disturb the lady do we?'

'Don't worry,' said Julia who though reluctant to speak felt herself compelled to say something.

'It's not just that,' said the woman. 'Look at 'is shoes. 'E'll 'ave 'is 'eels down in no time if 'e carries on like that. New they are too.'

Julia looked down at the gleaming and stiff brown lace-ups that promised to give the boy blisters by the end of his first day's holiday.

'Not that 'e's ours mind.'

'Excuse me, I . . . '

'No, 'e's our nephew on his 'olidays with us, aren't you Tom? Go on, Tom, say something to the lady.' Tom's head was still lowered and his mouth opened like the lips of a goldfish.

'Cors when you want 'im to 'e won't speak. Catch 'im with 'is friends and it's different. Can't get 'im to stop speaking then. But you try and get 'im to open 'is mouth to an adult. Blood from a stone it is.' She turned to face Julia for the first time since speaking and lowered her voice. 'We couldn't, you know, couldn't 'ave any, me and Albert. It's the choobs. Somethin' blocked,' she confided. ' 'Es not mine.' She nodded at Albert as if she were a doctor discussing a patient in a clinic. Albert was holding an unlit cigarette and toying with it in his fingers.

'Albert, did you ask the lady if she minds you smoking in 'ere?' Albert coughed. 'Filthy 'abit if you ask me.' Albert cleared his throat.

'I say, do you mind if I have one too?' enquired Julia. Albert looked for a moment as though he hadn't heard her correctly. Then a smile broke out on his face as he offered her a cigarette from his packet.

'No thanks, I've got my own somewhere,' said Julia, searching in her pockets and eventually finding a packet of cigarettes in her handbag. Albert's wife fell silent while they smoked their cigarettes, only speaking once to her nephew.

'Don't lean out of the window. Or that shirt'll get filfy.' When they had extinguished their cigarettes she tried once more.

'We're on 'oliday.' Julia nodded and smiled. 'We don't normally go this late. Usually we go in June but we 'ad to wait for 'im to finish school. Are you on 'oliday then?' she asked directly at last.

'I'm going to Guildford. Just for a few days.'

'That's nice. I've bin to Guildford. The right sort of people,' she whispered, no doubt including herself amongst them.

'Relatives is it?'

'Friends.'

'Ow, I thought it might be relatives.'

'There aren't any relatives.'

'It's just that I thought . . . Well, you are on your own. And I 'appened to notice that you aren't wearing a ring so I thought you might be going to stay with . . . Tom, get down off that seat. Sorry about that.'

'Never mind,' said Julia, crossing her right leg over her left knee and gazing out of the window. She saw the circular tanks of a sewage farm in flat fields for they had not yet reached the slopes of the downs. They passed a line of poplars through which Julia could see a man and a woman on horseback; they were both dressed immaculately in riding helmets – she could sense the soft stroke of the velvet – jackets and jodhpurs, stitched and crisp, boots, stirrups, saddles and reins – she smelt the tang of polished leather – shining with the sleek coats of their mounts groomed and burnished. This recalled another man on horseback more than twenty years before. The figures seemed to be his descendants, cantering away now across a field in a world that she had left but with which she still flirted, as she was doing on this journey, this last journey, to the home of her dead lover's daughter. She didn't know, how could she, that before her year ended there would be horses no longer groomed to perfection. Dying horses that would be clubbed to death, not shot, to save ammunition, and that then the bodies of these beasts would be lugged to form a shelter for riders who had never worn helmets or jodhpurs.

Albert coughed and glanced surreptitiously at Julia's ankles. The train stopped at Woking. No one got off but more families boarded so the carriages were bursting with suitcases and children. They stopped just outside Guildford, waiting for the signal to change under an empty hill where some three decades later a red-brick cathedral would be built, topped by a gilt angel and held in position with steel cables. Which would formally be consecrated in the presence of the monarch of the second Elizabethan age but as they waited for the signal to change nobody had thought of cathedrals and the hill remained empty.

The railway station at Guildford is near but not right in the 'vee' of the valley floor formed by the hills on which the town, later city, is built. It is the River Wey, tributary of the Thames, which occupies and slides through the bottom of the valley. Julia had to walk down to the river and over the bridge before she could climb the cobbled High Street down which her lover had rattled on the night he died. It was, and is, a longish and steep walk to the brow of the hill where she would find a branch of the Harrison retail business with its plump façade resting like a contented thrush on the edge of the well-kept High Street. She was carrying a bag containing her things for an overnight visit to Emily and family so by the time she reached the shop she felt a little out of breath and entered it feeling a shade dizzy. How cool and ordered it all seemed after the bustle and warmth of the street outside. The marble counters and polished wood of the cupboards exuded an air of discreet service akin to the waiting room of her Harley Street doctor, not at all what one might associate with commerce. No doubt, she thought, it was almost *de rigeur* to shop here on account for money should certainly not be seen to change hands. It should be just as if one were walking into one's own larder to fetch a necessary item. Bottles and jars, packets and cartons all looked so spick and span that each one might have been taken down every day and individually dusted before being returned to its place in the hierarchical system. Frequently requested items like teas or jams were stacked within easy reach of an assistant's hand, the more arcane, stuffed olives or walnuts pickled in brandy, say, were stored in cupboards on less accessible shelves forming a mosaic of labels and wrappings to display an assortment of foodstuffs which fell beyond the imagination of most people. French cheeses and German cold meats! As inaccessible as that Spanish artist Julia admired who painted people's eyes on the same side of their noses!

A man stepped forward.

'Can I be of any assistance?'

And Julia fainted.

Did Edward's face, wonders Virginia, frighten her so much, or was it solely that steep hill on a warm day?

Hours later Julia was sitting on the terrace beside Emily with Virginia at their feet. They were watching the gardener tie back a climbing rose, Paul's Lemon Pillar.

'I had forgotten how exquisite your shops are, Emily. I hadn't been into one for so long.'

'They're not all as nice as the one in Guildford. Nor as efficient now that we have a new manager there.' Julia seemed to Virginia to be uncharacteristically edgy and evasive since her arrival. Perhaps it could all be accounted for by her fainting fit.

'I don't know what came over me. It's never happened before.' Julia said nothing about the rose, one of her favourites. 'Did you say that he was a distant relative of some sort?' Emily smiled in disdain.

'My dear Julia, would I have a relative of mine working in one of my shops?' The question was rhetorical.

Mother's question stayed with me. I found Edward intriguing but would I have propelled myself into love with such vigour had her attitude been a different one? Was it to pay homage to Julia and to spite mother that I married him?

Julia's letter came, like Margaret's, from Spain but it arrived forty years earlier. And like Margaret's letter it heralded a shift, an ineradicable reversal. Julia had gone and never returned. The letter revealed nothing which, knowing Julia, was unpredictable or out of step. She had joined the International Brigade to fight against General Franco or rather she had gone with the brigade as an auxiliary nurse. Emily's response to Julia's departure was predictable.

'Charity begins at home and Julia never knew the meaning of the word. She could never stay still long enough to call a place home. Oh, she used to say, my home is wherever I am. That's nonsense of course. It takes years and years of hard work to build up a home with roots and connections, real ones I mean, not your easy here today gone tomorrow superficial charm, but Julia never had the patience. She always wanted quick results. You know why she volunteered for things? Because she was frightened of the commitment that working properly brings. Volunteering means no one can turn round and say, I'm employing you, do this and now. She wanted to retain her privileged status. It's a selfishness though if you don't examine her motives too carefully then it appears to be self-sacrifice.'

When Virginia put it to her that Julia had volunteered for a cause in which she believed Emily pooh-poohed the idea. 'Too easy, too easy to do that, my dear.' For Emily knew how hard it was to live with the almost-commitment, the edge of escape, as she had done for so long.

Virginia opens the Aga then throws in more logs from a battered wicker basket that sits by the boiler. She ought to go to the kitchen door and call for Cyril to come and fill the thing with more wood from the porch. She pictures Ronald with the basket under his arm. Dorothy was the grandmother, Anne was the sly fox, Cyril had agreed to play the woodman, and Ronald was Little Red Riding Hood. They had used the copse at the end of the garden, but only half-way through the walk to grandmother's cottage Ronald had grown frightened and run back to the kitchen. She had had to go back with him as Little Red Riding Hood's guardian angel to accompany him through the copse and ensure he arrived at grandmother's cottage safely.

* * *

IN AUTUMN 1936 Virginia found herself talking to Edward for the first time. She had seen him three or four times since his first appearance but on those occasions he had come to the house to discuss 'business' with mother. It could not have escaped an observer's attention that Emily had never before found it necessary to invite her managers to the house to discuss the affairs of her trade. And it did not escape Virginia's notice. Moreover, these visits invariably occurred when Charles was absent – not in itself an unusual event except that he was on shore leave for much of that summer.

Virginia was crossing the bridge over the River Wey when she saw Edward coming towards her on the same side of the street. Although she had expressed to herself an intense curiosity about the young man she nevertheless wanted to avoid such an unforeseen confrontation as meeting by chance at the foot of Guildford High Street. But it was too late and she had no choice save to acknowledge his presence, for he had already seen her and was visibly preparing himself to speak.

'Why, good morning, Miss Russell, what a surprise to see you in town.'

'I'm here to buy a birthday present for a friend.'

'What about one of our roast hams or a jar of Sharwood's mango chutney?'

For a moment Virginia thought that he was being serious, then he smiled, she laughed and so did he.

'Are you not working today?' she enquired then bit her lip; she didn't, after all, want him to think that she was spying on him and might report back to her mother, but he was quite unperturbed.

'One can't spend all day in the shop. I have to get outside at least once a day and clear my head. I was just going down to the river for a few minutes. If you'd care to . . . ' He gestured towards the towpath and told her weeks later that he had expected her to refuse the suggestion.

We sat on a bench by willows, trees with unbrushed and knotted lime hair. What could I say to a man who, operating in the mysterious world of work, would have, so it seemed, accumulated more wisdom than I could ever hope to gain? I chose the first adult topic that came into my head.

'Do you remember that lady who fainted in the shop? She's gone to Spain. To help the International Brigade.' Which then meant no more to Virginia than something vaguely associated with helping the less fortunate than oneself, like working in a soup kitchen.

'And what do you think about it yourself?'

'Her going? I think she's very brave. I think more people should be going to fight the Fascist dictator Franco.' She wasn't sure what fascist meant exactly but she had read the word in an article in the *Daily Express* she had stolen from Cyril. Optimistically, she had combed the newspaper from the front to the back pages in search of news about Julia and had been disappointed to find nothing, though it did appear that the paper too was not fond of this general. She continued, 'But mother doesn't think that. She thinks Julia's mad. What do you think?'

'I'm sure you're right that she's a very brave woman.'

Virginia was impatient with such a cautious remark.

'Well I know what I'd be doing if I were a man. I know whose side I'd be going to fight on.'

'Is that very patriotic? After all, the government's policy is non-intervention.'

'I don't know about that but they're killing thousands of people who believe in democracy.' Another word that had frequently arisen in the *Daily Express* columns.

'I suppose you could say that but . . . '

'Mother doesn't see it that way. She thinks they should all be shot anyway.'

'Mrs Russell is an extremely kind and generous lady.'

'To you, yes.'

Then I realised I'd already said far too much. I remember ducks splashed with iridescent emerald swept past on the current that seemed to be racing past, small branches and debris churning on its back.

'I'd better be going. Oughtn't you to be getting back to work?

'You're right, I had.' He said it with a hint of deference and alarm as though Virginia had suddenly reminded him of his position and had had enough of hob-nobbing with her inferiors. Which wasn't the case at all. She didn't intend to frighten Edward but he looked for an instant like a startled creature caught and frozen in the beam of a headlight.

In early 1937 Julia had gone to help the International Brigade, as a nurse she thought, though she had no idea what that might entail. She had been Emily's friend but with Emily – however much she protested it made no difference – incapable of accepting Julia once she learned that her friend had been her father's mistress, the friendship withered. Now Julia had slipped away from both generations of the Russell family. Virginia had been deserted for a cause. It was a measure of how Julia had been unable to commit herself fully to anyone after George's death. Attachment abandoned in favour of a principle.

Her departure from England had left Virginia bereft of any intimate contact. Margaret was already too much Emily's daughter and had accepted her opinion of Julia along with her views on almost everything else. Jean, when approached, would say nothing to her sister however Virginia pleaded. She refused to talk about her feelings for anyone, only expressed them for God who was the one subject capable of stirring her emotions.

How Virginia envied the glints of conviction that already lit her sister's eyes. Intractable, winking chips of diamond. As for Cyril, he still felt the tug of the cord that bound him to mummy and subscribed to the conspiracy theory which stated that all women and especially those in his family were out to get him. So Virginia's brief exchange with Edward gave her a hint where she might in future be able to address herself without inhibition or the restrictions that determined conversation among the Russell family.

Now I ask whether my sense of freedom and the ability to speak openly to Edward were not products of the difference in our backgrounds. He, the willing and docile listener who could contradict only within limits the gauche opinions and adolescent emotion of his employer's daughter, me! I took advantage of the situation and spoke to him with a candour and frankness normally reserved for use in the presence of nanny, cook or the gardeners. People who were not expected to respond, whose opinions didn't count. Tape-recorders that would only play back what you said to them. Or is this feeling a postponed guilt? Who, after forty years, can claim to understand their own behaviour any better than they could at the time? Am I not now another person trying to keep warm in the middle of the three-day week, recollecting a stranger and constructing motives, guessing at her actions?

Before they parted down by the swirling river Virginia said to Edward, 'I don't expect to mention to mother that we talked about Julia. In fact, I probably won't mention our conversation at all. Unless she asks, that is.'

He nodded. Which signified an understanding that not only this but future meetings would, if they happened, be held incognito and their proceedings kept secret.

An intimacy was then established which featured another – Julia – as much as themselves. The Julia that Edward came to know was, of course, mediated through Virginia. She came to exercise an influence over his life out of all proportion to his experience of her. She hovered as a resident but not in Edward's mind as a guardian spirit. He understood and could manage the pervasiveness attendant on Emily; she was, after all, his employer and a figure in his working as well as his emotional landscape, but he could not come to grips with this perpetual though unseen presence.

I realise now that I tormented, mocked him with an unknown woman in a foreign land. Had I been more astute I would have reduced you, Julia, to a more manageable scale for Edward's consumption. Then he might have felt your competition less keenly. I say might.

Their first conversation was brought to an end by Virginia hurrying along the towpath towards the bridge and Edward staring after her beside the green rush of water on its way to mingle with the grey of the Thames.

* * *

IT WAS A TRADITION that on the fifth of November each year a bonfire party was held in the grounds of the Russell house. In addition to local dignitaries and people from the church Emily would invite staff from those shops which were not too distant. She suggested to Edward that as Charles was away and Cyril could not be expected to take complete responsibility for ensuring that all the preparations went smoothly that he come and spend the day at Shalford. Then he could oversee the gardeners' activities and make sure that the bonfire was positioned in the right place – away from the trees but not too far from the house or it would mean that the food and drink would have to be carried further than was necessary.

Edward was flattered and delighted to accept the invitation. He walked up the drive of the house for the second time, not in the rain, but through a freezing light-blue steel which left his lungs aching and his hands, nose and ears smarting and numb. Although he had a scarf, a whorl of dark-grey smoke round his throat, his hands were stuffed into his pockets and he wasn't wearing a hat. With so little protection he would freeze throughout the day.

'You're not even properly dressed. You need someone to look after you.' Emily scolded Edward in the indulgent tones used with a favoured child. 'Come on, we'll find you a hat and some gloves.' She disappeared and returned with a trilby that belonged to Charles – 'He never wears it now' – and gloves that were Cyril's – 'He's got plenty of others. Here, hold out your hands and see if these fit you.' She slipped the gloves on to her manager's, her future son-in-law's fingers, pulling and pressing them into place.

'They'll do. Virginia, take Edward and show him where the gardeners intend to build the fire.' It was a comment that proved not that Emily had under-estimated the potential of Virginia's attraction for Edward but that she had altogether discounted its possibility. The fire was being thrown up near the vegetable garden wall where a cotoneaster grew.

As she looks up through the kitchen window Virginia can see the sage and silver leaves and the scarlet berries of its replacement planted a few years before by Cyril. She remembers how Ronald had once picked all its berries and used them to write RONNY on the ground. Like so many drops of blood.

Edward suggested to the gardeners that they rope off the fire to prevent the guests approaching too near the blaze. They questioned the need for this as it had not been considered necessary in previous years. Virginia glimpsed a profile of an Edward she had not known existed: he told them sharply that the mistress of the house had put him in charge of preparations and they would do as they were requested. He turned to Virginia.

'I couldn't forgive myself if there were an accident and I was responsible.' They helped the gardeners throw small boughs and sticks on to the scrambled but rising pyramid, working in silence except to ask each other where a certain piece of wood might fit or balance. When they had finished the structure was over ten feet high and as wide at its base.

'What about the guy?' said Edward.

'Someone's bringing it up from the village later,' a gardener replied.

'Goodness knows how we get it up there. A ladder I suppose.' They stood and admired the intricate tangle of dead or dying wood that might in another place and time have been a funeral pyre. Then Edward spoke.

'Why don't you show me some of the garden? I haven't seen it yet.'

Virginia led him to the southernmost edge of the landscaped garden where on Emily's instructions a stream had been dammed to form a pool from which a waterfall fed a second pool below. The water gushed through Westmorland stone which had been placed there to create and break its fall. The stream then ran through a marsh garden where the gardeners had ensured the spring and summer growth of yellow water flag, water mint or primulas. They sat on two outcrops of the mottled stone which Edward said reminded him of the Lake District. Virginia told him how she had visited the Lake District with Julia, how it had been her first trip away from home without Emily, how Julia had quoted poetry. She asked Edward which part of the Lake District he knew.

'I don't. I've never been there,' he admitted. 'I collect post-cards. The Alps, the Andes, the Pyrenees; mountains are my favourite.'

'And you've never been to any of them? Not even the Lake District or Snowdonia?'

He shook his head and she glimpsed a second unknown profile beside the face of the efficient retail manager.

'One day I'd like to. This summer I went to the coast.' He offered it as a poor substitute and continued to stare into the foaming stream.

'Do you mean you never went away with your family?'

He picked up a twig which he snapped in two and threw one part into the stream. Crows croaked in the elms and the air turned a greyer shade of blue. 'Look at that,' he said pointing to the twig that had wedged itself between two rocks and in spite of the battering it was getting from the water did not budge.

The orphanage had probably been better than most. He had not actively disliked the echoing corridors and dormitory, the clattering floorboards and the high-ceilinged rooms with their peeling paintwork and crumbling roses. In cold weather they had sat on exposed pipes and scalded their hands or legs. On Saturday morning they clutched the yellow-brown angles of their week's pocket money which left welts in their palms. They were allowed out to spend it in the High Street busy with shoppers. When he grew up he thought he would like to work in one of those shops and handle all those goods then beyond the power of his purchase. A shop that sold foodstuffs would be best for at the orphanage there was always an edge of hunger that gnawed at him even immediately after he had eaten a meal. Nobody on the staff was unkind to him and it seemed there was 'a benefactor, whose generosity' – the principal's words – allowed him to stay on at school after other children of his age in the orphanage had been obliged to start work. There were fixed times for meals, for playing games, for brushing one's teeth and cleaning one's shoes, for taking walks and reading books, for rising in the morning and for writing one's letters – except that Edward, like several others, did not know to whom his pages should be addressed. Nevertheless, they were told that it was a useful exercise in epistolary expression for the day when they might require such a skill, though the heart went out of it for Edward when he discovered a cache of his and other boys' unposted letters in a teacher's desk drawer. But all these acts established a routine that was half oblivion.

Edward's words rose in me, a bilious wave, when mother had me send Ronald to school, for I knew the pointless agony this would cause us both.

When Edward was fifteen and Ramsay MacDonald became Prime Minister once more it was deemed auspicious to dispatch the orphan to London. If the nation's leader could rise from such humble origins there was surely no limit to the heights Edward might attain. Taking his wishes into account he had been found a job as assistant in a hardware shop. He did not fully appreciate the nails and screws, the lengths of wire and the hammers, the sacks of grass seed and the smell of paraffin. He wanted to sell food so he went to work for that impeccably respectable company, J. Sainsbury's. After seven years in London he had had enough and wanted to go 'home'. The nearest he could approach to this was Guildford where the orphanage was situated. Virginia had first seen him trudging up the drive in search of work.

The twig lodged between the rocks was swept away by a gushing current of the stream. From the stones where they had been sitting a chill had leaked into their bones. They slipped from their seats and hurried back to the warmth of the kitchen in silence.

As the dusk gathered into night the guests started to arrive. Those who had parked their cars in the drive were invited inside to warm themselves by the fire before going out to watch the more eventful fire of the evening. The guests from the village who had all arrived on foot were, with the exception of the vicar, expected to wait outside by the unlit bonfire stamping their toes and flapping their arms against the cold.

'Ope they come and light the bleedin' thing soon.'

'They're all right. They got so much whisky in their veins they won't notice the cold when they come out.'

'Like as not they'll unbutton their coats and tell us 'ow warm it is.'

In the drawing room a sea of reddened faces was fortifying itself with spirits or wines in anticipation of the freezing night air. It was hard to tell whether it was laughter or glass that crackled and splintered. A lanky youth with a whinny like a horse was saying to Margaret, 'Orflee, orflee good.' She hadn't the least idea whether he was referring to the wine he was drinking, the party or himself.

Jean had cornered the vicar whose eyes were shifting round the room seeking the whereabouts of the whisky decanter which, when he had last glimpsed it, had looked dangerously low; all the while he was trying to concoct an excuse to escape Jean's questions about the Catholic and Church of England's differences in perception of the role of the Virgin Mary.

Cyril was shuffling from foot to foot because an old school friend was saying, 'What do you mean, haven't a job? Should've thought that if you play your cards right the business'll be yours in ten years' time. Then you can retire.'

A dumpy figure in a tweed skirt was asking Virginia whether she preferred hunting or point to point.

'Neither,' she said. The woman clucked furiously

'Well really, what do you do then? Do you breed?'

'I'm sorry I . . . ' Virginia hesitated.

'Breeeed,' said the woman growing exasperated. 'Dogs, ponies, anything!'

Virginia stared back at her, knowing full well what the woman meant.

'Do excuse me. There's someone I must have a word with,' said the tweed skirt and made off in the direction of a woman who in spite of the crowded room and the fire had not removed her headscarf. She plunged in again.

'Did you hear about Tommy's shin? A stone flew up. My dear there was blood everywhere. Pouring out. I thought he might go lame but we had it seen to in time. No. Tommy's not my husband, dear. Wouldn't have been so worried if he were.'

A short man with glasses and tufts of hair sprouting from his nose and ears simpered.

'And when's your daddy next coming home, Virginia?'

'I don't know. Mother hasn't said. I suppose she's too busy with other things.'

'Quite, quite.' The hairs jigged over the upper lip.

Across the room Emily was introducing Edward to a circle of faces eager for fresh blood.

'So this is the young man you've been telling us about.'

'Quite brilliant I understand.'

'Mastered the business inside three months.'

Edward coloured as Emily led him on from this group to the next.

I could see what she was thinking: here is my tall, handsome captive. See how he dotes and does as I wish. Look at the firm hands with their immaculately trimmed fingernails – you can always tell a person's character from their fingernails. Such delicious humility! What slavery and devotion! And in a vibrant figure that might be the stuff of revolutions. Instead, submission to me. Now I pity the need for attention that induced her naivety. Could she really have believed that Edward's courteous compliance was for her, for Emily Russell? And not for the person who paid the piper? With me he was able to slough that meekness and show a self.

Outside in the chilled air clumps stamped and shook, sucking and wincing the sharp air over their teeth and into their lungs. Among them were the gardeners and their families, several shop assistants – any managers present were inside – the handyman, the blacksmith – the vet warming himself by the hearth – Shalford's car mechanic, the sub-post-office manager who thought he should have been invited inside, the publican, butcher, postman and other sundries. Their children were growing impatient.

'When is it going to start?'

'When are they going to light the fire?'

'I can't wait.'

'I'm cold.'

Then came the tinkling of ladies' laughter accompanied by the booming bass of men's whiskied voices.

'Ssh, they're coming,' said the man who cut the grass round the stones and dug a new grave when it was necessary. Emily headed the procession, immediately behind her walked the cook, housekeeper and other helpers carrying stone jugs.

'We've brought something to keep you warm,' said Emily.

'Thank you, ma'am,' said the post-office manager, hoping to secure a place inside the following year by this rapid obsequiousness.

'About time,' growled the publican but he only expressed this view because he knew that he was standing out of earshot.

'And there's cocoa coming for the children and ladies if they prefer.' Was there no end to Mrs Russell's magnanimity, the sub-post-office manager asked himself. The butcher raised a mug to his lips and proposed a toast to Mrs Russell's health but no sooner had he tasted the contents than he spat them out.

'Christ, what is it?' he wailed.

'I thought we'd try mulled wine this year instead of rum toddy. I seem to recall that one or two of you almost fell into the fire last year.'

'What's wrong with beer?' muttered the publican.

Those gentlemen who had been inside were passing round hip flasks but none of the leather-swathed containers reached those on the far side of the rope.

'Perhaps, Edward, you would like to do us the honour of lighting the fire?'

Edward stepped over the rope and knelt at the foot of the pyramid. There were one or two torches and the glowing ends of cigars but it was too dark to sense anything more than the presence of others or the smudged silhouettes of the elms beyond the garden wall. The flames licked at the base of the piled timber and, as Edward had instructed the gardeners to douse the wood with petrol, quickly flared and soared skywards.

'By George,' cried the vet. 'I don't ever recall seeing a guy dressed like that!' The eyes of the house guests swivelled up towards the guy that was perched on top of the fire. It was dressed in one of Emily's frocks which the catalogue had described as 'neat and serviceable' in a fine Washing Poplin. At seven shillings and sixpence Emily had for once overcome her instinctive parsimony and purchased, not made, the mud-brown frock.

'It's a lady's,' spluttered the simpering man.

'Oh, isn't it ghastly,' said a woman who wore a fox fur coursing round her shoulders.

'I'd burn a frock like that if it were mine, though of course, I'd never own such a thing in the first place,' sniffed a woman next to her. Someone giggled.

'Oh it really is too frightful.'

Then the vicar suggested that the hat on the guy's head reminded him of one he had seen Charles wearing when he was last on leave.

'I say, Emily, do you think he'd mind? The thing looks as if it's only been worn a couple of times.'

Emily remained silent, the skin at her lips and nostrils stretched tighter. It was a hat she herself had bought for Charles and the very one she had lent Edward that morning.

'Sorry, Mrs Russell. I must have left it out here when we were building the fire.'

By this time the mulled wine had in spite of its hostile reception worked its way through the veins of the guests who had had to wait outside.

'Be all right if it were my mother-in-law up there,' said the car mechanic.

'Watch your tongue,' said his wife.

'Tongue? She'd be so busy talking she'd never notice until the flames was burnin' 'er feet!'

'Look. It's caught!' shouted one of the boy shop assistants. The sack-covered feet and legs of the guy were already on fire and the hem of the frock singed. People on both sides of the rope stopped talking and watched as what appeared to be Emily's trunk was consumed in the flames. A voice cried out, 'Confess and we'll reverse the verdict.'

'Ain't got many clothes left now, 'ave you?' jeered the publican.

As the hat went up the crowd cheered and there was laughter.

I saw Cyril smile quietly to himself.

Margaret was tipsy, having had two sherries inside and several nips of brandy. Jean was pale and tight-lipped as though she were witnessing the martyrdom of Joan at the stake. Emily was still silent until she found Virginia in the flickering light. Then she spoke as a ventriloquist, her lips not moving. 'How dare you! Go to your room at once and stay there.'

Though I wasn't guilty, at least not in the way she thought I was, I didn't mind. As I picked my way up the steps and across the terrace with the shadows of the guests jumping out at me I realised this small victory was mine, and not the last. Not the last, not the last.

The words spin round Virginia's head as she wonders whether she ought to plumb the depths of the vegetable basket in search of something for lunch. Though a tin of something would, she considers, be so much easier.

* * *

'THERE'S A LETTER FOR YOU,' Emily said to Virginia and held it out at arm's length as though she might otherwise contract some contagious disease from its presence.

'It looks like Julia's handwriting,' said Emily, knowing that it had to be hers. She continued, 'Who knows what tricks she's been up to now!' And the swivel of her shoulder as she turned from Virginia and the letter exhibited all the dismissive contempt she now bore towards her former intimate and what she considered her ridiculous actions.

No wonder Julia needed someone, me, to embrace.

The letter opened: 'Dearest Virginia, It has always struck me that it is absurd to begin a letter by saying things like "this may never reach you" but here I am doing it. I have written this in the event of something happening to me, hoping that it will be found and sent on to you . . .'

Numbness spread from my stomach, ran out through my limbs, the blood draining away. I had no need to read further.

Later Virginia was moved again by the ordinariness of the letter's contents: passengers being sick on the ferry, eating chocolate with bread, drinking table wine from the bottle, the abundance and cheapness of peaches, the white cubes of houses set in a hillside, a stork nesting in a bell tower, the gratitude of her hosts.

Now I needed Edward more than ever. It took me two years to prise him, barnacle, from the rock of mother's security. If I ever hear anyone say that economics play no part in the business of love, I smile. I don't contradict them. Perhaps they were lucky but with Edward the gold letters on a green background that proclaimed the Harrison retail business in almost every town throughout the Home Counties seemed, at times, to be branded on his forehead. He said that he wanted to have something to offer me. I pointed out that if it were money that I was after I would hardly be looking in his direction. I could not understand the fervour with which he clung to the notion of offering himself to me as a free agent who was independent of mother. Now I claim a measure of understanding which is, I suppose, only a guess. I took my independence for granted. What else would a girl from a prosperous merchant family do? Edward, an orphan, knew what economic security was because he had never had it but was, initially at any rate, determined to go some way to achieving it, so that he wasn't forever haunted by the whisperings that intimated he had married me for money.

What Virginia needed most was to tell Edward how her mother blew hot and cold and mostly cold towards her; that Virginia could find no rhyme or reason for this upset her. With Margaret, Jean and Cyril, Emily steered a consistent course, but with Virginia she was mercurial. On rare occasions she held Virginia close saying how sorry she was and asking her for forgiveness. What it was that Virginia had to forgive her mother for she never knew. Emily told her that there was something special about her and that one day she would explain to Virginia what it was, though she never did.

'Sometimes she gets angry with me,' Virginia told Edward. 'I mean angry for no apparent reason. Sometimes I'm sitting quietly by myself reading or looking out of the window. She comes into the room and says, "I might've known . . . " Here Virginia adopted the supercilious veneer of Emily's tone. "Can't you find anything better to do than pore over a book or stare out of the window?" Mother accuses me as if I were someone she employed to keep the house clean.'

Virginia often felt as though she were at best an accidental addition to the household who could not expect to be treated as Emily's own daughter, as if she had been taken in on sufferance. What irked her was that none of this was stated directly. When Virginia asked her mother why she was treated as if like Edward she were an orphan, Emily looked at her as though hearing a strange language, never heard before. She reserved for Virginia her bitterness, her frustrations and disappointments laced with a self-reproach that was too strong a mixture for her youngest daughter to stomach. An unexpiated guilt that might, had Emily not possessed such a strong constitution, have acted as an emetic and cleansed them both.

Virginia remembers how Emily once found her with dolls – she had borrowed Margaret's and Jean's – scattered all about the bedroom floor except for the one she was holding. Her mother surveyed the scene and then asked her if she would like to be flung in a corner of the room or abandoned face-down on the carpet. She did not reply. Like all children she thought the answer to the question an adult was asking to be so obvious that it was not worth asking in the first place.

'Would you?' Emily repeated.

Virginia shrugged.

'I said, would you?' There was still no reply forthcoming. 'Answer me, would you?' By this time Emily's hands were on her daughter's shoulders.

'Would you?' She shook Virginia for an instant then stopped.

'Would you?' She shook her again, a little harder this time.

'Would you?' She shook her harder and for longer.

'Would you?' She shook and didn't stop. 'Would you, would you, would you?'

Emily screamed, Virginia shook.

Virginia looks down and finds that her hands are trembling slightly as she unscrews the lid of the coffee jar. Is the water still hot, she wonders.

I used to see her after communion, a beatific smile through her face. Something I was endlessly promised but never received.

Emily would not leave Virginia alone unless she was working at something she had set her to do. As if work might in some way atone; Adam and Eve assiduously pruning and watering as if their busyness might win them back a sliver of grace. Idleness to Emily was a constant reminder of a laxity which she both feared and despised. Yet only by admitting that she had once inhabited a passionate landscape would she have escaped its tyranny and domination of her attitude towards Virginia. Instead it rested, clutched secretly within her, a hard, cold and unassailable diamond. To show it to the world would have entailed the introduction of too many disruptions. She tried to claw her way back to an innocence she had lost and her attempts to regain it meant that the only obstacle in her path, Virginia, was made to bleed.

'Perhaps she's jealous because you're more beautiful than your sisters or, more important, than her,' said Edward.

'Perhaps.'

'Or perhaps she was jealous of your friendship with Julia.'

'But it was her lack of warmth in the first place which drove us together.'

'Perhaps she senses that I'm fond of you?'

'That's something recent. She was cold towards me long before you arrived.'

'Perhaps' often arose. 'Certainly', never.

Virginia crosses to the Aga and finds that the water in the saucepan on the edge of the ring is no longer sufficiently hot – there are no bubbles rising – so she shifts the pan back into the centre of the hot plate remembering how on cook's day off Ronald had once helped her with the preparation of dinner. She had asked him to drain the boiled potatoes by pouring them along with the hot water into a metal colander standing in the sink; the potatoes were caught and the cloudy hot water drained away through the unplugged hole. There followed a howling from immediately outside the kitchen window. Ronald dropped the saucepan and ran outside only to return in tears. Virginia went and discovered one of the cats, which must have been crouched in the drain, still whining and nearly bald. With the attention of the vet the creature recovered yet she could never again persuade Ronald to drain water from a saucepan, help as he would in other ways around the kitchen.

* * *

'THE POOR BOY has no family to spend the day with.' So Emily explained why she had invited Edward to spend Christmas Day with them. Charles was at home for once and he watched as the young man whom he had never met walked up the drive towards the house. He noted that Edward's hands were not in his pockets though he did not wear gloves against the cold but swung his arms briskly in a manner that was reminiscent of a military or naval man. This, he thought, boded well for Christmas Day.

'Have you walked all the way from Guildford?'

'Yes sir.'

'I hear that you're a very astute young manager.'

'Thank you, sir.'

'Ever think of going to sea?'

'Not really, sir.'

'I would have thought a fine young man like you might have entertained the idea.'

'Yes sir.'

'Or one of the forces. Not that either is to be preferred before the navy.'

'No sir.'

'By some the Merchant Navy is regarded as unglamorous but as you're in trade you know very well that it's not.'

'No sir, I mean it's not unglamorous.'

'It's essential. We couldn't have done a thing without it. Been the backbone of the Empire for centuries. Ask me what our wealth is founded on. Trade, not warships. There's no point in taking a piece of land if you can't do business with it.'

'No sir.'

'That's what the colonies are for. Schools, hospitals, laws, roads and railways are accidents. We don't do it out of the goodness of our hearts, do we?'

Edward did not know whether he should say yes or no at this point so he said neither.

'Don't tell me about educating savages. Most of them don't need an education. They're as sharp as you or me. Take Chiang Kai-shek. Ever been to China?'

'No sir.'

'Shanghai – Chinese women know how to look after a man,' he whispered. Then his voice rose. 'Chiang's no fool. A twelve and a half per cent tariff on trade, he knew what he was doing! Got the Russians to attack us at Hankow and we ended up surrendering to Chiang who denounced our right to be there at all. Do you think he'd have been interested if we hadn't got the whole enterprise going in the first place?'

Yes, thought Charles, I'm going to enjoy Christmas Day, after all. Edward, of course, could say nothing about the matter of Chiang Kai-shek and trade. Whether Captain Russell's facts were right or wrong he had no idea, much less his interpretation of them. What he did know was that he was listening to his employer's husband and that he was not going to interrupt or contradict him. Virginia's father was delighted. Here was a young man in trade – albeit his wife's business – with whom he could talk about the world, men's affairs, what made the whole thing really tick. Cyril had never shown much interest in this sort of conversation so the opportunity was doubly welcomed by Charles who continued his peroration.

'At last they're beginning to realise the importance of the Merchant Navy. They've given us eighty destroyers to protect us from Franco's bullies but not before he's sunk a few of our ships. What about those who've already lost their lives in lawful trade with the Republic? I'm sorry to say that in spite of people like Emily's poor friend Julia, Franco's already on the way to winning. And now the very thing we wanted to avoid: Mussolini's alliance with Hitler. Only last month he signed a so-called Anti-Comintern Pact with Germany and Japan.'

Emily could see the distance in Edward's face as she had seen it years before in Bertrand's expression and Edward too would have allowed Charles to continue in this vein all morning while he occupied himself with his own thoughts. She decided – something she had never done while Charles had been rambling on at Bertrand – to interrupt.

'Don't you feel, Charles, that it's time we were getting ready to go to church?'

After a brisk walk they arrived to find the church already full. The Russells had over the years crept from sitting somewhere about the middle row of pews up to the front pew where only the supremely confident or ignorant are to be found.

Now when I take mother to church she finds the walk down the aisle too tiring and we sit at the back.

Heads turned as the seven latecomers swept down the aisle. Who, muttered half the congregation, is the handsome stranger with the Russell family? Those who knew, the other half, gave the silent response: Edward Wilkins, Harrison's shop manager, we do not know what brings Emily Russell to lead him here, into God's holy place on Christmas Day, and with her husband too!

Rumours. What are they? If one could pin them down they would cease to exist like snow melting in a clasped palm. So how can one in truth characterise these evanescent threads of fact and fiction bound together in one strong cord? One cannot. Nevertheless, rumour had half caught some spirit of the affair. There was justification for thinking that Emily's constant invitations to Edward showed a more than professional concern in the young shop manager; this thread was twisted along with those of Cyril's inability to play the role of only son and the long periods Charles was obliged to spend away from his family. These strands were so entwined as to exert a powerful tug on the imaginations of at least half of those in the congregation; in short, they were ready to be pulled in whichever direction the threads of rumour might lead them.

Edward slid into the pew first followed by Cyril, then Virginia, Jean and Margaret eased themselves along the worn oak and Emily sat next to her eldest daughter with Charles on her right beside the aisle. The church was packed and steaming with bodies constantly shuffling and readjusting. Virginia sensed the rustling of animals in a manger; the tread on concave tablets engraved, Here Lieth Lady . . . stalls, fences for God's creatures; hassocks ruby as communion wine where she should kneel in humility; octagonal columns of stone jet spraying up and fountaining down in restrained parabolas; translucent yellow, green, blue and red light pencilled in by lead – colours pure as a crocus petal in the robes of saints and the flanks of cattle; waxy green of holly wreathed round the pulpit and the font; an oceanic swell of bodies rising and dipping; the Herald Angels singing in their voices; sovereigns, pats of butter on the collection plate. And through all this Edward's face turning across Cyril to smile at her.

After shaking hands with the vicar they passed through the lych gate where Emily said to Virginia, 'I thought your behaviour in church left something to be desired, madam.'

Edward who was just behind them heard and said, 'Oh no, Mrs Russell, it wasn't Virginia's fault at all. It was mine.'

'I see,' said Emily. Who saw too clearly.

The seating arrangements for the Christmas luncheon had been planned with care by Emily: she was to sit at one end of the table with Edward next to her while at the other Charles would have Virginia on one side and Cyril on the other. As they were about to sit down Charles objected.

'Emily dearest, do you think we might change the seating arrangements? Edward and I were having such an interesting conversation earlier in the morning. I rather thought we might be able to continue it over luncheon.'

'But Charles, it's all arranged now,' Emily countered.

'What's arranged? It's only a matter of everyone moving round a bit.'

'This is not one of your ship's tables.'

'But Emily dear, how often am I home at Christmas?'

His wife adjusted the position of a fork on the linen and called for the housekeeper.

'Shall we ask Edward where he would prefer to sit? Edward?'

'Perhaps I will move. The conversation was most interesting,' he said, looking not at her father but at Virginia.

'Have it your own way then, Charles. I shall have Cyril, our son, next to me.'

And everyone duly moved round.

I knew then that he'd made the choice and from that moment he would be mine. It was only a matter of waiting. Which is how I ended up here. Still waiting for Edward, or someone, anyone, to come and take me away. It's so easy to let things slip by and then before you know it the opportunity's gone and there you are in your mid-fifties unable to move forward or to step back. So you remain where you are, most of the time forgetting what it is you were waiting for. And when, on occasion, you remember, you realise it's too late to do anything about anything; stuck, letting it all swirl round you, untouched. It was the past or will be the future but is never the present. Not today and not any more.

* * *

TIME. Who would want to talk about it? Especially not me in my position for that is all there has been since we were married. A wait which spans more than a third of a century. Time allowed us to close the gap and yet there was an unseen hairline crack somewhere in our sympathy which time has brought to an impassable abyss. Absence, though I strain to remember his presence which now runs too quickly through my memory like the blue sand through the pinched waist of the timer on that shelf. My store too is an enclosed one to which nothing further can be added and which I have to invert before it becomes active once more . . . Sundays were most precious.

'I've been invited to spend the day with Clare.'

'A Sunday?'

'Yes. Why not?'

'Sunday is a family day.'

'Please, mother. I haven't seen her for ages.'

'Just this once then. You may go after church.'

'Oh thank you. Thank you very much.' Virginia sounded so humble.

She ran and ran after the service so that she didn't miss the day's sole bus. The engine coughed and the body rattled but it was Virginia's limousine, carrying her to salvation. On the seat beside her the picnic basket jumped and its cloth billowed out. Emily had asked her why she was taking a picnic if she were going to spend the day at a girlfriend's house and Virginia had had to invent an excuse. No, she shouldn't whitewash, had had to tell a lie. The bus swung over the bridge and juddered into the riverside station where Edward was waiting to meet her. They walked past the willow and the bench where they had had their first conversation and continued along the towpath. Two swans, dollops of cream, cruised downstream. Edward had taken the basket and they clattered over the duckboards to hire their rowing boat. When she stepped in the craft rolled from side to side and she cried out, thinking she was about to be tipped into the river, but Edward's hands were on the bows. He rowed as one must with his back turned against the direction in which he propelled the boat and Virginia called out instructions telling him how far they were from the bank or when he should raise one oar and dip the other. They snaked their way through the meadows and deliberately ran ashore on the sands below the ruin of St Catherine's monastery where pilgrims had once sought food and shelter on their journey to Canterbury. Virginia slipped off her sandals and paddled in the green water. She lifted the basket from the boat as Edward dragged it half out of the water, its hull on the gravelly sand sounding as if the river were clearing its throat. He wound the painter round the trunk of a tree while she spread the ivory cloth under the lime-light fingers of another.

He drank a glass of cider and she had lemonade, then they ate the sandwiches and sausage rolls that she, not cook, had made. He fell asleep and she listened to the oars knocking, wood on wood, in the bottom of the boat. She picked a stem of grass and tickled him awake – he sprang to his feet, grabbed her and held her over the water threatening to drop her in fully clothed. She turned in his arms and they kissed. The scarlet breasts of sand-martins swooped under the trees and upstream they didn't hear the cattle splash in the shallows.

They sneaked lunchtimes too whenever Virginia could find an excuse to go into Guildford. They favoured sitting in the handkerchief-sized park by the castle keep. The bandstand seemed as evocative without musicians as when it was occupied – in the silence they could still hear the notes curling round the wrought-iron fencing, weaving their way in and out of the twisted metal. Down the slope the stubbed thumb of the Norman tower poked into the sky, at its top grass grew sprouting like untrimmed hair from a nose. From the bowling green, shaved in lemons and limes, resounded the firm clunk or click of bowls as they collided and spilled into the trough surrounding the perfect grass. To their left stood the house where the Reverend Dodgson had once lived a half-century before they sat on a bench holding hands as the sparrows dipped at the snowflakes of their sandwiches.

Now, thinks Virginia, they have built two outsize boards on which one can play draughts by hoisting the counters on something like a boathook and dumping them on another square. She had seen two youths, boys with long hair, seated there and laughing. 'Far out', one had said passing the other a hand-rolled cigarette which, she supposed, contained marijuana or hashish. She does not lament the imposition of the late image on the first. Although they are both composed of the same place they are, she knows, two entirely separate worlds nearly forty years apart, and her memory the bridge on which she tramps from one to the other.

When was the last time that I functioned solely in the present?

In the spring and summer of 1939 is the answer. It was after Edward had proposed marriage and Charles, to Emily's disgust, had telegrammed: Delighted. Let me know date. Congratulations. There was nothing for Emily to do at first save adopt a rational approach to the proposal.

'Do you think this is a good idea? After all you are very young. Edward has hardly established himself yet. Perhaps in four or five years when he has gained more experience of the business there might be . . .'

'But mother, he's marrying me. Not your business.'

'Oh really? Is that so?'

Later the cool rationality of Emily's response dropped in favour of a more outright assault.

How could she be so cruel? The question still comes to me as I am helping her in and out of the Maxi or tidying up the rose stems she has pruned and can no longer bend to reach. Or, like now, making her coffee.

'Do you think he really loves you? Is that what you think, you poor child? Let me tell you why he's marrying you. Why would a poor orphan boy choose a girl as immature and inexperienced as you? He knows that if he waited any longer, until you were older, you'd refuse him. You aren't even pretty.'

Did she mean like some small canary tweeting and ruffling its yellow feathers, stupid bird, thought Virginia. She was conscious that she blazed light, that she was strong, that she had the beauty that grows with age. What did it matter that her ears were not perfectly flat against her skull? That their lobes were not whorled as pearls. They were to Edward succulent as the strawberries they picked, helping the gardeners to save the fruit from the birds.

'Do you think he'd be marrying you if I weren't who I am? Answer me, child. Who provides him with his daily bread? And you think that he doesn't itch to get his hands on the whole loaf? He wants to be the "& Son". To replace your brother Cyril. Impossible!'

Emily's bitter harangues continued throughout the spring and into the summer. Then just before they were married they suddenly ceased as though she had relented and decided to give them a chance. But, as Virginia was to discover, she was only biding her time.

The Führer had already taken Czechoslovakia; Britain had promised to defend Poland's sovereignty; cook's *Daily Express* had said there would be no war in Europe that year or next when Edward asked Virginia to marry him. The wedding was in August when Cyril helped the gardeners pick the tomatoes every day and the Victorias – magenta globes hanging from the fan-trained branches against a southern wall – needed watching daily too. The gardeners spent dusty hours cutting the privet and formal stretches of box yew with their blades slicing through the butter light into the bottle-green hedging.

Margaret, once she realised that nothing would deflect her sister from marrying a shop manager, took all the arrangements in hand: the five-tier cake, its base a model of the house and grounds; the invitations in a silver copperplate; the silk dress which would puff in clouds round Virginia's shoulders before drawing itself in tightly at the waist then cascading out in fountains of silk with flowers embroidered in its streams; arranging the extra staff required to cater during the reception; the marquee; the cannas and campanulas, checking the fuchsias and the begonias were coming to their best, that the Prima Ballerina would whirl and flaunt her fragrant pink layers in petal after pastel petal.

'How do you feel about your youngest daughter marrying first?'

'She loves him,' Virginia heard Emily say and thought that her mother must believe it. Though it didn't stop her accusations, her recriminations, later on.

During the service only Jean could be heard crying as though she knew that she would never walk down an aisle to stand beside an earthly groom. Afterwards Cyril could not be traced, someone said that he was wandering in the vegetable garden – a retreat that came to be predicted at moments of high excitement or crisis. The laughter of the mistress of ceremonies – Emily had withdrawn and Margaret had taken on the role – threatened in its nervousness to splinter in the plump, warm air. Conversation bubbled through the guests:

'I expect Emily has been quite unable to cope with it all. It's traumatic enough when one's youngest daughter is the first to be married . . . '

'And at twenty years old before she knows her own mind.'

'But to a shop manager! It must have all been too much for poor Emily.'

'Margaret is managing very well. She is, I must say, a most capable young woman. Quite unlike that brother of hers, who wouldn't say boo to a goose.'

'Did you see the other sister?'

'My dear, how could I have missed that awful caterwauling? One might have been forgiven for thinking Judgement Day had arrived, not that she was at her sister's wedding.'

'Quite. It started with the March and continued right through "Let no man put asunder". She was still sniffling when they came out of the vestry.'

'I thought that Mrs Hewitt had done a marvellous job with the flowers.'

'More tea?'

'I'll have sherry please.'

'In particular the lilies under the pulpit.'

'The bride is looking quite radiant.'

'One has to admit that whatever his background he is a handsome devil.'

'Cake?'

'Thank you.'

'Sweet sherry.'

'I thought the reverend's words most appropriate.'

'In the circumstances what else could he have done but mention the humble?'

The women in shades of pastel, the men in dove-grey leads, stood in the marquee on one of the lower terraces listening to the words of Captain Charles Russell.

'Emily and I have known our new son-in-law for some time now and he has shown the qualities of industry, intelligence and application which we are sure he will bring to bear on his marriage.' Virginia thought that he spoke as if he were presiding at the opening ceremony of a new shop. 'And which, I am certain, will command our daughter's attention.'

That was not it at all. I needed someone to approach. Someone who would help me loosen mother's grasp on my life. I was choking.

'Our only regret is that Edward is here today on his own

and that none of his family were able to attend.'

The guests fiddled with their jewellery, looked down at their shoes, raised glasses to their lips, slipped food into their mouths – anything to hide their embarrassment at this insensitive allusion. After all, many of them thought that though Edward was a bastard there was no need to make such a pointed reference to the fact.

In the end I gave up asking him whether he didn't have a wish to find out. Like a hedgehog he would roll up in a ball with spikes out, bristling. If they had abandoned him, he would stifle curiosity and ignore them. I didn't believe him. Too much of the petulant child left out of the game. Who then says he didn't want to play anyway. The cowed, prickly posture of a badly hurt person. I wanted to hold him and stroke that away. He wouldn't let me come near, remained knotted in his own tense wound.

Edward realised that he would need some formal, if not personal, support on the day of their marriage and had sought out another orphanage boy who was not a close friend – Edward had none. The best man, an articled clerk in Croydon, was precise, with spectacles, and picked at his food like an underfed fowl pecking and scratching in the dirt. His hired morning suit was ill-fitting and the cuffs poked out from his jacket sleeves as if they were cardboard. Perhaps they were. His shoes were unpolished and scuffed. He spoke with a London whine that did not even possess the veneer of charm that is claimed for a Cockney accent.

'Mister, er Commander, er the bride's favver was not qui' raight when 'e said that Edward 'as no famly 'ere tedai. Standin' over there I can see the 'ead of the orfnidge oose just retired afta fawty years. 'Ee was like a faaver te uz oo 'ad none. I should say that ai fink of myself as er par' of Edward's family . . . ' He paused but before he could continue the reverend, who had been nudged furiously by Margaret, interrupted.

'Thank you very much. On the subject of families I will say that we are all God's children. Let us give a moment's thanks in prayer.' The head of each guest lowered in blessed relief.

Only Edward spoke to the point.

'I love her.'

He said it ignoring the guests and looking straight at me, and pierced the cluttered air of the marquee with a needle. Outside the plants, flowers, hedges, bushes and trees teemed with life; the mellow house looked snug or smug depending on where one was standing; the sleek bodies of polished motor cars glinted while their drivers manoeuvred on the gravel which cracked and spat like a fire coming to life. A little further away Chamberlain was about to sign a treaty with Poland; Halifax was attempting to keep Mussolini sweet; and by the end of the month Hitler had come to his decision.

* * *

IT WAS OVER. In two months Edward had sold his wedding suit for two pounds – fifteen shillings less than he had paid for it.

'You'll need all the money you can get now.'

And was posted to a training camp, Catterick, in what the Russells called The North. Virginia had soon realised how fruitless it would prove to argue further with Edward about his decision to enlist.

If only I hadn't praised Julia's courage in running off to Spain when I first met Edward. Fool! I'd held Julia in too high an esteem and shown him, too. He'd spent months agonising over the timing of our marriage only to hear the vile whisperings that ran like a virus, spreading the disease of suspicion about his motives. He wasn't going to stand accused of cowardice into the bargain.

Virginia looks out of the kitchen window but her eye is caught by the putty in the corners of the frame. It has dried out and cracked. In its corners mould is growing. She remembers how she was woken by screaming and had rushed into Anne's bedroom to find her daughter with fragments of glass embedded in her arm, blood on the windowsill and carpet. There had been a severe nightmare and the arm required several stitches. Emily will no doubt ask her again why she hasn't found anyone to replace Mr Woods who came to clean all the windows throughout the house every month. She hadn't wanted to tell Emily that Mr Woods no longer came because he had fallen off his ladder and was lying in The Royal County with a broken back. It didn't seem right. Mr Woods had cleaned their windows for nearly twenty years and Virginia couldn't summon up the energy to replace him. She prevaricated and allowed the windows to grow mould and gather dust.

'Being a shopkeeper is hardly a reserved occupation.'

'But Edward, darling, we need food. We must eat.'

'How essential are fresh Kenyan coffee beans to the war effort?'

'We have to keep up the morale of the civilian population.'

'How many people buy from us? Besides, if the war lasts there won't be anything left to sell. They won't have ships like your father's wasted on French wine or cheeses.'

There was nothing I could say that he didn't already know. We married to be together. How can I continue to live here without you? I didn't say it and he knew.

Edward said that he would prefer to leave unaccompanied and would rather Virginia stayed at home than come with him to the railway station. They said goodbye to each other in the porch where wood was already stacked for the approach of winter. Cyril and the gardeners had been chopping logs that morning. There were fresh creamy yellow chips scattered on the ground and an aching, primeval smell of split timber. Moments before this the rest of the family had said its farewells in the drawing room where even Emily had appeared to soften and had held him warmly. Margaret said that she knew Edward would do well but the trembling Jean could not bear to look him in the face when he kissed her goodbye. Cyril was not present and Edward claimed he would see him soon enough in any case.

There was a chill in the air but it wasn't truly cold. Edward had his overcoat on one arm and carried a suitcase in the other hand. Which he put down to embrace his wife who with her back to the house saw a flock of doves wheel over the tips of some conifers. Then Edward released her without a word and set off down the drive. He had refused to be driven to the station and insisted on catching a bus instead. As if the spool of his arrival walking up the drive was now turning in reverse. Just before he reached a rhododendron bush on the curve of the drive he turned, waved, and then disappeared in the channel of greenery.

I stood, autumn in my senses. I turned back inside to see the portrait of grandfather in the hallway. The grandfather I never knew. The slightly drooping eyelids, the full moustache, the heavy growth of stubble about his jowl, the skin stretched tight over its frame: the image of the man to whom I'd just said goodbye. Don't, I thought, let them tell you that history has nothing to do with it, it has everything.

Virginia had already guessed but not told Edward that she was pregnant with the child she was to call Dorothy. She had held back from saying to Edward that she had missed her period for she was trying in a misplaced fashion to act as a mature, adult, married woman. If she were going to have a child she did not wish – so she reasoned – to be accused of holding Edward back through some form of emotional blackmail.

How stupid I was! I should have used anything, everything to make him stay. My notion of freedom was so limited. This is how one behaves if one is a responsible, independent adult: don't tell, let him make his own decision unfettered by consideration for me. And he did.

In the meanwhile the Russell family had the business of war to contend with and it impinged most directly not in a lack of stock or a loss of profits – though both these things occurred – but in the shape of evacuees. Emily had agreed to act as billeting officer for 'those poor London mites' and found a home for the children with each of the gardeners, cook, driver, housekeeper, farm workers, then in Shalford the publican, mechanic, post mistress and other minor tradespeople were called on but she could not in the end resist the pressure and an evacuee arrived as the birth of Virginia's first child was imminent.

Nanny, who had returned to help Virginia with the child, was expected to look after this evacuee, 'urchin', she called him. She reported that she had found 'vermin' in his hair and that when he came back from his first walk in the fields he had asked whether they drank real milk – 'yer knaaw, the stuff wha' comes in bo'les' – or cow's milk. Yet this fair-haired boy, Graham, showed more devotion to Virginia in her pregnancy and a more persistent interest in the new baby, Dorothy, than did anyone else in the family.

'Put your hand here,' Virginia instructed him.

'I fel' it. It moved.' Graham was genuinely excited and whenever he saw Virginia asked whether the baby was wriggling about much that day and could he feel its movements.

'Wha' did the doctor mean when 'e said its 'ead's ingaged?'

'It means the baby will soon be born.'

When Virginia went into labour Graham insisted on cycling to tell the midwife and refused to return until she agreed to accompany him though she protested that it would be hours before she was needed. After Dorothy had been delivered he was allowed in to see the new baby and entered Virginia's bedroom white as porcelain.

'Are you all right? I 'eard you screaming. It must've 'urt.'

'Here, take a look.' Virginia drew back the shawl from Dorothy's head.

'Cor, dunnit look funny. Awl red and wrinkled. A bit ugly really.' The rest of the family had already said how pretty Dorothy looked and how she had Edward's eyes and Virginia's smile.

'An' I wouldn't knaaw. I mean if someone 'adn't said it was a girwl. She's got a sort of squashed-up nose.'

Graham was, of course, right. There was nothing beautiful about the new baby and his words accorded with the feelings of Virginia who was slightly revolted by the puce, squalling creature.

'Here, would you like to hold her?'

'No fanks, I might drop 'er.'

Days later when Graham had grown more confident he would look downcast if Virginia reminded him that he had already taken Dorothy for two walks that day.

'But the fresh hair's good for 'er. The midwife said that.'

Then he would go through the most elaborate ritual, packing her up in her perambulator as if she were some infinitely delicate and invaluable antique.

'There she is. Nice an' snug in the ol' alligater.'

He would disappear with Dorothy in the evening when the

bats were stuttering in the dusk and nanny would have to go off in search of them both. Sometimes she found Graham sitting on a stile pushing the 'alligater' with one hand while the other shaded his eyes as he scanned the darkening sky.

'I fought I 'eard a aeroplane.'

'Get off with you. That's wishful thinking on your part,' said nanny. 'I expect you'd like it if one crashed hereabouts or even dropped a bomb in a field.'

' 'Ow did you know?'

'Well if you don't get us inside before the blackout you'll probably get us all killed. And that means Dorothy too.'

Nanny's prompting reminded Graham that he was in charge of Dorothy's well-being and sent him careering down the lane muttering to himself, 'Awlright, we'll get you inside before anyfing 'appens to you.'

He would plead to be allowed to watch Virginia – not nanny – bathe her and take his turn at singing a cradle lullaby. And he always poked his head round the door of the room where her cot stood *en route* to his own bed. 'Just in case.'

Having spent nearly a year out of London when there was little danger, Graham was summoned back to the city by his mother into the worst of the Blitz.

'I'll send 'er a birfday card next year.'

'Thank God,' said Emily when he had gone. 'I thought my granddaughter would end up speaking like a London barrow boy.'

Virginia wrote to him twice but there was no reply.

I still like to think it was because he was too ashamed of his poor handwriting and not for any other reason that he didn't write. The letters Ronald used to send from school were in an exquisite hand. They flowed on and on and the discord wasn't in their form but their acid content. I could never read Anne's writing which always seemed to have been scrawled in a hurry with malformed letters sloping in all directions at once and lines veering off the horizontal. At eleven Dorothy's hand was strong and well-formed but it stopped there. Whenever she writes to me now I open the letter anticipating words from a grandchild, not the mature woman who is my daughter. Her hand shows nothing of that. Perhaps in graphology there is something like astrology. I keep meaning to borrow books from the public library then I forget.

At this time Margaret decided to make the break at last and went to live in London. Emily remonstrated with her.

'What about the bombs?'

'That's why I'm going, mother. I want to do something, to be involved.'

'But you can firewatch here. Plenty of girls from the local church . . . '

'Mother, it's not the same. Even the Palace has been bombed.'

And she left intimating that it was some hush-hush department vital to the war effort in which she was going to work. It was, of course, nothing of the kind but it mollified her mother.

Jean remained working for the WVS, the Red Cross, the church – anything which helped 'those less fortunate than ourselves'. A dedicated career ministering to the needs of others was being established. She now had an excuse for the complete neglect of her personal appearance. She had even been heard to say that she didn't know why women should worry about face cream or lipstick when there was a war on. It was the nearest her words ever came to criticising the behaviour of others. She limited herself to two frocks, one for winter and the other for summer, and gave away the rest of her dresses. As an act of charity she wrote to a girlfriend's cousin who was being held prisoner of war in a German camp.

On a visit home Margaret confided to them.

'Don't tell mother but I've got an American boyfriend.'

She described a magic palace, Rainbow Corner, which kept her supplied with nylons, cosmetics, bourbon – better than Scotch, she insisted – and Camel cigarettes which as she didn't then smoke she could barter for an evening gown or butter.

Cyril lost his single chance of an escape: enlistment. He was silent for weeks after failing his medical and when he did talk again his speech was almost invariably pared to a minimum. No one was certain why he had failed, not even Cyril himself who shrugged and turned away if anyone tried to discuss the matter with him. But one day after the war, as he was trimming the edge of the lawn with a turf cutter he said to Virginia, 'It was her. She stopped me going.'

'Who?' asked Virginia, knowing perfectly well who he meant but wanting to hear it from his own lips.

'Her. Mother. She stopped me from going to fight.' He brought down the turf cutter, slicing the air, the grass, mud.

There had been rumours that Cyril had been refused entry to the forces on account of some 'psychological unsuitability'. Now he was suggesting that Emily had somehow had a hand in helping the board to reach its decision. 'They couldn't find anything wrong with me. I passed all the tests. It must have been her.'

Whether or not this was true and Emily had managed to influence the outcome of the board's deliberations, what did matter was that Cyril thought it was true and that the possibility could not be discounted. Had Emily had the opportunity to bias the matter there is no doubt that she would have used it to the full.

The blade flashed in the air, slice, flash, slice, flash, slice, fla . . .

* * *

LEAVE is a word with more than one cutting edge. It is commonly employed as a synonym for 'depart' but it is also used in the sense of 'holiday'. The notion of Edward's leave was, for Virginia, not merely a break from his army service, but simultaenously a departure from her. This leave happened on two occasions.

Shortly before the first leave Virginia suggested the name Dorothy for their daughter in a letter to Edward who had objected and replied asking her why she had chosen it. 'On my father's side my grandmother's name was Dorothea. I never knew her. I thought it would be a nice way of remembering her but Dorothea seemed a little old-fashioned. So I chose Dorothy,' wrote Virginia. Edward's reply came back. 'I might've known, however hard I try I can't get away from your family. Its tentacles clutch everything, everywhere, even wrap themselves round the name of our child. Our unborn child.' How right Edward was, although he didn't know just how right when he wrote that. Virginia wondered what could have happened to bring such a bitter tone from her husband. It was this:

Edward was being squeezed by his army experience. By the other ranks he was treated with mockery and contempt on two counts. Edward was not wholeheartedly convinced that he had done the right thing in enlisting and his fellow soldiers could sense this though he never voiced his misgivings. His self-doubt and lack of inner conviction led to overcompensation – he constantly asserted that anyone who had failed to join up at the first possible opportunity was at least a coward if not a traitor. A second reason which led to their suspicion of Edward was that by marrying a woman out of his class they thought he must regard himself as somehow superior to them. It was as if his marriage had cast a slur on the ranks who had to work in peacetime as butchers, bakers or candlestick makers for their living. The NCOs on the other hand considered him an upstart with pretensions to grander things. And one knows how upstarts are treated by those who have pulled themselves up by their bootstraps.

'And how is our heir to a fortune this morning?'

'Very well, sergeant. Thank you, sergeant.'

'Good, good.' The sergeant's voice was caressing.

'Is Private Wilkins feeling fit and healthy?'

'Yes, sergeant. Thank you.'

'I think I'd be fit and healthy if I had all that money in the bank. If it isn't too much trouble perhaps you'd like to strap your pack on.'

'Yes, sergeant.'

'Now, if it isn't too much trouble.'

The sergeant watched as Edward struggled to put on his pack.

'Here, let me help you. There, is that more comfortable?' He helped Edward adjust its weight.

'Thank you, sergeant.'

'Now, heir to a fortune, I want you to do me a little favour.'

'Sergeant.'

'Let's step outside.'

They went out into rain that was being driven across the yard, waving like fields of wheat in a high wind.

'You see that fire escape over there?' The sergeant pointed across the yard.

'Yes, sergeant.'

'I've had a report that it could be unsafe and that it should be checked. We wouldn't want anyone to come rushing out of a burning building and find the fire escape give way, would we?'

'No, sergeant.'

'That's right. So how would money bags go about checking it if it had to do the job?' The sergeant had to shout into the private's ear to make himself heard against the wind and rain.

'I'd inspect it, sergeant.'

'How?'

'I'd shake it. If it felt safe I'd try it out myself.'

'Good. Not just a big bank balance, a big brain too. Now would you go and do just what you told me?'

'Yes, sergeant.'

Private Wilkins walked across the open yard to the cast-iron fire escape while the sergeant stood under cover and watched him. Wilkins grasped one of its rungs and shook but it didn't budge.

'Seems to be all right,' he shouted over his shoulder.

'Go up and see if it's all right,' the sergeant replied. Wilkins began to climb. 'Right to the top,' he called. When Wilkins had climbed to the top and come down again the sergeant called out, 'Do it again. Faster this time.'

Wilkins obeyed.

'And again,' came the sergeant's reasoned voice. 'If we had a fire there'd be hundreds of boots rushing up and down those steps.'

'And again.'

'And again.'

'And again.'

'And again,' shouted the sergeant each time Wilkins reached the ground. On several occasions Wilkins slipped on the wet rungs. Once he cracked his forehead and blood trickled out. The sergeant continued to shout, 'And again. Faster.'

When it became evident, even to the sergeant, that Wilkins's legs would take him no higher because it was the fifth or sixth time he had collapsed in trying to climb beyond the second rung the sergeant walked over and said in a quiet voice, 'Now get back to your other duties, money bags.'

Wilkins picked himself up and stumbled towards the bunk-house. Behind him the sergeant's voice screamed, 'I don't want to see any fuckin' shirkin' for the rest of the day!'

And the harder Edward was squeezed the more determined he grew to prove his worth and make a success of being a soldier. He had been trained from an early age to please those in authority and understood nothing else.

So Virginia waited with trepidation for Edward's arrival, knowing that something was amiss but agitated because she did not know what it was that was forcing the change in Edward's tone.

Edward in his uniform was admired by everyone including Emily who told Virginia that she thought it suited him better than a manager's collar and tie. Cyril came in from the garden where he had been digging up turf so that more vegetables could be laid. He looked wistfully at the khaki, thick and ugly like a horse blanket.

'When are you joining up?' Edward asked him. Cyril blushed.

'I can't,' he muttered.

'What do you mean, "you can't"?'

'I tried but . . . ' Cyril shrugged.

'But what?' Edward asked in a direct, no, more than that, thought Virginia, a forthright tone which sounded unfamiliar on his lips.

The Edward I married was circumspect, oblique to the point of obscurity.

'They wouldn't have me for medical reasons.'

Edward's lips formed a silent 'O'.

'What was the problem?'

But Cyril had gone back to the garden so Edward turned to Emily.

'What's the matter with him?'

'Nothing. Nothing at all is the matter with Cyril.' She placed the emphasis of the sentence on her son's name, almost spitting it out in the process.

Edward turned to Virginia.

'What have you got to say? Why hasn't your brother joined up?'

'I don't know but Edward, darling . . . '

'Don't "Edward darling" me. You all sit here making money while the rest of us are fighting for our country.'

It was the argument of a man trying to persuade himself of the worth of his own action and the strain could be caught in his voice which mimicked the tone and phrasing of a stranger. Virginia's cheeks were flushed.

'Have you forgotten all your shop-manager's economics? We're not going to get rich on people buying two ounces of tea a week.'

The first time we argued. I cried for something broken.

Emily turned away towards the french windows as if embarrassed by these strong words which might have been none of her concern for the contemptuous air with which she treated them. Had anyone observed her at that moment they might have glimpsed the ripple of a smile flicker through her face but even a trained detective could not have sworn to it, so slight and quick was its movement.

This difference between them was never alluded to either by Virginia or Edward and no further open breach took place during Edward's first leave. Had there been a similar recurrence and a second confrontation, the way open to another level of understanding might have been taken. In place of this there was a mutual closing down of areas which signalled a potential danger; such backing off avoided conflict but spelled an end to the richer intimacy which Virginia had assumed to be the purpose of marriage and most certainly of their marriage.

Virginia dutifully enquired about the trivia of army life. What time do they make you go to bed? What do they give you for breakfast? Do they give you free time on Sundays? What happens if you do something wrong? Edward had already answered these questions in his weekly letters but he responded with the information politely enough as though he were telling an absent-minded and aged aunt things she had already heard but which she had soon forgotten.

I wanted to put his other life at a distance, I hoped that by ignoring the pain it would go away. Soon but not soon enough I realised it was a mistake to act as though Edward's new life didn't exist. I hated its existence and swept it from my thoughts. Of course, it reappeared later on with an immediacy that was starker for having been kept out of sight for so long.

Edward took Dorothy for walks in her pram, pushing her up, down and round the drive. He helped Virginia bathe her and would, if no one else was about, even change her napkin. In considering his daughter's needs he showed a meticulous attention to detail but Virginia considered there was a sharp edge of professional detachment in all his responses and missed Graham's immediate enthusiasm for the infant.

In the course of Edward's leave the strawberries ripened followed by raspberries, gooseberries, white and red currants and loganberries – soft fruits easily spoilt by cold weather, the rain, a virus, birds' looting, or the gardener's inattention allowing them to over-ripen and rot. And then he was gone.

Waiting for her second child Virginia took care to write asking Edward to choose the name. Anne for a girl, Ronald if it's a boy he replied, without offering any explanation for his choice. Virginia remembered Edward's suggestion when her third and final child was born. But this second was a more difficult pregnancy than her first had been or third would prove. Virginia had to spend hours, sometimes days, in bed. She was in labour for more than a day and the child was dragged out with forceps between the Blitz and the introduction of clothing coupons.

And people, thinks Virginia, still ask how one spent the war. Waiting for Anne to be born. Waiting for Edward. Waiting for Ronald to be born. Waiting for Edward. Waiting for it to end. Waiting.

* * *

LETTERS FROM NORTH AFRICA . . .

the desert is not at all monotonous as some will have you believe. Once your eye adjusts it is full of variety and colour. Someone shot an Italian soldier's dog, mistaking it for one of the enemy. The poor thing was yelping so we had to shoot it dead and put it out of its misery. It was odd to think we had to go such a long way round to get here. I was seasick for the first ten days and after that I felt queasy all the time. I was glad to feel my feet on dry sand! We went and saw the pyramids, of course, which were magnificent outside, but inside in the narrow passageways I could hardly see a thing. All the guide had was a stinking taper which threw stuttering shadows on a few scratches in the walls. Did you realise that they, the pyramids I mean, were built to mirror the sun's rays? And that they're on the west bank of the Nile because that's where the ancient Egyptians believed the sun started its journey?

The Italians are on the run now and it looks as though we might well have the upper hand. At least, that's the rumour here – a desert Christmas. Supplies are short, we're a long way from our supply base now, but our Corporal Jackson managed to come up with some flour from somewhere and concocted something he called pancakes. If we couldn't have Christmas cake or pudding then we'd call it Shrove Tuesday instead. Tomorrow we continue pushing eastwards, I think.

Virginia waited for messages from this strangely familiar world. Edward might have been on a tour of the eastern Mediterranean from Benghazi to Greece.

I am being taught how to operate the radio wireless as a reserve in case anything happens to Fletcher. We have moved south with Stukas on our tail pitchforking us all the way down.

What, and where?

which has been the worst so far. Bombers followed by parachutists then troops in gliders. We were overwhelmed. They took us off by sea and I was one of the lucky ones. Thousands of Greeks and even more of our own troops were abandoned. Corporal Jackson is dead.

Anne, your second daughter, has just been born.

Back in the desert it seems that all the gains we made last year and earlier this year have come to nought. We have been pushed out except for one pocket which is being held by Aussie troops.

To and fro, to and fro Edward seemed to shift back and forward across this stretch of desert like a goatherd in search of a little grazing and water for his flock. His letters became less frequent and when they did arrive more impersonal, wrapped up in a war which he now took for granted. Virginia could barely follow the crazed sequence of its assumptions.

Virginia did not learn until much later that Tobruk had finally fallen. Rommel was closing in on El Alamein.

Happy birthday Dorothy and Anne.

The first of the brussels and parsnips.

We have three hundred Sherman tanks from the Americans. Rommel's panzers won't be able to move over the salt flats. After two weeks of shelling the German General has retreated. In the end we couldn't catch him because of the rain. In the desert! They say he lost more than four hundred tanks. It is rumoured that American and British forces under Eisenhower are about to arrive. We caught Rommel and gave him a hiding. Now they've scuttled back to join the Italians.

Cyril has taken the runner beans in their boxes from under the glass to toughen them up before planting. Spring cabbage and purple sprouting broccoli are harvested.

On a newsreel Virginia saw how a quarter of a million Axis troops surrendered on a narrow spit of land, Cape Bon, by Tunis. The Allies crossed to Sicily. Mussolini was thrown out. Sicily bent and they leapfrogged over to the Italian mainland. The new Italian government surrendered unconditionally.

The marrows have swollen. There are some late raspberries and the birds are squabbling over the black mulberry tree which Cyril has to shake to bring down its berries. The last potatoes are lifted and stored.

The newsreel whirrs. They have climbed the spine of Italy. Most of the Italians are co-operating with the Allies but the Germans are still defending every ridge, every river. Cassino. St. Benedict's Abbey.

Which proves a devastation, though neither knows it, echoing some – Warsaw – and rehearsing others – Dresden.

The picture flickers: the road has led them to Rome.

Leeks, swede and beetroot are sown, potatoes earthed up.

Sorry I missed your birthdays.

* * *

WREATHED in a mist like candyfloss Edward went on leave for the second time in November 1944. The mist was not sweet and whichever way they twisted or turned it hung about them like a shroud. And the more vigorously he turned the more tightly it wrapped itself around him. In Virginia's nostrils and throat it was acid and bitter, leaving her dry and with a bilious aftertaste. Jean asked Virginia what the problem was between them. Whether she wasn't pleased to have her husband back with her.

'Of course I'm happy he's come back safely.' This answer was not sufficient for Jean or, in truth, for Virginia herself. The sister who was so physically reticent accused her.

'You're so cool towards him. I used to be embarrassed by your spooning. Now you seem to be glad if I'm there to keep you apart.'

Virginia was not inclined to argue with the accuracy of Jean's observation. There was, she felt, a North African desert and the ridges of its dunes, the escarpments and gorges of Italy separating them now in spite of their longed-for proximity.

Edward had done as he wished and proved himself to be a courageous soldier in defiance of his first sergeant's expectations; there was a citation for the Military Cross though he had shown more than bravery – he was being put forward for a commission. In overcoming certain inhibitions – sensitivity, a sense of deference – and turning them on their head he had lost himself to Virginia in the process.

It was an afternoon when the light was thick and soupy. Virginia stood by their double bed with its green feather eiderdown when Edward came into the room. Without a word he pressed into her from behind, kissing her neck and putting his arms round to squeeze her breasts through her cardigan and frock.

He had never tried to touch her in this way before. He leaned his weight forward and pushed her face down into the eiderdown so that it was difficult for her to catch her breath and she wanted to sneeze. With Edward sprawled on top of her she felt pinned down and staked out like one of Cyril's moths. She protested but Edward ignored her half-choked cry and pulled her frock up her thighs to the small of her back. His fingers were at the clips of her suspenders and he released the tension of her stockings with a surprising deftness, she thought, for a man who had not been with his wife for so long. A hand was cupped under each of her hips to raise her buttocks from the eiderdown and she had a moment to catch her breath while he slid her knickers down to her calves. At some point in her struggle he had undone the waistband of his trousers which had fallen round his knees. He stood, leaning against the edge of the bed, and pulled her towards him; until this moment she had not made a full resistance, believing that he would stop. Now with his fingers seeking what she in schoolgirl argot still called her slit she realised that he was intent on fucking her like this but the knowledge arrived too late. He was already forcing his way up her dry walls and she cried out in pain which he might have taken for pleasure. He soon finished his business and withdrew. While she lay sobbing into the eiderdown he pulled up his underpants and buttoned his trousers. She heard nothing until the disapproving tongue of the door clicked in the mortice, a final remonstration.

I had waited so long for some tenderness and when I most expected it there was something brutal. Was it something which had rubbed on to him from the soldiers like the stench of garlic he couldn't smell on himself? I wanted, Ronald, to make it up to you for the lovelessness of your conception. As one might make allowance for a child born with some infirmity or handicap.

This abuse, the last occasion Virginia allowed a man near her, spins in her head and makes her dizzy as she unscrews the top of the Nescafé jar. Her vice is to keep two jars of instant coffee; for herself the Nescafé Gold Blend, which Emily claims is exorbitantly priced – there is some truth in the assertion – and which she swears is no better than her own house brand – which is quite false. Virginia must be careful not to confuse the two cups; not that she imagines her mother's palate retains such a fine discrimination but so that she can tell the truth if mother asks what coffee they are drinking.

Virginia lay half-choking in the eiderdown, bruised and trying to fathom her husband's behaviour. Her mind ranged from the tawdriest affair in Cairo: an archway leading into an alley where a rotting wooden door swings into a small courtyard open to the sky and with a bench in one corner; rats scurry on the flags as the whore pulls up her skirt and lies down on the bench with her knees raised and legs apart; in one hand she still clutches the packet of foreign cigarettes left by her last customer as payment, a few *piastres* echo on the stone before she receives, unflinching, her next customer. From there Virginia travelled to the most sumptuous and ornate boudoir which, she was certain, existed somewhere in Rome in spite of the restrictions imposed by a war; a bottle of chilled white wine sits on a silver tray in a red and gold room; the elegant woman wears silk stockings, an ivory cigarette holder dangles from her carmine nails, the fragrance of orange blossom drifts round her and yet she is no less, more in fact, pliant than her Egyptian counterpart; when he says, 'Turn round, lift up your skirt, lie face down on the bed' – which has a satin spread, scarlet of course – she does precisely as he instructs, and smiles too.

Such were the places where Virginia thought Edward had learned the role he had just played out with her. She had not then discovered that there are brothels which do not exist in streets or between walls but somewhere behind the eyes. When she tried to catch Edward's eyes they slipped away, avoiding her grasp like an eel at the bottom of a pail. Her sight then had to content itself with a soupy light swirling round the house as if someone were throwing buckets of the stuff from the rooftop.

The intervening years have brought dreams in which she inflicts all forms of abuse and sexual humiliation – bondage, whips, urination, defecation – on an unidentified man giving neither party the slightest pleasure, masochistic or otherwise. Now she wonders whether these will be replaced by dismembered male torsos and for the first time a wave of revulsion swells through her. She remembers glimpsing Ronald through his bedroom doorway; he was naked and lying on top of his bed with one leg crossed over the other, his penis tucked out of sight between them. He kept smoothing his hand over his hairless pubic area. This was in the summer holiday after his first year away some twenty years before and it is the first time that Virginia has allowed or found – she is not sure which – the image floating in her consciousness.

In the new year Edward had gone sweeping northwards with Montgomery across the Rhine where pleasure steamers had once cruised and would do so again. The river was completely cleared by the time Cyril's tomato seedlings were sprouting under glass nearly two inches tall. By the end of the month Munich had fallen. Montgomery then accepted unconditional surrender and Cyril helped to plant the remainder of the maincrop potatoes. The war in Europe was for the time being over, and the Axis defeated.

I waited. There was no news from Edward. I waited and waited; somewhere on another continent a cloud mushroomed trailing VJ in its wake. I waited. In the end I suppose they were obliged to write, though I sometimes felt I would rather have had their silence than their 'missing presumed' and they didn't elaborate or write again. I had no idea of where or how. Or for that matter with a war all but over, why. They had won and I had lost.

* * *

THIRTY YEARS LATER, almost, that sense of waiting clings to me still like a bad dream that won't be shaken off by the day's trivia or philosophy. Waiting which brought us to a late autumn of Republican bombings: The Tower, Woolwich, Guildford and the Horse and Groom in North Street opposite the library where I went that same morning to change books for mother. She insists on Large Print now. The assistants treat me with the muted deference generally reserved for the elderly or sick. It gives me a glimpse of a future. She makes me read to her. At the moment Agatha Christie is her favourite; she often interrupts my reading and offers a theory of her own about the identity of the murderer or the execution of the crime. Sometimes she dozes for several minutes on end and then insists I read the undemanding paragraphs again and as a result there are passages I half-know by heart. Could Hercule Poirot solve the mystery of the mutilation of my son? Who made the waiting easier in its first few years until mother's purse strings tied him, tied us all up. I'm paying, I'm paying, I'm paying, drumming in my head until I thought the skin would burst on its frame. The unspeaking and anonymous, they to whom I address these thoughts, say, But you have other family. Your sisters, for instance. How wrong they are.

Virginia recalls one of Jean's letter from the Gold Coast as it was then known. You know what they call this up-and-coming leader; Osageyfo, which means the Saviour. She described how the Saviour had his portrait printed on millions of yards of cloth so that big women with enormous hips and baskets on their heads would waddle down the street with the Saviour's high-domed forehead shining from their bottoms. Jean had patiently explained that while he talked about African unity and socialism as leader of an emergent Africa, there were far too many infant deaths, too much malnutrition, malaria, beri-beri, and that was before one had even begun to consider housing and the lack of education.

Jean's earnest grasp of Christianity had led her into action at least as radical as any gesture Julia had ever made, and yet to Virginia Jean's behaviour lacked the excitement and spontaneity which accompanied everything Julia had done. There seemed to be something automatic in her movements as if she had switched on a self-regulating mechanism somewhere and she no longer had to think through each decision afresh. It was a mode of behaviour which Virginia in an uncharitable and blinkered fashion attributed to all committed Christians. A free will, she once thought, hedged in by the narrow prescriptions of a religious creed is an illusory freedom. It was only later she understood that she had confused spirit with dogma.

Jean once told her how she had found the houseboy spitting on the veranda and told him she did not consider that to be proper behaviour for a Christian. The houseboy had replied that he thought it was cleaner to spit than to put it in one's handkerchief and carry it around in one's pocket all day long. Jean had told the anecdote in a straight-faced manner without the slightest hint of humour but Virginia knew that her own faint sense of superiority was false when Jean stayed on and on. She remained while the Gold Coast became the second black African state to achieve its measure of independence and did not budge when the first coup toppled President Nkrumah who had flown to Hanoi to proclaim world peace and then found he was not welcome back in his own country. She outlasted the Generals and Colonels, the Majors and Lieutenants clad in their uniform rhetoric and tumbling one after the other in coup after coup. She came back every three years or so to sit in the pew near the church door and under the tapestry she had helped to weave as a member of the Women's Institute before the war. 'Though I walk in the Valley of the Shadow of Death' still hanging on the wall as she had sewn it.

Jean had gone to Africa escaping the prisoner of war with whom she had, for the sake of charity, begun to correspond. When he was released and returned to England she discovered that he was blind – a fact that had remained unmentioned in his letters which had been written for him by a friend. They had tortured him and whether on purpose or not had blinded him in one eye. They had threatened him with loss of sight in the other eye but he refused to believe they would act in the same way again. He was right in a sense for he was not tortured. A local anaesthetic had been administered and an operation conducted. He told Jean, 'The last thing I saw was the face of a young woman doctor leaning over me and she whispered, "Don't worry, there are others worse off than you are. You will be all right."'

Jean nursed him back to health. The body recovered quickly enough – in a matter of months – but it took longer for other parts to heal. Then one day it dawned that she was no more the concerned and caring though distanced professional who was taking delight in the recovery of one of God's creatures. She discovered that there had grown within her like a pot plant in a dark and forgotten cupboard an attachment, stronger on his side perhaps but nevertheless a mutual growth. She grew wary and started to withdraw while he held on more tightly, eventually with a grip of desperation. She was anxious. There were other things she had to do in this world besides devote herself to the care and attention of a single individual. It had come to her without her seeking or wanting and she could not accept it. There was a tinge of envy in Virginia but she quashed it and remained magnanimous.

She was being offered what I craved, one man's devotion, and turning it down. I willed her to accept it and him. I couldn't understand. I thought that she, like me, could only be truly happy if she gave herself to a man who wanted nothing more than her. I sensed that she was momentarily tempted. She asked my advice. I wanted to say take him, take him with all you have, all your heart, but I was too conscious that that was what I wanted for myself.

Instead, I said, You must make up your own mind. Is she a little bitter like me now? I doubt it because she had what she chose. I had what I didn't choose.

Virginia went with Jean to Liverpool and stood on the quay vigorously waving her sister away in the drizzle. Jean was standing on the upper deck of the SS *Apapa* but Virginia couldn't distinguish her in the throng lining the rail. Nevertheless she continued to wave, wave at a part of her departing until her arm grew too tired to hold up any longer. Later came letters which featured beef tea and rugs on knees in the Bay of Biscay; these were exchanged for boaters and deck quoits tossed through the sizzling air into concentric white circles painted on the blistering planks of the deck. Then she melted into the deep green shadows with the molten splodges of cocoa pods scarring the dark like gold fillings in a cavernous mouth.

But your older sister, Margaret, surely she has been a prop and comfort to you, they mutter. No, wait a minute. Margaret left with her American from Rainbow Corner in search of a crock of gold. They went to golden California where I imagined the trunks of redwoods reflecting the primrose air turning to orange with just the faintest smear of pink in the setting sun later shot with grenadine. Even the Californians' skins are dusted with gold.

That, at least, was how it appeared to Virginia when Margaret had made her last visit a decade ago. Her hair was styled in imitation of Jackie Kennedy's; bouffant, back-combed and in the right shade too. It was altogether different from what Virginia had anticipated – a few years before Margaret had sent a photograph of herself in which she could be seen with her hair cut short and bleached a radiant blonde.

Margaret talked about Catholicism and how perhaps after all there might be something more in it than first met the eye. Margaret, thought Virginia, had always been aware of how she might best take advantage of the current climate.

During her visit President Kennedy was shot and she cried, saying, 'I wanna go hoam.'

She had renounced her British citizenship and carried an American passport. Virginia was not sure she now knew who this woman was, sobbing and slumped in one of their deep leather armchairs.

'I wanna call Gene. See if he's OK!'

It was unclear whether she meant Gene or the President she had never met. She saw the incomprehension on Virginia's face and misinterpreted it.

'Don't worry about the cost. I'll call collect.'

From that moment she had lost Virginia who wondered how her sister could conceive that no other disturbance than money might move her. Virginia pondered a country founded by religious exiles still looking for Saviours even in its politicians. Margaret straightened up in her chair.

'I guess I should tell the boys.' Then she burst into tears again.

'Poor, poor Jackee,' she croaked as though later she would be commiserating with the President's wife in person. Margaret's boys, Andy and Larry, came in, Virginia withdrew and as she was closing the door she could hear the voice of the woman who had been her sister slur and choke, 'They've shot our President . . .'

The following morning Margaret went into Guildford and came back with a large stiff paper carrier bag, Harvey's inscribed on its side.

'I couldn't find a decent dress shop anywhere.'

She pulled out a black dress.

'I thought I'd wear it on the day of his funeral.'

Virginia nodded.

'It seems kinda decent to show some respect.'

'Mmm . . .'

Could Margaret's skin have thickened to this degree of insensitivity? It appeared so. Virginia had written to Margaret telling her that their father had a tumour. That she might like to see him. Margaret had arrived not realising the gravity of his illness and she had remained quite oblivious of her father's condition. When she first saw him sitting in a wheelchair she said, 'Pop, you look swell. We'll have you on your feet in no time.'

Her brash cheer had irritated Virginia. Who was she to breeze in, transatlantic, with her skin glowing and her talk of good health. It occurred to Virginia that in adopting her country's optimism, Margaret had taken on board an unconscious belief in an immortality of the flesh. When Kennedy died something in her trembled and wavered, held together a few more days then shattered. Virginia found her kneeling on the bedroom carpet sobbing again but with a deeper resonance this time. She was clutching her new black dress and rocking backwards and forwards. Kennedy was dead and now her father was going to die. It came to this naturalised American with large diamonds on her fingers and a ruby brooch in the shape of a heart pinned over her own that life was not going to last. It was finite. A terrible thing for a woman of fifty to discover. For a moment she and Virginia were together but then she had gone and Virginia was left with her parents and Cyril. In the ten years since Margaret had lost more – a son in Vietnam, her marriage to Gene failed.

Now she sends a letter from Spain telling mother what Ronald has done, as if I didn't know and she might gain something by being the first to let Emily know. I remember her taking a film of Ronald in the garden. She said she didn't know what had got into Anne who refused to appear in front of her camera but Ronald, she said, would do anything in front of it. I hated the way she drew out an exhibitionism in him like some performing freak at a circus.

They interrupt me and say, But there was your father. It must have been a blessing to have him back home after so long. There they are a little nearer the mark. When he did finally come home for good there was affection, it's true. But he'd been away too long. He didn't know my past or understand my present and how that was the result of day heaped on day like an invisible accumulation of grains banked up by the wind to form a dune.

Through the kitchen window Virginia sees Cyril striding past, hunched over with a length of wire in his hand going to repair a fence in the vegetable garden.

Charles Russell tried to help his son in the garden where he now spent all the daylight and some of the darker hours too. But he had neglected Cyril for so long that at this late date the son would turn silently away when he sensed his father's approach and only grudgingly tolerate his presence in what he now considered his garden. Cyril had been left, like all Charles's children, in Emily's orbit and he was not going to let him edge his way in now that he had returned. Cyril, since he was born, had been the only man in permanent residence: Charles's visits, though lengthy, were sporadic; Edward only lived in the house for a few months; Ronald had been dispatched to school before he became old enough to prove a threat, so no one now was going to attempt a coup and end Cyril's reign in the grounds of the house.

Father must have found Cyril grown gnarled and twisted out of recognition, like one of his own pear trees. Poor father who came home from a life at sea expecting to come to grips with things now that he was ashore on *terra firma*.

Virginia would find him in the mornings sitting by the french windows with a copy of *The Times* on his knee folded open at the half-completed crossword around which he had doodled with his biro.

'Why aren't you outside?'

He would shrug and when she pressed him answer, 'I don't know where Cyril is and I don't know what I should be doing out there anyway.'

'Why don't you go for a walk? It's nice out.'

'I've already been for one.'

'What about mother?'

'She's at a meeting. Won't be back until late this afternoon.'

'I need a letter posting. Could you take it down for me?'

He sucked his pipe and without looking up from his paper nodded. He reminded Virginia of a dog being made to beg for a titbit it didn't want in the first place. She watched him walk – I'll be the fittest man in Shalford, he would say – down the drive knowing that he would linger in the post office and talk to the post-mistress, spinning out the minutes until he could, he felt with some justification, make for the Sea Horse. She wondered if the faint mockery of this quaintly named public house was not lost on her father who had spent all his life at sea without ever having seen a live sea horse himself. As he walked in under the sign with its turquoise-tinted sea she pictured the grey Atlantic waves crashing on to the deck of the merchant ship: their ferocity a jagged, vicious mouth vomiting over the rails then sucking back waving trails of foam, saliva dripping over the bows; idiot ship! Which seemed to her infinitely more terrifying than anything the enemy might cast. Wasn't there something more tangible, predictable, about the white scar of a torpedo cut under the surface of the sea? That could be understood and because it was man-made, possibly avoided, unlike the more complex ruthlessness of the shark. Like the boards of all public houses the Sea Horse's sign was impossibly romantic.

Virginia rattles open a drawer to the left of the sink and picks out a teaspoon with the robed figure of Christ forming its handle, which Jean had presented for Ronald's christening. Virginia herself has already forgiven her son. She wonders how the Deity would have reacted had Jesus turned to Lucifer but that was, fortunately, not part of his story. Would he have forgiven his Son for siding with Satan? She doubts it as she spoons the instant coffee from two different jars into the cups.

It was customary for Charles Russell to have his pint and a half of Gales Ale and then walk back to the house in good time for lunch. One day he did not appear at his usual time or even a few minutes later. There came a telephone call from the publican who told Virginia that she would be advised to come down to Shalford and collect him. Virginia found him in the Sea Horse half-shouting at an empty bar-room.

'Khrushchev hammers on a table at the UN with hish shoe and they say Khrushchev? He's a Russian, isn't he, what else would you expect from a Communist? Macmillan in Cape Town, winds of change, Nigeria independent. Good riddance they shay. Should we apply for membership of the EEC? They shrug. They don't know. What about immigration policy I asked them. They had no idea.' Then he fell silent.

'Take me home please,' he croaked.

He could barely walk to the car and Virginia had to hold his arm. He removed it with exaggerated politeness.

'I can manage quite well thank you. I didn't spend fifty years at sea without learning how to cope with a little roll now and then.' His voice was tight, wound like a spring. He swayed backwards but managed to reach the car door.

When they arrived home and Virginia had switched off the engine he said, 'I'm going to stay in the car for a little while.'

Virginia left him expecting that he would fall asleep but when she returned half an hour later he was wide awake, staring in front of him through the windscreen where he had cleared a small hole on the fogged-up glass. She could distinguish his outline through the misted screen but not his features. When she opened the car door she saw that his cheeks were wet and that he had made no attempt to dry them. She held out her hand. He took it and eased himself out of the car without a word, his face glistening.

If I had seen him cry before . . . there might have been contact. Tears of a man who'd discovered too late that lives were happening around him while he talked about the world out there.

'I had a dream last night. I'm going to die next year.'

Virginia nodded but made no comment, contemplating a mild absurdity. Yes, he liked his life to run smoothly: radio news broadcast, breakfast, walk, newspaper, correspondence, pub, lunch . . . and she understood how one set of rigid patterns might with ease be exchanged for another; the rhythms of one lifetime could not be completely jettisoned when work came to an end. But how could such precision be carried over into the timing of one's death? Yet within a year he had died.

How did he know? Was it an inspired guess, an accident, or something he'd planned? And telling me an instance of his genius in prophecy. Can one's own death be planned? I don't mean suicide. He wasted away as if he'd made up his mind he had nothing left to stay for.

Charles Russell had come back to a house whose spirit he no longer, if he ever had, possessed. It belonged to his wife who was selling produce to those who'd never had it so good; and the attendant guardians were his son who ruled the grounds and his youngest daughter who had locked herself inside and refused to discuss her brother's emasculated angle of vision; and one of his granddaughters, Anne, was he felt sure having more than was good for her; he could see it in the way she walked.

Did he give up in disgust, loneliness, regret, sorrow? I suspect all of these and more. He spent his life like me waiting for something that never arrived. A family wheel in which he, clasped with his partner, was at the hub.

But Emily was absent, surfing on waves of rising wages, car ownership, abundant television sets and washing machines, supermarkets and frozen foods; out riding on waves of foaming but not yet bio-degradable detergent.

They say, 'But you can't tap some disease or illness on the shoulder and tell it that you're ready. Can you?' Among others the word tumour was written on his death certificate. Yet I think he died of a broken spirit.

Nevertheless, in spite of all this, there are two daughters. Some compensation. Dorothy lives in Aberdeen with two children and her husband who is something in oil. Virginia has been there once but it was too cold for her though she admired the sparkle in the buildings' granite. With each invitation Virginia had used her attendance on mother as her reason for refusal and now the invitations are made perfunctorily if at all. Anne, like her Auntie Jean, is a traveller. Amsterdam, Hamburg, the Greek Islands, Turkey, Iran, India, Nepal. Emily traces her routes in the atlas and sticks the postcards which she receives in an album. Once a year or so Anne comes back for a long visit, usually with a different friend each time. They stay up late at night – the records they play penetrate Virginia's dreams – and rise late in the morning. In a few weeks they have disappeared, exotic creatures who are unable to adjust to the habitat of this house. Virginia admits to herself that neither Dorothy nor Anne occupies the circle closest to her heart. Though his absence preceded his sisters', Ronald's has been that presence she has always, still does cherish. Should she try to persuade him to return to the home he's never had? Should she?

She finds the saucepan of steaming water in her hand and pours it into one cup then the other. For a moment she panics. Which cup holds the Gold Blend? Yes. The one nearest the sink. Tray. Down in the gap between the Aga and the wall or by the vegetable rack in the pantry? She crosses to the primrose door of the pantry and raises the latch. The rush of cool air reminds her that away from the Aga the rest of the house is cold and she wonders whether mother is warm enough. Perhaps she should offer to light a fire though they have been holding back from doing so in the day to preserve their dwindling heap of coal. She remembers how she had once blacked her own face with the dust and jumped out at Margaret in the dark. What a fright she'd given her. Now Margaret's letter attempts to exact some measure of revenge on her sister.

Round and round the garden, like a teddy bear. One step, two step . . . but Cyril would never let her or anyone else come close enough. Even as a child he harboured too much resentment and assumed humility for approaches to succeed. And yet as he was the sibling who had stayed along with Virginia, their lack of harmony, their distance apart, is a constant goad and reminder of failure. She still tells him to remove his cap inside the house and sullenly he still obeys. She remembers him sleeping with his light on because he was afraid of the dark while the others, older and younger, showed no such fear. She half expects when she takes mother her coffee to find Cyril harbouring in the shadows cast by her skirt, cringing and looking for affection, encouragement. She recalls the longest speech he ever made:

'I was there before you were born, standing in mummy's bedroom, light coming through a crack in the curtains, the carpet tickling my bare feet. Daddy was away but there were two figures humped like sand dunes under the covers. Two, not one! That was you, that was you!'

Virginia didn't understand what Cyril was saying then, only later, when he talked about mummy and daddy's friend, was the seed sown. And now it hits her like a rush of heat from the Aga when she opens the door. Bertrand and her mother. Surely not?

'And pee trickled down my leg and soaked the carpet. Wet like when I knelt in the snow. That woman Julia whispering in mummy's ear. And mummy's laughter, like walking on splinters of glass. None of you knew but I stayed with her and heard how that wicked woman's words broke her into thousands of fragments. That's why I've stayed with her. Not like you because there was nowhere else for me to go, but because I understood; and she needed my protection.'

Virginia had scorned and laughed at Cyril's words. Then he was a man but still a boy, trusted only in the garden and not permitted to wander along the road leading away from their mother. And this constriction had in its turn led to Cyril restricting his own gestures of emotion to the point of an almost absolute stillness and silence. The garden had become the sole area in which he might exercise control and have some expectation of success in the nurture of living things. Now Virginia questions whether it is Cyril who has failed. Certainly she has not succeeded. It may be, she thinks, that the measurements of her rule were in the wrong dimensions. Which should she choose? After all, it is Cyril who is now outside what is Emily's immediate orbit, the house, and she, Virginia, who is confined inside like some minor planet held in place by the attraction of her mother's force.

* * *

BECK AND CALL. Virginia has to wait on Emily now. The obligatory chores jump up at random: awkward buttons that mother can't reach any longer, a supporting arm up the stairs, the adjustment of a pillow, a search for her glasses, tucking the fading rug under her legs, attendance on her cries in the small hours, changing the channel from the news to the ice skating. In spite of these habitual dependencies, Emily refuses to let go, especially of the empire she has built out there. That chain of shops everyone has entered at least once in their lives if not once a week. Virginia wonders what will happen to the business mother has so meticulously nurtured for more than half a century. Not that she expects, not that she wants to shoulder its burdens, but once upon a time she had thought Ronald might inherit. Now she doubts whether mother will wish to hand over to her . . . grandchild is how they will have to think of him now.

Beyond the sweating kitchen window the slate-blue and pink of a chaffinch darts at a net sock filled with nuts and dips away in the corner of Virginia's eye.

She should take mother her coffee. What is there left for Virginia but to wait on mother? She puts the cups of coffee on a tray from the kitchenware department and picks it up.

Bowed at your altar, bent in your service, I am coming, although I know it has taken me an age.

Bearing the tray Virginia crosses to the sitting-room door which she opens and then it clicks in the mortice after her.

As soon as she sees her mother in her chair by the french window opposite the empty one where Charles used to sit Virginia makes a guess at what will happen now. Emily will ask her about Ronald, his change, why she had to hear it from Margaret instead of Virginia herself; there will be questions about the purpose behind Ronald's action. Which Virginia will make no pretence to try to explain. Emily's list will include references to Virginia's father and to Virginia's husband. When accusations are being dealt Emily always ensures these two men at least receive a full hand of recrimination. She could never leave them out. Virginia puts down the tray on a small side table.

'Here's your coffee. And biscuits. Your favourite.'

'You've been such a long time. What've you been doing?'

'Only making coffee for you,' says Virginia, glancing at Margaret's letter in her mother's lap. She does not bother to prepare herself to listen to the hurt in Emily's voice which she has heard for so many years now it no longer holds any surprises. Or, at least, that is what she thinks until her mother begins to speak.

RONNY

AN EASY BIRTH I heard someone say much later. 'Slipped out just like a wet cake of soap out of your hand.' There was no anticipating the trouble and heartache I would bring in my train with such a smooth and well-timed arrival. They told me later that I came on the exact day that everyone had said I would in August. Unless, of course, you take into account the retained afterbirth as heralding trouble in my wake. I was even found to be the right weight – nine pounds twelve ounces, they liked their babies bigger then in those retricted, austere days. Large, healthy babies, the bigger the better – this is how the future will be – large-limbed and glowing with all the fuel we can muster to send it on its way into the world. An embodiment of the vitality and optimism of our times.

Years afterwards, bloated with an insubstantial affluence, we demanded that they slim down and were born leaner, lighter and more muscular, fit to run the world's race. Oh yes, we suddenly realised there was competition but I was born in a country that still had no qualms about using the epithet 'great' in front of its name. Great, yes, great babies for a great country in a world that was great and that was going to be even greater. Just recently it seems to have shrunk a little. Somewhat dwarfed now but not me, not then.

My mother turned to the nurse – my father was not there, not in the delivery room, of course, it was 1945, but not outside pacing or fidgeting in a chair and jumping up and shouting, 'Is it a boy or a girl?' And not at home looking after my sisters and wondering if everything was all right and whether it was a boy or a girl. And not in a shop or a factory or at sea saying to himself, 'Has it come yet? Is everything all right? Is it a boy or a girl?' And not as far as was known any father anywhere asking, 'Is it a boy or a girl?'

So in the glare my mother held out her arms and asked, 'Is it a boy or a girl?' 'It's a boy,' said the midwife wiping away the blood. 'My first,' she breathed. 'And he's really bonny, A good nine and a half. Here, you take him.' My mother folded me in her arms and put me to her breast straightaway where I had no hesitation or difficulty in fastening on to her nipple and sucking mother's milk for the first time.

In months to come she would say again and again to a friend or neighbour, 'If he doesn't stop soon that child will suck me dry. He can never get enough.' And, of course, it was excruciating for her when at the end of an especially long and demanding feed I would cry for more which she did not have to give. I bit on her already sore mamilla with my gums – the teeth forming below giving them an extra hardness – and I drew blood. I would pummel her breast and turn puce in my rage and frustration that there was nothing left for me to drink. And how she tried to feed my thirst. She would wake in the night and sit bolt upright staring into the orange sodium light which bathed the room through the half-open windows. Had she heard me crying or was I just turning over? I was her third child and yet she slept as lightly as if she anticipated that something momentous would happen any minute – I sensed then from the time of my birth mother in an almost perpetual state of agitation and excited by my presence – she woke when I made even the slightest of movements in my sleep to find me breathing peacefully. Not considering that she could go back to sleep again she turned and took a shallow dish from the bedside table.

Years later she picked up this dish with its dark-brown glaze and held it under my nose, saying, 'What was in here was for you and now look what's happened. Look what you've done,' and she started to shake and dropped it on the linoleum. Surprisingly it didn't shatter, only cracked. Last time I saw it, it was on a mantelpiece filled with dandelions and forget-me-nots she had picked herself. The yellow and blue flowers were overshadowed by the darkness of the glaze which seemed to have grown more sombre with age and the flowers were wilting, for my mother would not put water in the dish. She claimed that since it had fallen and got cracked (she said 'fallen' not 'dropped') it would not contain liquid for any length of time: that she had tried and the liquid had run through the crack – invisible on account of its darkness – and left the dish bone dry so there was no point in filling it any longer.

So while I lay asleep in my crib she took this dish and, opening the flap on her nightgown, which my grandmother, Emily, had designed and made for her, she placed it under her breast and began gently but firmly to express the milk from her engorged breast. She hoped that by doing this she could build up a reserve of milk and get ahead of my thirst.

It is said that if the milk supply is stimulated this will cause more milk to flow, with more flowing more will be drunk thus causing a renewed burst of milk production and so the cycle is stepped up another gear each time. On this basis one mother could in theory feed all the world's babies with her infinitely expanding supply of milk. Yes, I was born at a time when there were no horizons to the fields of endless expansion where everyone walked.

My mother believed in this limitless expanse too (who didn't?) so she sat squeezing her milk into a dish to feed me later with an extra dose of what her body could give. In the orange light, with the cries of children playing late on a summer's evening among the darting bats trying to catch the insects the swallows hadn't managed to snap up, she continued to fill the dish. She refused to admit that she would never produce quite enough to feed me and that my diet would have to be supplemented from an artificial product, i.e. powdered milk. It was a time when there was no question of disgrace or stigma attached to using a glass container or rubber teat with only one hole for the new-born, three for an older or greedy baby and even in those she had to prick a fourth with a darning needle to quench my thirst. She didn't want to give me the man-made product, not because she thought it was unhealthy or unsafe but because she wanted everything to come directly from her to me without interference. Although she had living proof in the shape of my two sisters that she was no Virgin Mary, somehow the idea of anyone else having had a hand in my creation seemed to fade as I grew older and by the time I am able to recall – about three years old – she had so enclosed me in her world that father, my father anyway, simply ceased to exist. If there were men they were viewed from within mother's compound and her stance at the gate was as protective as that of any soldier.

* * *

UNCLE CYRIL was my mother's brother. Uncle Cyril was a magician. Not a professional, though doubtless he would have liked to become one had circumstances permitted. That phrase 'had circumstances permitted' was my grandmother's refrain, a note of lament on Cyril's behalf. Cyril could have done this, done that, done anything had events walked a certain path. Or, 'more accurately' she once said, 'had he wanted'. Uncle Cyril thought that he could have been a magician if only his family had allowed him to become one. At least, that is what he used to whisper to me in the vegetable garden or the glasshouse.

Family in this case meant my grandmother. Grandfather went to sea and stayed there for most of the year, year in year out. He felt safer there than in the surface-calm waters of home where he could never negotiate the undercurrents set swirling and skilfully navigated by my grandmother. He could cope with slippery decks, with a ship listing at forty-five degrees in tumultuous seas, with (earlier on in his career) dry biscuits and brackish water, with cajoling and threatening the ordinary seamen to work harder, with weeks at sea and no sight of land, with the rough homosexual practice below deck, but he could not manage my grandmother.

Once we were assembled to say goodbye to him, before he set off on another voyage. It seemed to me that we were forever saying 'hello' or 'goodbye' to him and never encountered him except in the circumstances of homecoming or farewell. We were all gathered together in the garden of my grandparents' house where I was brought up. There were my grandparents, Uncle Cyril, Auntie Margaret, Auntie Jean, my mother, my sisters, two American cousins (Margaret's sons) and myself.

It was hoped that this was the last voyage my grandfather would make before he retired and my grandmother said to him, 'Knowing you, you'll go and get yourself drowned just to spite me after all these years.' A watery smile from under my grandfather's beard.

'What are you smirking at? Pour me another cup of tea, Cyril, please.'

'I was just thinking,' said my grandfather.

'When did you ever think about me left at home all these years?

You've roamed the seven seas as if there was no tomorrow. God knows I've been patient enough waiting for you to come home after months on end and then you disappear again before I've had time to blink. Though you had time enough to leave me with four children to bring up on my own. Cyril, ask your sisters if they'd like another cup of tea.'

And Cyril, my uncle who wanted to be a magician, obliged his mother by leaning over to my mother and her sisters, asking them all in a voice with just a tremble of resentment, 'Margaret, Jean, Virginia, would you like another cup of tea?'

'Oh, yes please,' said Jean, always polite.

'Sure, that'd be great, Cyril,' boomed Margaret, leaning forward in her deck chair and handing him her cup, tinkling as china does on a shaking saucer. Her hand was unsteady, I thought from bending forward in a deck chair that sank and swung in the soft lawn. I glanced up and saw that my mother and Auntie Margaret had tears streaming down their cheeks. They were flushed from laughing at some private joke which fell like a shadow across Uncle Cyril struggling to raise himself from the striped orange, green and yellow deck chair.

I was splitting daisy stems with my thumbnail and threading them through one another to make a chain but I let them fall on to the grass and stared at my Uncle Cyril. Come on, what are you waiting for? Do it. Cast some spell. Throw some magic over them. Make them all dissolve in a puff of sulphurous smoke. Or turn their tea instantly cold and bitter. Or unhook the deck chairs' wooden catches and send them sprawling on to the lawn – grass stains on their frocks and tangled limbs.

For an instant as he struggled out of the chair Uncle Cyril looked me in the eye and then with a grunt he was out and bent over the tea trolley busying himself with the cups and milk and sugar and pouring the tea through the silver strainer. Grandfather was saying, 'You pour, I'll hand the cups round.' I went back to my daisy chain and at the far end of the lawn I could hear my sisters giggling, beyond them the shouts of the two American cousins sounded like the cries of exotic creatures from an unknown continent. I sensed the deck chairs were still faintly shaking. Magician, where were your changes, your transformations?

'Girls,' cried my grandmother over the roses and down to the end of the lawn, 'gather round.' She neglected to summon her American grandsons which was, I sensed, a quite deliberate omission and a shame too. For I found their strange spiky haircuts and nasal voices quite alluring. So my sisters came skipping across the shaded draughtboard of the lawn, holding hands and kicking up their summer frocks – a confusion of nature in the pastel tones of blue and pink against the relentless emerald of the grass.

It had taken Uncle Cyril all morning to push the mower in the criss-cross grid demanded by my grandmother.

'It would be nice to have the lawn looking right today, Cyril. It is your father's last day home and for once we are all here to say goodbye to him. No, don't start it yet, the grass is still too wet.'

So Uncle Cyril had laboured to reduce the grass to symmetrical shapes alternately light and dark green and was still raking up the last of the cut grass when grandmother, standing at the french windows, clapped her hands and called, 'Haven't you finished yet, Cyril? Do hurry up. There's a good boy.'

'I love the smell of fresh cut grass, don't you?' said grandmother, addressing the crescent of her daughters in their striped deck chairs. They all agreed that the perfume of newly mown grass was one of the highlights of summer.

Auntie Jean said, 'I do love the smell, I think the Garden of Eden must have been like it. Smell of perpetual summer. Only it is such hard work raking up the grass afterwards. I never manage to get it all up and then some of it turns yellow and spoils the effect.'

'What you need is a mower with a hood on the front to catch the grass as it spins up through the blades,' said Uncle Cyril without raising his head from the business of pouring tea.

Grandmother snorted. 'Nonsense. A bit of raking never hurt anyone.'

You could see it in the way Cyril bent over the teacups, hunched up and wound like a spring almost to the point of snapping and sending the works flying everywhere. Then why don't you mow your own bloody lawn or at least help me to rake up the grass?

Grandmother again, 'You should take a leaf out of Cyril's book. He enjoys the exercise, don't you?'

Uncle Cyril went off into the house to fetch more hot water in case anyone wanted a second cup of tea. His training was almost perfect. Grandfather called after him, 'Do you want a hand?' Uncle Cyril passed between the french windows and into the cool gloom of the house without appearing to have heard his father.

'Our gardener says it doesn't harm the grass in any case if you leave a few cut blades on it. And he says if you rake it gently that's good for it,' drawled Auntie Margaret.

'How often do you have to cut the grass over there?' asked grandfather. Margaret showed her big, strong teeth.

'That depends. It can kinda creep up on you quick in summer.'

'Quite,' said grandmother.

My mother was silent.

Grandfather started to hand round the cups of tea. First grandmother, then Auntie Margaret followed by Auntie Jean and Virginia, my mother, my two sisters – Anne after Dorothy – and last grandfather himself, heaping sugar into his cup as if to make up for years of deprivation. Grandmother nodded in the direction of the sugar bowl. 'And too much of that isn't good for you either.' As Uncle Cyril was still in the house his cup sat on the trolley with a finger of milk in the bottom waiting for its tea.

The rigid order of the tea's distribution was a precise measurement of the family hierarchy, from the summit of my grandmother down through her daughters and granddaughters to the base of grandfather and Cyril. I, along with my American boy cousins, was not offered tea or anything else to drink.

Grandfather eased himself into his chair and following grandmother's lead everyone raised their teacups to their lips. My mother interrupted the rhythm of the movement to say the first words of hers I remember that afternoon, 'What about Ronald? Don't you think he might be thirsty too?' My grandmother paused, frozen in mid-gesture like a conductor who has just noticed that a member of the orchestra is playing in the wrong key. She returned her cup to its saucer, not a drop of the chestnut liquid (she liked her tea strong) drunk. The sound of china on china echoed round the summer garden like a gunshot.

At the moment Uncle Cyril appeared at the french windows holding a jug of hot water. Grandmother smiled at my mother and then looked at me hidden in the shadow of mother's deck chair.

'Poor thing. I'd forgotten all about him. Of course he should have a drink.'

'I'll get it,' said grandfather, about to climb out of his chair once more.

'No, you stay there. Cyril! Fetch your nephew a drink.'

Please, Uncle Cyril, pull one out from behind your ear, your pocket, jacket tails. Yes, on a special occasion like a father's farewell, a jacket even in midsummer. 'Put it back on after you finish raking the lawn but before you set out the deck chairs – some under the Orange Pippin please, you know your sister Jean finds the direct sunlight too strong to sit out in.' Emily had instructed her only son and he had obeyed.

But before Cyril could get away to finish the lawn grandmother stopped him in his tracks. 'Don't you remember how your stupid father once took you all to Worthing for the day and when you came back she was like a lobster and then a tomato. And I had to sit up with her all night, your father wouldn't, said he was too tired from the sun and fresh air, all night dabbing calamine on to her braised skin with wads of cotton wool. Used up the whole packet. She moaned when I put it on and moaned even worse when I didn't. She kept you all awake, well, you all had restless nights. Though that might have been too much sun, I suppose. Your father said how could he be expected to know that she'd burn so badly. He always thought plenty of fresh air and exercise would keep you all happy. But what did he know about children and how you treat them and bring them up and look after them? All very well for him to come home and take you all out to the beach and let your sister Jean stay out in the sun too long. Is that the way you look after a redhead? Oh, they burn so easily when their skin's the colour of pale copper. Where did it come from, he said, that colour? There's no one on my side of the family with red hair and ginger freckles, it must be from yours. And then he couldn't sit up with her. Exhausted from shepherding you round all day. Had a headache. You wouldn't think he was a sailor which is what I said to him. He laughed and said it was easier on board in charge of sixty men than out at the beach with four children. I think he went back to London the next day though for all I know he wasn't due to sail for another week and had just gone there for a rest and God knows what else before he was confined to ship again. So he left me with Jean looking like she'd just come out of a gas oven mark five and I swear that she's never been the same since about the sun. Can you blame the poor child? Roasted alive. Even when she goes out into the garden now – and you know how fond she is of gardening – she has to wear a cardigan so she doesn't get burnt. I'm sure her skin has never recovered. I ask you, a cardigan on a hot summer's afternoon. That is why she finds gardening so tiring. She loves it but can only do a little at a time and then she's exhausted. After the time in Worthing she always chose to sit in the shade when the rest of you were out playing in the sun. Even at the seaside I had to make sure that we took an umbrella or sunshade or sit her in the shadow of the breakwaters and that meant moving camp half-way through the day. And it was with the greatest difficulty that I could persuade her to go swimming and if she agreed it was only if I covered her up completely. So she would walk across the stones hobbling and with one of your father's old shirts flapping in the breeze. It came right down to her knees so that the only part of her showing was her calves – white skinny calves covered in fine auburn hairs. And then she'd float around in the water like a jellyfish with the air billowing up and around the shirt. Afterwards, when it grew heavy, it pulled her down to the bottom. Don't you remember how you once had to rescue her even though she was your older sister who could swim long before you could? But she went to the bottom like a stone and you had to pull her out. Your father wasn't there, of course, but when he heard about it weeks later he said it was a disgrace her sinking like that. I'll say that for him – he did teach you all how to swim, though I don't know if teach is the right word. He'd swim out into the middle of the baths with you holding on so that you were quite happy and then he'd let go. You all survived it and learned to swim so I suppose he'd say that it worked. Even after you had dragged her out and I had run over the rocks towards you both, cutting and bruising my feet, she still refused to sit in the sun. She sat shivering up against the dark-green breakwater and out of the light her skin looked green too. You'd think that someone who'd just been flailing around under-water would want to be out in the sun to get some warmth and put their blood back into circulation. But she wouldn't. I don't know what we would've done if we'd had Jean in a country where it was sunny all year round. Just as well for her that our summer isn't usually a long one otherwise she'd have to spend most of her time indoors. And then she'd really miss the garden . . . so do make sure you put at least one deck chair under the Pippin where she can enjoy sitting out with us in no danger of getting burnt.' Emily then waved Cyril away to finish his raking and put out the deck chairs.

Uncle Cyril, a sparkling clear glass of water is all I want, whipped from out of the air by a loop and a twist of your wrist, curving like some mysterious distant snake. And if you can't produce it like that I can do without. It wasn't me that asked. I was keeping quiet here behind my mother's chair when she asked your mother. Emily, my grandmother, has asked you and no one has consulted me at all. I could've made do if it means you have to fetch it yourself. Your father Charles, my grandfather, offered to go and get it for me but was told to stay put.

'After all, it is your last afternoon tea with the family.'

'Yes, father, do sit down. Cyril will fetch Ronald a glass of . . . what is it he wants?'

Nothing really. I don't want to trouble anyone, least of all my Uncle Cyril who teaches me card tricks when my mother and his mother aren't looking. My mother asked me, 'Ronald, would you like a nice cold glass of milk? I'm sure there is some in the pantry and it stays so cool there . . . '

My sisters giggled and I could see in the way they nuzzled into each other what they were thinking: our younger brother Ronald, look at him playing with daisy chains and too shy to speak when asked a question in front of a group of adults. Poor thing! We will have to help him. Dorothy spoke first. 'Mummy, Ronald doesn't like milk.'

'I know, dear, but it is so good for him.'

Then Anne, 'Couldn't he have something else just for once, Mummy? It is like a holiday with grandpa going away to-morrow. Please.'

'What would you like, then?' asked my mother.

Over her shoulder I could see Uncle Cyril hovering in the background by the french windows holding a jug of hot water.

I felt that at any moment he could walk out and pour it over the nearest flower bed, scalding its pink roses. (Peace, I know now.)

'Nothing, I don't want anything,' I whispered into the grass.

'But you can't have nothing, you will wilt away in this heat,' my mother insisted.

She had insistence off to a T, always making it sound to everyone except myself that she had only my best interests at heart. Perhaps insistence is an unavoidable corollary of motherhood that a child may have to suffer. Though my mother never appeared to demand that Anne or Dorothy do anything against their wishes. They floated through their days whilst I negotiated mine, being prodded this way and that. Parental assumptions in collusion with expectation – how much they have to answer for and explain . . .

Uncle Cyril was still standing as patient and resigned as a butler at the french windows.

'Water,' I croaked.

His mother called across the lawn, 'He'll have a glass of water and make sure you run the tap first so it's cold.' Uncle Cyril's ghostly face splintering back into the shadows of the house. There, it seemed, was the true magic: Uncle Cyril shattered like a glass by my grandmother's voice pitched on the very note which could pierce him and no one else. Who could fail to notice the effect which her tone had on Uncle Cyril's behaviour?

I knelt up and whispered to my mother, 'I don't really mind. I'm not very thirsty. I can do without.'

'No, you can never do without,' she said, 'never,' and she took a handkerchief from somewhere in her sleeve and dabbed it on my forehead. 'You look so very hot. A drink will cool you down.'

And how I need cooling down in this room in Egypt. When the window is open the air-conditioning starts up more and more often with its whirring and churning digging into my half-sleep. Leila comes in and closes the window. Hearing her footsteps I open my eyes and she smiles.

'Please open the window.'

'But if the window is open the air-conditioning makes a lot of noise.'

'I know but I'd rather have the window open.'

She shrugs her shoulders and opens the window for me. 'What is it they say? Mad dogs and the Englishman.'

'Men, not man. And that no longer applies anyway.'

'You're crazy. You complain about the heat and then go walking about in it as if it was an English spring day.'

'I don't think I'm up to walking just yet.'

'You know what I'm talking about. You say you dislike the heat but you . . . you encourage it.'

She was trying to look stern and make her voice sound cross but just as some inject venom into the most innocent of phrases she was incapable of disguising the true intention of her words – kindness. It flows out of some through no purpose or deliberation of their own and they can no more help it than you can stop water pouring out of a tap. You can turn it off for a while but it is still there waiting to offer itself. She had learned her English from such a good teacher that she was capable of, no, comfortable in, saying exactly what she didn't mean.

'But if the window is closed I feel enclosed, cut off from what is happening outside. At least with it open I can hear something.'

'What can you see from there? Tell me.'

'Flat roofs.'

'They don't need any other type. No rain.'

* * *

GREEN BLADES scything each other on the hillsides and the bluebells standing their ground in the June rain – a wind blowing it across in thin slanting gusts. The clouds, mushroom texture and colour, nibbled away at their edge by the sun which then takes a big bite out of one. The cloud dissolves in sunlight and at last we can run out from under the gloom of the pine trees and yews, mainly yews with their green under-water light-deadening sound – we glide through them like ivory figures, Dorothy and Anne ahead of me. The pale shades of their frocks flitting between the deep yellows and browns of the wood. They flash on and off like fireflies tricked by the darkness into thinking it is night-time. Running along the path worn smooth I trip and graze my knee but I stand up and refuse to cry. I will be brave and catch my sisters.

Swimming through the olive air their frocks flashing pink and primrose – tropical fish in a tank darting in and out of the weed – and then suddenly as we approach the edge of the wood a trickle of light filters through as if from the side of the tank. The outermost yews let their branches curve almost down to the ground and to escape from the wood I can see Dorothy raising a branch (she is taller than Anne) for Anne to slide under and out into the light and the long sweet grass. Then she follows and lets the branch fall behind her like closing a curtain on a summer's evening when you can still feel and sense the light beyond.

'Yes, Leila, I must have the window left open even if it means the room is hotter.'

So I am left in the dark, still running yards behind them down the slope when I reach that branch sweeping down to the ground. I hardly pause, but bent over and scuttling sideways like a crab on the floor of the sea bed I expel myself from the wood into an explosion of light bombarding the meadow. Where have they gone? I can't see them – only the buttercups, ochre smears in the grass, thousands of concentrated suns pulsing at me. There is a line in the grass leading diagonally down and across the meadow to another line of trees. Could that be the path they have taken or are they hiding somewhere off it? Or could they, as soon as they left the wood, have turned along its border and cut back in as I left?

Go on, down. They wouldn't have gone back into the wood. They didn't like it either, found it spooky, too, though they won't expect me to copy them. Not copy them at all.

Remember once when you heard Dorothy screaming and ran up the stairs two at a time. It was coming from the bathroom. Electricity and water flashed through your mind though you weren't sure whether that would make her scream or just knock her out. The bathroom door was locked. Dorothy stopped for a split second to catch her breath before she could start screaming again.

'What's the matter? It's me. Ronald. Let me in.'

She screamed again, louder than before. You banged on the flimsy door panel with both fists, shouting, 'Let me in. Why won't you let me in?'

She was scrabbling with the bolt and the screaming had subsided to a sobbing. Opening the door she pulled you in and pushing you in front of her pointed at the bath.

'There, it's in there.'

It was a spider. Quite a small one as spiders come. You knew at once what she expected of you.

'Do something!' You were frozen stiff, unable to move, so you shrank back into Dorothy's warmth. You were terrified of them too and yet there was your elder sister shoving you forward and whimpering.

'Ronald, do something. I can't stand them. I hate them. Please, please.'

You had to take your terror and hold it at arm's length and pretend that if it was there at all (which didn't occur to Dorothy) you could with no trouble put it away on the shelf. She didn't see that it was the same for you as it was for her. She was older but she was a girl and you, you were a boy who could put spiders on the back of his hand and let them run around – that was the very least of your capabilities; surely you, the only male in the family, carried live frogs in your pocket and would even pop a squirming newt down the inside of your own shirt to exhibit your bravery just as Victoria Transome's brother had done.

'Get rid of it!'

You closed your thumb and forefinger round one of its pencil-line legs to pick the thing up and the leg came away. Why wouldn't she do it herself? Couldn't, she said. You couldn't either but you had to because she demanded it.

'Pick it up.' It was trying to climb up the side of the bath but sliding back down the enamel at each attempt.

Now. Your open palm came down on it and scrunched it up into a tight ball with white knuckles. You drew the fist out of the bath and walked to the window as if you were holding a bomb that could explode at the slightest provocation. Tense, lips hardly parted.

'Open the window, Dorothy.' You a ventriloquist's dummy with the voice coming from elsewhere. 'Carefully.' Your hand moving slowly outside the window, unclenching itself tentatively in imitation of a hand testing itself to check whether anything is broken after an accident. With your hand palm down the spider should have fallen but somehow it stuck there, flexing its seven remaining legs and you had to shake it off. The release as it fell away, wafting from side to side as though suspended on one of its own invisible threads, was as if someone had unwound a prickly blanket wrapped round your head on a close summer's day. Dorothy stepped forward and hugged you.

'But you're so hot and shaking too.'

Later Dorothy and Anne began to realise (unlike your mother until it was too late for her and she grew irreconcilable) and they expected something different. Though it was only Anne who showed the flexibility to accept fully the demands of altered expectations. Dorothy clung like your mother to the old order.

No. They weren't in the yew wood. They wouldn't have gone back. Too gloomy and elvish. They might have expected me to go back but not themselves, not on a shimmering day when a meadow stretches sweeping down and away from your feet to the welcome dapple of a deciduous wood in the valley where the light falls in pools between the tree trunks. The scene so perfect a recreation of the fragile and chimerical nature of an English summer's day.

Run down the meadow past the tangle of the wild rosebush like a woman more beautiful because she has forgotten to put a brush through her hair. The grass still damp from the shower. Wait a minute, the stalks are newly flattened and bruised to one side of the path. Stop and listen with your eyes darting everywhere as if suspended on the ends of elastic bands. Step forward on the path a couple of paces and just as you are about to continue there is a rustle from somewhere behind. Is it the rosebush in the breeze? Or the fat underbelly of a blackbird scraping along the ground before it skids and whirrs away into the soft air? Look carefully through the bush at its edges where its scribble is less dense. There is at least one pale shape beyond the confusion of stems, brambles, leaves and flowers. It is camouflaged until you stop and see that it is not a mass of flowers on the far side of the bush but the outline of a pink frock criss-crossed by the bush. Anne, it is Anne who was then still wearing pale pink.

Playing hide-and-seek, this was the moment I savoured most. I knew where they were hiding but they didn't know yet if I had seen them or whether I would continue down the path. They were in doubt about whether I could find them at all but I knew I had. Until this day, this Coronation summer, when we had played hide-and-seek it had always been Dorothy and Anne hiding or seeking together, not Dorothy and Ronald or Anne and Ronald and yet I longed to hide with Dorothy or Anne, to lie huddled in the grass behind a bush holding hands and whispering, 'Ssh, I can hear someone coming. Keep still. Don't move.' And then my sister's arm shaking with the excitement and suspense of possible discovery.

There was nothing malicious in my sisters' behaviour as a unit which left me to operate on my own. It was an assumption inherited as much from my mother as from the time in which we lived and what was expected; boys didn't want to hide with girls, they wanted to go out and find them giggling together behind the wild rosebush. They wanted to go away from them and achieve great things in the world like their fathers and grandfathers had done before them. Well, perhaps not literally speaking, but you could assume the mantle of maleness without there being any father to pass it on.

I once said to my mother, 'Tell me about my father. The father I don't know, who I am supposed to inherit.'

She looked at me as though I had said something obscene and then went back to her quilting. Quilting had apparently become a solace – how bitter a one I couldn't have guessed – and she would sit for hours stitching like a lady in a medieval romance waiting for her husband to return from the battle or quest.

The music from Anne's record player could be heard swirling round the house. *Love Love Me Dooh, You Know I'll Be True, So Please Love Me Dooh.* I spoke to mother.

'He was a hero, wasn't he? That's what they say.'

'Who is "they"?'

'Grandad told me years ago.'

'What did he say, then, about your father?'

'That he was a very brave man and that it was a tragedy he disappeared in the service of his country and freedom.'

'Yes. Do you like this?' she said, holding out a cushion cover with a chocolate brown and cream mix of threads.

'Yes what? Yes it was a tragedy, or yes he was a brave man, or yes . . .'

'Can you see what it is?'

'No.'

'It's a flock of sheep. Look, here are their little black faces and there are their hooves.'

'Why won't you talk about him?'

'I think I might have it finished in time for your grandma's birthday. I think she'll like it, don't you?'

Anne was playing the same record over and over again so that *Love Love Me Do* not only underscored our conversation but became an anthem for the day.

'If I was born in August 1945 how could my father have died during the war?'

'He could have. He could have, don't you see? Count. Go on, count backwards from August 1945.' It was the first time she had ever spoken to me about a father, my father, and she was vehement. It was like opening the valve on a pressure cooker and trying to avoid the hiss of escaping steam threatening to scald. 'Have you done it yet? Have you counted?'

'It comes to December 1944 – the war was more or less over by then.'

'More or less,' she muttered and withdrew to her needlepoint and the fine concentration of her quilting. Her fingers were poised but did not move and her eyes were fixed, staring at the cover as though she had lost the thread. 'Please go and tell Anne to turn down that noise, I can't concentrate. And I'm sure your grandma doesn't like it any more than I do.'

The very door of Anne's room seemed to be rattling in the mortice. Knocked, no answer, knocked again, no answer. Why did she have to have it so loud? Open and enter. They were on her bed. Two of them. Anne and a boyfriend. I had forgotten. A tangle of knee, shin, upper arm, hair, thigh, waist, elbow, palms, lips jumped out at me. Clothes on the floor, on the bed, round ankles and necks and *Love Me Do* screaming from the corner of the bedroom. Out, back out before you are seen. And that was what I did. They didn't even hear me shut the door and I crept away on tiptoe although at that volume the Beatles would have drowned the sound of boots on a parade ground.

Just before lunch, in winter always taken at half past twelve at Emily's insistence, there was a hush which fell over the house as if someone had died. They had finally stopped playing the record and I thought, they've finished. It's all over. She's done it at last. How happy she must be. How relaxed and content. Another initiate. But what is this silence creeping round the house and laying its dust over everything? Perhaps it had only happened because they were trying to keep warm. Anne and her friend snuggling close together on a late October morning in her cold bedroom. If you wanted to blame anyone Grandma could be held responsible. She would neither install central heating, though she could more than afford it, nor would she allow a fire to be lit in the bedroom until after five o'clock in the evening.

I put on a coat and went out into the vegetable garden. There was Uncle Cyril bending over in the distant and shrouded greenhouse examining pots in the cap he had taken to wearing since he had started to go bald. It was silent out there too and Uncle Cyril's presence muffled and enclosed behind the smoking glass which was patterned in whorls of frost only underlined the quiet. My breath rose in steaming clouds.

It was all grey and subdued under a cloak of drizzling mist. This is what it might have been like when . . . when . . . in the thick air ill-defined shapes which could have been dinosaurs, mammoths or pterodactyls turned out on closer inspection to be rhododendron bushes, the trunks of trees or their branches. How did Anne feel? Did she have some sense of emerging out of a murk into a greater clarity with more space and more light, or did she still feel herself surrounded by a clamminess that made her shiver? Please put that record on again and break through. Nothing. Wet leaves and a lawn squelching. A broken hoe and a spade leaning, dying in the clods. Anne in her thinness (born after rationing was introduced but before the scent of a possible victory was in the air) with her skin pulled tight around its frame like a tent stretched over its poles; she always gave off a translucent sheen as though somewhere inside her someone had turned on a light that wouldn't or couldn't be turned off. Her straight fair hair parted in the middle and shining with lacquer that she would later abandon as a symbol of . . . artificiality? . . . consumerism? . . . capitalism? It was to become long and untrimmed with its split ends showing in the sunlight like a barbed-wire fence glinting. I used to picture myself, imagine how I would look with her hair. How it would have transformed my face and the way I held my head. It would have changed the very manner of my walk and lent me that gloss which Anne was soon to neglect.

* * *

REMEMBER THE FUSS in Harvey's when I tried on a hair-piece? 'Just for fun,' I said to Dorothy who having just had all of her brown curls cut off was looking for a consolation and protection in the form of what she called a 'false coiffure'.

'Has she gone and bought one of those wigs?' said grandma, spitting out the word wig. 'I told her she'd regret it. A woman cutting off all that God gave her is bound to end in unhappiness.'

'You shouldn't,' whispered Dorothy, amused in spite of herself. 'They'll throw us out. That doesn't suit you. Look, try this one.'

She took a magnificent cascade of ash-blonde curls from its stand. I stood in front of the mirror and adjusted it around my face, turning my head from one side to the other as a bird will cock its head on one side when listening. I pouted a little as I had seen both her and Anne do when they thought they were unobserved or when I was in the room – it made little difference to them since they believed I gave such gestures scant attention.

'Oh, but it does suit you!' She was in hysterics, not only forgetting what had brought us there but that we were in a store in a town, Guildford, which later in the year would count its votes quickly so that it could become the first Tory seat in the new government.

Dorothy forgot that was where we were and where Harvey's was and continued to prance around me as if we were in our own green room getting ready for a pantomime. That was always her way of doing things (unlike Anne and myself).

'Ignore them. Pretend they're not there and they'll go away,' she once ordered me when two gypsies approached trying to sell us pegs or heather.

'Lucky for you if you buy some, young miss.' Sticking a basket under her nose which she then held even higher and walked on in disdain. You could see it in the gypsies' eyes, 'A curse on you for your high-and-mightiness,' but they said, 'Nice day, miss, good day. That your brother, is it? Don't he want no luck? No? All right, good day to you.' Further up the road I looked back and saw them holding their chins in the air and mimicking Dorothy's walk but she was quite oblivious to their mockery and contempt.

'See, if you carry on as though nothing out of the ordinary has happened then you're home and dry.'

Looking in the mirror at my face framed by a waterfall of curls I noticed an assistant watching us from behind a glass swing door. Her face had that same look as the gypsies' faces. The superciliousness of someone who is at the same time obliged to be humble and bow down is a look that is especially bitter and distorting. It has been my misfortune to endure that look much too often though for different reasons than Dorothy. She has for the most part been unaware of any such gaze and on the rare occasions when it has come into her field of vision has been able to disregard it, assured of her own rightness and superiority in the matter.

The door swung open, scattering its reflection of our backs round the room. The assistant came forward, her hands clasped in an attitude of beatification. 'Can I help in any way?'

'We're just browsing.'

'Quite, madam.' She looked at my shorts. What is this boy doing in my section? Why is he trying on, no, playing with one of my precious wigs? Can't his sister keep him under control? I suppose she is his sister. Much too young for his mother though you can never tell nowadays. You'd think someone of her age would have a greater sense of responsibility. You couldn't expect a boy of twelve or thirteen but her, she's positively encouraging him. You don't know where that sort of thing might lead . . . boys trying on wigs. And what's more, what if he damaged it in any way? As it is he's probably getting his sticky little paws all over it.

'Doesn't he look funny? I think it quite suits him, don't you?'

'Was it something for a fancy-dress party that you were after, madam?'

'Oh no, not really. I thought as I've just had all my own hair cut off that I might like to try one of your false coiffures. But then it's so hot and I don't think I could bear it after all. So sticky and itchy. That's why I had mine cut off. Such a wonderful summer we're having. It seemed a shame not to take advantage of it and have as much of your skin as possible exposed to the sun. I don't suppose this weather is very good for your business.'

'You'd be surprised, madam. People, ladies that is, come here in all sorts of weather. You can't predict it. And often they come looking for, say, a demure little grey piece, neatly trimmed and all that, and they go away with an absolutely ravishing auburn like this one.' She took the piece from its stand, handling it with all the care and trepidation that a rare museum exhibit would warrant. 'This is absolutely devastating,' crooned the assistant.

'No, I don't think it's really me.'

'Try it on, You don't know until you try. A piece like this can work miracles. Effect an utter transformation so that you won't know yourself.' She was too sleek, too smooth and rehearsed. Her phrasing smacked of I've said this a thousand times before and will say it another thousand.

I stood to one side forgotten by Dorothy and ignored by the assistant. The ash-blonde wig which I had taken off after the assistant arrived hung limply in my hand like a dead animal. The assistant, I noticed, was not wearing a wig. Her own hair was frizzy and looked as though it had had too many permanent waves. It was dry and thin. But when Dorothy put the auburn wig in position all my criticism of the assistant evaporated. She was right, it was a magnificent piece of work whose colour, texture and shape transfigured Dorothy's plain face into something quite unrecognisable. She looked like a model for Dante Gabriel Rossetti and I felt like telling her that 'the stars in her hair were seven'. Dorothy knew what had happened to her though she said nothing. The assistant stepped back, folded her arms and smiled in professional triumph. I felt too hot in my flannel shorts – flannel even in summer, grey woollen socks too – and the ash-blonde wig slid out of my hand on to the floor. I gasped for air. Dorothy said, 'Yes, I think I'll take it.'

I was suffocating, my head was spinning and I slumped to the floor.

'Oh dear, could you fetch my brother a glass of water? I think he's fainted.'

And for the rest of the summer she haunted me in that auburn wig. I would look out of my bedroom window in the evening when I heard a car pull up in the drive outside. My elbows resting on the sill and wearing pyjamas, flannel still, I heard the front door open and bang to, then saw Dorothy half skip to the car, the flame of her hair trailing behind her. A tall figure emerged from the black saloon and she took his hand and led him back to the porch. They disappeared into the house below me but I could still hear Dorothy's laughter tinkling up the stairs. How many times this happened I lost count. Whether it was always the same figure stepping out of the same saloon I am not sure. What fixed itself was the way in which she leaned against the man as she took his hand and then the afterglow of her fiery wig like the retained image on your retina following an intense flash of light. The way she leaned for support and comfort accompanied by the auburn 'false coiffure'. Then mother would come in and say, 'Aren't you in bed yet?'

'But it's so light I can't get to sleep.'

'All right, go downstairs and say goodnight to grandma and grandpa.'

They were sitting by the open french window looking out across the lawn which was immaculately razored. Grandpa had just bought Uncle Cyril a new power mower, 'horrible, noisy thing. I don't know what was wrong with the old one,' said grandma. They were at an angle to one another, their fields of vision cutting across to different parts of the garden. I looked between them, straight down the centre, and there was Uncle Cyril kneeling and doing something to a bed – sprinkling slug pellets, perhaps, he often complained that the garden fed more slugs than any other he knew but as he had never gardened anywhere else I didn't know how he could be sure.

* * *

I ONCE SAW HIM when he thought he was alone, attacking a

slug with a sharp spade which he brought up and down, up and down until the slug had been hacked into slivers. His face was a knot of concentration but as he finished this intimate savagery a calmness flooded through him, his jaw went slack and he smiled weakly to himself.

This time he looked as if he were doing it in the proper and recommended gardener's way by spreading the little green poisonous pellets around. He was, of course, in full view of the house with my grandparents able to observe his scientific reasonableness in the business of slug destruction. Would he do the same on the other side of the wall in the vegetable garden where he was out of sight? In any case neither grandparent seemed to be watching what he was doing but, unspeaking, each was lost in different aspects of the garden. They were beginning to sit like this together more and more as if they were both waiting for someone to arrive or something to happen and they had no need to talk about what they both knew too well. I broke into this mutual acceptance.

'What is Uncle Cyril doing in the garden?' Grandpa took his pipe out of his mouth which was unnecessary for he could talk perfectly well with it between his teeth.

'Hello. What are you doing? Couldn't sleep I expect. Cyril? I've no idea. Bashing slugs probably.' I stood between them in my pyjamas and bare feet. 'Does your mother know you're down here? You'll catch cold like that,' grandma said, making a move to stand up.

'It's all right, he can stay here for a few minutes,' said grandpa, holding out his hand to direct me on to the arm of his chair. His pipe was still fuming gently – he told me once how he'd kept it alight for a whole night when they thought they might collide with another ship in the fog – and as I leaned against him there was both a comfort and a thrill in the smell of his tobacco and in his bulk.

'Have you seen Anne?' grandma asked. I shook my head. 'In her bedroom I suppose. Reading or mooching. I wish she'd take a leaf out of Dorothy's book and be more sociable, enjoy life more.' But when she did this later on it was not at all to grandma's taste.

'She's only sixteen,' grandpa said.

'That is exactly what I mean. It'd be far healthier if she were out playing tennis or something like Dorothy instead of sitting cooped up in her room on an evening like this.'

Grandpa laughed and his whole body shook. 'That is not what I've heard you say about Dorothy's boyfriends or friends.'

'Oh that. That is not what I was talking about. In any case you shouldn't be talking like that in front of your grandson,' and this time she did stand up. 'Well, there are still things to be done. You haven't forgotten that Jean is coming home tomorrow, have you?'

'No, I haven't forgotten,' he said.

At that time, as there were seven of us and seven bedrooms in the house, it meant that whenever anyone came to stay someone had to move out and share a bedroom. It was usually me and I invariably shared my mother's room or Anne's but there was talk of going in with Uncle Cyril. Grandma had said, 'After all, he is in his second year at school now. And he is used to a dormitory with other boys. And he is thirteen years old. And it really is time. . . .' And when it was Auntie Jean who was coming to stay it was for a matter of weeks, or months even, but never days.

So the question of who was to share a bedroom with whom was not insignificant. I recall this visit of Auntie Jean's in particular because it was the last time mother won the tussle with grandma and I was allowed to share her bedroom. Ever after when I was home from school I had to share with Uncle Cyril. This used to agitate me as much as sleeping with boys in a dormitory did and I always slept badly, if at all.

* * *

WHEN AUNTIE JEAN was staying you could go into a room and think there was no one there but yourself and you might pick up a book or newspaper and begin to read. Then minutes later you thought you heard a shuffle or a creak. No, it was just the wind or the furniture drying out. There it was again so you put down whatever it was you were reading and looked about. You had chosen to sit near a window for the light, which on that day might have been brown and muddied, hardly giving you enough of itself to see by. It certainly did not reach into the recesses and alcoves of my grandparents' 'quiet room'. Another muted rustle. You stood up. The carpet seemed to wheeze with years of gathering dust. And then a dry voice whispered, 'Why is it always so dull and grey when I come back?'

'Aah, Auntie Jean, it's you. I wondered what it was.' Then, following the path of her voice, you could see the crown of her head between the wings of a chair. Her hair was coiled into a bun and it was wispy, arid and bleached not by anything other than the sun. It was so brittle-looking that you thought it could snap in the wind outside, that is, if she dared to go out there. You might come across her sitting at the unlaid dining table and staring into its polished oak as though she were trying to read something in the grain of the wood. This visit was when Uncle Cyril had asked you to fetch him a ball of twine from the garden shed and you found her in there poking about in a battered tea chest with Elder Dempster Line stencilled on its side in thick black lettering.

'I'm looking for something,' she said, without my saying a word. 'I don't suppose you've seen it? A shoebox, cardboard, green, Clark's. It's got some papers in it.'

'No, I'm sorry, I haven't. Is it important?' She didn't answer but simply shrugged her shoulders. 'I don't know where . . .' Turning over more things in the tea chest.

'I'm looking for a ball of twine. I don't suppose . . . '

'On the second shelf at the other end,' she replied, without raising her head from the chest. Oh yes, she noticed things. Saw them once and then they were caught and held by her until she saw fit to let them go. And yet she looked so frail and desiccated, like a specimen of a stick insect which was ready for mounting in its case. At times you thought that she had stopped breathing altogether for she could be so quiet and unmoving. Had you not known otherwise you would have suspected her of practising yoga or Buddhism or some other form of philosophical exercise that called for stillness and absolute harmony with one's surroundings.

She was dried out because she had gone to live in a place under the sun, or that was the logic as it appeared then. Yes, under the sun! Unable to sit out under an English summer's sun without protection she chose to go and work in Africa! Grandmother, everyone, thought she was joking when she announced her plans. But Jean did not joke. It was a self-inflicted punishment which no one (then) could fathom. When she came home on a rare but lengthy stay she was on leave from her last tour of duty and on each occasion she looked more dehydrated than on the previous visit. And it was the kind of dryness and shrivelling something gets when it is out of the sun and living in the shadow. Leathery like a reptile. Grandmother pleaded with her to stay and not go back. Said that life was passing her by. Slipping away and running through her fingers like sand through the waist of an egg-timer. She usually said little or nothing in her own defence. 'Perhaps you're right.'

'You will never, never meet anyone there. What will you do when you are too weak, too old to work? What if you catch some disease? Cholera? Malaria? (She already had.) Leprosy even. What will you do then?' Grandmother persisted in her belief that Auntie Jean was only biding her time and in a sense she was right though not for grandma's reason – waiting for a husband. What more should her daughters want? And then mother. 'We'd love to have you back. It would be so nice. Come back here and live here with us.'

'There's no room for me.'

'Nonsense. We'd make room. We always do. Anyway Dorothy may leave home soon.'

Grandpa: 'Why don't you both leave her alone? If she wants to come back she will. If she doesn't then nothing you say will make her change her mind.'

Grandpa with such a clear-cut notion of what made Jean (and everyone else) move. Who's to say he was wrong? He had spent so much of his time away from his family, any family, how was he to understand or appreciate the finer pressures that may come to bear? Or was he more aware than anyone else of the nature of Jean's decision? They both had a sense of exile in common. Such a decision must be made and adhered to without wavering. Away from home doubt must not be allowed to undermine what is an already vulnerable and often rootless life – that of the foreigner and expatriate. If uncertainty is allowed to enter you must either return home or bear your exile like a cross but without the consolation of redemption or salvation. Grandpa had gone to sea and settled for a sort of in-between life and his daughter Jean had gone one step further by crossing the sea and staying on the other side which was the Gold Coast. Her final words before each of her returns to Africa, 'There's still work to be done.' And grandma had to suffer that in silence for it was she who had encouraged Jean, and all our family, in the Christian faith.

* * *

'LEILA, are you religious?'

'Me? Why?'

'I wondered if this bothered you at all?'

'Why should it?'

'I mean you could see it as going against creation. Altering what God has given us.'

'They're not all cases like yours.' ('Not all' – how many then? One? Two?)

'Most of them are quite straightforward.'

'But even a nose job is a change in what's natural. So are drugs and most other forms of medicine. Why do we treat people for cancer or heart disease? To make their lives longer, more comfortable, maybe happier? Tell me, what is the difference between heart surgery and a nose job?'

'Perhaps you can't survive without one but you can without the other.'

'Survival! We are not animals to talk about survival. We can survive in a cave without music, without poetry or painting. Do you want life without those things? Without those achievements? Do you want to live just at the level of a beast that only exists and accomplishes nothing? Why did you come to this clinic? To survive? Nonsense! You came so that when you leave here you will start to live as you have never lived before. You will be one thousand, no, one million times the person you were before. And if you leave here a person who is more in tune with herself then you will make the world a better place.'

Oh, the sweetness of the girl! Herself! How I hoped she would say that, but I did not dare to think that she might really defend me from my own doubts and questions which seemed to deflate me just as my hope was beginning to take flight. Why did I always let the self-questioning creep in as everything else was going smoothly? A defence mechanism, a rehearsal of what I had to face. Marshal the enemy's arguments and have them at your disposal ready to reduce them to tatters. God knows I hate to talk in terms of war but I have rarely had much choice in the matter. And for that reason I am in debt to Leila who expressed my own argument with a clarity and conviction that I too often lacked. It is true that to get as far as the clinic and pursue my intention required a certain amount of determination, especially when Dr Dupont (a name artificially constructed to disguise his identity as his re-working of the appearance of others changed theirs) showed me the photographs.

In ninety-nine per cent of 'normal or routine' operations there is no need for photographs. The patient is rarely concerned with how the stomach wall will look after the removal of an ulcer or whether the replacement heart-valve is yellow, green or striped. What the patient wants to know is whether it will feel more comfortable and whether it will work or not. Even with scarring as a result of the surgeon's knife or some accident the patient, as far as I know, does not see photographs. In those rare but unfortunate cases where scarring can occur in the facial region the patient is still not offered photographs. This is, of course, because she wants the result of the operation to restore the body to its previous condition as nearly, if not exactly, as possible. The patient hopes that the body will be a nearly perfect replica of what it was before the operation and has an accurate image of what this is – it is the accustomed body, always lived with and one to which they would like to return. There is then no call for photographs since the patient knows the parts of his or her own body better than any photographic image.

This is not the case with the field of medicine loosely referred to as 'plastic surgery'. The patient may have an idea, even a clear image, of what he or she wants and may envisage what she anticipates the surgery will achieve. But this is dangerous ground for the patient's picture of how a retroussé nose might look if it is turned down may be quite at odds with what the surgeon has in mind. Therefore, a photograph or photographs are used as a common and easily referred-to source.

'What about this one?'

'No. Too beaky.'

'And this?'

'Not bad. Can we have a look at some others?'

'Now this is very nice.'

'Yes, but is it me?'

'My dear, we are looking for something that is not you. I think this one is rather aristocratic.'

'Yes, but won't it make my lips look too big?'

'Sensual, not big. You forget that big lips are now considered sensual not common. But if you want this nose and you're worried about your lips I can always tighten the skin a little round your lower lip which would raise it a fraction.' Here the surgeon lays a photograph of a pair of lips under that of the nose they have been looking at. 'There. What about that combination?'

'Yes I like it. I like it very much.'

'Take the photos with you and think about it then come back when you've made up your mind,' he says, handing the client the prints. And the client takes them away and decides Yes or No and they have something definite on which to agree or disagree. Then after it is all over the surgeon can point to the photographs and say, 'Look, I told you that this nose with those lips would make an excellent combination. What do you think?'

'Very good. Very good indeed. Quite beautiful. Thank you so much.'

And the client is happy, knowing the product paid for is the one she wanted.

Now in my case I was shown photographs not only of the finished product but of the means to the end. That is, I saw photos of what would happen to me during my operation. Once more this is different from standard medical practice. It will be explained to a heart patient how the operation is to be performed, he or she may be given a simple outline of the steps that will be taken, may even be shown a few sketches or diagrams and perhaps rarely a photograph. But the purpose of this last item is to give confidence to the patient and, by increasing knowledge, to lessen fear and provide encouragement. My photos were the opposite. They were shown to me to generate, not quell, doubts and fears.

A large brown envelope with Egyptian stamps decorating half of it. Bent in the post. The photographs slid on to the table. At first glance mainly black and white. My eye caught by part of a letter that ran, '. . . enclosed are some photographs which I would desire you to study at your leisure. Please examine them very carefully and think about what they mean before you give a definite reply. If you are unable to confront these then it is unlikely that you would be able to stomach what will happen to you if you are determined to go through with this operation. If after careful deliberation you are still committed to the idea then please return one copy of the contract with your signature giving permission for the operation to be carried out. Keep the other copy for yourself. I await your early reply. Yours with best wishes. Signed . . . Dupont.'

There were seven photographs, only one of which was in colour and evidently the most recent. They all showed the lower half of the male trunk down to the thighs. Four of them had been taken with the body horizontal and the thighs apart and two with the torso in a sitting position, the thighs also apart. One, the colour, was taken with its subject standing and this showed more of the torso and thighs than any of the others. The four photos of horizontal sections had all been taken while the patient was on the operating table, in two of them there was no penis or scrotum at all between the legs but a ragged hole, in the other two the penis was in one case half dismembered and in the final photo the penis had gone but the scrotum remained intact. In all of these four photos there were dark pools and to varying degrees lumps of flesh torn away and hanging, presumably ready to be sewn back by the surgeon. Thus, the four photos presented a procession of steps from part-severed penis to a male torso without one. The two photos taken with the patient sitting must have been shot post-operatively. The thighs rested on the edge of a bed, there were no dark pools or torn flesh and where the base of the penis should have been were clean and stitched wounds which appeared no more or less gruesome than any cut sewn together in another part of the body. In the colour photograph with the patient standing the wound had healed completely and the pubic hair had grown around the area of the scar almost disguising it though through the dark tangle one could make out a red line where the flesh had knitted together – its redness indicating that the photograph had been taken not long after the wound had healed.

They had been sent to test my resolve. What would the reactions be of a 'full-blooded' man to photographs depicting the loss of the pinnacle of manhood? I suspect that the standard response would be a sense of nausea perhaps so intense that one could not bear to look at such scenes and would have to turn away without having absorbed their detail. I too felt a sense of loss and waste, of compassion and sympathy for the suffering of these poor men, but I was not moved in the way that I am moved by the loss of an eye or limb – parts of the body common to us all. I mourned for the dismembered but not for myself. The notion that 'this could happen to me too' which is a kind of sympathetic selfishness born of fear and a sense of relief was not what occurred in me. This, if you are a man, sounds heartless and cruelly devoid of any sense of belonging to the male fraternity. That is true. But if you are male consider how you might respond if you were told that a woman has lost a breast – with regret and compassion – but can you truly say that the notion touches you at your quick as does the thought of losing a penis? If it does then perhaps you (along with all of us) ought to examine your ideas and emotions about what it is to be male or female.

That I was able to review (what for some would undoubtedly be the horror of) the photographs so dispassionately seemed then, as it still does, an indication of my nature which satisfactorily passed the doctor's test. Oh, I admit to feelings of squeamishness bordering on a nauseous fear at the thought of the operation. But these feelings were the same as if I had been about to undergo surgery for the removal of a tumour or a cancer which was in the end what I regarded my penis to be. Had I been able to anticipate the pain involved I might have wavered but photographs, like all other forms of representation, can only hint at the dimensions beyond their surfaces.

And so part of my reply to Doctor Dupont ran, '. . . and whilst I appreciate the pain that must inevitably accompany this operation I am determined to go through with it. Your photographs are, medically speaking, revealing and I feel for the suffering of the men involved, at least, I assume that it is suffering and the patients are unwilling and unfortunate victims of accidents or you would have shown their faces. Nevertheless, your photos have not dissuaded me, only made me more determined. There are . . . ' I did not appreciate the pain but I was right that the photos were of men who had all lost their penises in accidents. I have described them as clearly as I can but, excepting the later colour one, most of them had been taken many years before. They were beginning to curl and split at their edges and some were already screened by a yellow-brown film that gave them a sepia effect as though they came from a period primitive in the reproduction of its images.

* * *

ANNE, after a certain age, never liked having her photograph taken. And it was not that temporary coyness that appears in girls who have recently had their first period and believe the world sees all their little blemishes as if through a magnifying glass. Auntie Margaret was holding her ciné camera and shouting at everyone to 'act normal and just carry on as if I wasn't here.'

That, especially in Auntie Margaret's middle age, became almost impossible. Auntie Jean would, if she could help it, never come to stay when Margaret and her own family were at grandma's house on account of Margaret's increasing desperation to direct all those around her and loudly too.

'That's it, Cyril. Carry on getting rid of those nasty little weeds. Beautiful. Beautiful,' and she pointed the camera at Cyril, holding it on him for a few seconds, and then panned up and down the rosebed he was stooping over.

'Hey! Those roses are gorgeous. How about a shot with the watering can, Cyril?' Cyril muttered. 'What's that you say, Cyril?'

'I said you can't water roses in the middle of the day. You've got to wait until the sun's lower.'

'That's OK. Get the can and swing it round empty. It'll look like you're watering them anyway. I'll tell 'em back home that the water here is so fine, like champagne, you can't see it.' She laughed and it was an explosion, making the pigeons shoot out of the trees and clatter through the torpid summer air. Uncle Cyril stopped his weeding and went off towards the shed to fetch his can like the estate gardener receiving his orders and submerging his own opinion on the nature of his sister's request.

Anne and I were sitting on the grass with our backs against a horse chestnut tree which, as it was in full flower, would soon become Margaret's next focus of attention.

'Who does she think she is? Ordering Uncle Cyril around like that.' Anne could never resist championing the underdog.

'He doesn't have to do it if he doesn't want to,' was my simple (fatuous) adolescent view of how things worked. A view I still retain and it gets me labelled even in the most flattering terms 'naive' or 'selfish'.

'He's oppressed. He doesn't have any choice.'

'Oppressed or repressed?'

'Stop playing with words. You know quite well what I mean.' Cyril returned with the watering can.

'Oh darling, that's wonderful. Move it around a bit. That's it. A bit nearer the roses. Yes, they'll love that back home.'

'Where does she think she is?' said Anne, who was forever full of rhetorical questions that I nevertheless attempted to answer. 'She can hardly call this home any more. She hasn't lived here for more than twenty years. It's that awful Americanism "back home" that I loathe.'

Dear Anne, in so many things a snob though she zealously denied the charge whenever I made it. Her sense of egalitarianism did not extend as far as transatlantic speech though indeed many of her enthusiasms and the causes she took up were American in origin and often in expression too. She nodded at Margaret's ciné camera which was still sweeping across the beds with the house as its backdrop.

'If she comes anywhere near me with that thing I swear I'll break it over her head.'

'I thought you were non-violent, pacifist . . . '

'This is the exception that proves the rule.' Margaret had finished with Cyril and his empty can and swung round on to the chestnut under which we were sitting. At first she failed to notice us, partly because we were hidden in its shadow and also on account of her eagerness to capture the tree with her camera.

'That is just fantastic. Those flowers are just like little waterfalls. Don't you think so, Cyril?' He appeared not to have heard her and was moving away to return the can to his shed as if he were computerised and had not been programmed to respond to emotion or spontaneity but simply to execute routine tasks with maximum efficiency. This was naturally Uncle Cyril's bearing but if you looked hard you could see that his knuckles were white from gripping the watering-can handle more tightly than was necessary.

'Why does everyone ignore Cyril's feelings and pretend he hasn't got any?' was Anne's third question.

'Because he does the same himself. If he won't admit to his feelings how can you expect others to?'

'Darlings.' Margaret had spotted us under her little waterfalls. 'Why don't you both come out from under there? It would make a perfect picture.'

'Why don't you stick your camera right where it belongs,' hissed Anne so that I but not Margaret could hear. Why did she so often begin her utterances with 'why'? Was it because she had not really thought the answers out for herself and needed help? Some of us are incapable of thinking clearly to ourselves and conducting our own internal dialogues. We have to do it out loud and in the company of others. Was this Anne's case? Did she expect any answers? Anne, perpetual instigator of questions, provokes so many too.

'Why have Americans always got to take pictures of everything? Why can't they leave us and everything else alone?' We could hear Margaret's camera whirring outside the tree's parasol. 'It's as though they've got to record every moment, every image otherwise no one'll believe they've been where they say they've been or done what they say they've done. As if they're afraid they themselves might forget and their memory play tricks on them later. And it's also very pompous and self-centred to think that "the folks back home" are going to be interested in your brother holding an empty watering can over a rosebed. And . . . '

'I think you take it all too seriously and should humour her. We see her once every three or four years. This was her home and she probably feels sentimental about it. Why not?'

'That is all she seems capable of. Nostalgia and an indiscriminate gush of pathos.'

'You're too hard on her. She's lonely. Don't you think she might be lonely? Stuck in America which isn't really home. Unable to come back here.' Outside the compass of the tree the whirring stopped and Margaret's voice broke in.

'What are you two doing under there? Come out so I can take this movie.'

A thrush scuttled away across the lawn with her approach.

'I don't mind. I'm going out even if it is for the "folks back home".'

'There's something morbid about photographs, especially when they're movies trying to pretend they've got the scene exactly as it was. But they never do. I hate them for their glib surface, for their recall of things as they aren't. And when everyone sits round and says, "Oh, isn't that just like her." And in fact it isn't like her or anything else at all. It is never like that. But they are all ready to believe that it is.'

'I'm waiting.'

'Yes, Auntie Margaret, I'm coming.' I shuffled out from under the tree leaving Anne to brood on her dislike of photography.

She thought, I suppose, that it was the high point of technology without depth or substance and in the end nothing more than a trick achieving the appearance of dimensions without really having any. Her intensity propelled her into the non-material, the spiritual (rather than the religious) which was already souring into a dismissal of and contempt for the humdrum which ordinarily entertains most of us. She had to be different and appear to be so, as though to seem content with the ordinary was a sort of stigma which could only be erased by unconventional behaviour. This meant that, superficially anyway, we had much in common and we were often identified together as 'different', 'outlandish' and, finally, 'grotesque and sick'. But truly this was because neither of us was understood. I felt that as things stood I was different and that by entering the clinic I could restore my normality and return to the status quo. This is what I wanted, whereas Anne found the notion of such conformity depressing and claustrophobic. It was my freakishness which cut me off from the rest of the world and distorted my relations with it. I grew determined to erase my sense of inborn unorthodoxy, albeit by somewhat bizarre means, and correct that imbalance between the world and myself, but Anne was set on a path which led her as far away as she could possibly get from a mutual comprehension or sympathy between herself and her fellows. So she sat under the tree cursing Auntie Margaret's transatlantic eagerness with her ciné camera which was hurting no one, except Uncle Cyril who anyway regarded all his contacts with people as though they were designed to add another weight to the load he felt himself to be carrying.

So I went out to humour Auntie Margaret. Perhaps that is one of my faults, a willingness to please and keep people happy which leads them to believe that I concur with everything they do. Then when I act otherwise from what they expect they feel hurt and betrayed. But where is the effort which one makes at friendship and sociability to stop? If it reaches the point where your own identity is submerged in another person's or other persons' then what is there left you to offer? I once used to do that so often that it became unclear to me who I was. When I decided that I should define the limits of compromise and act honestly in accordance with myself I was called 'Judas' by many who I had thought my friends.

But walking about in the garden and giving Auntie Margaret something on which to focus seemed the smallest of considerations that Anne was unwilling to make because it did not accord with her view of the world as it should be rather than as it is.

'Isn't Anne going to walk around with you?'

'No. She's tired.'

'It would have been nice to have my nephew and niece together in the garden of the house where I used to live. But never mind.' Her unflinching optimism again. 'Walk over there towards the french windows. Slowly.' And I began. 'When you get to the top of the slope turn round so I can see your face.' She was absorbed in the mechanics of her camera, one eye squinting and the other in the viewfinder. 'Hey Ronny, did anyone ever tell you that you've got a really nice pair of legs?' I was walking already so she could not see my face and when I reached the crest of the slope I turned to face the camera as she had told me. 'That is one hell of a smile. Keep it up. Lovely, just great. OK. Come back down the slope now, slowly, and walk over towards the sundial. When you get there stop and pretend to be reading the time.'

And all the while I imagined I could hear Anne muttering under the chestnut to herself. Pretend. Do this. Do that. Do anything as long as it's for the camera and not what you'd do in the normal course of things. But in spite of my natural sympathy for Anne I discovered that I was enjoying myself in front of Auntie Margaret's movie camera. It could seem, and some will have you believe, that out there in front of the camera rather than behind it you are no more than a dupe, a pawn moved about by the cameraman's (or here woman's) hand, submissive to and exploited by an unseen director. And I think that until that moment I would, if I'd thought about it in any way, have agreed with the notion that the power lies behind the lens and not in front of it. But watching Auntie Margaret hunched in concentration it was obvious that she was following my every movement and gesture and was oblivious to herself. I, on the other hand, was supremely aware of myself. Where I was making for. What speed I was going. How I was carrying myself – upright, relatively small steps for the length of my legs, head tilted just a fraction to one side so that my face gave more than a flat ninety-degree profile to the camera, position of hands and fingers, the left in the pocket of my shorts, the right swinging free and brushing my thigh, the rocking motion of my pelvis on its ball joints, the lock of hair swinging across my forehead and grazing my eyebrows, the sandy velvet of the grass under my soles – I always discard my footwear whenever there is an inviting lawn, carpet or beach – even the down on my jawbone and that was so fine that it was invisible and could be guessed at by the lightest of fingers, even that in some obscure manner had captured Auntie Margaret's attention and imagination.

I understood then that there are moments, in rare personalities extended over considerable periods, when there is nothing but the person in front of the camera and that whatever is claimed later the person operating is nothing other than an extension of the machine which records. Don't let them fool you, I said to myself, that the figure whose hand directs the camera is the person in charge; it is you here, walking across the lawn, who holds the influence, the charisma that draws everyone, everything else towards it. Later they may say, 'But you are nothing without that person recording, directing you . . . ' Don't believe it. At that moment they are in thrall to you and who wants 'later'? Sorry, Anne, for I know you too subscribe to the malcontent's theory of 'later and afterwards', but for me in front of the camera it was one of the first instances of self-realisation, knowing among other things that I liked being watched and admired. This had implications for behaviour and actions later on and led me to think, not forever but from time to time, that Van Gogh was defined by a starry night at Arles, by sunflowers and cornfields, by his room and bed and chair and that he in no way defined them. I wanted to be the starry night or the bed and chair and not the person who only came alive through them, who was measured by these things and not the other way round, as I thought it should be, for me anyway.

* * *

AND HERE in my bed all this – the pain, the blood, the bandages – is only an adjustment of myself to the notion of the harmony of things in complete alignment with themselves. Not that I am vain enough to think I can ever achieve that completely but all this is a step towards it.

Leila comes into the room, shutting the door behind her with almost theatrical deliberation and care, thinking I am asleep. I never cease to wonder how (to my eyes anyway) stagey and melodramatic the conduct of many Near and Middle Easterners seems – I love it, it suits my own temperament or what I would like my temper to be more often. You can get cowed too easily in my position and I need the grand gestures of emotion inspired by its own bravado to carry me along. You squabble, you shout, you get excited, you even throw things about.

Remember your mother and grandfather once:

'I will not have you mention him to Ronald again. Do you hear me?'

'But my dear, he is or was the boy's father.'

'Never.'

'After all, it's only right and proper that he should know something about . . . '

'Nothing. Don't you understand me? Nothing. Nothing,

nothing, nothing!' And here a crash. The teapot? The toaster? They were in the kitchen. A door slammed and then sobbing.

If only my mother had allowed herself to be like that, to come clean more often. Perhaps then she might have shaken off a demeanour suggesting she had grown intimidated by the facts of a situation she felt powerless to change. And it was, of course, from her that I learned how to conceal and hide things that mattered to me.

That is why it took me nearly thirty years before I was able to come to this clinic. I needed to love myself first before I could manage to love others. But even then there has been something secretive, hidden, inherited or learned from mother. I have sneaked away to North Africa when I might have chosen London. Why Egypt and not Toronto or New York? Or London itself? The sophisticated centres. Better care, more advanced techniques, I hear people say. And there's nothing to be ashamed of any longer. In the fifties or early sixties perhaps you would have had to trail along the southern shores of the Mediterranean in search of what you wanted. But to go there now? You're crazy or hiding something. Well, I suppose I am. I'm too well-known in those places. I had a need to be anonymous. I wanted it to happen out of sight, away from friends or family. When I go back to it I want to arrive in their world transformed. But the messy business of the birth itself is mine alone, kept here with the wonderful Leila and the surgeon away from the curious eyes of all those who might want to peer at me through the wired glass of some Western hospital door. The secrets of alchemy are not displayed before the public, they are performed in obscure rooms removed from the open bustle of the market place.

Forget the difficulty in finding a doctor – that was a concrete obstacle overcome with relative ease. No, the greatest problem was overcoming myself or what I took to be myself. Having done that, although imperfectly and at times unconvincingly, and said here I am, this is what I can and will do to make sure that I no longer have to hide from the facts of my own life; then I could hardly creep, furtively, on yesterday's repressed route. I had to pick things up and talk clearly, confidently, loudly, even about my past, my present and future. The strength to do that sometimes fails, deserts me. And in my mother's case the courage, the willingness to face certain facts, whatever they are, was only glimpsed at points of crisis or what the cool and placid English might disdain with epithets such as 'over the top, hysterical, melodramatic'. That is why I like the hysteria and melodrama of other nations – they signify a release, lack of inhibition, a throwing off of suppression and restraint – something I have tried, am still trying, to do both within myself and the rest of the world. And yet such behaviour, whilst often appearing aggressive, insensitive or unsubtle, only confirms in my mind the true vulnerability and childlike nature of a person who is not conversant with guile or deception when emotion is uppermost.

Leila is one such person (my grandmother quite the opposite) and she is whispering huskily to me, 'Is there anything you want?' I don't open my eyes at once but enjoy listening to her glide about my room. What is she doing? Opening or closing the window? The tone of a workman's hammer has changed though I can't tell whether it is louder or softer. Now she is doing something around my bed – adjusting the height or simply tucking in a loose sheet? Without opening my eyes I hold out a hand and she takes it in both of hers. As she caresses I feel the ridge of a ring on one of her fingers. I stop her from moving her hands and with my eyes still shut examine the ring beween my thumb and forefinger. What metal is it made of? Almost impossible to guess. Is there a stone or anything else set at the top? No. Plain. Does this signify wedding or engagement ring in the Arab world? Though, of course, I must remember that although she was brought up in Beirut and lives in what is a predominantly Moslem country, she is, I assume, a Christian at least in name if no more. So that further complicates the issue. Does she follow the mainstream of the culture and country in which she lives or does she prefer the customs of a minority? I don't want to ask her just yet. I like exploring the possibilities, the implications. Can I feel on which finger, or hand for that matter, she is wearing this ring? The left I think but I can't be sure. The finger next to the little finger – that would add weight to the adoption of a Christian habit in a Moslem country, wouldn't it? Why don't I just come out with it and ask her? Is it that I would rather not know? Not that.

This conjures up a small group of us: Dorothy, Anne, a young man in a tweed jacket – one of Dorothy's boyfriends – and myself sitting in a semicircle on the rug in front of the fire. It was four o'clock, the grandfather had just chimed, and it was already dark outside. Dorothy stood up and went over to draw the curtains. I noticed the young man's eyes following her calves and the scissors of her thighs and buttocks under her navy-blue skirt, grandmother's preferred winter colour, as she moved.

'Come and help me please, Anne. You know how heavy these curtains are.' Anne would have sat there all evening oblivious to the night smudging the windows. I imagined going up to bed and coming down the next morning to find Anne in the same position, sitting by the ashes of the burnt-out fire.

'I'll do it,' said the young man jumping up, tweed tails flapping. He helped Dorothy draw the Prussian blue velvet curtains which grandmother put up in the autumn, 'October the first and not a day before, mind you,' and then replaced, claiming the arrival of spring, 'March the thirty-first and not a day after,' with lighter, creamy cotton curtains printed with pale pink and blue flowers. Does anyone still change their curtains with the season?

The young man, a Simon in my memory but possibly not, was behind Dorothy, leaning over her to draw the curtains above her head. His tweed jacket rose up as he bent forward to grasp the velvet – what a delicious contrast of textures! I could sense him pressing into Dorothy from behind as she fiddled about trying to get the curtains to hang straight. (I doubt whether Anne ever knew what the fall of a curtain was.) The gap between the top of his flannels and the jacket revealed a narrow band of skin – somehow his shirt had ridden up too, unusual in those days when shirts had long tails that might reach the back of a boy's knees.

Oh, I had seen plenty of skin, much more than that, whole, or seemingly so, bodies in showers looming up and out of the steam – here a grazed knee, a rose-coloured buttock, a glistening and curved shoulder blade, there an eyelid dripping, wrinkled finger tips, the dark triangular bush with its pale stick – there was nothing with which I was unfamiliar anatomically speaking, though what a difference there is between the physiology which was known and the psychology which was, in conscious terms anyway, a mystery to me. This was, after all, happening after my first term at school when I had seen a modernist display of limbs, joints, pallid skin, often bruised, almost certainly scratched, grazed or blotchy, hairs (which I didn't have anywhere except on my head) and knuckles, elbows, ankles which came shooting, scurrying up at me in the light, twilight and dark. In short, every moment and others of my waking and sleeping there was and still would be a collision, a criss-cross of boys', adolescents', young men's bodies.

No. A small strip of skin above a waistband was not in itself enough to make me sit up and take notice but then why did I find myself turning away from the coals, up off my elbows and swivelling round to concentrate on Simon's lower back? Context was all. The proximity of Dorothy to this piece of exposure (although she could not have been aware of it) put it in quite an extraordinary light – literally too; with the curtains drawn any remaining daylight was shut out, there was a dim fringed standard in one corner which was supplemented only by the glow and occasional flicker from the coals. Simon stretching over her, part of his back exposed – Dorothy must have sensed the body under the clothes straining towards her even though she couldn't have seen it like I did.

I realised then how a man's body would forever strain, arch, in the direction of a woman's. Before this the male figures, shapes – mere outlines – in the showers, washrooms and dormitories had seemed disembodied as though they were waiting in limbo for something to bring them to life. At that moment I realised what that waiting was. It seemed a cruel mockery to have them circling each other, endlessly frustrated and resentful, not fully understanding what they were doing there but apprehending in their own limbs and restricted movements that something was wrong, like animals in a zoo. I didn't feel that I myself was one of these restless bodies forever pacing through the school corridors or out on the playing fields waiting for another body to match mine. I was not straining to escape this land-locked sea of maleness in order to find that missing femininity which would complement my lack but rather because I was aware, though at this time unable to formulate it, that my own femininity could not possibly be complemented by hundreds of males *en masse*. It was like being confronted with such choice at a supermarket that you walk out again, empty-handed and unable to reach a decision.

But Dorothy was too alert to succumb to Simon's gentle pressure. She always saw even the slightest of her movements as a stone dropped into a pond with ever widening implications and long-term repercussions. Oh, she could appear carefree and spontaneous but if she seemed so it was invariably as part of some larger design. She was not devious, did not set out to fool people. It was as if she said to herself, If I do this that will happen or if I don't do that . . . and so on. She wanted to get things clear in her own mind so that she knew where she was going. And she didn't want to hurt anybody either. So she giggled and said to Simon, 'Don't you think we ought to continue the game?' As she moved away from the curtains and he followed I could see the blood rushing round his head signalling his embarrassment. And I tried to think, analysing before we all got caught up in the game once more. What is my reaction here and how do I feel? And is that any different from what it 'should' be or how people say they and most others respond? Take me. Eleven years old. My first term 'away' just finished. Back for the Christmas holidays, playing a game in front of the fire with my two sisters, Anne and Dorothy who is older than me by five years. In any case starved of their attention and affection – my suitcase is still upstairs opened but unpacked on the bed, a measure of my urgent need for their company. As we have just seen, 'a man friend' makes a feeble and clumsy attempt at a pass and this is done as though Anne and I were not in the room, let alone that we can, and I do, watch every move he makes.

According to all accounts both substantiated and anecdotal my response is likely to be one of the following: feelings of repulsion coupled with disgust and fear; this attributable to a naivety about sexual relations alongside the shocking discovery that someone, someone moreover close to you, indeed part of your family, not only appears to take such behaviour in their stride but might even be seen enjoying flirtation or something a little stronger. Another reaction might be one of protectiveness in tandem with outrage. How dare he treat my, yes my, sister like that! Keep your hands off, you nasty little man. (Even if the 'nasty little man' is several inches taller than you and commands your sister's affection, not pestering her as you would like to believe.) This, of course, is the initial and maybe last response too, of many 'adult' men, married or not. Only substitute girlfriend or wife for sister: attributable to insecurity nurtured by fear . . . fear of a comparison proving relative incompetence and underlining the failing stimulus and lack of excitement provided by the male partner himself. In the case of an eleven-year-old this would produce a fear of the family fabric being ripped to shreds leaving him without visible support. A third possible reaction could be one of identification with the male and his behaviour. Quite advanced for an eleven-year-old. This would show a degree of sexual knowingness and would only happen if the younger brother felt secure and confident in his sister's affections. Did I feel secure and confident in Dorothy's affections? Yes. Was this my response? No. It is this third, most recent and 'liberated' response in which the old regime, subscribing to the first two, could find something perverse or indecent about a young boy regarding an approach made towards his sister's sexuality as something quite normal, perhaps even to be encouraged, certainly not to be discouraged. This, I suspect, is what most 'forward-thinking' people would agree on as acceptable. But none of these were mine. There is a fourth dimension resulting from the third one but which is nevertheless quite distinct. I identified surely enough but not with Simon's low-key advance on Dorothy. I was drawn into sympathy with Dorothy's position. Ah, you say, we're back to the first two. Was it fear or loathing I felt? Neither.

I saw myself struggling with the Prussian blue velvet and Simon leaning over to help me – body trembling, shirt rucked up – I half turned round, smiling at Simon who was pressing forward a fraction more. I could feel the roughness of the tweed on my bare forearms; unlike Dorothy I was wearing a sleeveless frock not a long-sleeved blouse and cardigan – it was pre Dorothy's auburn hairpiece days. My frock was made of some shimmering material. Satin? And in the flickering light of the fire it kept changing its colours: aquamarine, emerald, turquoise, sapphire. Simon was by now face to face with me, his head less than two inches away and with the length of his whole body gently moulding into mine. I could feel his flannels flapping, brushing round my shins and the small of my back against the door handle of the french windows. He grew heavier against me and the curtains tautened like sails which had been waiting for a wind to fill them. His lips were by my ear. More weight on me. Something creaked. Over his shoulder I could see Dorothy and Anne sitting on the rug watching us and whispering in the firelight. I desperately wanted to hear what they were saying but the falling coals and Simon at my ear prevented me. There was a noise of tearing. Then a quick but ear-splitting rip as if a rifle shot had cracked through the room. We fell backwards, splintering glass and wood on our way down. We tumbled, caught up in the velvet curtain which wound itself round, binding us together . . .

'And what are you smiling at?' asked Dorothy as she and Simon, who was still pink, sat down on the rug. I was silent but she prodded. 'Hmm. . . ?'

'Nothing.'

'Dreaming just like Anne I suppose . . . '

'Thinking you mean.' Anne, speaking for the first time in an age, took the poker off its stand and started to stab at the fire through the grate. Was she jealous of the attention that Simon was giving Dorothy? The movement suggested some sort of resentment. Was she feeling what I ought to have felt according to the theories of normality? But for no reason. She and Dorothy shared everything. Anyway, I always thought, and still do, of Anne as a tiger to Dorothy's cat – one wild, the other domesticated – and she could have had a dozen Simons for her tea.

'Whose turn is it?' said Dorothy, picking up what had once been a peg bag.

'Mine, I think,' said Simon, holding out his hand.

'Go and find something then.' Dorothy spoke to him as if he were a five-year-old and he jumped to his feet and paddled off in his brogues like a spaniel gone to fetch the newspaper from the front door mat.

'I can't stand him,' said Anne, 'he's so limp.' So that was it or what she said at any rate. Perhaps she was finding fault with him because she was jealous. If she hadn't been jealous, shouldn't she have been either happy for Dorothy, loving her as she did, or amused at his antics, knowing that she and Dorothy shared a common view?

'Oh, he's all right. Better than the bull in a china shop type.'

'Worse if you ask me. Look at the way he tried to sidle up to you when you were drawing the curtains just now.'

'I didn't think you'd noticed.'

'I couldn't help it. And right in front of Ronald too. What sort of idea is that going to give him?' If only she had known that it wasn't a question of giving me ideas but what was already there in the blueprint.

'Don't be such a little prig, Anne.' Dorothy was right. Anne was being unjustly pompous – she must have been hurt in some way and this little nugget of moral rectitude was her defence mechanism coming to the rescue. What was the exact nature of the hurt? Did she consider, for instance, that Dorothy's neutrality in the matter (neither encouraging nor repelling Simon) was a sign of her weakness rather than strength? Or did she consider herself so intimate with Dorothy that any approach made to her sister was one made to herself which she was unable to respond to – as if Dorothy had to behave by proxy for her and on this occasion had failed to get it right? It was one of the first times I had glimpsed a crack in the cement holding them together. Or was it as straightforward as she had indicated? I know you too well to think that Simon has anything to offer you except perhaps a little amusement. In other words, Simon is beneath your contempt. Shame on you for thinking anything else and on me for letting you think it. Or . . . or . . ?

* * *

WE ARE ALL AMATEURS in this – the way in which we try to detect motives or construct them for ourselves where maybe they don't exist. Some difference between detect and construct. But who is to say where fact (detection necessary) shades into hypothesis (construction obligatory) in the matter of motivation? If this is true for oneself, and I find it so, how much harder it is when talking about others, even those we claim to know well.

Example task: examine my own motivation for coming to the

clinic. Can I detect it or must I construct? There were and still are certain biological facts which I can point to as propelling me here and obliging me to undergo the operation – although some already have and many more will dispute what I know to be true about my body; for example, comparatively hairless, voice unbroken, minimal development of male genitals, significant development of breasts and so on. These can be considered as facts fuelling my reasons, indeed, they themselves are part of the reasons for coming to a clinic and undergoing a particularly harrowing operation. But then there are other reasons too. For example, the sense of alienation from myself. This is for me a fact though it can't actually be detected anywhere. Have I then constructed my own alienation? No, I don't think so. If I didn't make an effort to think about it, to talk about it, I would still feel the same way even though I hadn't put any of it into words. Some people say that it wouldn't be there if I didn't conceptualise. Nonsense. I know how I felt before at fifteen years old. I started to delve into that alienation rather than ignore it, or try to pretend it wasn't there. And it was the same before and after the words, the thoughts. Oh, they helped me to explain what I was feeling but they didn't change the feelings themselves. The words, the explanation of my alienation as one of the motivations for my behaviour are a construction for you, doubtless later on for the courts and anyone else who requires classification of what I've done, am doing. It seems then I detected that alienation in myself as soon as I felt it but that in order to justify to everyone else what I was doing I had to construct it as a theory. Detection then for our own motives but construction to explain them to others and sometimes to ourselves too. Fooling ourselves means constructing motivations before we have done the detective work on ourselves.

A figure appeared in the doorway, hesitating. 'Here's Simon. What are you waiting for, Simon? Do come in.' Dorothy being motherly. 'Have you found something?'

'Yes, yes, I have,' he said excitedly, breathless. How could a man who wore tweed and brogues act like this? He wanted so much to please. Had he been unpopular at school? Unsuccessful in whatever job he did?

We were playing a game that involved someone finding an

object and putting it in the peg bag unseen by the others. It was then passed round and each in turn felt the object through the bag. No one was allowed to speak until the bag had gone full circle. Then everyone had to write down what they thought the object was. It could be anything but was, of course, limited by the size of the peg bag. The trick was in finding an object that resembled something more usual which it would be taken to be. For example, a coiled wire might be taken for a necklace or a dog's round nametag for a coin.

The bag came to me first. What was in it was small and circular. Hard, too, with a hole in the middle. No, not so much a hole, a space. Or rather whatever it was seemed to be almost all round space held in by a circular band. Definitely inflexible. Porcelain? Wood? Metal? Size? Be more exact. Finger size. Yes, it could be a ring. Too obvious. What about a curtain ring?

'You have to write down exactly what you think it is,' Dorothy had once said when I wrote down shoelace and it was a lace from one of her tennis shoes. Could it be some sort of fishing weight? I thought I'd heard an outside door open when Simon was out of the room. Could he have gone down to the summer house where Uncle Cyril kept his fishing tackle? Look, there was some mud on the soles of his brogues! Fishing weight I bet.

I passed on the bag to Anne and wrote down fishing weight on my paper. Wait a minute. Can fishing weights be that shape? Don't they just have a small hole for the line to go through? Or are there some special kinds? What else then? Should I go back to curtain ring? He could have found a box of those in the shed. I crossed out fishing weight and wrote down curtain ring. Anne barely fingered the bag before passing it on to Dorothy who smiled when she felt it and then scribbled her answer.

Simon collected the pieces of paper and studied our answers as if he were trying to crack a secret code. 'Who's nearest?' I asked.

'You are,' he said. 'Anne's nowhere near it. She's got pig's nose ring. It's far too small for that. Unless of course it was for a very small pig, a piglet.' He waited for Anne to laugh but she wouldn't. He couldn't see that Anne had been making fun of him by writing pig's nose ring.

'Now Dorothy's got washer. I can't see that at all. It's not flat enough. And the hole's too big.'

'I know,' said Dorothy, 'but I heard you going outside and I thought you might've gone to the shed. And I couldn't remember exactly what a washer was like. But I thought it was something like that.'

'Ronald here has written down curtain ring which is pretty close.'

'Let's see then,' I said. Simon picked up the peg bag and loosened the string at the top.

Remember doing that for mother? Cold numb fingers in January. So stiff you couldn't get the string undone and then dropping some of the pegs on to the ground. A robin watching you pick them up and mother saying, 'Careful now. We don't want to get the washing dirty, do we?' And then as she hung it up watching the robin hop closer on the frozen sleet-covered ground until you thought you could reach out and touch it. Somewhere in the house a door banged and it flew away. Uncle Cyril clumping past in his wellingtons muttering, 'Cold, it's freezing cold this morning.' On his way to the shed.

Simon took the bag by its corners and tipped it upside-down as if he were shaking out a pillow case. Nothing. He shook it again and something tumbled on to the rug, rolled a short distance and came to rest. Anne and Dorothy watched it closely and then, looking at each other, started to giggle. I was concentrating on the mystery object. Their giggles grew louder.

'What's the matter? What is it?' asked Simon. The giggles exploded into laughter. A pinkness suffused Simon's face. Tears ran down Anne and Dorothy's cheeks. They were united again. I continued to stare at the object of our guessing game.

'I don't see what's so funny.' Simon's voice sounded a little strained. Anne and Dorothy groaned and held on to each other for support. 'Ooh . . . ooh . . . ooh . . . ' I picked it up. It was a plain gold wedding ring, which was evidently worn but had no other distinguishing features except for its hallmark.

'It's not funny.' Simon's voice was close to breaking. He stood up and moved towards the door. I slipped the ring on to the middle finger of my left hand. Simon started to cry. 'It was my mother's.' He left the room. Anne and Dorothy's groans subsided into occasional snortings. The ring was a little too big but felt comfortable on my finger.

* * *

STILL FINGERING Leila's ring which brings a welcome coolness (like the woman herself) to my own fingers that feel sticky and hot. I don't know why they feel like this for she bathes my face and hands every hour or so when I'm awake. She doesn't have the fingers of a working woman, a nurse who has to turn bodies and sheets, but more the fingers of a highly selective manicurist who accepts only favoured clients. They are both yielding and pliant yet responsive and firm, able to hold on tight and grip whatever they want – something like the ideal vagina. The doctor wrote again and again, saying '. . . while I can, as much as one is able with any kind of operation, more or less guarantee successful removal of the member and testes, the second phase, construction of a vagina, is quite a different kettle of fish.' (Where did he learn his English?) And again, almost as soon as I had arrived and we sat tearing open the little packets of Nescafé and pouring them into the hot water in our cups. 'I will tell you once more that we are on dangerous ground with the second part of the job. It is impossible to judge what kind of sensitivity you will have. It may be excellent, better than is usual or it may be . . . ' He looked into his coffee as though he might find an answer in its muddy swirl. 'There may be very little sensitivity.' 'Do you mean sensitivity or sensation?' He licked his moustache, a gesture which I have always found disturbing to the point of erotic.

'I assume that you are talking about the possibility of orgasm?' I nodded and crossing my legs noticed that his eyes followed their movements. 'Look,' he said, leaning forward for the first time, confidentially as though the conversation had until then been about the weather or the colour of my dress. 'I don't need to tell a person of your undoubted,' his hand circled trying to churn up the word, 'undoubted experience, that orgasm in a woman is not simply a matter of sensation. It can come from feeling, from emotion as much as from any physical source. With us men, unfortunately, we . . . you know what happens to us, we are like children who cannot control themselves.'

'You mean that there is every chance?'

'Every chance. I will provide a network of tissues, of blood vessels, of nerves, but the rest, the most important part, is up to you. You will provide the spirit for the new body I am helping to make and that is a far more difficult task.'

I stared into his brown eyes and then quickly looked away. I felt faintly embarrassed, like a prospective bride who goes to the vicarage in order to arrange the details of her wedding day only to find the vicar talking about religion. There had been none of that in his letter which had been so professionally impersonal that I was relieved and thankful. I had had so much advice from so many quarters that all I longed for were some medical facts, hard or otherwise. Now here he was like some scientist who had glimpsed undreamt of worlds just within his grasp if only . . . The light in his eye made me think absurdly of those horror films with mad doctors and inventors clapping their hands in glee as their creation rises from the table and moves on to terrorise the world in a new body with a complete lack of conscience or any moral sense at all. Only here for a moment it seemed that the reverse was true. I had come to the clinic prepared, as far as I could be, for all the horrors and torments the surgeon's knife might inflict on me, but I was in no way ready to undergo any sort of spiritual or related kind of exercise. I knew that there would be all sorts of psychological self-examinations, not to mention social pressures, later on. But just then it was the body and nothing else that I felt wanted attention and yet here was the surgeon himself talking about 'spirit' for the body which he was about to service.

He licked his moustache again. It was flecked with grey. How old was he? I found it difficult to guess as much because I couldn't be sure of his racial origins as anything else. He seemed to be a mixture of Middle Eastern and Asian bloods but I couldn't tell which one was uppermost. He had the complexion and features (the large hooked nose, for example) of an Arab, perhaps from the Gulf, though his skin was smoother, his face not as heavy jowled as many Arabs. His speech had a formal, almost over-elaborate quality about it, at times verging on the faintly archaic or ridiculous, as though he had learned it as a *lingua franca* on the Indian sub-continent twenty years before. This mattered for guessing his age in as much as I had been wrong before.

Once a lined, dried-up face came close to mine, saying, 'And I have only thirty-two years as well as the five children.' It was hot, I couldn't see very well, the sun was in my eyes and I had lost my sunglasses. My head was spinning. 'Thirty-two!' I thought he was fifty.

An oil-well Christmas tree shimmered in the background and I could make out a few Bedouin tents pitched in the scrubby desert with the open mouths gawping like fish on the gritty sand. I wanted to glide into the cool chambers of the tents only I wondered what the reaction would be: a European (a man apparently) in the midst of the women. Looking into the dark rectangles out of the pulsating light I could see nuggets, splinters of gold floating in the depths, like coins winking at the bottom of a wishing well. It was, of course, the bracelets, the finger and ear rings and other jewellery of the Bedouin women which they kept close to them as their security, their insurance against the instant divorce permissible under Islamic law.

The Bedouin whose face was pressed up to mine pulled a packet of Marlboro out of his robe and offered it to me. 'No thank you,' shaking my head. He insisted and I lit up, feeling light-headed and then dizzy under the sun. 'We will go and drink coffee,' he said in Arabic. As I swam through the thick air towards the tents the gold glinted in spurts – matches struck in the dark – but by the time I reached the tents it had disappeared as though it had only been a trick of the light. (The cackle of a television from somewhere, the clinic?, breaks in on me. The first time it has happened. I am, I suppose, feeling a little stronger.) I sat cross-legged on a carpet and from somewhere, a fold in the tent, a hand appeared holding a tray with two small, handleless cups and a coffee pot with its spout arched, a crescent moon. He poured the coffee for us but the women remained hidden. Only once I thought I saw the white of an eye flash in a pillar of sombre cloth but otherwise all that I glimpsed of the women was a line of black posts stretching like a fence as they made their way to the next tent where they would sit away from the men. Now, when I leave here I can, if I wish, join that dark line of women separating themselves from the men. What would the ancient-looking Bedouin say if he knew that I had crossed the dividing line so clearly drawn for him and the rest of orthodox Islamic society? Oh, I've seen them, even the modern ones who take their wives to Europe or America. They lock them in the hotel rooms with the children and then go out to the clubs and bars on their own. They don't even take them out to eat but scour the city until they find some food they think the women and children will recognise, Lebanese usually. Then they ferry it back to the hotel rooms in plastic carriers and eat it off bed-spreads laid on the floor. Cultural routines and patterns are hard to break, fish and chips on the Costa Brava, and who's to say they are wrong to have the women grouped out of the sight of other men in hotel rooms? It is a paradox that Islam which draws the boundaries so sharply between men and women is, albeit unknowingly, allowing me to cross that boundary. Thanks be to Allah!

But the age of the surgeon? Late thirties? Early forties? Did it matter? Somehow yes. If he had said 'But I am only twenty-eight' I think I might have got up and walked out. I needed to put myself in the hands of a man of experience and not some eager young thing who was still experimenting. This raised the whole question of just how many operations of the kind he had done.

As if he could read the direction of my thought he continued, 'We get people in here who think that all I've got to do is a bit of cutting, a bit of hormone treatment, some hair removal and that is it, the work is finished, and they can walk out a new person. I am telling you that the new person comes from in here.' He tapped the region just above his heart. 'I do nothing major, irreversible, unless the person proves to me that they themselves have changed. And not many have proved that so I tinker with their bodies for the sake of their vanities and they leave here fundamentally unchanged.' I must have appeared apprehensive, frightened even, for he smiled.

'I know what you're thinking. You're worried that you're the first. You're not, but you are rare. It happens that maybe once every three or four years I am convinced enough to change someone's sex.'

'And what is the success rate?' He burst out laughing, not maliciously but as one laughs when a child says something funny that it does not fully understand. 'From my end one hundred per cent. But you should ask the patients, not me.' He looked at me, narrowing his eyes. 'You think you're not going to have any problems after this. You're wrong. There are problems, only of a different kind.' He looked down. 'You have good legs. Better than most of the other women who come here.' I knew from his letters that the bulk of his work was plastic surgery. Without it he would not have been able to deal with cases such as mine. 'They are vain, superfluous . . . '

'Superficial you mean.'

'Yes, they are interested only in their bodies but in a case like yours . . . ' He was struggling for the words. ' . . . I can use my skill to put your self, your spirit, back in touch with its right body.' Did he believe in reincarnation? 'But I'm sure you are tired.'

He stood up and called softly through the open door, 'Leila.' She entered, smiling, emanating a comforting warmth like a radiator of human affection. I sensed then that whatever happened to me she would be there to console or chivvy as the need might arise. 'Please show Ronny to her room.' But there was no need for him to ask. She was already holding out her hand which I took, she led me away and I felt as if we were two sisters who had not seen each other for years and who loved each other dearly.

So, still holding her hand and exploring the possibilities of the ring, I finally open my eyes and ask, 'What's he like?'

For a moment she looks puzzled, bewilderment snaking across her forehead which is normally clear and untroubled as glass.

'Oh, the ring. There is no one.'

'Why then?'

'Try telling an Egyptian that you are married without it.'

But I can see that she is lying. Not about the pressure and hassle for an unattached girl living alone in Egypt but about her 'no one'. There is something too quick and definite about her answer. Something that she wants kept hidden away. 'Are you sure?'

'Don't be ridiculous. Of course I'm sure. You try living in this country on your own. See how long it takes you before you are fed up with the men. They want only one thing.'

'I'm sure you're right. I was talking about the "no one" who gave you the ring.'

I have touched something for she turns away.

'Tomorrow we may be able to get you out of bed. You'd like

that wouldn't you?' Her shoulders are shaking and her voice is choked. When she turns round again I can't see her face clearly for light is pouring from the window into my eyes. It takes them a few seconds to adjust while Leila stands with her head lowered. When I focus I can see that there are tears cascading down her cheeks.

I hold out my arms and whisper, 'Come, come here.' She sinks into me, burying her wet face and hair in my neck. I rock her gently until the tears drain away, poor darling, understanding that, as the surgeon says, there is more, much more to my new self than a change of body – and I rock, her forgetting my own pain until the lightness of her breathing tells me that she has fallen asleep.

EPILOGUE

AN APOLOGIA

You should know that I am writing this in the eighty-sixth year of the century, a dozen years after grandmother, then mother, read Margaret's letter in Mr Heath's long winter. What has happened since then? Looking back from my humid balcony at the heart of this vibrating city the twelve years telescope in bizarre, alarming fashion. This is how Alice must have felt as she shrank or grew extraordinarily out of size. The standard perspectives have long since been eroded. After the operation and its aftermath a hundred and forty-four months is too brief an incarnation. I could have taken you along the glossy steps of the path leading from my change of sex – the villas in the south of France, Andalusia, Tuscany; the modelling and photographic assignments in Peru, Noumea, Iran; the clubs and restaurants as owner, entertainer, guest, client; the jewellery, the dresses, the drugs, the clinics and other retreats; and so on, but such details, if not strictly mine, are available to you in a thousand and one magazines and supplements which portray their hollow beauty far better than I could have managed.

Have I, have you learned anything? Or is such a question misguided? Should we seek anything beyond a narrative peppered with descriptions and events to spice our jaded palates? I wanted to try to grasp the nature of those pressures in a family history like the accumulation of layer on layer in formations of rock, one stratum moulded by the last and in its turn forming the next. Can an individual be explained, in particular its sexuality, by tracing that pattern of others' lives as they impinge, pressing up against and into it? Or was, is, anyone's self the creation of a random selection of accidental and quite unrelated collisions? I didn't know when I began and I still don't.

At what point their history – Emily's, Virginia's, Julia's and that of the others told here – stops and shades into mine it is impossible to gauge. I intended to draw some conclusions about where the personal ends and the public begins but I find I cannot. Was the death of Bertrand in the General Strike of 1926 a private or a national affair? Was Margaret's marriage to an American in uniform a matter solely of the heart? Somehow I doubt it. After all, why was the soldier here in the first place? Was the success of my grandmother, Emily, in the retail business hers alone? Of course not. It was part of the wider ebb and flow of an economic tide washing through the country and a good portion of the Western world too. It is like trying to determine where the pink runs into the red runs into the orange runs into the yellow of a sunset. My vision is only able to distinguish where the extremes of colour throb not the point at which they melt. Your eyes perhaps are more finely adjusted, can pick out the precise points at which one colour merges into the next.

As a result of the Great War Emily's husband, Charles, was away at sea for longer than he would otherwise have been. Then was the birth of my mother, Virginia, through the liaison of Emily and Bertrand, a result directly or partly attributable to that war? It would seem so. And yet how to measure what influence that had on me? My sisters, Dorothy and Anne, were the offspring of my parents also, but for all their differences they shared a sexual certainty which I lacked. Was it our father's absence? Or was it that the sole model of masculinity was weak and reclusive Uncle Cyril? Which created me? I am, I feel, no nearer to finding the exit from that labyrinth than I was at the beginning of this account. I am lost in trying to discover whether it was an accumulation of all these details, a single one of them, or none at all. Instead I fear it could be a nuance that has completely passed me by.

The demarcation between the public and the private, the weight of a family and its history, the personal and sexual identity of an individual; all these perhaps can be pondered but not in the end resolved. Some things remain a mystery forever. Our all too frequent assumption that nothing is insoluble if we work long and hard enough in teasing out its threads leads us into specious fictions which we swallow in preference to . . . a blankness, and a nothing.

I think you must have had almost enough. I have. Let the others disappear first.

the first, the biggest, the healthiest of her generation. She seems to command more room than the others, her skin glowing, on fire with energy and zest. The Old World was too small for her sweeping, confident gestures. It could not, it seems, contain her. She demanded a new world where she might breathe more easily and deeply, those healthy, elastic lungs filling and expanding with the purest Californian ozone. I go swimming every day, she once wrote to us. I can no longer recall whether the strokes were made in her pool or the Pacific Ocean. She joked that she used to stand on the beach expecting her father, Charles, to come sailing over the rim of the horizon and anchor his vessel offshore. Though, of course, he never did. Had he done so she was sure that he would have been proud of his daughter and her boys, her house and motor cars. There was no doubt that she was her mother's daughter writ large with the Englishness vaporised. There rolled no words from her tongue on creating wealth for the nation or providing opportunities for more employment. 'Money,' she drawled, 'what do you want the stuff for if you don't spend it on yourself?'

After my change she wrote to me from Spain saying, I always knew. I mean, you've only got to look at yourself in that movie I took. The way you wiggled your hips. I could've told you there and then. Margaret was always wise after the event. I hear her after her marriage had broken up. 'It was inevitable that we were gonna split. How could I go on living with him? What class had he got? He didn't understand English women.'

I imagine her later sitting on her balcony from which she can see the Mediterranean. More of a lake really if you compare it with the Pacific, she thinks. The rings on her hands feel heavy, impossibly large. She removes them and places them on the table beside her gin and tonic. She tries to remember whether she has swum in the patch of blue out there. She can't. How long has she been here? But her skin, her shining succulent skin is parched and cracked! Wrinkled too. It doesn't seem to make any difference how much lotion she uses these days. It must be the sun. It doesn't caress like the Californian sun. It dazes, squeezes one dry. That's why her skin is so thirsty these days. The sun.

But it wasn't the sun that attacked her liver. I wasn't sure what they meant so I looked it up '. . . cirrhosis: a condition in which fibrous tissue forms around and within the lobules of the liver . . . in the late stages of the condition it generally shrinks . . . symptoms caused by the failure of the cells to function properly, blood is not subjected to the normal detoxicating action . . . neurological effects like mental confusion may be observed.'

From her Spanish balcony, I'm coming home tomorrow, next week. The mother country. Are those Germans or Swedes? – I can never tell the difference . . . But she never went home. Her life shrank within her until it was riddled with holes and then nothing but one large thirsty hole poisoning itself.

JEAN

lay on approximately the same longitude but further south. They had brought her from upcountry, Kumasi way, down to Accra on the coast. They had said it might do her some good but they knew it probably wouldn't. She rallied once and they took her down to the sea where she sat watching the breakers foam over the rocks and surge into the swimming pool. She felt quite happy in her striped deck chair, though she noticed that some of the others could not be used for the wood was infested with termites, making them crumble as soon as one tried to sit down.

I imagine her remembering how they had had to take the roof off her bungalow not long after she had first arrived. The joists had proved rotten. Termites then too. But she hadn't minded. That's why she had come. To help.

The rocks glistened with salt crystallised from sea water. There were a few scrubby palms behind which the ground rose steeply. Beyond these grew spiky clumps of grass which looked as though they had been glued there as an afterthought in the red laterite. People she knew played tennis on courts rolled from this red earth. She had gone to watch them play and the ball left skidmarks in the dust every time it hit the ground. Hundreds of insects whirred and fluttered in the floodlights – it was too hot to play at any other time. On another occasion someone had lent her a pair of tennis shoes and she had played badminton. If one hit the shuttlecock hard and high it disappeared and then dropped out of the night again like a dead bird caught in the moonlight. But it was unusual for her to play such games. She only came to Accra once or twice for a few days' local leave and where she worked further north the only sport was football. How shocked she had been to discover the boys playing in tattered khaki shorts without shirts; when she had first seen them she thought they looked like matchstick men scurrying about as though their spindly legs might snap at the first barefoot contact.

She climbs the steps cut through rock and away from the pool thinking how Europeans seem bloated, oversize in this landscape. She notices that the whitewash is flaking from the wall on which she has to lean every few steps under the shadow of the rouge hibiscus. A fly buzzes in her ear, this the last she hears twisting in the shrouds of bed linen.

You see how we wrap them up and try to tidy them away and though unseen they remain known to me as does

CYRIL

who somehow never filled out to be more than a shadow of what he might have been, forever his own silhouette. Cyril as a magician soon disappeared to become a garden recluse.

I see him crouching in the furrows weeding potatoes. Striding through the emerald shadows of his runner beans splashed with drops of scarlet. Casting nets as if he were fishing for soft fruit. Dropping rotted compost in a trench. In the greenhouse spraying against aphids. Handing over to cook a basketful of July's first tomatoes. Seated on the steps near the stone statue of The Fiddler, cap on his knee while he wipes the moisture from his forehead.

It is true that he did not live up to my early anticipation of his magical powers but he did grow and grow things – there are too many worse occupations for a man to pursue and too few for him to do better. Weak? Repressed? They seem irrelevances from here and now. I have to admit that he did not love but then he hurt no one either. Perhaps this is what made him . . .

Mother had gone into the garden to find out why the chain saw had been droning on for so long. Dusk was printing itself in the light when she found him at the end of his fence wire gently knocking on one of his apple trees, an enormous Howgate Wonder, which he had tended for most of his life.

MY SISTERS'

stories were for me their early ones. After all, it seems that they shaped my world less than the generation before us had done. We lived side by side for a few years but as much through someone else's world as our own. There were occasions we thought special and ours alone but these seem now to be holidays from a history others had made and were still making for us. In those moments sandwiched between the times others had given us we formed our own histories which would later gather their own momentum and force, enough to cough us up so that we were as much ourselves as we might ever expect to be.

Their differences are readily apparent so I should not lump them together. Dorothy conventional, Anne radical, Dorothy large-boned, Anne slight though tall. Dorothy living in a Gulf sheikdom where her husband earns more in a month than Anne ever earned in a year. Anne living I'm not sure where, but if the last time I saw her is any indication, making no attempt to free herself of an addiction to heroin. But my purpose is not to elaborate their dissimilarities. They are alike in that the role they played in me was, though I didn't know it at the time, a small one. Our lives had already diverged and in the larger sweep their effect on me was diminished beside that of

EMILY

who like her business is dead now. She put the thing in trust and it came at last to mother who inherited a faltering enterprise.

Even before she died its profits were declining though Emily knew nothing about it. What had started life as a small number of exclusive food shops and had in the fifties and sixties expanded to cover most aspects of the consumer goods trade became, when mother quickly sold it, a minor subsidiary of an American conglomerate – as if the course this business took were a model for the history of Britain's twentieth century.

And yet the woman herself lived through her life as a monument to those apparent virtues of the Queen who had dominated the entire existence of her father, George. She found her consolation in a dedication to work: the work of family, the work of money, the work of controlling and disciplining emotion, practising the self-abnegation one associates with the daily penance of those who have gone into retreat from the world as a means of mastering it. As though she had to spend the succession of her time in atonement for a few minutes' indiscretion at the base of a tree one freezing, damp December. The manner in which she clenched herself, held herself in after that, owed more to the temper of her father's century than the one in which she had to live.

This guilt was heaped on all her children. The discipline of work was the only way she knew to scour the stain which obsessed her. Yet the harder she tried, the more it hurt, the tighter she became. She had to punish herself for the aberration she had allowed, forgetting that it had given her a momentary glimpse of other worlds. If her own days were to be dictated by a rule of torment and torture then so would the hours of those about her. Suffering was not an option, it was a necessity.

In particular her resentment was directed against those like Julia, and later Margaret and Jean, whom she could not bring to heel. She despised their freedom, regarded it as an easy forgetfulness. Julia's sin had been, Emily felt, so much greater than her own that it lay beyond her comprehension how her one-time friend blossomed, rather than withered in the radiance of its wrong. Emily's triumph was, of course, Cyril – the supreme paralysis of another's will.

She did not relent. In the half-dozen years she survived after my operation she never forgave me for what had been perpetrated, as she put it, on the last descendant of the male line in our family. Masculinity in her version had been lacking all along – an absent Charles, a dead Bertrand, a missing Edward, a withdrawn Cyril, a dismembered Ronald – so she had had to provide it through her own efforts. And she did. Right to the end she would call out and Virginia would scurry in from the kitchen.

She refused to release her grip on a single individual; even the dead were not beyond her control. She continued to chastise Margaret for her abandonment to what she considered a life of unbridled West Coast hedonism. She asserted that it bore all the worse and none of the best – whatever they were – aspects of an avid consumerism. A neat twist in the career of a woman whose enterprise at its peak fed, clothed and otherwise catered to millions of customers throughout the British Isles. Jean was similarly reviled for the excess of her behaviour in throwing it all up to work in faith and charity. However often Virginia reminded her mother that the country had been called Ghana since independence Emily persisted in using the colonial name.

'Gold Coast!' she would snort, 'not much gold for Jean there!' Emily thought that her ethereal daughter was running away from the obligations that a daily routine in the Home Counties would have imposed. In a sense she was quite right. The diurnal round for Jean under her mother's roof would have proved no less arduous than missionary work upcountry.

My mother, Virginia, was despised more vigorously than the other children by Emily as the embodiment of her fall from grace. Even in the final months Virginia continued to cower under the lash of Emily's bitter tongue and had to suffer the recriminations implicit in the enforced silences of her mother. As time ran out Emily made more demands, not fewer. It was too cold, draughty; there was not enough sugar in her coffee; when was Virginia going to take her out? (never mind the doctor who had said it could kill her); had Virginia spoken to the accountant?; why hadn't he come to see her?; why couldn't her slippers be warmed for her before she got up in the morning?; Virginia was not to enter her bedroom unless asked to do so although on four occasions she had found her mother on the floor unable to raise herself or move at all. Death did not stalk Emily gracefully under camouflage. It made a noise, saw no point in remaining hidden. She became tentative, uncertain there was any more, the lines in her face grew more bitter by the hour.

Sitting at the window where she now spent all her time a jay flashed in Emily's eye, kaleidoscopic. Her children skipped and sang across the lawn, skirted the rosebed with Margaret in the vanguard, Jean and Cyril trailing behind. Virginia peeled off and made towards the house while the others disappeared from view. Then her youngest daughter was on the gravel path on the other side of the pane. Virginia held the hand of a small boy, Emily's grandson, Ronald: me in a flannel-grey shirt and long dark-grey shorts, head cropped of its hair. As my grandmother watched my hair shook out, growing luxuriant, abundant, the shirt and shorts melted away, I was wearing a dress of pale lemon with pink roses round its hem, my skin transfused soft as a mouse.

'Get out of my sight! Go away,' Emily screamed but we stood our ground staring in through the glass while it was Emily who left us, rising higher and higher. She hovered over our heads while we turned up our faces, squinting up at her until with a visible slowness she faded from our sight.

She had outlived all her children with the exception of my mother.

VIRGINIA

who talks now about moving away from the house in which save for a few months she has always lived. It was already too large even before Cyril and then Emily died. But where would she go? She wants me to go back and live with her and seems to have sudden crazes. What about the Lake District? Would you come and live with me there if I bought us somewhere easy to manage? Or the coast, you like the sea, don't you? Or we could stay in the same area, just move somewhere a little smaller, Sussex way perhaps. I can't predict where she might next suggest though it certainly won't be outside England.

It's too late for that, she says, and charges me with spending too much time away from my own country. But at the moment she stays in the house which is half closed up and with a garden that is beginning to ramble over its own lawns and beds. She is no more unhappy than any other widow whose family has grown up and left her alone. She lacks company but she doesn't fuss. She knows that she is more fortunate than many. She is not a recluse and she still takes care of her appearance. There are holidays more or less where and when she wants. But none of this is as she would want it in her heart of hearts. She would turn the clock back and, if she could, do it differently. She is not bitter but she will tell you this if you ask her. She hopes and waits for

ME

at last. Who sits on my balcony overlooking the city. Behind me the fan, which I prefer to air-conditioning, whizzes. I am especially fond of the huge rain tree I can see silhouetted in an adjacent garden like some enormous mushroom. The light swinging on the end of a crane I can't see looks like a spaceship about to land nearby. The yellow elastoplast in the sky is, I think, an illuminated hospital cross. The grenadine tracer of city lights fizzes in the moist blue dark while below the purple bougainvillaea bobs in a light breeze which heralds a storm. Whirrings spatter in the light that spills from the room behind me; a frog croaks in anticipation of rain. In the bowl of sky behind the city limits lightning switches itself on and off like the flicker of a fluorescent tube.

Has my optimism been justified? Or is optimism rather an end in itself, needing no strictly worked-out rationale? I wouldn't, unlike mother, reverse and start again had I the choice. In spite of the pain and sorrow. The court case, for example, which some of you read about. Its absurd ruling which meant that legally I ceased to exist and became a ghost haunting no man or woman's land. After that lost battle what was left me? The obvious benefits of some fame and at periods a lot of money. But you observe that I refer to the world out there which I can see from my balcony. What about that matter of the heart?

I thought it was going to be all right. We wanted children but they wouldn't let us adopt. We had seven happy years to show – more than many clutch in the palm of their hand – but in the end he was driven away. One shouldn't underestimate the forces that can be brought to bear on two people who taken together appear self-sufficient. I miscalculated. There are always others who will neither leave you alone nor help you.

There were plenty of admirers after that. Too many of the curious, the prurient, willing to take me on board for a while, but no one who cared enough to stay for long enough. Looking in you might ask whether the world out there hasn't compensated me in its other ways? There are women, I heard a woman say, who would have given an arm or a leg for half of what she's had. But the one thing I wanted has eluded me. This has been, not just for the others in my family, a love story with love appearing at best short-lived or missing altogether. Though it made me more vulnerable I don't regret the change from man to woman. It was an act which helped me to admit not only what I was but what I wanted. Love.

My mistake was that I thought the world might change with me. I thought that my change would be everyone else's too. But things are the same. Dear sweet Leila, for instance. They are still butchering her country, her people in the Lebanon. Was it foolish of me to think they might stop? The metamorphosis, was, after all, only a personal affair. On the borders of the country where I sit there are guerrillas, insurgents, liberation fighters, call them what you will. I don't dispute the justice of their causes, only I had hoped that by now there would have been a change in man. I was wrong.

The rains have started and the twisting brown river threatens to burst its banks and slough its cargoes. There is indiscriminate building and one can taste the lead in the air. Perhaps it is time for me to go back to England, to home, to mother, who might say:

your father, Edward,

was Julia's son

your great-grandfather, George,

was Edward's father too

Which would, I suppose, explain it.

Or she might say nothing at all.

Which would, from my point of view, prove no more or less satisfactory.

The rain is now gusting along the edge of the balcony. I think I had better go inside and close the shutters.